An Epic Retelling of The Phantom of the Opera

Chanson de l'Ange

Book One:
Orphan in Winter

PAISLEY SWAN STEWART

Chason de l'Ange
Book One: Orphan in Winter
By Paisley Swan Stewart

©2011 by Paisley Swan Stewart

Cover Design: Frances Wheeler
Cover Text: Nathan Allen Pinard
Interior Design: Linda Boulanger

ISBN: 978-1-61752-141-6

Also available in eBook publication

Published by TreasureLine Publishing
www.TreasureLineBooks.com

The following is a work of fiction. Names, characters, places, and incidents are fictitious or used fictitiously. Any resemblance to real persons, living or dead, to factual events or to businesses is coincidental and unintentional.

The views expressed in this work are solely those of the author

PRINTED IN THE UNITED STATES OF AMERICA

Bill, as we journey along the everlasting way,
I love you with all my heart and soul.
Never forget: one day we shall dance on the stones of fire!

"Let me first say the preface from the author was pretty much a "prequel" for me as to how this book would unfold. She laid her heart bare & I felt such powerful emotion behind her words that I knew the same would go into her book. I was not disappointed! This book truly comes from the heart,& through her words you could feel the love, pain & torment of Christine & Erik's story. This re-telling of the classic love story captured me right from the start,and while staying true to the story & the characters, the author has a style of her own that made this book so much more enjoyable. I felt through her book the pieces that were missing in the original were put into place and there was much more explained. I felt I got to know the characters better, not just Erik & Christine but the others as well. She gave them more "personality" and to me made the story much fuller. As for Erik, my heart cries out for you once again, and I cant find the words to explain how the author makes you feel such pain in his heart for the things he cannot have or share. Many a times I cried through the story. This book has so many elements to it, mystery, passionate romance, madness, a tormented soul that cries to be heard. A beautiful, wonderful, powerful story!!! This is a MUST read for fans of Phantom Of The Opera! " ~Sandi~

"I've read hundreds of POTO stories in the past five years. I'd rate ten percent of those worthy of reading again and again. I'd also rate ten percent of those a story that cannot be let go of. It lingers, it bothers…it just won't leave a person's mind. This is one of those stories. The depth put into this story is amazing. The emotions are written in a way that a person FEELS what the character feels and knows what the character is seeing in THEIR mind and soul.

Paisley Swan Stewart is a wonderful writer who manages to 'take us away' to a world of sorrow, pain, joy, innocence and triumph. I recommend this book and it's follow-on books highly. It's a must read for any loyal POTO fiction reader." ~Pertie~

"When this book was recommended to me, I took a look on line and was intrigued. Upon reading it, I have to say that it surpassed all of my expectations! What I was concerned would happen, and what I think would be so easy to do, is someone writing a sappy love story to fulfill their own Erik fantasies and make him the perfect man instead of the conflicted man he was meant to be. Ms Stewart writes him realistic, making him the Erik he was intended to be, not just the Erik of our fantasies we might have preferred. Her story captivated and lulled me in from the start – it was like getting an intimate view into the lives of the characters we have grown to know so well – it was never a "spin" on Phantom – but a gift of allowing me to grow even closer to those portrayed. I am so looking forward to the next book. I could not have been happier with this work which has honored the PTO story." ~Erin~

"Brilliantly coloring the classic story of The Phantom of the Opera, Stewart paints a passionate picture of each of her characters. As she delves deeply into their psyches, her readers begin to understand Christine's confusion and the thought processes and memories that shape Erik's trend toward madness. Ms. Stewart has a knack for describing deep emotions in a way that readers can relate. I was so moved that I actually felt Erik's heartbreak and became angry with Christine for her indecisiveness. Chanson de l'Ange, Book One: The Bleeding Rose, defines the term "page-turner," and is a must read for all Phantom of the Opera phans." ~LLea~

Dedication

I dedicate *Chanson de l'Ange* to my husband Bill, who is the love of my life and who has taught me the meaning of true love, faith and trust. Without his support and encouragement, *Chanson de l'Ange* would have been nothing more than a short story posted on a message board. Bill, as we journey along the everlasting way I love you with all my heart and soul.

To Nathan Allen Pinard: your musical compositions have created a beautiful and atmospheric orchestral soundscape for this retelling. Thank you for creating the perfect music to underscore my story. I love you and I am so proud of you.

To my best friend Melissa: my inspirational forever friend and earth angel. You have always been there…always.

To my sister Reba and my mother Dottie: you two have always been my biggest fans. Thank you for believing me. I adore you!

To Gabriel Micheal: you are the friend and angel overlooking us all from heaven.

And finally to my Lord and Savior Jesus Christ: Thank you for your mercy and grace, and for loving me when I was just a Phantom lost in the Shadowlands.

Acknowledgments

If Gaston Leroux had not created the original *Phantom of the Opera* novella from which all other *Phantom of the Opera* fictions are drawn, *Chanson de l'Ange* would not have been written. I offer my admiration and respect to Monsieur Leroux for giving us our "Poor, unhappy Erik."

My love and appreciation to Frances Wheeler, for her breathtaking cover designs.

Thank you to my dear friend and beta, Alison Joy Tippetts-Driggs. You not only assisted me with edits and advice, but also provided spiritual encouragement along the path to publication!

I must acknowledge a few others who have inspired me: Gerard Butler, Andrew Lloyd Webber, Hans Christian Anderson, CS Lewis, Colleen McCollough, Josephine Leslie, Ellen Gunderson Traylor, Charlotte Brontë, and Harper Lee.

Preface from the Author

Growing up as a lonely and introspective child, I recognized man's cruelty to his fellow man and was profoundly disturbed when children were ridiculed and bullied by others because of their physical appearance.

As a skinny and physically awkward little girl, I did not fit with other children. I was unhealthy, my eyes were too big behind thick glasses, and my complexion was too pale. I rarely played outdoors and chose to remain indoors while the neighborhood kids played kick ball and hide-n-seek, and thus I was nicknamed "the mole."

My preteen years remain shrouded in family secrets and my stepfather's escalating alcoholism. I sought to escape his negative influence through books, movies and music, gravitating to musicals and movies from the 30's 40's and 50's. Often staying up late into the night, I enjoyed the old black and white horror films like *Dracula*, *Frankenstein* and *King Kong*. I was sympathetic to these monsters, perhaps relating personally to their outcast stories.

The first time I saw the Lon Chaney silent version of *Phantom of the Opera*, I was about eleven. I was frightened but equally fascinated by the masked Phantom, the movie's man/monster whose real name was Erik.

Later I came across the colorful film adaptation starring Claude Rains, and I developed my first crush on a movie character. His voice floating through the mirror enthralled me, and the melancholy melody he played on the violin was unforgettable. I thought him so handsome in the mysterious mask and was captivated by his efforts to win the trust of the young opera singer.

In the early 90's my husband and I attended an LA based performance of Andrew Lloyd Webber's stage musical starring Michael Crawford. I shall never forget the first commanding chords played on the dark organ as the gold and crystal chandelier rose above the gasping audience. When the Phantom first appeared in the mirror I forgot everything else around me; the audience, the auditorium…they all receded into the swirling mist as he beckoned Christine through the glass.

Dressed in elegant tails and black opera cloak, he gracefully prowled across the stage, with the half-mask erotic and spell binding. I watched breathlessly as the tragic story came to life through Webber's soaring music. The performance was hypnotic and deeply sensual, but for me the drama resonated beyond its Victorian romance and beautiful score.

The Phantom is a man of superior intellect and artistic intelligence who, because of a hideous facial deformity is denied acceptance and love. He is forced to remain on the outside looking in and can never know the warmth of human touch. His soul is twisted and his psyche damaged through his self imposed isolation in the opera house cellars where he exists as a shadow, a ghost...a haunted creature to be feared and obeyed.

But the Phantom is no monster. He is only a man who desires to walk unmasked in the daylight, who craves someone to share his music, his heart and his body. Underneath the ugly skin, Erik longs to be loved just like the rest of us.

In December of 2004 as I watched Joel Schumacher's film version starring Gerard Butler, in my memories I was once again awash in the flickering light of an old black and white television where a lonely little girl wept real tears for the *Phantom of the Opera.*

My own story however, will have a happy ending because despite my emotional and physical scars, I found true love and a deep abiding faith in God. As I grow older my own need for masks and disguises diminishes, and I am learning to love myself for who I am...as alas, poor Erik never could.

~ Paisley Swan Stewart

Prologue

Looking back on the events of those early days, I concede it is only now, through adult eyes, that I can describe what happened to me. Childish innocence has faded into sepia photographs, hopelessly romanticized by the passing of time and my aging memory. The girl I once was is little more than a stranger to me now, a far removed shadow of the woman I am today.

I often wish I could have prepared, and yes, even warned her about the events which were to come. But even if I could have, would I? And would it have changed anything, if she . . . if I had chosen differently; if I had understood and known the truth? Or was I in some way destined to make that strange journey, irresistibly drawn to him for a greater purpose than I could have possibly imagined?

My woman's heart willingly embraces the truth now, and I must tell it, and though even after all these years it threatens to split my soul asunder, I must speak of it.

They say that pain is a patient teacher; that a wound burns and bleeds to purge the body of life threatening infections. Pain is a warning against danger and alerts one to escape further injury by avoiding the behavior which caused the pain. If treated swiftly, most wounds heal over time, perhaps leaving only the slightest scar, hardly visible…but emotional pain is a vicious tearing force, capable of inflicting wounds so deep that no balm and no stitching together of flesh can bring wholeness to the sufferer.

These invisible scars mar more than the surface of the skin, burrowing deep into the recesses of the mind and deforming every pure intention. This pain paralyzes the soul and renders one the shell of a human being, who desperately reaches out through a haze of devastation and inconsolable grief for a reason to live.

No one knows for certain why some souls must endure pain

and suffering, whether self-inflicted or carelessly caused by others, or why some creatures are chosen for sorrow and others destined for joy. We do not choose our place or time in the world, nor can we change our past. Each soul is blessed with the spirit of life and with the ability to make the best of what it is given; the ability to love or to hate, to heal or to wound, to draw the darkness of hell up into the world . . . or to reach beyond our heartache for the strength to lift our eyes heavenward, and to make the music of angels.

Chapter 1
Orphan in Winter—1873

The bleak sky hung gray and heavy, forecasting a winter storm. Barren trees, thick with ice, were bent unnaturally in the silvery sheen of late afternoon, and huge snow-dusted monuments encompassed the gravesite. Ominous winged angels, statues of saints, and mysterious creatures whose forms might have turned to stone under enchantment stood watch over the dead. They stared with hollow eyes, unblinking, their frozen hearts numb to my grief.

With acute emotional pain, I watched my father's coffin lowered into the grave. The wind whipped strands of hair against my cold cheeks, and clutching a bouquet of red roses in my gloved hand, I watched in horror as darkness swallowed him. Shivering in my black dress and heavy winter cloak, I tightly held onto the hand of Madame Giry, a woman I barely knew, whom Father had chosen to be my guardian. Scriptures spoken by the minister echoed eerily through the mausoleum, and there Father would lie forever below those benevolent stargazers, whose cold countenances made me shiver beyond the chill of the day.

A burial plaque was all that marked the thirty-seven years of my father's existence on earth; a stone marker with engraved name and dates, saying nothing of the man who lay there. There was no mention of the life he had lived, the places we had traveled or the music he had created with his beloved violin. They don't engrave memories on markers, for only we who are left behind can truly tell the story of a life. He had been my only companion, both father and mother to me, and his music would live in my heart forever. But on that winter afternoon as I watched the ground steal him away, his beloved face began to recede from my inner eye.

Memories of Father playing gypsy melodies and the music of Mozart drifted through my mind as snow flurries began to swirl, and gazing upward I squeezed my eyes closed as snowflakes melted on my lashes. Looking down with an ambiguous expression, Madame Giry took my hand and led me to the grave's edge where, with vapored breath, Reverend Manning recited the last scriptures. He spilt a handful of earth into the grave, and I flinched, wishing to have covered my ears from the sound of dirt striking the coffin. The few living souls attending the service offered a final prayer, and then Madame Giry instructed me to release my roses into the grave.

At only ten years of age, I could not comprehend the finality of death or understand how quickly a living being could be reduced to a six-foot box in the ground. I wanted to throw myself down onto the coffin and beg God to bring him back, but I could only whisper goodbye as the roses fell from my hand.

Father was lost to me as I slowly turned away, and with the sound of shovels piercing stone cold earth, Madame Giry led me through a massive iron gate where we boarded the carriage that would take me to my new home.

The carriage wound its way through cobbled streets and wide avenues. But for a few beggars who hovered in doorways, shops and markets were deserted. The Christmas holiday found families and merchants comfortable in their fire-lit homes, and as the winter storm gathered force, bitter wind began to howl, sending brittle leaves spiraling up into the air. Tree limbs crackled as frozen rain pelted the already slick street.

"We are almost there, my dear," Madame Giry spoke quietly. I could feel her eyes but kept my attention straight ahead and nodded without speaking. Gently she tucked her hand under my chin and turned my face toward her own, patting my wet eyes and cheeks with her cotton handkerchief.

"I know how difficult it is for a child to lose a parent, Christine," she told me. "Gustave was a decent man and a wonderful father who will never be replaced in your life, but I promise I shall be good to you, and in time you may even come to think of me as a mother, or at the very least a friend you can trust."

Nodding my head I stared out the window and answered dutifully, "Yes, Madame."

A mother. I repeated within myself, fresh tears making silent pathways down my cheeks.

Her words stung as I thought about my real mother and the mystery surrounding her death. I knew only her beautiful name, Katrine Daaé, and that she had been born and raised in Paris. Father never spoke of her, and there had been no reminders of her in our Parisian apartment or our home in Sweden. No photographs or mementos of Katrine Daaé were among our family treasures, and now my only portrait of Father lay with my belongings in a small suitcase, on its way to my new home.

I had been told that Mother passed away shortly after I was born, but beyond that I had no knowledge of where she was buried or how she had died. Late at night when he thought I was sleeping, I often heard Papa playing his violin, lovely gypsy melodies that were both beautiful and melancholy. I would wonder what could have been the cause of so much beauty and sorrow, and I would lie in my bed listening, comforted by the violin's haunting music. Father had promised that when I was older he would tell me more about my mother, but as our carriage journeyed to The Paris Opera House, I knew I would never know her story.

I held my breath as the horses trotted up to the largest and most beautiful building I had ever seen. Father and I had traveled extensively before coming to settle in Paris. Our travels had taken us to great cities throughout Europe and Scandinavia, but Paris boasted some of the finest architecture in the world, and this ornate structure was the crown of Parisian artistry and skill. Blinking my eyes, I craned my neck, placing the palms of my gloved hands on the window.

Corinthian columns framed the building's massive entrance and supported the arches of the theater's dome. Wreathed by engravings of flowers and cherubim, the arches were suspended between earth and sky. Voluptuous bare breasted angels perched atop the highest edifices, seeming to have dropped down from heaven to grace the world of men. Stone gargoyles crouched in the shadowed archways as if they had crawled up from deepest hell. Webbed bat-wings wrapped around their grotesque forms, revealing only a glimpse of malevolent mouths and eyes.

In time I would come to learn that angels and demons both shared guardianship over that magnificent palace, a garish monument to music and humanity. Both light and darkness sought influence in the comedies and tragedies of the souls who inhabited the opera house, where the human condition was little more than a drama played out on a stage of choices. Humans could embrace the light within or be seduced by the hissing caress of darkness. Each soul was expected to make choices that would ultimately lead to eternal life and joy, or to disaster and damnation. I couldn't help feeling that my life would never be the same once I walked through those doors.

Snow was steadily falling as we pulled to a stop, and Madame placed her hand on my knee, pointing up to the roof. "If you like, Christine, my daughter will take you to see the statue of Apollo," she said, trying to engage me in conversation. As I looked up to the gigantic figure overhung from the very pinnacle of the opera's roof, I could only stare in silence, feeling powerless and afraid of what lay ahead.

Madame Giry took my hand as the driver assisted us down from the carriage. Father's violin case, along with my bags, was carried by a porter up the granite staircase while the driver tipped his hat and waved us away. With each step toward the grand entrance, dread inched icily up my spine. Dark and nearly deserted, only a small staff of maids and chamberlains had been left behind to oversee the building. The opera would remain closed during Christmas, to re-open on New Year's Eve for the annual Bal Masque. With dreary daylight giving way to winter gloom, gas lamps and torches lit the grounds, and I clung to Madame Giry's hand as she led me up the snow-covered stairs.

"Tomorrow you shall have the grand tour of our lovely lady," she said with a smile, "but for now, we must get you settled in your room."

With the opening of the massive doors, I drew in a sharp breath as we entered The Grand Foyer. Only a few lamps reflected on the marble and golden surfaces, but even in near darkness the beauty and size of the place was spectacular. From the main floor, we proceeded to the left of the grand double staircase and entered a long, narrow corridor to the very back of the building, and then on to a plain wooden door. Madame pulled a set of large keys from her handbag, and with a quick twist, the door opened into yet another narrow hallway. I was immediately struck by the contrast between this quarter of the building and The Grand Foyer.

Whereas, the foyer sparkled with Parisian wealth and luxury, I could sense the age of these corridors, the damp musty odors souring my senses. Taking an oil lamp from a bracket seated in the wall, Madame held my hand as we wound our way down a flight of stairs. Her silk skirts and woolen cloak brushed the walls as the porter followed behind with my belongings. The stairway curved downward through rough stone walls on either side, giving me the sense that I was descending into an ancient castle. Reaching the bottom, Madame smiled and tugged on my hand gently as we looked down a long stretch of wooden doors, each painted a different color.

"This is the dormitory wing, where you'll be staying just a few doors down from my apartment," she said, guiding me to the end of the hall. A torch flared and smoked, casting elongated shadows across the plaster ceiling, and the hallway was quiet, with only the sound of muffled silence greeting our arrival at a rose-colored wooden door.

"I chose this room especially for you, Christine," Madame informed me cheerfully, slipping a key into the padlock. "Most of our girls must share common quarters, but now that I am your guardian, I've made arrangements for you to have your own room close to mine."

She led me into a small room furnished with a coal-burning stove that glowed from the corner. A single bed was draped in layers of quilts, with a pink lace coverlet overtop. The room also came equipped with a small chest of drawers, a cedar trunk, and a stuffed armchair upholstered in worn damask. Filling out the modest but homey furnishings, a rose-patterned carpet lay atop the wooden floorboards, and a rose-colored stained glass window embellished with brass fittings was set high in the wall above the bureau.

As an only child I had always slept in my own bed, even if it was in makeshift quarters behind a kitchen pantry or my own little corner in our small apartment, but I wasn't certain I wanted to be left alone on my first night in the opera house.

Though it wasn't fancy or richly appointed, the room was inviting and cozy, and I was tired, longing to unpack my things and crawl beneath the covers. Trying not to let Madame see my childish fears, I sat down on the bed, yawning repeatedly as the porter deposited my suitcase and violin on the floor.

"What do you think, my dear…will it do for now?" Madame asked, seating herself beside me.

Gazing about the room with another yawn, I nodded my head and whispered wearily, "It is very nice, Madame. Thank you."

The room's one truly remarkable feature was the floor-length mirror that dominated the wall opposite the bed. With its unusual size and golden embellishments, the mirror seemed an odd fit to the room's shabby and girlish decor. Light reflected from the mirror, causing strange shadows to dance on the ceiling and across the floor.

The porter took his leave, closing the door behind him as Madame helped me remove my boots, the hooded cloak, and my dress. I was an emotionless and obedient automaton as she opened my suitcase and pulled out my night clothes, slipping the nightgown over my head.

"I see you've noticed the mirror, Christine," she spoke soothingly, doing up the little buttons on the back of my nightgown as I pulled off my stockings. "It is very old, and has been hanging somewhere in this opera house since before the ballet dormitory was added many years ago. This room was mine when I was just a few years older than you, Christine," she explained, rising up from the bed and walking gracefully across the carpet. Caressing the golden frame, her slender fingers slid along the detailed leaf and vine carvings, and she glanced back at me, speaking with a hushed voice, "I once danced before this very mirror for hours at a time," she said wistfully. "You will find many mirrors in the opera house, Christine, but this is my favorite."

"It is beautiful," I answered sleepily. With my eyes feeling heavy, I dangled my legs over the side of the bed and asked her, "But, Madame, why do I need such a big mirror?"

There was something unsettling about this mirror, and I wasn't at all certain I wanted those strange reflections and shadows looming over my sleep. Gliding back to my bedside, Madame shrugged off her heavy coat and draped it across the footboard.

Turning down the blankets, she unpacked my cases and stored my clothing in the bureau.

"Christine, my dear," she answered with a patient sigh while emptying the carpet bag, "It was your father's wish that you master all the performing arts under my care. You will be a student of dance, of voice, and of theater, and one day, if you work very hard, you may even perform with the opera company."

Unable to grasp her words, I looked up, wide-eyed, with my mouth gaping open. At only ten years old I could not imagine how I would ever fulfill Father's wishes. With him gone the very notion of performing was out of the question, and my only thoughts were of his loss, and not of a future he could not share with me. Letting my shoulders sag, I folded my hands in my lap and tried not to cry, staring at the rose designs woven into the rug.

"A dancer must have a mirror, child, and a great singer must observe her reflection while she sings," Madame instructed as I puzzled over her words. It was in that moment when I began to realize just how different my life would be in the opera house. I had never attended an actual opera, and now I was being groomed as a professional singer. Performing with Father at country fairs and in small concert halls was far less intimidating. I had always loved singing with my father on those small stages for farmers and merchants, but what would it be like to sing on a real stage with lights and a large audience? The very thought terrified me.

Madame sat down beside me and unwound my braids, combing her fingers through the length of my hair as I closed my eyes and rocked my head back with each gentle tug. Removing a hair brush from a drawer in the bureau, she brushed out the tangles, and I found comfort in her hands on my scalp and neck. Separating my hair into equal sections, she expertly combed my chestnut waves until they shone, and again my eyes drifted back to the mirror's reflection of myself and the strange woman who would now be a mother to me.

Following my gaze, Madame Giry remarked breathlessly, "Mirrors are enchanting things, are they not, my dear? One could almost believe them magical," she sighed, twisting my hair into two new braids and fastening them with ribbons. "Well, I expect that is because they are often depicted as such in myths and stories," she added, tying the ribbons into bows.

I looked up at her face, fascinated by her features and startling posture. Even when sitting, Madame's spine was perfectly straight, her shoulders back and chin erect. She seemed never to slouch, and when she walked across a room there was no hesitancy or clumsy bounce in her fluid movements. Following our move to Paris, I had seen her from time to time in our apartment, but I had never actually been bold enough to observe her beauty. Now with her close proximity, I studied her physical appearance in admiration. Her hazel eyes were kind and mysterious, reminding me very much of the tabby cat owned by Madame Valleria, Father's wealthy patroness. Madame Giry's eyes could appear either green or golden, depending on the color she wore. Her ivory complexion and high forehead were smooth and luminous in the room's soft glow, making her appear younger than her twenty-nine years. A thick braid trailed gracefully down her back, its rich auburn color accentuating her feline features.

She smiled at me and set the brush on my nightstand as I pulled my feet up onto the bed. "Christine, would you like tea before bed?" she asked kindly, cradling my cheek with her hand.

Shaking my head, I drew my knees up to my chest, for although I had eaten very little in the past two days, my stomach felt oddly full. "No thank you, Madame, I am not hungry at all," I answered.

"That is understandable, dear," she replied with a nod. "I will bring your breakfast in the morning, and after you've had time to adjust, you will take your meals with my daughter and me in the dining hall."

I slipped my toes under the heavy quilts and lay my head back against the pillow, grateful for the bed's warmth as my legs stretched under the soft layers. Madame pulled the blankets up to my chin and bent over to kiss my forehead.

"You'll see," she said, pulling matches from her pocket and

lighting the oil lamp on the bureau. "You will be happy here, and tomorrow, Christine, you shall meet my daughter. Her name is Margaret, but she prefers to be called Meg, the nickname her father gave her," Madame added.

When I did not immediately reply, she stood regarding me for a few moments, then turned toward the doorway. "Good night, my dear," she said over her shoulder as she gathered her cloak, took up her lamp and tiptoed across the rug. "If you need me, I am just down the hall. Mine is the blue door on the right."

"Good night, Madame," I answered, yawning and rubbing my eyes. With the soft rustling of silk, the door closed behind her and I was alone.

The room was deathly quiet and I lay with the blankets pulled up to my chin, trying not to look at the mirror. I considered bolting out the door to Madame's apartment, but I did not wish anyone to know how truly frightened I was. How would it look if I cried out for Madame on my very first night? It would surely shame my father, who had taught me to look after myself. With all our travels to foreign cities and villages, I had often slept in strange houses, and sometimes we even camped out-of-doors. Surely I was grown up enough to stay in this room on my own.

But the terror of the moment and the weight of the day's nightmarish events suddenly bore down on me like the heavy lid of Father's coffin. With my heart pounding, I could scarcely breathe and jolted upright, throwing back the blankets in a panic! Panting breaths came hard and fast, and I clutched my arms around my body as the memory of Father's death rose up in my mind.

Pain gripped my belly as I gagged back the meager contents of my stomach. Tears flowed in a sticky mess as I sobbed violently, rocking back and forth until the neck of my nightgown was soaked through. I simply couldn't comprehend that Father was gone.

So quickly he had taken to his bed with fever, his violin ignored as Madame Giry brought a succession of physicians to his bedside. To no avail, potions were poured down his throat and tinctures rubbed over his feverish flesh, but day by day, I watched him change from a strong and handsome man into someone I barely recognized. In the hours before his death they allowed me into his sick room, where he lay dressed only in his nightshirt. He was shriveled and dusky, his once handsome face now gaunt, with his eyes sunken and his lips drawn back to reveal his yellowed teeth. He gasped in short breaths as his frail hands clasped the sheets, then gestured for me to approach. Oily sweat clung to his skin, and losing consciousness, he rose up from the death throes just long enough to gurgle my name.

His voice was so weak that I had to put my ear to his mouth, and his breath smelt like death.

"Christine, I will not leave you alone," he panted, with a strange sucking sound in the back of his throat.

I could only lie across his chest, my little hands clutching his face as I begged him not to leave me. "Papa, please don't die," I whimpered. "Please don't go!"

"I promise," he forced between gasps, "I will send the angel."

"But I don't want an angel. I want you to stay here with me!" I cried, holding onto him in desperation. Burying my face in his nightshirt, not caring that he was unwashed and sweaty, I prayed for God to let him stay. I didn't want an angel! I wanted my father to get better, to leave his bed and play his violin. I wanted him to eat meals with me, to sing with me and tell stories like we used to.

What good was an angel? No matter how holy or beautiful, an angel could never take the place of my father. I had heard the legend many times, the story of the Angel of Music who appeared only to the most deserving of souls. The legend taught that the angel was sent from heaven to watch over special children who had been given the gift of music. Papa had explained that it was the angel's duty to protect and nurture that sacred gift. He was never visible to the child and often appeared when a child was lost and heartbroken. The angel would come to comfort her, and suddenly his celestial voice would call out in the night. Father said that those who were visited by the angel would experience an ecstasy unknown to the rest of mankind, but proud and foolish children were denied visitation because they were not found worthy. Only the humble and the gentle could be blessed by the angel's holy presence.

I had always imagined the Angel of Music to look like the

stained glass seraphim in the chapel windows; with flowing robes, white swan wings and golden hair. But now I wanted my father's gentle brown eyes and soft dark hair. His tattered work clothes and his calloused hands meant more to me than any old angel!

"I don't want an angel!" I repeated stubbornly, "I want you, Papa! Please don't go away!"

Father moaned and writhed in his bed as Madame Giry tried to comfort me. He drifted in and out of consciousness for another hour, intermittently opening his glazed eyes and twitching violently. They wiped his brow and parched lips with a damp cloth while I hovered in the corner, as Madame wrapped her arms tightly around me. Finally, with a shattering wail as his back arched in rigid spasms, he called out my name. I ran to his bed and he took hold of my hands, looking into my eyes for the last time.

"I love you, Chris..."

And then he fell back onto the mattress, his body going limp, the muscles and lines of his face becoming relaxed and smooth as if he were only sleeping. I waited, wanting him to move, watching for breath to fill his chest...but there was no movement. The only sounds in the room were my sobbing and a ticking clock. I lay across his chest for some moments, clinging to him, listening for that familiar thrum of blood pumping through his heart, but there was no sign of life.

A mysterious, dark power had taken my father to a place where I could not follow, and my grief was unbearable as I clung to his lifeless body.

"Papa!" I wailed. "Papa!"

All alone in my opera house room, the memories of his death were too vivid and I could not bear them. Choking on my tears, I slipped down from the bed and knelt before the mirror, folding my hands in prayer as I had done nightly throughout my childhood. But Father had always been at my side, waiting to tuck me in and kiss me goodnight. Now he was gone and who would hear my prayers? I believed in God, but on that night even God seemed too far away to hear the longings of a frightened child.

"Dear God, please let me hear his voice again!" I begged.

My prayer was met with silence, and I had never felt so alone.

Drawing my knees up to my chest, I sobbed into my hands, trying to stifle my tears in the sleeves of my gown. With all the loneliness of the world crushing me, I remained on the floor until my body ached with the cold.

Chapter 2
The Bleeding Rose

The night of my father's burial seemed to drag on endlessly as I huddled on the floor in my room, but sometime in the night I had crawled back into bed and drifted off to sleep...yet even in sleep I could not escape the horrors of my father's death nor the terrifying image of the frozen graveyard. I awoke fitfully hour by hour, sitting up with a start, not remembering where I was or what had brought me there...but gradually, exhausted, I snuggled down into the bedcovers, reciting a prayer to St. Michael.

The next morning, sunlight from the pink window awakened me, its rose-tinted rays casting warmth across my bed. As my swollen eyes slowly opened and adjusted to daylight, without warning the image of my father's funeral assaulted me like a blow to my stomach, and once again those waves of devastation broke my heart afresh.

"Oh...no...I can't believe...I can't believe he's gone," I cried, clutching my fingers around the sheet. "Papa, my papa!"

Turning over onto my stomach, I buried my face in the pillow. I couldn't understand how the tears kept coming, but on and on they rolled down my face without reprieve, wetting the bed linens and leaving my nose raw and congested. I reached for a handkerchief and blew my nose until the pressure made my ears ache, but with no relief, I turned over onto my side, sobbing until, unexpectedly, my tearful gaze was drawn to the great mirror across the room. As I rose up on one elbow, I looked at my reflection and hardly recognized myself. A stranger with a white anemic face and dark circles under her eyes stared back at me. Only months ago I had been a happy little girl, flying kites with my father on the seashore, collecting shells and singing songs around the campfire. Now those happy days were grains of sand that had slipped through my fingers.

The mirror seemed to show me who I had become, what my father's death had made of me, and I doubted that I would ever smile or laugh again. I tried to look away but somehow the mirror captivated my attention and I found myself pulled to its reflective power. In the dark of night, the mirror had both fascinated and frightened me, but in the rosy glow of morning it was merely a beautiful old piece of furniture. There were no shadows or eerie reflections to be afraid of, and so I scolded myself for behaving like a child and lay there sniffing and blowing my nose until a soft tapping on the door disrupted my dark thoughts.

"Christine, are you all right, dear?" Madame Giry muttered from out in the corridor. "I thought I heard you crying...may I come in?"

Very quickly, I sat up and tried to wipe away the tears with a handkerchief, but my face was dreadfully red and puffy, so what was the use of pretending?

"Yes, Madame," I answered, clearing my throat and shocked by the frailty of my own voice. "I'm awake now...you may come in."

Madame entered with a smile, carrying a large tray of fruit, bread and cheese. With one look at my condition, her brows knit together and the smile immediately gave way to a look of concern as she sat the tray on the bureau and came swiftly to my side.

"Oh dear, my poor child. I never should have left you alone!" she cried out. With regret threading her voice, she sat down on the bed and held out her arms to me. I immediately flung myself into her embrace, and with my head tucked beneath her chin she rocked me gently as I softly cried into her fringed shawl.

"I can't make it stop, Madame. It won't stop!" I cried.

"I know, darling. I know. It is hard," Madame soothed me. "But you must not be brave for our sake, Christine. It's all right to cry, and even though it hurts desperately...let the tears flow."

Madame's words made me cry harder, and into the softness of her shawl I gave myself to the grief, letting it wash over me.

"There, there, child...you poor darling," she consoled me.

Father had always been affectionate with hugs and kisses, but affection from a woman was a rarity in my life. Snuggling closer into Madame's arms, I closed my eyes, sniffling and sobbing.

Unlike many women I had known, Madame Giry did not speak with a high pitched nasal voice. Her voice had a soft, low register and was very pleasant to my sensitive ears. She was a petite and delicately boned woman, and yet as she held me in her arms I could feel the physical strength from her years of dance.

She did not rush me away and we held each other for some moments until finally, my tears began to abate and I lifted my eyes to hers. With her hands stroking my braids, Madame's voice dropped just above a whisper as she tried to explain herself.

"I looked in on you a few times last night, but you appeared to be sleeping so I thought it best not to disturb you. I'm so sorry, Christine. I should never have left you alone. But your father insisted you would want your own room, and I suppose, well...I simply wasn't thinking clearly," she said with a hint of sadness. "But I promise, Meg and I will make room for you in our apartment and you may move in with us immediately."

Unsure how to reply, I merely laid my head against her chest, utterly confused and afraid of a life without my father. It mattered little now, whether I had my own room or shared someone else's. I knew only that Father was gone and nothing, not even prayers, would bring him back.

"I'm sorry, Madame, I do not mean to be a bother," I apologized, as she gave my face another pat with her handkerchief.

"Oh, Christine, you are no trouble at all," she assured me. "We are so happy you've come to live with us. As a matter of fact, Meg is beside herself with excitement and very anxious to meet you. But of course, if you are not ready we shall do it another day."

I wasn't ready for any of the changes happening around me, but Madame was a lovely and kind woman, and I was curious about her daughter. Father and I, traveling as often as we did, had never stayed in one place long enough to make many friends. There were acquaintances and brief encounters with girls my age, but my only real friend was a boy I had met during last summer's holiday in Perros. I let my mind drift to Raoul de Chagny's sweet face, wondering what had become of him. Our time together had been all too brief, and I doubted that I would ever see him again.

Dislodging myself from Madame's embrace, I nodded and

tried to sound cheerful as I said, "I would like to meet her, Madame, but maybe I should dress first."

With her smile returning, Madame stroked the side of my cheek as she stood to her feet. "Splendid!" she exclaimed, folding her hands together. "You change and I'll bring Meg with the tea things. The two of you two can get acquainted over breakfast."

As I watched her leave, Madame seemed to float across the carpet and out my door. I stretched and yawned, looking about my room at the unfamiliar furnishings, then shuffled on my bare feet to the bureau, exploring its drawers and compartments. Madame had already folded and stacked my few frocks and dresses neatly in the top drawer. Setting aside heavy stockings and a dark blue frock with a white lace collar, I raised my arms and pulled the nightgown off over my head. After I had changed my pantalets and chemise, I slipped on the dress and fastened the little buttons on the bodice. Finally, I tugged on my winter stockings, and with a glance in the mirror, I set about tidying the room, making the bed and finally exploring the cedar trunk.

She had placed my boots and hat-boxes in the trunk, along with the carpetbag containing Father's photograph, my silver locket, and my music books. Opening the bag, I searched until I found a little drawstring pouch. After untying the cords, I spilled the silver locket into my palm, then slipped the necklace over my head. Closing the trunk, I turned to the mirror and polished the locket with my sleeve. I wanted very much to open the locket just for a moment, but I knew that seeing his photograph would make me cry again, and I didn't want Madame's daughter to see me crying. I stood gazing at the locket in the mirror and jumped slightly when there was a knock on the door, with Madame's pleasant voice announcing, "Christine, I've brought Meg with the tea."

Turning away from the mirror, I was uneasy and shy about meeting someone new, afraid she might not like me, but as I cautiously opened the door my eyes fell upon the prettiest blond girl I had ever seen! She carried a tray brimming with dainty tea cups and matching saucers.

Madame's daughter was two years older than I, but we were nearly the same height, and I couldn't help comparing my dull brown eyes with the flashing cornflower blue of Margaret's. Her dimpled cheeks flushed pink as she tiptoed in white satin ballet slippers, wearing a tulle skirt over a white dance camisole. Margaret's hair was pulled back with a wide satin ribbon, and a fringe of blonde bangs set off her blue eyes and perfectly shaped brows. In her dance costume she appeared older than her age, and I felt myself dull and ungainly in her sunny presence.

Madame stood behind her daughter, grasping the handles of a smaller tray that contained a steaming teapot, cream pitcher and sugar bowl. "Christine, this is my daughter, Margaret," she said cheerily. "She is training as a dancer at the academy."

"Good morning, Margaret," I said politely, as Madame and her daughter swept past me into the room.

After setting the tray on the bureau next to the fruit and cheese, the young girl spun on her toes and ran toward me with a flourish of pink tulle and ribbons.

Taking hold of my hands, she giggled and grinned. "Please, everyone calls me Meg. I am so glad you have come to live with us, Christine. We shall be great friends!" she said with a giggle.

"Thank you," I replied shyly, surprised by her outgoing demeanor.

Meg took my hand and led me to the bureau where Madame Giry was cutting a few slices of cheese, arranging them on a plate with fruit and chunks of bread.

"I'm afraid this will have to do until lunch, girls," Madame informed us. "Cook is off this morning."

I watched as Meg poured three cups of tea, then glanced up at me with a smile. "How many lumps?" she asked. At first I wasn't sure what she meant and I could not help but smile a little when I finally realized she was referring to the sugar.

"Oh, just one, please," I answered clumsily. Using a set of tiny tongs, Meg dropped a cube of sugar into my teacup and offered it to me, as Madame held out a plate of fruit and cheese.

My stomach was still unsettled, so I told her, "Oh no, Madame, I'm not at all hungry."

I saw the concern in her expression as she gently insisted, "Now, Christine, you must eat something. Just a few bites and some tea, yes?"

Receiving the plate from her hands, I obediently broke off a piece of bread as Madame sipped her tea. I still had no appetite, but nibbled the bread and cheese to please her. My heart was heavy, and from one moment to the next I felt on the verge of tears, but meeting Meg had brought much needed light into my otherwise grim world, and I loved her immediately. The more time I spent with Madame Giry, the more comfortable I felt in her presence, but there was something about her that troubled me; a certain aloofness and a hint of mystery in her eyes. As Meg and I nibbled our breakfast, I watched Madame through the corner of my eye, wondering why Father had chosen her to be my guardian and how he had come to know her.

Half an hour later, setting her teacup down and making her way to the door, Madame placed her arm around Meg's shoulder and announced, "Well girls, I have some business to attend to, so I shall leave you two young ladies alone to get acquainted...and Meg, darling," she added, looking over her shoulder as she turned the doorknob, "how would it be if you stayed with Christine for a few nights while I make room for her in our apartment?"

Nodding her head enthusiastically, Meg grabbed my hands and did three little bounces on her slippered toes, "Oh yes, Mama! I would love to. That is, if it's all right with Christine!"

"Yes, of course," I answered.

After Madame had left the room, Meg immediately drew me to the bed where we sat together and chatted easily over tea and breakfast. Despite my grief and heaviness of heart, she managed to engage my attention with her intriguing tales of the extravagant and often scandalous life of the opera house. She spoke in awe of the twenty-one year old Italian diva, La Carlotta, and of the many singers, actors and dancers who made up the opera's flamboyant company.

She told me about the scandalous romance between Carlotta and the tenor, Piangi, and of the opera's managers, Poligny and Debienne. According to Meg, these two men were known less for their refined musical taste than for their fat wallets. I was enthralled by Meg's eccentric stories, her blue eyes growing larger and more luminous with each outrageous tale. She seemed to have uncanny knowledge of the opera's many secrets and intrigues, and was anxious to avail me of them all. She giggled and shushed herself for fear that Madame would catch us talking of unspeakable things, and I found myself enchanted by her cheerful company.

Suddenly, looking around the room she leaned into me and cupped her hands over my ear, then began to whisper a story that rivaled even my father's tales. "Christine," she teased, her voice intense and eyes wide, "did you know that the opera is haunted?"

"Haunted?" I questioned, leaning back and staring at her incredulously. "You mean by a ghost?"

"Yes!" she enthused, obviously pleased about the information she was about to impart.

"Strange things happen all the time that no one can explain!" she informed me, her expression somber as her eyes darted all around the room and then back to me.

I listened, enraptured and frightened all at once by Meg's tale of a creature she called the Opera Ghost. According to Meg, the "ghost" pulled little pranks on the opera company and its managers. In the beginning they were small incidents, like missing sheet music and props that kept disappearing from sets under construction. Elaborate drawings would appear on previously blank canvases, and ballet girls reported strange shadows in the third basement where discarded props were stored. Food often went missing from the kitchen, and articles of clothing from the wardrobes were always being "misplaced".

When anonymous notes first began to appear beneath the managers' office door, giving specific orders as to how the opera should be run and demanding an extravagant salary, the joke began to wear thin, causing the entire opera house staff and its managers, Poligny and Debienne, to wonder who was responsible for the ruse.

Remembering the stories Father had read to Raoul and me that summer by the sea, I was momentarily distracted from Meg's gossip. On warm summer nights we had built large bonfires on Madame Valleria's beachfront property, and as Raoul and I huddled in blankets by the fire, snacking on chocolates and dried fruit, Father would play his violin and mimic the voices of all the characters. His stories were like little plays as he gently wove his spell into our vivid imaginations. From the days of my earliest childhood I had loved the dark legends of ogres, goblins, and nisse who lived in the enchanted Black Forest.

My heart began to grow heavy again as I remembered that lovely summer holiday, and suddenly, Meg's chirping voice faded as fresh tears rimmed my eyes.

Turning my gaze away from her, I thought it strange that as she continued to speak I no longer heard her words. My father had been healthy back then, his skin tanned from the sun, his wavy brown hair threaded with golden strands, and a genuine smile lighting up his fine features. I was desperate to forget the images of his deathbed, and needed to recall what he looked like during that magical summer.

Fingering my locket, I sadly remembered it all. That summer had been like a dream as we did whatever we wanted each and every day. There were no worries over money or employment during those blissful months. Through Madame Valleria's generosity, Father and I had lived like royalty; enjoying parties and performances for her friends. We slept in the most luxurious feather beds, dining on the best food, and drinking the finest wines.

Suddenly, Meg's voice broke through my happy recollections, and I heard her repeating my name. "Christine, Christine," she called out to me. "Have you been listening at all? Are you feeling all right?"

Blinking back the tears, I looked up and replied, "I was just remembering."

"Were you thinking about your father, Christine?" Meg asked sincerely, grasping my hands.

"Yes," I answered, lowering my chin so that she would not see me cry. "I'm so sorry, Christine," she spoke gently, sliding closer and placing her arm around my shoulder. "Christine, Mother says your father was a great musician."

As I absently looked at the violin case lying in the overstuffed chair, Meg followed my gaze and inquired, "Is it yours, Christine?"

"No," I answered bleakly. "It is…I mean, it was my father's.

"Is it very beautiful?" the inquisitive girl pressed. "May I see it?

"If you like."

I walked over to the chair and reverently picked up the violin case, setting it carefully on the bed. As if it contained a priceless treasure, I flipped open the brass fasteners and pulled the lid up slowly, revealing an intricately hand-carved violin nestled in blue velvet lining. Lovingly stroking the instrument's old pegbox and scrolled neck, I inhaled the comforting aromas of rosin, wood, and lemon oil. The fingerboard was scraped and worn down to bare wood where my father had skillfully pressed the strings, and there were small chips around the *f*-holes. The bow was rough and dull where he had held onto the whalebone grip, and the horsehair was frayed with errant strands. I lifted the violin from the case and tilted my head, tucking my chin onto the ebony chin rest. Plucking a single string with my index finger, I paused as it softly reverberated.

Rising up from the bed, Meg joined me and gently touched the scroll neck. "Christine, it is very old, isn't it?" she remarked with awe.

Caught up in the memory of Father's music, I began to softly hum an old gypsy tune we had performed together in the markets and squares. The bittersweet melody vibrated gently at the back of my throat as Father had taught me. As I hummed the tune, prickles traveled up my arms and I was beginning to think that Meg's stories of the haunted opera house had spooked me.

"Christine, what is that music?" Meg asked as I continued to hum softly, my eyes drifting to the mirror.

"Just an old gypsy song, Meg," I answered, plucking another string.

Meg followed as I padded across the carpet to stand before the mirror. Imitating my father's performance stance, I looked at my reflection, humming the song's pretty refrain. Standing just to the left of me, Meg's voice dropped to a whisper as she inquired, "Is it a song your father played?"

"Yes, many times. It is my favorite," I answered with another pluck on a string.

Meg stepped around until she stood between me and the mirror, then placed her hand on my shoulder and questioned, "Will you sing it for me, Christine, I mean the whole song?"

For years it had been my favorite song, and now it seemed almost a sacrilege to sing it without my father. Making excuses, I responded to her request, "I'm afraid my voice isn't very good right now, Meg, with all the crying…and well, I'd rather not."

Not ready to drop the subject, Meg pressed me further, her fingers gently tugging on my puffed sleeve. "But, Christine, wouldn't your father want you to sing it for him?" she suggested with a beguiling smile.

Grasping the violin's neck, I lifted my chin off the rest, then dangled the violin at my side. "Do you think he would hear me, Meg?" I questioned, slowly backing away from the mirror and moving toward the bed.

"Of course, Christine!" she replied without hesitation. "Mama says my grandpapa watches me dance from heaven, so why wouldn't your father be watching over you?" she asserted with startling confidence.

Having very little confidence of my own, I placed the violin safely back inside its case. "I'm not sure, Meg. I've prayed for him to hear me. But do you really think the dead can return?" I asked her.

I leaned over the bed and set the bow in its brackets as Meg came up behind me. "Of course I do, Christine," she affirmed cheerfully. "They come back to look after their loved ones."

Shutting the case, I snapped the fasteners closed and considered her statement, desperate for it to be true. With a heavy sigh, I turned around to face Meg and acquiesced, "Well, I don't suppose it would hurt. If you are right, and he can hear from heaven, well, what would be the harm?"

"Oh, Christine, what's it called?" Meg asked me as I turned away from the bed and faced the mirror.

"*The Bleeding Rose*," I answered.

As I moved across the carpet, Meg lowered herself onto the bed, folding her hands in her lap. After clearing my throat, I softly hummed the melody. I could already hear the fatigue in my voice and I knew I would not sing it well, but with my fingers grasping the locket around my neck, and with thoughts of my father, I began:

An Angel sent from heaven
Came to a garden fair
Searching for a flower
To wreath her golden hair
A lily grew in splendor
Radiant and white,
Dazzling in the sun
Shimmering of light...

I watched my own reflection in the mirror, mouthing the song lyrics as my eyes rimmed with tears. Behind me I could see Meg seated on the bed, her chin upturned and her eyes downcast. There was the strangest feeling around me, a tingling sensation on the top of my head...and for a moment I wondered if Father was near. Was this merely my imagination, or perhaps the fulfillment of his final promise that he would send an angel to guide and protect me? I wasn't sure if it was just the spooky old building or Meg's stories fueling my fancy. I knew only that I was compelled to sing.

When a single blood red rose
Caught the angel's eye
Dark and mysterious
She could not pass it by
Crimson petals beckoned
Beautiful and rare
The angel chose the red rose
To wreath her golden hair
But when she plucked the blossom
Was pierced by savage thorn
Blood poured from the flower
The angel's heart was torn...

My voice became more steady as I warmed to the song, and forgetting my fatigue, I thought of my father looking down into my room through a celestial portal. In my imagination, the ceiling of my room seemed to dissolve and the roof of the opera house vanished, revealing a brilliant starlit sky and the very vaults of heaven. I drove my voice beyond my grief, willing the song to reach higher and higher, soaring upward and outward.

> *She cast it onto the ground*
> *And then she did dispose*
> *Choosing the pale lily*
> *Instead of the bleeding rose*

With the song's completion, I was riveted to the mirror, tears rolling down my face with my heartbeat drumming in my ears. Jumping up from the bed, Meg flitted across the room and threw her arms around me as if we had know each other forever. "Oh, Christine, Mama told me about your beautiful voice, but…well, I didn't know you would sing like that!" she declared breathlessly.

"Thank you, Meg," was all I could say to her, using my sleeve to wipe my eyes.

"Christine, your father must be so proud. Really, you sing like an angel!" Meg praised.

Before I could utter a word in reply, the door opened and Madame Giry breezed into my room with a set of large keys jingling in her hand. She had changed from her morning gown into a fetching pearl gray frock, with a cuirasse bodice and a graceful pleated train flowing down the back. Her braided hair had been twisted and coiled on top of her head, with tortoise shell hair-picks pinning the coiffure in place.

Her smoky eyes immediately fell on the two of us with our arms wrapped around each other in a sisterly hug, and she sighed with a smile. "I am so pleased you two are getting acquainted. I just knew you would be like two peas in a pod!" she said cheerily.

Grinning at her mother, Meg rose up on her toes and grasped my hand. "Oh Mama, you should hear Christine sing! She sounds like an angel!" she exclaimed.

I could feel the blood rushing into my face and stared down at the floor self-consciously as Madame approached us, her train dragging behind her. "So I've been told," she said, one corner of her mouth turning up into an elusive smile. "Perhaps, Christine, you will sing again later but for now, would you like to tour the opera house?"

Meg's eyes widened as she awaited my reaction. In truth, my little performance had drained me and I was tired. But I did not wish to disappoint Meg or Madame, who were obviously anxious to show me my new home...and I was curious about the opera house, having never seen a world-class auditorium.

"Thank you, Madame, that would be nice," I responded with forced enthusiasm.

Placing her arm around my shoulder, Madame leaned down, and peering directly into my eyes, said, "This afternoon, after our tour and a bite of lunch, perhaps you and Meg would like to nap."

"Yes, Madame," I agreed with a nod.

The moment I stepped out from the narrow, dark corridor of the ballet dormitory and up into the bizarre and magical world of the opera's bohemian backstage, I was amazed and overwhelmed, for surely this was no place for a ten year old girl! Networked with spiral staircases and catwalks, tiered balconies led to the upper regions of the theater's backstage world, and as Meg pointed out, all the way up to the opera's roof. Reserved for the principal cast, ornately painted dressing room doors lined the main floor, while the community dressing rooms for chorus and the corps de ballet were located in the stuffier upper levels.

Large open bays were utilized for every facet of the opera's production. There was a gigantic workshop where plaster artisans formed molded figures of animals and oversized statues, whose eyes seemed to watch from their empty sockets, following us as we toured their realm. Every surface was coated in fine white dust, while disembodied heads and nude forms hung from the rafters in various stages of painting and finish work. The scenery bay, a vast structure at the farthest end of the backstage area, was used to construct giant canvas flies and backdrops. Blank or partially painted canvases and paint supplies littered the floor, with the atmosphere saturated by turpentine and linseed oil fumes.

As Madame Giry led us through the maze of studios and workshops, I couldn't help but feel the excitement of this colorful

27

world to which I now belonged. Though all was quiet, tomorrow the place would overflow with activity as the cast, crew, and workers returned to prepare the opera house for the Bal Masque, only five days hence.

We were just about to enter the wig room when a rotund, red-faced woman with a measuring tape draped around her neck came bounding toward us. Her chubby arms overflowed with yards of colorful fabric and costume pieces, stacked nearly to her double chin. As trims, tassels, and beads spilled to the floor behind her, two giddy young women followed, scooping up the mess as fast as they could.

"Madame Giry! Oh, Madame!" she shouted hysterically, nearly out of breath.

Folding her hands calmly, Madame inquired, "What is it, Marie?"

"Madame, he has struck again!" the portly woman declared.

With a faint smile and a glint in her eyes, Madame questioned the agitated woman. "Calm down, Marie, and tell me what has happened," she asked patiently.

I was to learn that although Madame Giry was only the ballet mistress, she was highly regarded, and even loved, by members of the opera and its company. If anything was amiss in any department, it was generally Madame who was called upon to assist in catastrophes, and then expected to resolve the crisis. Yet she never received credit from the mangers when her skill and patience had succeeded.

Madame's talents were not limited to dance. She was also known for her good head in business affairs. As a gifted young woman, Madame had dreamt of becoming a prima ballerina, but a whirlwind romance and family tragedy had forced her to give up the stage and remain behind the scenes. Unlike many women in her position, Madame did not grow bitter; but rather, she embraced her duties, loving her students and serving as mother to all. She was known never to speak of the tragedy which had thwarted her dreams, and very little was known of Madame's past. There was an air of mystery beneath the dignified grace and poise which set her apart from other women.

Madame Louise Giry had entered my life a year or so prior to

Father's illness, but I was only vaguely aware of their prior association. I knew that she sometimes managed his business affairs, and that she had helped him procure a teaching position in Paris…but beyond that, she was the kind woman my father had entrusted to become my legal guardian, and I was beginning to feel more comfortable around her.

Madame helped to steady the toppling bundles in Marie's arms as the woman breathlessly told her tale. "Madame, it is him!" she exclaimed, her eyes wide open with fear.

Taking hold of my arm, Meg led me a few paces away where, whispering in my ear, she announced with a playful grin, "It's the Opera Ghost!"

We listened to Marie's panicked account as spools of thread and trims continued to tumble onto the floor.

"As you know, Madame, the mangers' costumes for the ball have been labeled and stored in the wardrobes until the unveiling on New Year's Eve," Marie warbled.

"Yes, Marie, go on."

"I was reviewing my checklist, Madame, preparing to make some last minute alterations on Monsieur Debienne's costume. But when I opened the wardrobe to retrieve it, the costume had vanished!" she shouted. "Monsieur Debienne's costume is missing, Madame Louise!"

Shaking her head, Madame's eyes narrowed. "Are you certain, Marie?" she asked. "Perhaps it has been misplaced."

Still struggling to hold onto her goods, Marie adjusted the bundle and grunted, "No, no, Madame, I have turned the wardrobes, dressing rooms, and workshops upside down and inside out! I assure you the costume is nowhere to be found!"

A small muscle jerked in Madame's cheek as Meg and I listened with fascination. "Well then," she said, "perhaps it *is* the Opera Ghost!"

Marie's eyes widened and her cheeks turned red as she spoke in exasperation, "But why would he steal Monsieur Debienne's costume, Madame?"

"Well, Marie", Madame Giry grinned with a wink, "I suppose he approves of your skills with a needle and thread…and in any case, my dear lady, I'm sure it will turn up."

"But what am I to tell Monsieur Debienne?" Marie questioned, as her young helpers scooped up more of the sewing debris.

Thinking a moment, Madame regarded Marie's bundle of supplies, and then suggested, "Simply tell him the costume is not up to his standards and let him wear last year's pirate ensemble. Judging by the hangover he woke up with last January first, I doubt he even remembers what he wore!" Madame laughed.

Marie nodded her head, and snorting with laughter, she agreed, "You are probably right, Madame, right indeed!"

With another catastrophe averted, Marie and her helpers trotted down the hall, as Madame turned to Meg and me with a devious sparkle in her eyes. "Come, come girls," she clapped her hands, "we have much more to show you!"

We continued on the tour, and I could not help my fascination for this Opera Ghost, who apparently had a devilish sense of humor. His pranks seemed perfectly harmless…but still, I disliked the idea of someone sneaking about in the shadows. I furtively looked all around our surroundings as Madame led us through a series of locked doors and long hallways. With so many levels of twists and turns, the building was practically a maze, and having no sense of direction, I wondered how people managed not to get lost!

Finally, we arrived at a short staircase that was lavishly upholstered in deep red and lit by crystal wall sconces. Meg grabbed my hand and grinned at me like a Cheshire cat as we reached our destination. "Now, Christine," Madame announced, beaming down at me, "you shall see the heart of our lovely lady."

With the click of lock and key, Madame opened a heavy mahogany door and we entered into a small chamber draped with rich red velvet curtains. Lush golden cords with fringes and tassels trimmed the heavy hangings, and quilted velvet theater seats were arranged for as many as twelve patrons in the little alcove. With a grand gesture Madame pulled the thick cord and the front curtains opened onto a full view of the opera's resplendent auditorium. I stood wide-eyed, barely able to take it all in, stunned by its grandeur and golden opulence even when lit by only a few gas lamps.

Father had occasionally taken me to small concert halls, but this was beyond anything I'd ever seen in its beauty and scale. Wide-bellied balconies beehived the theater's perimeter, reaching nearly all the way up to the ceiling. My gaze traveled the balconies until, leaning back with a soft gasp, I caught sight of the tremendous chandelier high above the main floor. The blue and copper dome was frescoed with clouds and cherubim, and I could imagine how the chandelier would sparkle when lit with live flame. The fixture was strewn extravagantly with hundreds of tear-drop crystals and strings of iridescent beads, and golden harps formed the framework for its glittering six-tiered casement.

I leaned over the balustrade, looking down at the rows of theater seats on the auditorium's main floor. I let my eyes wander through the entire theater until they fell on the spectacular stage, which was framed by a carved relief of gold-leafed angels. Scarlet drapes trimmed with gold fringe hung in graceful velvet pleats across the Proscenium arch, and figures of angels and gargoyles loomed above the orchestra pit.

Gold and copper statues of Isis, Amphitrite, Hebe, Pandora, Psyche, Thetis, Pomona, and Daphne encrusted the theater walls. These gods looked down with haughty indifference upon the world of mortals as Madame remarked, "She is magnificent, no?"

"Yes, Madame," I whispered, in complete awe of my surroundings.

"And one day, Christine, you will perform on that stage," she spoke quietly, looking down at me as I stared ahead. This was said as a statement of fact, but I could not comprehend ever doing such a thing. My thoughts were suddenly interrupted as Meg began bouncing on her toes and clapping her hands. Blurting out for all to hear, she squealed, "Mama, if we go down to the stage, Christine could sing her song right now!"

Mortified by Meg's suggestion, I looked to Madame for an escape but was surprised to see from her smile that she was not at all shocked by Meg's request.

"Why, I think that is a wonderful idea, Meg! I would love to hear Christine sing."

"But, Madame," I protested, "here, on this stage? Now? I can't!"

Leaning down to me, Madame placed her hand on my shoulder and spoke in a whisper, "Of course you can, Christine. We have the theater to ourselves until tomorrow, and no one will hear you but the two of us."

I gazed about the huge theater, overwhelmed by its size and the very notion that I would dare sing on a stage where famous opera singers had performed. Compared to those illustrious ladies and gentlemen, my voice would surely sound dreadful. Singing at fairs was one thing, but singing on that stage was out of the question.

I shook my head and lifting my face to hers, I objected, "But Madame, I'm not good enough for such a stage!"

Placing her arm around me, Madame steered me toward the door and turned the knob, as Meg followed behind and chattered in approval of her mother's comments.

"Nonsense, Christine, my dear. I have it on good authority that you sing like an angel. In any case, your voice training shall begin after the New Year, so why not give it a try? It might take your mind off unpleasant things."

We started down the stairs and I found myself extremely nervous as Meg and Madame led me to the main floor.

"Yes, Christine, sing for your father like you did this morning!" Meg persisted, tiptoeing down the corridor that led underneath the stage. In spite of my nerves I felt somewhat obligated to fulfill their wishes because after all, they had taken me in and had shown me nothing but kindness.

With my stomach in knots and weariness creeping into my body, I decided I'd best be done with it.

"Well, I suppose I could, if you will stay here with me," I gave in, tugging on Madame's sleeve.

"Of course we will," Madame assured me. "You've nothing to fear from this auditorium, Christine. It was your father's dream that you live and perform here, and I promise you he would be so very proud."

Pausing before we entered through the door, I nodded and sighed to myself as Madame led the way to the stage. As we stood under the catwalk, I leaned back to gawk at the complex system of pulleys, flywheels, and cables high overhead. Meg took my hand

and practically dragged me onto the stage, where I continued to gaze upward, feeling utterly dwarfed by the massive backstage environment.

Looking down at my feet, I took notice of markings and patterns etched into the stage floor and wondered how the trap doors could possibly open and close without injuring the actor. An uncanny sense of magic and illusion surrounded me, and I wrapped my arms about my body as a gust of cool air swooped down upon us from the rafters.

"How about right here?" Meg suggested, leading me closer to the footlights where I could look down into the orchestra pit. From that vantage point the auditorium's rows of theater seats and balconies gave the impression of a giant city rising up around me, and I held my breath as their footsteps echoed into the wings. Folding her hands together at her waist, Madame smiled and nodded her head in my direction.

"Do not be afraid, Christine," she encouraged me, "It's just the three of us now."

"And your father!" Meg blurted out, garnering her mother's frown. Again, staring down at my feet, with chills spreading up my arms and my heart pounding, I began to sing *The Bleeding Rose*.

Chapter 3
The Ghost of Don Juan

Throughout its years as a palace to the performing arts, The Paris Opera House, then known as Théâtre de l'Académie Royale de Musique, had survived a series of political and military hostilities, culminating in its use as a field hospital throughout the Communard and Republican conflict of eighteen-seventy. The building had been spared significant damage, but the lowest cellars were seized by the Communard troops as an arsenal for weaponry, food stuffs, and kegs of gun powder.

It was believed by the present day authorities that gun powder was buried in the vicinity, but they had failed to discover its whereabouts. The search was called off when one of the soldiers did not return. His body was never recovered and it was believed that he had become lost in the underground passages.

The third level of the cellar's complex was used for repositories of lumber, masonry, and other building materials. Discarded set pieces, flats and backdrops were stored down there, together with a costume storage facility that was seldom visited.

Only the bravest of the ballet rats would wander below the second level, and no one in their right mind would dare take the ancient winding staircase all the way down to the fifth level, said to be haunted. Not much was known about the fifth level except that, during construction of the opera house, underground streams had been found on the site, and it was rumored that a lake existed somewhere in the limestone vaults below. However, no one had been able to find it and even if they had, they had never returned to divulge its precise location, or so it was said.

Located on the fourth level, boiler rooms provided the opera's central heating system, reminding one of *Dante's Inferno* as workmen with their silhouettes, black against the fiery ovens, shoveled mountains of coal into gigantic glowing burners. Day and night, these soot-covered men toiled so that the opera's patrons and residents could enjoy the comfort of warmth even on the coldest winter nights. Occasionally, the rat catcher lurked about the place; and as he loped through the darkness with his traps and burlap bags, one could always see the glow of his lantern even before his crouching form came into view.

That oppressive sector was known for its close proximity to underground Roman catacombs where, during seasonal floods, human remains routinely washed up, leaving unearthed skulls and bones scattered about.

Small rooms in the fourth level had been used as torture chambers and to warehouse political detainees. The stain of human blood on brick and mortar was still visible with torchlight, and anyone who ventured down there was chilled by its spiritually dark imprint. Where corridors networked with sewage canals leading to the city proper and the River Seine, the tunnels had also served as an escape route for a few fortunate prisoners of the Communard.

The fifth level's only occupant had made certain his legend was well publicized among the opera house inhabitants. On the fifth level beneath the opera house, he had established his domicile in a large subterranean cave, where the underground lake was fed by a tributary of the River Seine.

At the heart of the grotto's extensive three-cavern formation stood a massive organ whose tarnished pipes and fittings jutted upward, nearly reaching the ceiling's stony height. The black walnut console was splotched and caked with hardened candle wax, and five tiers of manuals and stops formed the organ's archaic keyboard.

A carved music stand stood beside the organ, with sheet music spread across its harp-shaped easel. Leather-bound manuscripts were stacked knee-high against the back wall, and tattered Persian rugs were spread haphazardly across the stone floor. A small mahogany table was occupied by a variety of musical instruments, with a violin resting alone in its leather case.

To the right of the organ, stone steps led up to a bedroom, with black velvet drapes framing the chamber's entrance. The old four poster canopy bed was also draped in black, lending the room an atmosphere of a gloomy funeral parlor.

To the left of the organ was a library, furnished on one side with eight foot tall shelves of books and antiques. Looming against the library's back wall was an assortment of floor-length mirrors, but their reflective glass and gilded frames had been carefully concealed behind heavy canvas dust cloths.

Illustrations of costumes, set designs, and bric-a-brac lay scattered about on small tables, with a large desk and high-backed leather chair anchoring the library's center. The desk was piled with detailed blueprints and books, together with a Persian monkey music box that had been perched atop a thick pile of fresh manuscripts.

The underground caverns were dimly lit with oil lamps and brass candelabra, and the fragrance of candle smoke camouflaged the sour odors of the dampness. The implied opulence of his surroundings was informed by the ambiance of a dark palace; however, for the Opera Ghost, the grotto's silence had long been his solitary confinement.

He emerged from the shadows and sat down at his organ, a large sheet of manuscript paper held in his left hand, and an ink quill clutched in his right. He laid the manuscript across the keyboard, dipped the quill in an ink pot and set about scribbling musical notes and signatures across the lined paper. Hunched over the organ in rapt concentration, he filled one sheet of paper after another, tossing them to the floor upon completion.

Scratching his pen furiously across the parchment, he muttered to himself as candles receded into pools of glossy wax. Absorbed in his composition, he barely took notice when a faint alien sound drifted across the lake. Pausing momentarily, he raised his head, but upon hearing nothing more, returned to his work with his head bent down and his pen scratching away. Eerily, the sound echoed once again, and again he lifted his head, but this time his pen stopped moving. Setting the quill down on the console, he rose up and strode to the water's edge, straining his ears as he listened for what he was certain had been a female voice. From somewhere above, a voice echoed down the winding stone stairway and passed over the lake; an exquisite voice that softly invaded the expanse of the cave until it reached his critical ear. He listened, transfixed.

He stood, listening for some moments as the voice waxed clearer. Closing his eyes and standing perfectly still, he sucked in his breath as his arm began to sway in subtle movement, a slight tremor traveling through the slender fingers of his right hand. Music from the opera house occasionally disrupted the peace of his sanctuary, but never had he heard a sound more distinctly untainted. This voice was not the over-stuffed warbling of a diva. This voice was something unprecedented.

With his curiosity piqued, the dark figure walked around the lakeside, but by then the voice had grown fainter, until it was no longer discernible. Disappointed, he slowly returned to the organ, seated himself and continued his work. The hours passed with alternating sessions of writing and playing, until by mid-morning he had exhausted himself. Clearing away the ink pot and manuscripts, he rose from the organ and walked wearily to his leather chair, where he sat down and leaned back with a tired groan.

As he began thinking up entertainments for the evening, in the grotto's silence he became irritable. Forcing his eyes closed, he stretched out his legs and fell asleep. As the noon hour approached, he awoke with a start and glanced up at the clock. Thirsty for a cup of tea, he groggily unfolded his lanky body from the chair and stood to his feet, turning in the direction of his pantry, when out of nowhere the angelic female voice resumed. Pausing midway between the library and the pantry, he ran down to the edge of the lake where he listened again, but this time he did not hesitate to act.

He turned sharply and rushed to a rock outcropping where he kept a small rowboat. Lifting his black opera cloak from the cushioned rear seat, he swept the garment across his shoulders, stepped into the boat, snapped the rope free, and pushed off. As he traversed the lake, he used the pole to steer the boat in the direction of the voice, journeying deep into the opera's gloomy underbelly. Mooring the boat beside a massive winding stone stairway, he stepped out and followed the voice up to what appeared to be a solid stone wall, then tripped a concealed device until an opening appeared before him. He crouched down and entered an ancient Roman tunnel, and slowly winding his way upward, he arrived at a breezeway located between the ballet dormitory and the theater.

The breezeway was used for transporting materials on mechanical lifts, and was also connected to the stables that housed the opera's twelve prized horses. When the horses were used in an opera, they were led through the breezeway and behind the theater for a backstage entrance.

Within his first few years of refuge beneath the opera, he had discovered every hidden passage undergirding the cavernous structure. These were convenient locations where he could conduct his business discreetly, but of all the opera's secret haunts, his favorite was his own personal seat in box five; his chosen roost from which to view the operas, ballets, and concerts. With the majority of the opera's employees still on Christmas Holiday, he was comfortable in taking long, deliberate strides, listening intently as the female voice drew him up the stairs. The cloaked man unlocked the door, slipped the keys back into his pocket, and moved directly to the balustrade where, careful not to be seen, he parted the heavy velvet drapes.

Peering through the curtain's narrow opening, he shook his head and squinted his eyes, shocked to see that the source of this unusual voice was no more than a skinny little girl with long dark braids and an extraordinarily pale complexion. From what he ascertained by her appearance alone, she was somewhere between the ages of eight and eleven.

He listened in awe, captivated by the child's upturned face. Her brown eyes were large, and the song sorrowful and lovely. Slipping past the curtains, he leaned over the balustrade and gazed in fascination, but then withdrew back inside the dark of the draperies to speak his thoughts.

Stroking his cheek, he swore to himself, "Damnation! Who is this child? How could that voice possibly come from such a skinny little thing? Does no one feed her?"

He allowed the question to hang in the air as he slowly released his breath. "Perhaps she is a new protégé," he commented to himself. "I shall make it my business to find out all about her."

In his estimation, he was at least twenty years older than she, nearly old enough to be her father. He wondered what good fortune, or perhaps misfortune, had brought her to the bohemian world of opera. Although she was very young and her voice undeveloped, he marveled at its power and clarity. Her delicate soprano was warmed and mellowed by rich woodwind undertones, and already she infused her nearly perfect pitch with artful vibrato. Her eyes were glassy and fixed on the ceiling, and she appeared to sing for an unseen listener, as if someone were watching her from above.

"Why the look of sadness? What is she looking at?" he mused, puzzled by the waif. Her breath was erratic, inducing infuriating gasps at the end of uneven phrases.

"No, no, that is all wrong, my dear!" he spoke in a harsh whisper, his voice muffled by the heavy curtains. "Do not take shallow breaths, girl! Support the voice with your diaphragm!"

He doubted her tiny rib cage and lungs could support the breath needed for such a dynamic voice. She needed training, and soon. If she were entrusted to him, what beauty he would inspire from those inexperienced vocal chords! What immense pleasure it would give him to mold and develop that voice, drawing out the flute-like tones of a soaring upper register, while deepening the lower register to an even richer timbre! A remarkable instrument was hers, but she lacked discipline and confidence. He was certain that, under his expertise, the girl's voice could be transformed into a magnificent force of nature!

"She is a gifted child," he sighed, his gloved hands bearing down on the balustrade. "Christ, if she is not properly trained, she will develop bad habits and we shall have another Carlotta on our hands!"

As his eyes momentarily roamed away from the little girl, he spotted Madame Giry and her daughter, Meg, watching the child's performance from the wings. Muttering to himself, he resolved that he must speak to Madame immediately! He must know the girl's name, where she had come from, and why she had been brought to the opera. What was Madame Giry's connection with her? How old was she and how had she come to be blessed with such an extraordinary gift?

She fascinated him, and as he contemplated her remarkable performance, he could not account for an odd sense of foreboding in connection with her.

Moments later, when Giry and the girls had left the building, the dark figure left his post at the balustrade in box five and sank back in an armchair, his hands clasped lazily behind his head, with the brown-eyed girl's angelic voice still resonating in his ears. Softly he hummed the haunting melody she had been singing, commenting to himself as he sang.

"Rather a childish song," he remarked dryly, "but I quite like it." Having already memorized the entire piece, with eyes closed he sang the final verse:

> *But when she picked the blossom*
> *Was pierced by savage thorn*
> *Blood poured from the flower*
> *The angel's heart was torn,*
> *She cast it to the ground*
> *And then she did dispose*
> *Choosing the pale lily…*
> *Instead of the bleeding rose*

It had been three days since his last sojourn up to the opera house and he sat, exhausted, at the organ, his elbows planted on the keyboard and his head drooping into his hands. With tousled wig hair hanging wet in his eyes, beads of sweat glistened on his forehead, and his ink-stained fingers ached with the hours of abuse they had suffered throughout the night. The *Don Juan* opera had consumed him for over a year now, and was by far the most ambitious work he had ever attempted, but the more time he spent in its service, the more he feared that the piece would ultimately defeat him. He could not seem to find the soul of the work, and although the plot was quite simple, the composition had not measured up to his expectations.

It was a marvel that he had not simply given up and concentrated his efforts on a symphony or concerto, but he refused

40

to surrender to defeat. *Don Juan* would one day be his crowning achievement and if, even in death, his stinking remains were discovered with the completed score grasped in his skeletal fingers, then so be it! In either case, he would finish the damn thing! But he wondered, what was it that shut down his confidence at the precise moment when the music was its most powerful?

In the service of *Don Juan,* his dark chambers had shaken with the ominous wail of the huge pipe organ, his voice articulating the hardened masculinity and the insatiable lust of his hero. At times the score seemed to write itself as he characterized the primal sexual urges of the male, performing strident chords and primitive rhythms that flew across the keys in unparalleled speed and accuracy.

This opera was informed by his own sexual starvation; but it was the role of Anelinda that confounded him and sent him into a demented rage! What did he know of a woman's mind? How could he, a man who had never even touched a female, give voice to the gypsy girl? How could he know her heart and reveal its feminine secrets through his music? What did a woman want? he wondered. What were a woman's needs? How could he express the soul of such a mysterious and frightening creature, when women were a complete enigma to a man who had only watched from afar?

He was all male in every way, with the same driving physical needs and passions of any man; and indeed, he often wondered if isolation made his lust burn hotter than most. Reading numerous volumes on female sexuality had made romance seem clinical and remote, so therefore, in an effort to understand the love and passion found between a man and a woman, he had studied the romantic poets and memorized flowery sonnets and songs. He watched women from his hiding places whenever given the chance, but he had never seen a female completely naked, or held or kissed or loved one, and he feared that he never would.

He was far too particular and well-bred to pay a common whore for sex, though he had considered the idea on several occasions. But he wanted more than a body to slake his lust. He longed for a beautiful, intelligent woman who would share his music, his soul, and his bed. He desired a voice to fill his silence and he wanted a companion who knew his mind. Like any man, he dreamt of someone lying beside him in the night; a woman whose eyes would darken in his embrace. But he knew that no woman would willingly accept an embrace from him. What female would desire his lips on hers, his hands on her body or his breath in her hair? He was a freak of nature, plain and simple.

Suddenly, the blood surged up into his neck and face. His lips quivered with the rapid intake of breath as his temper flared. No woman would let him near her, but that truth did not prevent him from wanting one. He wanted a wife! Like any other man, he wanted a goddamned wife; someone to live for, someone to compose for, and someone to love him!

"Is that asking too bloody much?" he raged.

The muscles of his body went taut and he could feel the anger coiling. He shot to his feet and waved his arms wildly, savagely kicking over the organ bench with a curse. Grinding his voice in the back of his throat, he stomped across the Persian rug to a floor-length mirror, and taking hold of the dust cover, he yanked it down from the gilt frame and tossed it to the floor with mocking laughter.

Self-contempt spewed out in cursing, and he glared at his half-normal visage in the glass before ripping off his mask to reveal the other half's repulsive twin. Losing control, he threw the mask to the floor and shouted at his own image, thrusting his accusing finger at the man in the mirror.

"Who the hell would marry you, you bloody freak?"

He squeezed his hands into hard fists at his sides, the veins of his neck bulged, and his mouth twisted into a snarl until his whole person resembled the monster he believed himself to be. He hawked and spit upon the smooth surface of the mirror, his saliva sliding down over his reflection.

"Ignorant fool!" he roared, "You do not deserve what you want, so stop wanting it!"

The tension in his body was unimaginable. The mind-numbing solitude had become a physical torture. He dug his fingers into the flesh of his upper thighs until his knuckles turned white, while images of the past drove his darkened thoughts into complete blackness.

How could a woman hate her own child? Was it his fault that he had been born deformed, or that his face was a thing of horror? Why hadn't his mother loved him? Or better yet, why hadn't the bitch just let him die? Death would have been so much more merciful than the life she had condemned him to.

The memories were painfully vivid as he tortured himself with the same questions over and over. How could a mother abandon her own child to be exhibited in a freak show; to be laughed at, pissed on, and treated more brutally than any animal? Hell, Djordji treated his monkey better than he treated his freak. The freak had envied the monkey, who was given fresh fruit and vegetables, while the freak ate gruel and stale bread.

Gentle with his monkey Djordji was, yes…but with those same hands he inflicted pain and humiliation on the freaks. Daily humiliation climaxed in the final act, with Djordji ripping the mask from the face of the freak to the applause and laughter of well-dressed ladies and gentlemen, who had paid well to see the entertainment. Plummeting more deeply into darkness, he spiraled down into early his childhood. In his mind he saw a boy of not more than twelve, caged behind metal bars in his own filth, watching a parade of human faces pass before him.

"God! Oh God!" he moaned. "The cage, the stinking cage!"

They glared at him, laughing and mocking; children and adults hurling food and mud at the cage. The stench of pig excrement rose up in his memories, as they poked him with sticks and kicked at him through the bars.

"Oh God," he cried, "Make them stop!"

And then there was that certain humiliating night after a performance, when the prettiest gypsy girl had been allowed into his chamber. She had flowing, dark hair, red lips, and alluring eyes; and was sixteen years old to his twelve.

Swaying her hips, she had bent over to reveal the swell of her breasts, smelling of sandalwood and spice. She lifted her skirts and exposed her naked knee, murmuring her enticements, "Touch me, boy, I won't hurt you!"

He hadn't known what to make of her advances. He knew only that she smelled sweet and that her company was far more pleasant than the men in the camp. Looking up at her timidly through the mask's eye holes, the boy had not resisted when her slender fingers stroked his mask gently. He had closed his eyes as her long hair tickled his arm, and he had let her pet the top of his head, as if he were a dog or cat. But all at once, she had grabbed hold of the mask with her fingertips and then had heartlessly ripped it away! Then came the laughter, and the flashing of white teeth as she had spit in his face!

Sneering at the mirror, memories of the gypsy girl drove him to the brink of insanity. Tears of rage burned his eyes and he couldn't catch his breath, stumbling backward and grasping his head in his hands. He panted as he opened his eyes and focused on his organ and his music, until slowly his vision cleared and the demons receded. He was back in the grotto. Safe. No longer a boy in a cage. No longer a child.

"Damn it to hell, I've had enough!" he gasped as if awakening from a nightmare.

He had to get control and resist these exhausting fits of rage, so steadying himself, he took a few deep breaths and wiped his mouth with a handkerchief. Removing a comb from the pocket of his trousers, he smoothed back his hair, tucking it neatly behind his ears. With a heavy sigh, he bent over and picked up his ivory leather mask from where he had dropped it onto the floor, then slipped it effortlessly onto his face.

The mask effected an immediate change in his posture and demeanor. Throwing his shoulders back, he thrust out his chest, stretched to his full height, and just like that, with his practiced mannerisms restored, the Opera Ghost was himself again!

Tossing the cloth up over the mirror, he walked calmly back to the organ, pulled the cork from a brandy decanter and poured a glass half-full. Swirling the dark amber liquid, he took a sip and let it coat his tongue before swallowing, then opened his mouth wide and expelled a grunt of satisfaction. The brandy began to ease his black temper, and for some moments he stood holding the glass, waiting for his hands to stop shaking.

"That's better," he sighed, as he slowly inhaled the residual taste of his libation.

With the glass still in hand, he looked around at the evidence of his artistic and sexual frustration: a growing pile of crumpled manuscripts spread across the floor, and the organ bench lying over on its side. Reaching down, he set the organ bench upright and with a brandied voice he announced, "I shall have to fire my maid."

A restless frame of mind had taken hold. He felt isolated, needing fresh air and an escape from the suffocating darkness of *Don Juan*. He wanted to hear human voices and to see human faces, and there was a private matter that required his attention.

He lifted his opera cloak off a high-backed chair, draped it over his shoulders, and leaving the library, took long strides to the edge of the lake. He then stepped into the boat and began to pole across the green waters, silently gliding under the darkened vaults toward the stairway, while amusing himself with the thoughts of his thievery the previous evening.

In an effort to convince his managers that O.G. was in charge, he had been preparing a harmless entertainment for the Bal Masque and had stolen a costume for the event. The theater had been practically deserted that night, and it had been too easy, really…no challenge at all. He had slipped into the wardrobe room and removed Monsieur Debienne's costume right out from under Madame Marie's nose, and now it hung in his own clothes closet awaiting his personal use. Of course, the trousers were two inches too short, but his knee boots would solve that problem quite nicely. As his mood began to improve, the brandy having mellowed his temper, he smirked with a low chuckle. As he contemplated the crime with satisfaction, he thought about the letters he had sent to those two fools, Poligny and Debienne; just friendly reminders that he meant business when it came to the matter of his salary, which was late in payment! His considerable savings were intact but his monthly income had dwindled, a fact that weighed somewhat heavily on his mind.

Arriving at the expansive breezeway that divided the ladies three-story dormitory wing from the theater's rear staging entrance, the sound of singing interrupted his cynical commentary. Silently, he slipped among the large props that had temporarily been positioned against the back wall, and listened again to a voice he would never forget. Judging from its direction, he was able to guess the approximate location of her ground floor room.

Within his first few years of refuge beneath the opera house, he had uncovered many 'secrets' devised by stagehands and sceneshifters who had utilized their stage crafting skills to spy on the young ballerinas. Taking a few steps through, and behind the props stationed along the back wall, he easily located and then gently pressed against a small embedded stone. A spring door opened inwardly, revealing a dark chamber just large enough for one grown man, framed by a large, eight foot floor-to-ceiling two-way mirror. To his disappointment, the girl had stopped singing, and she now sat on the bed beside little Meg Giry. With their eyes focused downward and their heads close together, the two of them were engrossed in turning the pages of a large book. Squatting in front of the two-way mirror, he stroked his chin thoughtfully, frustrated that the girls spoke in hushed voices.

It struck him as ironic that he had disapproved of the stagehands doing exactly the thing he was about to do, but he told himself that, unlike those perverts, he was utilizing the device for honorable intentions and had no inclination to spy on children. No, he was interested in this girl for her voice alone.

After a few moments of watching little Giry and her brown-eyed friend, he became restless, but vowed to return again; and in the meantime he would personally contact Madame Giry, who had been his source of opera house news for years. Drawing the cloak up high around his neck, he backed out from the secret chamber and made his way as he plotted the evening's entertainment.

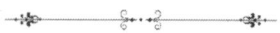

The opera's managers, Poligny and Debienne, stood with their heads bent over the mahogany desk, chuckling as they examined a heart shaped velvet jewelry box. The roomy office was well-appointed in fine leather furnishings, with massive book cases and framed opera posters lining the walls. Hand-loomed rugs carpeted the hardwood floors, which had been polished to a mirror finish, and the room smelled of leather, pipe tobacco, and freshly brewed coffee.

Debienne, the co-manager of The Paris Opera House, was congratulating himself on a recent acquisition, taking great pride in an exquisite diamond and ruby necklace; a gift for his young wife. The necklace had been purchased from one of Paris' most exclusive jewelers, The Rue Mogador, and was to be presented to her at tomorrow evening's Grand Bal Masque.

He was feeling rather smug, convinced that this bauble would smooth over a recent difficulty in his marriage. It had been a serious blunder when his wife had somehow discovered that Mademoiselle Jammes, the little blond from the corps de ballet, had recently captured her husband's attention. Debienne could not afford to have his little wife running home to mummy and daddy, when her parents were secured investors; but knowing her as well as he did, he had little doubt she would accept his gift and forget the whole matter.

"It is perfection!" Poligny exclaimed to his handsome partner, "and no doubt will do the trick, my friend!"

"I should hope so!" Debienne replied, raking a hand through his thick hair. "I paid a small fortune for this thing!"

Debienne was about to close the box, when someone rapped lightly on the door.

"Yes. What is it?" he grumbled, snapping the lid closed, and quickly depositing the box in the desk drawer.

Madame Giry entered with an envelope in her hand, folded and sealed with a red wax death's head. "Good morning, Monsieurs," she greeted the gentlemen with a curtsy. The moment the managers caught sight of the red stamp, they realized the purpose of the letter, and both rolled their eyes as they cursed under their breath.

"Oh, not again!" Poligny moaned, combing his fingers through thinning hair.

Keeping her thoughts to herself, Madame Giry replied, "Yes, Monsieur, a letter from the Opera Ghost."

Debienne slammed his hand down on the desk and sucking on his pipe, he demanded gruffly, "Well, what the hell does he want this time, for God's sake?"

Keeping her eyes downcast, her shoulders back and chin

erect, Madame Giry broke the seal and read the hand-written script aloud, "Fondest greetings, Gentlemen. I trust you enjoyed your Christmas holiday and are prepared to take up the business of managing my theater, which brings me to my salary."

She looked up briefly from the letter, suppressed a smile and continued to read as the two men glared at her, "I am aware that the advancement of age can adversely affect one's memory, which I presume is why I have not yet received the twenty thousand francs you owe me for my services. I have therefore arranged a little entertainment for tomorrow night's ball as a friendly reminder of our agreement. I anticipate a memorable evening. Your obedient friend, O.G."

The two men stared at each other in disbelief as Madame Giry dropped the letter on the desk and folded her arms across her chest.

"Advancement of age? Loss of memory? How dare he imply that we are tottering old men!" Debienne groused, grinding his teeth.

"Is this some kind of joke? What does he mean by 'entertainment'?"

Poligny shrugged, looking irritably at his partner.

"I haven't the slightest idea!" sighed Debienne, "but I suppose we are about to find out!"

"Really, Debienne, this business of the Opera Ghost has gone too far," remarked Poligny, rifling through the pages of a ledger. "After the New Year's party, we must discover the identity of this extortionist and have him arrested!"

"I couldn't agree more!" Debienne affirmed, pouring a cup of coffee.

Madame Giry was enjoying the discomfort O.G.'s message had inflicted on the two gentlemen, while privately hoping that O.G. would not go too far with his entertainment. His pranks at the opera house had been escalating with greater risk, requiring more boldness on his part, and she feared for his safety. If the man became careless, he might find himself in prison! She would therefore immediately alert him to the danger, and perhaps he would reconsider his actions.

"Well, I shall leave you gentlemen to your work," Madame

replied as she turned to leave…then paused to look back over her shoulder, adding with a lilting tone, "Oh, I nearly forgot, Monsieur Debienne, Madame Marie asked me to inform you that she has reassigned your costume for tomorrow night's ball."

Without looking up, Debienne stiffened as he held onto O.G.'s letter.

"Reassigned my costume? For heaven's sake, why?" he asked, chewing on his lip. "What was the matter with the first one?"

With only her eyes betraying her mirth, Louise kept a straight face and suggested, "Well, Monsieur, it appears someone has misplaced it."

With that, Debienne's head snapped back as he waved his arms in exasperation and shouted, "Good heavens, more missing props, more missing costumes. This business is getting on my nerves, Poligny! Fine, fine," he sighed, "just so long as I have something to wear…now, Madame, will that be all?" he asked, his nerves beginning to fray.

"Yes, Monsieur. Good day."

Waiting until Madame Giry had closed the door behind her, Debienne quickly thrust out his key and with an aggravated grunt, locked the desk drawer.

Meg and Christine sat reading a book on the faded lace coverlet of Christine's bed, while Madame Giry was arranging a fancy wardrobe screen in an empty corner. Their recent visit to prop-storage had enabled them to furnish and decorate her room with the screen and a collection of small ballerina paintings.

"How is that, girls?" Madame smiled, stepping back to appraise the new additions.

Gazing at the screen with a perplexed expression, Christine wrinkled her nose and inquired, "It is lovely, Madame, but what is it for?"

With her usual grace of movement, Madame floated across the room and sat on the edge of the bed, cupping Christine's chin with her hand.

"What is it for? Christine, a proper young lady must always disrobe in private," she explained, while Christine continued to study the fancy screen in curiosity. As the only daughter of a man with no wife, Gustave's furnishings had tended toward the practical, with few flourishes and in no particular style, so Christine was unaccustomed to living with such finery.

"But why, Madame?" she questioned again.

"Because you are growing up, my dear, and one day you shall be a young woman," she explained, touching the tip of the girl's nose with her slender index finger while Meg giggled.

"Besides," Meg added, "you can use it to pretend that you are a very famous actress. La Carlotta has one just like it in her dressing room!"

Meg struck a pose, mimicking the diva's famously snobbish posture, and Madame Giry laughed over Meg's theatrics, while Christine sat with her hands demurely folded in her lap. She was trying to adjust to life at the opera house, but was struggling with all the sudden changes. She sensed that they were merely occupying her time to keep her from dwelling on her father's death, and longed for a moment to herself. With all the bustling about in preparation for the ball, she was constantly being pulled from one event to the next, when all she really wanted was the quiet of her room.

Meg had spoken of little else but the Grand Bal Masque, describing the dress she would wear, and giggling over the outrageous fashions expected to be worn by La Carlotta and her guests. Christine had never attended a ball, and couldn't imagine the sight of ladies dressed in flowing gowns dancing with their handsome partners; and apparently this was to be a masked affair!

Suddenly, Madame Giry rose from the bed and held out her arms, with a strange smile lighting her hazel eyes. As if she were about to share a secret, she leaned down and spoke with a hushed voice, "Now girls, I should like to speak to you both about tomorrow night's ball."

Bouncing off the bed, Meg blurted out with undisguised interest, "Yes, Mama?"

With her eyes glittering, Madame resumed speaking in that mysterious hushed voice, "I have decided the two of you will attend."

"Oh, Mama, do you mean it?" Meg interrupted, bouncing back onto the bed while clapping her hands.

"Meg Giry, do not interrupt!" Madame scolded with a chuckle. "Yes, you and Christine may go but you will not be permitted on the dance floor, you must watch from the orchestra mezzanine, and you will be in bed by nine o'clock sharp."

According to Meg, the ball was held each year on New Year's Eve and was the talk of Paris. It was sponsored by the opera company and wealthy patrons as a fund raiser for the conservatory. Over the years it had earned a reputation as a bawdy, lavish affair, where the champagne flowed freely and guests danced until dawn. The city's renowned artists and musicians all attended, contributing to the bohemian madness and revelry. Christine's head was spinning as she contemplated what tomorrow's evening held in store.

Again, Meg bounced excitedly off the bed. "Oh Christine, it will be so exciting!" she squealed, spinning on her toes.

Despite herself, Christine forced a smile as Meg leapt across the floor and pirouetted in front of the mirror. Observing the girls with her hands clasped behind her back, Louise Giry was pleased that her news had brought a smile to Christine's wane features. She was wise enough to know that the child would grieve over the loss of her father for a long time; and hoped that keeping her occupied would help to ease her from dark introspections.

The opera house would soon be abuzz in its production of *The Magic Flute*, after which Christine's training would begin. Although Madame Giry did not know where exactly the funds for Christine's education would come from, she was determined that the very best instructors be obtained. The conservatory had already completed the student enrollment for the next season, and the late addition of Christine would be a drain on the school's limited resources, as the money raised from the ball never fully covered budgeted expenses.

Christine had inherited nothing after her father's death, and in fact, he had accumulated a sizable debt by the time of his passing. Consequently, Madame Giry was prepared to offer what she could toward the child's education and personal needs, but feared it would be insufficient.

Lifting her chin with a sigh, Louise let her eyes fall on Christine's hunched little form, sitting so quietly on the bed, her skinny legs dangling as Meg whirled and bounced around the room like a toy top. There could be no doubt that Christine was an unusual child, who perhaps was prone to dark thoughts more than other girls her age. That first morning, during Christine's tour of the opera house, Louise remembered watching, transfixed, as the child stood center stage and sang in a voice unlike any she had ever heard. She had seen many talented girls with beautiful voices who went on to achieve success, but Christine's voice was a gift beyond measure.

Contemplating Christine's future, Louise closed her eyes, resolved that she could work out the details of Christine's education later; for now she was tired and tomorrow would be a hectic day. Louise nestled into a stuffed armchair next to the bed, preparing to cat-nap for a moment, but just as she lowered herself down onto the threadbare cushion, she heard something crinkle in her skirt pocket.

What is this, she wondered, her hand patting down the folds of her skirt. Reaching into the pocket, she discovered that the item in question was an envelope, and she had a sneaking suspicion who had placed it so near to her person.

What are you up to now, she mused, observing from the corner of her eye as Meg waltzed Christine across the floor. Reading the contents of the letter in silence, a slow smile turned up the corners of her mouth.

My dear, Madame Louise,

I trust you are well, and I thank you for delivering my missive to Poligny and Debienne. As always, your service is invaluable. I wish to discuss the matter of Christine Daaé, the child you brought to live in the dormitory four nights ago. I am aware that the child is recently orphaned. I am also aware that her father was a musician, and that the girl herself is remarkably gifted. I should like to offer my services as her benefactor, and I shall make arrangements with my accountant to release the funds for her educational and personal needs. I shall rely on you, Madame, to see that the girl wants for nothing. I will, of course, remain anonymous.

As to her education, I have no doubt that the opera conservatory will damage her voice and instill a lifetime of bad habits. I shall, therefore, tutor the child myself. I shall communicate my future plans for her development at a later date, as presently I am preparing for tomorrow night's Bal Masque!

My warmest regards,
Your devoted friend, Erik

Chapter 4
Dark Side of the Mirror

Restless and irritable, Erik contemplated the following night's festivities while lying stretched out on the sofa, the monkey music box lifting and lowering with each intake of his breath. The music box gradually wound down until the cymbals clinked sluggishly, with the pings and gears grinding to a slow stop. He wound the key until the cymbals clanged again, its bells and pins restored to full tempo.

Having no desire to compose, he closed his eyes, engaged in a mental accounting of all he had accomplished and what was left to be done. The games of cat and mouse were merely a diversion from the monotony of the grotto, but he actually enjoyed devising clever schemes for making his presence known, and tomorrow night would be a test of sorts; an opportunity to prove to himself that he did indeed have the upper hand. This would be his boldest performance thus far, and he clasped his hands behind his head, musing on whether or not he had the balls to follow through.

All was in readiness for the Bal Masque, and the ingredients for the evening's festivities were concealed in his costume pocket. He was quite certain that no one would recognize Debienne's stolen costume due to the improvements he had engineered. The Persian costume would add to the illusion of his performance and enhance the power of suggestion for his chosen victim.

Thinking about the ball inevitably brought to mind memories of his years traveling with the gypsies when, as a twelve-year-old boy, he had obtained experience in illusion and trickery. His exceptional mind and his ability to mimic voices had made him an avid pupil, and in order to survive he had become a consummate performer.

Apart from his talent in sleight-of-hand, he had become an expert ventriloquist and could throw his voice into any object, alive or inanimate. Consequently, experimentation with ventriloquism had led to the startling discovery that his voice was endowed with hypnotic qualities, and certain individuals seemed highly susceptible when he sang. Females, in particular, seemed easily charmed by his voice as long as his face remained hidden.

By his fourteenth year, Erik had absorbed enough knowledge and skill in the art of illusion to convince even Dijordji of his crowd-drawing talents; and as Dijordji perceived that the little freak could attract a higher paying audience, Erik used the gypsy's greed to his own advantage. The boy was extensively featured in the carnival's magic tents, and as audiences lined up to purchase tickets, Dijordji's purse grew heavier while Erik secured additional freedoms, which then led to the gypsy's unfortunate demise and Erik's escape.

He preferred not to think about the first time he had killed, but the event still haunted him despite his efforts to forget. It was a horrific and desperate act for a fourteen-year old boy, and he would never forget the odor emanating from the poison or the sight of Dijordji's face as he sat there slack-jawed, his eyes bulging in their sockets as the wine took immediate effect. The big man doubled over, with foam oozing from his mouth, but death would not come for hours. While the gypsy succumbed to the poison-laced wine, Erik had searched the tent for food and supplies. Stealing a knife and a loaf of bread, his eyes had fallen on Dijordji's monkey box.

Erik then recalled the early days of his captivity when he would lie awake in the confines of his cage, listening as the eerie lullaby would drift from Dijordji's tent throughout the camp. Carefully placing the prized music box into a thick burlap sack, Erik had slipped away into the night.

He had found himself wandering the streets of a massive city, and three days after his escape a young ballerina had discovered him in the rain, filthy and half starved, hiding behind the garbage bins outside the servant's entrance to The Paris Opera House.

She had taken pity and given him food, showing him the underground tunnel to the lakeside domain he soon called home. That night he had built a small fire, curled up under a pile of blankets given to him by the ballerina, and had slept in peace and safety for the first time in two years. The next morning, it had been a stroke of luck when he had discovered a secret compartment in the music box, a hidden drawer where Dijordji had deposited all his jewels, his gold and silver coins.

From his reclining position on the library sofa, Erik took hold of the music box, gave it a shake and listened for the familiar rattle, then continued his introspection with the monkey perched on his chest. In his early twenties he had traveled outside France intermittently; to India, Rome, London, and various locations overseas; but for the most part The Paris Opera House had been Erik's sanctuary, and Louise Giry, the little ballerina who had assisted him, had gradually become a loyal friend.

Communicating with her mostly through letters, in those early days he had seldom spoken to her in person, preferring his privacy, and having no wish to endanger her position at the opera house. She had helped him over the years to procure his needs; food, clothing, cast-off furniture, and manuscript paper.

His thoughts turning again to the present, Erik smiled to himself, remembering the note he had slipped into Louise's pocket earlier that evening. He was enlisting her help in the matter of the Daaé girl and hoped that his letter had pleased her.

Now bored with the music box and weary of his memories, Erik set the monkey down and stood to his feet, his earlier smugness deflated by self doubt. Stuffing his hands in the pockets of his robe, he glanced up at the clock, realizing it was suppertime. He hadn't eaten since breakfast, but he wasn't hungry and had no interest in dining alone. It was always the same, day in and day out, trying to fill up his time with composing; and when he became bored or frustrated with his music, he would read, or paint, or talk to himself incessantly. But it made no difference what he did, for regardless of how he chose to occupy his time, he was always alone.

Dragging his fingers down the length of the mask, Erik sighed heavily, wishing that the long hours ahead would simply vanish; that it was the night of the ball. At least then he would be among other people. Even if tomorrow night was a complete disaster, that would be preferable to the same old routine.

"Bloody hell!" he cursed, anxious and jittery.

Scratching his chin, he clasped his hands behind his back and paced back and forth over the rug, his eyes darting toward the library where his sketchbook lay open on the desk. He'd been working on costume designs for *Don Juan,* and thinking perhaps he might resume his sketching, he plodded down to his desk and began flipping through the sketchbook, only mildly interested.

He eyed the decanter and his empty glass, then poured a brandy and inhaled the fumes as he swallowed. Smacking his lips and chuckling to himself for no particular reason, Erik sat down and stared at the drawing of *Don Juan's* act two costume. He selected a piece of charcoal from an open drawer, bent over the parchment and began to sketch. As the silence of the grotto seemed to throb around him, he pondered that it was a strange thing how, for days at a time, he could compose around the clock, with no thought of loneliness or of leaving his quarters, but now suddenly, out of nowhere, and far more frequently than in years past, his grotto would begin to feel like a tomb from which he must escape. As he angrily slammed down his fist, the charcoal broke in his fingers and smudged the paper.

"What is wrong with me?" he groaned.

In the midst of this brooding state of mind, an idea came to him. He fought it at first, but as his blackened fingers worked to blend out the smudge he had made on the drawing, Erik tried to convince himself that there could be no harm in going back up to the opera house, just to see how the little girl was adjusting. He had no intention of accessing the mirror on a regular basis, but he needed fresh air…and perhaps she might even sing again.

Her voice had somehow elevated his mood that morning when he had first heard her sing on the stage, and in all his years beneath the opera house, nothing had ever instilled that peculiar lightness. He could not account for how a little girl's voice had affected him so…but it had, and he wanted to hear her sing again.

Thrusting out his chin and cocking his head back for another swallow of brandy, Erik laughed, "Why the hell not?"

His mind was already made up, and with the image of Christine Daaé standing center stage, and the sound of her voice vibrant in his memory, Erik vaulted up out of the chair and bolted toward the bedchamber for a change of clothes.

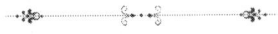

Madame Giry had returned to her room hours ago, leaving Meg to spend the night with me, but Meg had been much too excited for sleep and pestered me with endless chatter about the Bal Masque. I didn't mind, really. It was rather enjoyable listening to her go on about how she intended to wear her hair, and offering suggestions for my own coiffure.

Half a dozen times she had looked through my bureau, searching for an appropriate dress for me to wear, but since I had outgrown the one party dress Madame Valleria had purchased for me, she announced that we could have Marie find something appropriate.

Meg had exhausted herself dancing wildly around the room, and now as she sat beside me in the glow of the wood stove, the two of us were absorbed in hushed conversation. We had changed into our winter dressing gowns, and as Meg braided my hair, she talked to me of her dreams of becoming a famous ballerina. She spoke, too, of missing her father, and of her wish that he would come back from America. It seemed that she had never given up hope of her parents reconciling, and was convinced that so long as her mother still wore her wedding ring, Anton Giry might one day return.

Feeling drowsy, I lay on my back with my head on the pillow, staring up at the ceiling as Meg asked questions about my father…and so I spoke of my early childhood while she listened.

"I wish you could have heard my father play, Meg," I sighed dreamily. "My happiest times were listening to him play his violin."

Meg turned over on her side and moved closer, her wide-eyed gaze fixed on me as a tear slid from the corner of my eye. I found it impossible to speak of him without that now familiar ache squeezing my chest, yet at the same time, to not speak of my father seemed wrong. How could I keep silent about the man who had been the center of my world? It hurt desperately to relive those memories, but to not remember was far worse…and in either case, I could not escape the grief.

"I still can't believe he's gone," I whispered breathlessly, as Meg reached out and touched my hand.

Through the mutual loss of our fathers, a common bond had

been strengthening our new friendship, and without her even trying, just having Meg there and speaking openly about my grief did make me feel better. With Meg, I did not have to pretend a strength I didn't possess, and with each new day in the opera house, she and I had grown closer.

"Christine," she said, clasping my hand, "why don't you sing for your father again? It always seems to lift your spirits."

I nodded my head and wrapped my arms around myself, knowing that what she said was true. I suppose that somehow, whenever I sang, even though he was gone, I did feel closer to him.

"My father loved hearing me sing, Meg," I told her, sitting up in the bed. "When he first got sick, the doctors even let me sing to him."

I closed my eyes, leaned against the headboard and spoke about the days when Father was still young and smiling, just as he was pictured in the locket I wore around my neck. I described all the places we had traveled, the people who had gathered in market squares to hear him play; and I watched as a winsome smile lit Meg's face while I spoke of the concert halls and the applause.

I told her of the times he had read to me…my head resting on his shoulder and his strong arms about me. I spoke of the many nights he had read folk tales and Swedish legends, and I whispered about having felt so protected and loved when he carried me up to bed. Recalling the laughter and the joy of the summer before Father's death, I wistfully spoke of Madame Valleria's house by the sea.

Resting her back against the headboard, Meg hugged her knees to her chest and listened as I rose up from the bed and softly began to sing *The Bleeding Rose*. My voice was tired and uncertain, but by the second refrain I was drawn away from the bed and toward the mirror. Goose pimples prickled up my arms as I stood before the mirror, secretly praying that my father would hear me, and that he would send some magical sign to tell me that his spirit lived on.

Riveted by the girl's angelic singing voice, Erik had been watching from behind the mirror. Something about the child had inexplicably warmed his heart, and he was enchanted by her delicate, almost transparent, porcelain face. Her eyes were rimmed with thick lashes, and dark braids hung down to her waist. She bore an expression of other-worldliness, with a vaguely disturbing uncommon sorrow in her eyes.

This time, he chose not to critique her voice or listen for its flaws. Instead, he closed his eyes and let her voice soothe him. Minutes after her song had ended, he could not dislodge himself from the mirror. Removing his cloak and gloves, he leaned his long form against the side wall of the mirror chamber, and listened as the girls spoke long into the night.

He watched Christine with profound curiosity, as though observing an alien life form under a microscope. Contact with human beings had been so severely limited in his underground world that he found himself fascinated by everything she did. Her shy manner of speaking, the complex expressions that played across her features, and her emotional attachment to Meg charmed and enlightened him. The mirror had suddenly become his window into a world that the Opera Ghost had never inhabited, and he did not want to leave.

As I looked at my reflection in the mirror, I could not help seeing Father's face in my own features. Singing for him as Meg had suggested had momentarily eased the grief, and I backed away from the mirror, seating myself on the edge of the bed.

"Was he very handsome, Christine…your father, I mean?" Meg inquired, sitting cross-legged on the mattress.

With a faint smile I nodded my head, remembering how handsome Papa had been, dressed in his best suit. When performing in the market squares he wore the clothes of a working man, but whenever Madame Valleria arranged performances in small concert halls or for private parties, Father had worn his evening clothes; and I always thought him so handsome in his spectacles and black tailcoat.

"He was very handsome, Meg, especially when he played the violin," I spoke wistfully, trying to push away the image of my father when he was ill.

"Do you have a photograph of him?" Meg asked.

Leaning back against the wall, I pulled the chain from underneath my nightgown and carefully snapped open the locket, revealing the immortal image of my father set in a tiny oval frame. He was wearing a black formal waistcoat and white ascot, and his dark wavy hair was threaded with silver strands. He appeared just as I remembered him, and I cupped the locket in my hand as if it were a fragile butterfly about to fly away.

"Madame Valleria arranged for this sitting," I explained. "I shall keep it always."

"Oh, Christine, he is…he was very handsome," Meg sighed, her finger barely brushing across the image. "You have his eyes!" she added brightly.

"Yes, I have his eyes and his dark hair," I agreed, twisting the end of my braid absently around my finger. "I wonder if I look anything like my mother?" I added sadly. "Father would never talk about her, but Madame has told me that I do have my mother's pale skin. She also says that my mother had golden hair and light eyes. I don't have a photograph of her, but once, when he didn't know I was listening, I heard him say that she was beautiful."

"I take after my grandmother," Meg said, glancing up at her reflection. "But I wish I had red hair like Mama; it's so much more dramatic, don't you think?"

Scooping up a rose chintz pillow, I squeezed it against my belly, with tears blurring my vision. There were so many questions racing through my mind as I thought back on life with my father. The only times he had ever seemed happy were when we were performing, or when we stayed at Madame Valleria's beach home, where he was more carefree and where those sad lines on either side of his mouth seemed to disappear. Even though I was only a child, I had somehow always been aware of his unhappiness, and I suppose, like most children, I blamed myself. It wasn't something I voiced, just a feeling that ate away at me, but with Meg sitting beside me and with the locket in my hand, I suddenly blurted out what I had feared all along.

"Meg, it's my fault Papa died!" I cried out, clutching the pillow tightly to my body as Meg's eyes widened.

"After we moved to Paris, he hardly ever left our apartments except to play and teach. He missed Sweden so much, and he hated Paris. He was always tired. He didn't sleep well and sometimes he would stay awake all night playing the violin. Maybe if he hadn't had to work so hard…maybe if he hadn't had to take care of me, he wouldn't have been so ill."

I broke into sobs, feeling my grief profoundly and wondering if this sadness would remain with me forever. I could still hardly eat, and in my sleep I dreamt of my father's lifeless face, of bones in a grave, and of his coffin. Memories of his death could not be pushed away, and my stomach physically ached from trying to forget.

"Christine, please don't cry…it wasn't your fault, Christine…it wasn't!" Meg tried to comfort me as I buried my face in the pillow.

We were silent for a few moments, until Meg asked another question.

"Tell me about your favorite memories, when you were the happiest," she chirped in my ear.

I rose up from the bed, strangely drawn to the mirror once again. The lamplight painted my face with highly contrasting shadows as I spoke of the past.

"When Papa played the violin and told stories," I answered quietly, touching the gilt frame with my fingertips. "Those are my favorite memories."

"What sort of stories did he tell? Were they fairy stories?" asked Meg.

Standing up from the bed, she struck pretty ballet poses behind me, which made her appear older and more mature than her twelve years. Whereas, my arms and legs were skinny and awkward, Meg's graceful frame was more typical to ballerinas; her limbs lean and well-formed, and her hips narrow. You could tell merely by looking at Meg that she was stronger than I, and I envied the grace and power of her body.

"Some were fairy stories, and some were old Breton tales about goblins, korrigans, and witches," I answered, trying to mimic the curve of her arm in the mirror as she posed behind me. "But my favorite legend was the Angel of Music."

"The Angel of Music...how beautiful! Will you tell me the story, Christine?"

Turning my back on the mirror to watch Meg as she stretched, I recited Father's story from memory:

"From the time I was three years old, Father told the story of the Angel of Music, who came only to good children," I murmured, wrapping my arms around my body. "The Angel of Music is sent from heaven, Meg, to watch over children who have the gift of music. It's the angel's duty to protect those children, but Father said that proud and foolish children can't see the angel because they are not well-behaved. You must be worthy and very good to hear him, Meg, but he will never let you see his face. He appears when a child is lonely or sad, and when he sings, Meg, Father said that the angel's song makes even God in heaven weep!"

Closing my eyes, I padded across the rug in my house slippers and pulled a book from off the bureau top. Sitting on the bed with the book in my lap, I turned the pages, gazing at the beautiful illustrations. As a child, the story had given me comfort and I had been enchanted by the notion that someday I might be visited by the angel. Before he died, Father had promised me that the angel would come after he was gone...but somehow, in my heart, I no longer believed the story.

"Oh, Christine, that's a lovely story! Maybe someday your father will send the angel," Meg affirmed quietly, sitting on the floor with her legs now in a full split.

"No. It's just a story, Meg," I resolved, beginning to tire as my mouth opened wide in a yawn.

Looking directly at Meg, I clutched the book in my hands and reiterated in a drowsy whisper, "Father promised the angel would come, but it's just a fairy tale, Meg."

"God watches over us both, Christine," Meg said, yawning and stretching. Leaping up off the floor, she climbed into bed beside me and whispered, "And even if the Angel of Music is only make believe, God is real."

I lay back against the pillow and pulled the blankets up to my chin, as the book fell from my hand to the floor.

"Why did he have to die, Meg, why?" I mumbled, closing my eyes as my body began to relax and settle into the softness of the mattress.

Meg's blonde head sank down onto the pillow and she held my hand in hers as my eyes grew heavy with sleep. She blew out the candle on the nightstand and pulled the comforter over us both, then kissed me on my cheek.

Erik had been listening from the darkness behind the mirror, and he now understood the reason for this child's sadness. She was obsessed with her father, who had apparently been her only source of love and security. From what little she had said about her mother, he surmised that the woman had died when the child was very young, and now this poor girl was literally suffocating in the cocoon her father had spun around her with his strange gypsy music and primitive horror stories.

Having never experienced the steady guidance of a parent, Erik was no expert on family dynamics; but through his own observations it was becoming quite clear that Christine's father had intended to keep her a child forever. She had been denied a proper education, having traveled from village to village in near poverty for most of her early childhood. Erik found himself disturbed by the fanciful upbringing of this troubled girl and concluded that the father deserved a good lashing, dead or alive.

The poor child was now motherless and fatherless, left to grope her way through the world without the only love and security she had ever known. *Well, at least she has Louise and little Meg*, Erik affirmed to himself.

Of all people, he understood how alone she felt and knew the suffering of losing one's parents. When he was a child, he had made living beneath the opera house without parental supervision, rules, or adult guidance of any kind into a game. Yet as he had grown into his adolescence, he began to realize the abnormality of his life compared to other children who grew up with real families where the father and mother lived in the same home, and loved and cared for their children properly.

Christine, it seemed, would never have those things either, and he felt sorry for her, wishing to comfort her. Unlike little Meg, Christine rarely smiled, and her pale face was frequently drawn into sad expressions. Generally speaking, Erik had no interest in the children living under the opera's roof, but this girl and little Meg were the exception.

As Meg blew out the candle, Erik leaned against the chamber wall and softly whispered the dark-haired girl's name, "Christine."

For some reason beyond his comprehension, this child had stirred up unfamiliar yearnings, and he found himself wondering what it would be like to father such a sweet child. Naturally, he would never marry, and therefore fatherhood was out of the question. But if, by some miracle, he could escape the opera cellars, and if he found someone to love and marry, what would it be like to have a son or daughter? At thirty-one years of age, he was not yet too old to father a child. He growled in the back of his throat and dismissed the idea, scoffing at the image of himself as a father. The very question of fatherhood shocked and confused him, for he had rarely been around children, much less cared for one; and as for his own father, he had barely known the man.

"I must be losing my mind," he hissed, raking his hand through his hair. "What do I know of fathers…or families, for that matter?"

He found himself in a quandary. He had already committed himself to training the glorious instrument that was her voice; and it stood to reason that in order to teach her, he must make his presence known at some point. He would have to find some means of communication; and even then he would never permit her to see him.

Eyeing the sleeping girls through the two-way mirror, Erik pressed the flat of his hands against the glass.

"Why not?" he muttered to himself, his eyes scanning the darkened bedroom.

Why couldn't he conduct her voice lessons from behind the mirror? If she stood close enough, their voices would carry through the gaps around the frame, with his voice enhanced and magnified by the chamber's acoustics. In this way, perhaps in time she might even come to think of her teacher as a father figure. He had already made himself her benefactor and was planning to provide for her financially, so what would be the harm if, over time, she came to trust him as something more?

Stuffing his hands into his pockets, Erik backed away from the mirror, remembering Christine's fervent prayer that her father would one day return. Her father, she said, had promised to send an angel; someone to watch over her and protect her musical gifts. Erik leaned against the chamber wall and dragged a knuckle hard across his mouth as an idea began to take shape in his mind.

What if he could convince her that her father's spirit had returned from the dead? As ridiculous as it sounded, this child dreamed of hearing her father's voice again, so what would be the harm if he sang for her? He had heard that gypsy tune enough to sing it from memory.

"I could sing to her," he mused with a whisper. "I would let her believe that mine is the voice of her father, or her Angel. She would never see me...only hear my voice, never knowing my true identity. I could accomplish it all from behind the mirror, rather like play-acting. I could use my voice to portray her father, or her Angel...whatever she prefers."

Suddenly, a dull warning arose from the back of his skull. It was his voice, and yet different from his voice.

Do not do this, it warned. *Do not pursue this course of action; you'll only hurt her.*

Laughing it off, Erik scowled and contradicted the voice. "I have no intention of harming the child. I only wish to help her with voice lessons, and to give her some small measure of happiness. How could that be wrong?"

Why couldn't he become this child's father returned from the grave? Just until she had recovered from the loss of him; only until she outgrew her need for angels and fantasy. Then he would simply vanish from her life like a forgotten childhood dream.

Contemplating the future of this girl, Erik felt a warming

sensation just behind his breastbone and visualized in his mind how he would first introduce himself. The longer he mulled over the possibility of teaching Christine, the more intriguing the outrageous scheme became. She needed him, and no one had ever needed him before. It was a most pleasant, yet foreign, concept.

Finally, raising his head and straightening his back, Erik pulled on his leather gloves and flung the dark cloak across his shoulders, shivering as the wool enfolded his cold body. Despite a gnawing sense of foreboding, he had already made up his mind; but there was much to consider before he could take any action.

The Grand Bal Masque was tomorrow night and Erik was devilishly tired. He had been standing behind the mirror in tight quarters, and was stiff and chilled by the chamber's damp atmosphere.

"Damn, it's cold! I need a brandy," he remarked dryly. "And the next time I venture up here I must remember to bring a bloody stool!"

So that was that! He would become Christine's tutor through his voice alone; but first he must devise a plan to earn her trust. He must proceed cautiously, so as not to frighten her. He must watch her carefully, listen to her and acquaint himself with everything about the child and her father. It would require time and patience on his part. He must not rush, and at the opportune moment, when she was ready, he would make first contact. With his plan taking shape, Erik stretched his body, looked over his shoulder once more at the sleeping children, and then left the chamber.

Chapter 5
Masque of Illusion

Showers of gold, pink, and white pyrotechnics exploded above the opera house. Iron torches lit up the courtyard, where dozens of horse-drawn carriages were arriving for the annual Bal Masque. Men and women crowded into the promenade, arrayed in resplendent formal wear, their voices raised in laughter as they spilled through the opera's entrance into the Grand Escalier. The dance floor swirled with ladies in flowing ball gowns, and the room was awash in vibrant reds, yellows, and blues as tiaras and glittering masks sparkled in the mirrored walls.

Tiny, corseted waists and daring necklines enhanced the ladies' creamy cleavage, while gentlemen in top hats sashayed their partners across the floor. Attendees danced in masks of peacock feathers, furred animals, exotic birds, and purely mythical creatures, as the chandeliers twinkled overhead and children rained confetti down upon the dancing guests.

Dozens of banquet tables were heaped with trays of steaming duck and roast pork, garnished with fruits and vegetables that had been cut and peeled into shapes of flowers. Souffles, iced cakes of every size, and decadent chocolates were stacked high on silver trays, and the winter feast was illuminated by a veritable forest of tall brass candelabra. Steeping food and wax candles filled the room with extravagant aromas, as champagne flowed freely from a life-size fountain featuring the naked sculptures of a goddess and her maidens.

The entire opera company was in attendance, with La Carlotta wearing a feathered pink gown, and followed by her admirers. Her escort for the evening, Signor Piangi, was handsome in formal wear, top hat, and a leopard mask. Accompanied by Marie and her assistants, Madame Giry was beautiful, but understated, in her copper satin gown. They were all engaged in animated conversation about the opera's new season, as Christine and Meg watched, enthralled, from the mezzanine.

Although Christine had never seen anything like the gorgeous spectacle unfolding before her eyes, she was oddly distracted by the music of the orchestra; her attention drawn away from the dance floor to stare at a young violinist. She found herself mesmerized by the movement of his hand on the bow and the gentle swaying of his body to the waltz's tempo. How easily she could erase this man's face in her mind, and project the face and form of her father in its place! She could just see him, with his smile of ecstasy, his eyes closed, and his bow making long, sweeping strokes across the strings.

Meg, on the other hand, interrupted Christine's concentration, pointing out her favorite gowns and chatting endlessly about whose masks were the most beautiful. Christine listened to her friend politely but drifted into daydreams, resting her chin on the tufted balustrade and watching the violinist's every move.

Activity on the dance floor slowed as the opera's managers, Poligny and Debienne, entered on the arms of their wives, to the applause of the guests. Marie had redesigned last season's costume, and the handsome Debienne wore flamboyant pirate regalia. His rotund partner, Poligny, was appropriately dressed in a powdered wig and courtier clothing, with his plump little wife in a matching gown of pink satin and lace. But it was Debienne's young wife Lisette, who outshone every women in the hall, with her face partially hidden behind a feathered swan mask. The tall, stately beauty wore an iridescent red, off-shoulder gown, with a diamond and ruby necklace gleaming across her decolletage.

Debienne had glided his wife across the floor half a dozen times before retiring to the gentlemen's lounge for a brandy and cigar. He and his partner now stood with their heads bobbing closely together, discussing the matter of the Opera Ghost's letter. Meanwhile, as the evening's tempo quickened and the guests grew giddy with champagne and wine, Madame Debienne spun from one dance partner to another, virtually ignored by her husband.

All at once into this dizzying kaleidoscope of color, to the audible gasps of the revelers…a tall figure emerged at the top of the stairs. Costumed in Persian robes, he stood a foot taller than any man present, and lifted his chin with arrogance, strutting down the stairs slowly as his gaze swept over the guests. He wore a floor-length black and silver brocade robe that emphasized his masculine and menacing physique.

Red satin lined the robe, the flowing sleeves and hem trimmed with silver metallic braid and jeweled embroidery. Black breeches hugged his long legs and thighs, and the heels of his black knee boots struck the marble floor as he sauntered coolly across the room. Green eyes mocked from the eye openings of a black leather domino mask that was perfectly molded to his obviously handsome features, with only his mouth and chin visible beneath the mask's rim. A black turban was wrapped around his head, with a large red gem and black feather plume attached at the turban's crown, investing him with an aura of exotic royalty.

From up in the mezzanine, Christine had observed the Persian's dramatic entrance. The moment she saw him her stomach tightened as he aroused a sense of mystery and an unshakable feeling of dread.

Whispers could be heard throughout the hall, with everyone wondering who he was and speculating that he must be a person of some importance. Women fanned themselves, completely taken by his darkly sexual charisma. The tall Persian then brazenly approached the lovely lady in red, deliberately fixing his leering gaze on her cleavage. It seemed that Madame Debienne's husband had stepped out for a smoke, and Lisette Debienne was now in need of a dance partner. For her part, his attention was not unwanted. She blushed as he bowed low and languidly held her hand to his lips, brushing her knuckles with a kiss. Placing his left hand in her white gloved fingers and wrapping his right arm firmly about her waist, he led her to the center of the dance floor as the orchestra debuted the *Danse Macabre*.

The Persian spun his partner with grace and agility at the center of the dance floor, while other guests withdrew into the shadows to observe and comment. The lady easily succumbed to his charm, flirting coquettishly as a smirk played across his lips;

and all it required was a few carefully whispered words in her ear before she was bound to the resonance of Erik's voice.

Around and around he twirled her across the floor to the music's mad pace, until she grew dizzy. His masked face soon became a blur, and the room and the dark music were like a dream spiriting her away! She surrendered to his insistent touch as his fingers brushed the hollow of her neck, and she gazed up at the mysterious mask, determined to know his name.

Gasping for a breath, she tried to keep pace with his demanding tempo, but suddenly, with her body spinning madly, the Persian abruptly withdrew from her grasp, and she cried out as he released her to whirl on her own.

Searching the crowd for him, Madame Debienne gasped as a blinding flash of blue light and billowing red smoke erupted where she and the Persian had been dancing. "A-ha-ha-ha-ah-haaaaa!" a peal of maniacal laughter cackled as the orchestra lost their marks in the score, with the violins and cellos screeching to an awkward halt! Madame Debienne let out a blood-curdling scream as gas lamps throughout the building went dark, sending the guests into a panic! Finally, her husband bounded into the hall, half drunk and shoving his way through the startled guests.

The remainder of the dancers froze in place…until an additional explosion of red smoke and flashing lights brought more screams and pandemonium. Terror struck the crowd and many of the revelers ran for the exits, while others stood half blind and unmoving. Dazed and dumbfounded by the smoke and fireworks, no one even noticed that the Persian had vanished.

Debienne tried to question his screaming wife, and happening to glance down at the floor, his eyes narrowed at the sight of an exotic music box; bearing the figure of a monkey in Persian robes and a turban, playing little toy cymbals. Stooping down on his haunches, Debienne examined it, thoroughly confused as to how a child's toy had made its way onto the dance floor. He gave the thing a shake, listening to the clockworks rattle in its base, then wound up the key and set it back down on the floor with a shrug. A haunting melody issued forth from the box, calming Madame Debienne's nerves almost immediately…that is until her fingers strayed to her neck, where she discovered that her necklace was missing!

"My jewels…oh, my heavens, he has stolen my jewels!" she shrieked. Gawking at his wife through the semi-darkness, Debienne shouted at her, grabbed her by the shoulders and glared at her bare neck, "Who stole your necklace?"

Every woman in the room instinctively clutched her throat, while the men rushed about shouting for the police!

"The Persian!" Madame Debienne shouted back, "The Persian has stolen my necklace!"

Within minutes, the hall was overrun with torch-bearing, armed policemen who began searching throughout the opera house, but there was no trace of the necklace or the dark Persian.

"No one leaves this building until that necklace is found!" Debienne ordered over the mayhem. "Inspector, I want every single door and exit in this building bolted shut!" he commanded, his voice booming over the sound of his wife's hysteria. Uniformed men rushed about issuing orders as Debienne's instructions were followed, with each remaining guest subjected to a thorough search of their person.

Ladies and gentlemen were indignant as handbags, pockets, and cloaks were rifled through; but the necklace was not recovered. After an hour of interrogating guests and searching the foyer, the inspector finally dismissed his men, who unlocked the doors, allowing the partygoers to return to their homes. Debienne and his wife left the ball hurriedly and boarded their carriage, while other guests spoke in hushed tones, clustering in groups around the banquet tables.

Discreetly leading Christine and Meg down the Grand Escalier, Madame Giry paused to collect the Persian's forgotten music box. Maids and chamberlains blew out candles and began cleaning up the mess, while Maestro Reyer picked up his baton and instructed the orchestra to play. Sluggishly, the musicians retrieved their instruments and performed a subdued waltz, but the remaining guests were already filing out the doors.

The Bal Masque of eighteen seventy-three was over before the clock struck midnight!

The morning of January second found Debienne with a blistering headache, staggering out of his carriage with his cloak collar pulled up to hide his face. He stormed into the opera house, stomped up the stairs and glowered as he passed by the secretary's desk. Opening her mouth to greet him, she then closed it immediately when his condition became apparent. On his way down the hall, as he passed the offices of employees and department heads, no one dared speak a word.

Behind closed doors, gossip and speculation were rampant as all the opera's occupants and workers ignored their duties, gathering to discuss the events of the Bal Masque and dying to know the identity of the Persian. It had been reported that Madame Debienne had accused the mystery man of stealing her necklace; but as yet there was no proof that he or anyone else had perpetrated the crime. Certain guests of the ball implied that Lisette Debienne was beside herself with vapors and delusions, insisting that the dark Persian had somehow hypnotized her! Some even suspected that she had made the whole story up in order to take revenge on her philandering husband; nevertheless, the Persian had been witnessed dancing with Debienne's wife by everyone but Debienne himself, who had escaped to the lounge shortly after the dancing had begun.

Debienne unlocked his office door with a curse, then slammed the door behind him, groaning when the miserable sound only increased the pounding in his head. His appointment with the inspector was in less than an hour, and all he wished for was to draw the drapes closed and flop down on the sofa; however, the crime and his wife's injured sensibilities must take priority over his two-day binge.

Lumbering over to the cadenza, Debienne picked up the coffee pot, poured a cup of coffee and drank it black. Waiting for the brew to bring him back to his senses, he squinted his eyes in the direction of his desk, where a flash of red and silver suddenly caught his attention. Hardly believing his own eyes, Debienne stared, slack-jawed...for sitting on his desk in plain view was his wife's diamond and ruby necklace!

Beside it lay a parchment, sealed with a red wax death's head, which Debienne immediately recognized. "Son of a...!"

Drawing his hand up to his mouth, his eyes darted around the room as he rushed back to his desk. He gawked for several seconds before snatching it up, then roughly grabbed the necklace and stashed it safely inside the inner pocket of his waistcoat.

"What the hell!" he swore, his head throbbing miserably. Tearing open the sealed parchment, Debienne read the missive to himself:

> *Fondest greetings, Monsieur,*
>
> *I do hope you enjoyed my performance at the Bal Masque, and lest I forget, sir, thank you for the use of your costume! It certainly did stop the show, as we like to say in the theater! Perhaps now you will take my warning seriously by delivering twenty thousand francs to Madame Giry first thing tomorrow morning; and hereafter, on the first of every month as previously recorded in your memorandum. In addition, I require that box five be permanently reserved exclusively for my use.*
>
> *A pleasure doing business with you, sir,*
>
> *Your humble servant, O.G.*
>
> *PS: Ah yes, perhaps you have wondered how your wife discovered the unfortunate indiscretion with Mademoiselle Jammes? Be forewarned, Monsieur. I am aware of all that transpires in my theater, and in the future, I advise you to be more attentive to your lovely wife, and less to the corps de ballet!*

Three nights after his triumph at the ball, Erik sat in his high-back chair, with the monkey music box seated in front of him on a small table. He had brought the gypsy relic back to the grotto, glad to have his old friend nearby. A distant look glazed his eyes as he wound the key, listening absently to the familiar melody while the old monkey clanged its cymbals.

He was now determined that his business must be conducted by letter only; and that future entanglements in the affairs of men would not be permitted. He could not afford to act recklessly as he had at the ball, and therefore, he must once again constrain himself to his work and a solitary life.

The Bal Masque…a triumph? Erik scoffed to himself. Yes, it had been a triumph of sorts…but it had cost him dearly, for unbeknownst to those who had attended the ball, another of Erik's maddening talents had surfaced for their pleasure. He was now a consummate actor…oh yes; he had convinced everyone of his powerful and mysterious persona.

Their eyes had been riveted on the Persian from the moment he had entered the hall; just as he had planned it…precisely as he had envisioned the scene. Every action had been devised with maddening attention to detail, the illusion having the precise impact he had desired. But behind the black domino mask and the Persian robes, Erik knew that he was a fraud.

The real Erik was not that man, but was someone else entirely. Beneath the suave and confident guise of the Persian and throughout the entire farce, he hadn't taken into account how devastating it would be to hold her so close to him, to smell her perfume, and to become drunk on his power over her.

Madame Debienne was a beautiful woman. Her skin had been soft and radiant in the glowing light, and the effect on his body had been immediate when he had taken her gloved hand in his. As his masked eyes had roamed across her bare shoulders, her neck, and the swell of her breasts, her physical closeness had ignited an embarrassing erection.

While he had appeared to glide her effortlessly across the dance floor, only Erik had been aware that on the inside he was shaking, his cocky self-assurance on the verge of crumbling. Hell, he had never danced with a real woman in his life! He had watched men and women dancing on numerous occasions, theorizing that dancing was a simple matter of coordinating one's steps and body movements to music. Convincing himself that dancing was an art he could instinctively master, he had practiced with a mannequin. But it had not been until he was actually holding a real woman in his arms that he had realized what a chance he had taken. The mask had concealed more than his deformed face. It had also hidden his fear.

The moment his fingers had opened the clasp of her necklace, he had let them brush lightly on the back of her neck, the soft sensation nearly driving him mad. The feel of his arm around her waist, their bodies moving perfectly to the music, the control he had felt with a woman in his arms…it had all been intoxicating.

And she had wanted it! She had relished dancing with him, had flirted with him, and had been completely taken in by the Persian's sexually charged magnetism. She had been attracted to him and had found him handsome beneath the mask.

"Erik is a master of illusion," he mocked himself, leaning his head back against the chair.

As the music box wound down, Erik cranked the mechanism yet again, his mind drifting back to his mother who, when she was young, had been just as beautiful as Madame Debienne. He thought of the hatred that had always darkened her eyes whenever she had refused to let him crawl up into her lap, or to touch her in any way. He remembered the fear, the contempt, and the hardness of her mouth whenever she had regarded his face; and he remembered the mask she had made him wear to cover it.

Like any child, he had only wanted his mother to love him, but from the moment of his birth she had pushed him away; refusing to nurse him or to attend to his needs. Instead of being coddled by a loving mother, he had been left in the care of an emotionally detached nanny.

Letting the music box play on, Erik arose from his chair and began to pace aimlessly through his chambers. Dragging his feet across the stone floor and over the Persian rugs, he trudged down to the library where his desk was strewn with charcoal sketches of architectural elements from the opera house. For as long as he could remember, he had loved to sketch buildings, statues, and architectural embellishments.

Erik's father had been a master architect whose extensive travels had kept him away from home for the majority of Erik's early years. Unlike his wife, the father had tried to give the boy a decent upbringing; and despite what he had referred to as "the boy's handicap", Erik's father had encouraged his son's ravenous appetite for knowledge. Against his wife's protests, he had insisted that, in his absence, she educate the boy with highly paid tutors and challenging activities. At only five years of age, when Erik began to display his dazzling musical aptitude, his mother had begrudgingly taught him piano and violin...but no matter how much he had tried to impress her, she had opined that he needed more discipline and practice.

Regardless of her coldness, as a young boy Erik had cherished those moments, seated by his mother on the piano bench where he had been close enough to smell her perfume. He had loved watching her dainty white fingers flitting over the keys, and had found it thrilling when his own fingers could mimic hers precisely. However, when he had outgrown her considerable musical expertise, she had hired private instructors, and from then on she never again attended his lessons, and rarely showed interest in his progress.

On the rare occasions when he had been permitted to play for her, she had cruelly remarked that such genius was wasted on a child with no future. When performing Mozart on the violin or singing the music of Handel, he had once made his nanny cry, but his mother had never shed a single tear over him.

Erik often wondered how someone so outwardly beautiful could have been so cruel. His mother, Nadine, had been a cold woman...yet he had always wanted to love her. Even when she had threatened to send him away after his father's untimely death, yes, even then he had tried to love her.

Shuffling through the stack of sketches, Erik sank back into the chair, dropped his head into his hands, and dug his fingernails into his forehead. Beginning to feel the dark gravity of those memories, he considered a drink of Brandy or glass of wine, but decided against it. Alcohol numbed his pain, but it also clouded his mind, and he needed his wits about him to compose. Drinking made him groggy, and he was determined to complete the *Don Juan* score before spring.

Raising his head, Erik pushed back memories of his mother, slowly unfolded himself from the chair, and walked to the edge of the lake. He crouched down on his haunches and trailed a finger through the water's green surface as the scent of algae and mud roiled up into his nostrils. His thoughts were a whirlwind of images;

images of his mother's face on the face of Madame Debienne.

He visualized Madame Debienne as she had looked that night at the masquerade, with her eyes downcast and her painted lips slightly parted. She was not a cold woman like his mother had been…and irrationally, ridiculously, he had convinced himself that he could have had her…that under different circumstances, he could have taken her from the ball and spirited her away to his chambers. How easy it would have been, he thought, to have seduced her with his hypnotic voice. As long as the mask had remained fixed on his face, she would have wanted him.

Shaking his head with a bitter chuckle, Erik struck the surface of the lake with his fist, watching the water as it splashed upward, then formed ripples outward from the impact. He was only fooling himself with these childish fantasies. If Madame Debienne had seen what was hidden behind the mask, she would have fled from him, screaming, just as any woman in her right mind would have done.

"God, I'm sick of this!" he spat bitterly, rubbing his hand across his mouth. "I'm sick to death of this slimy rat hole. I'm sick of this life!"

He had grown accustomed to his uneven tempers and dark moods, and could generally satiate his darker passions through music; but even music no longer had the power to calm the beast within.

"Is there to be nothing for me?" he murmured across the water.

Walking up from the lakeside, he dangled his arms loosely at his sides as his shoulders sagged in defeat. He wandered down to the library and stared at the rows of shelving, cluttered with manuscripts that were now yellowed with age and mildewed by the damp. Concertos, symphonies, operas…the outpourings of his soul were growing old and decrepit, just like their maker.

His music would never be enfleshed by an orchestra, by musicians, violins, cellos, and harps. His arias would never be performed by a warm and soulful human voice, and he would never hear his works applauded by a live audience. A few minor pieces had been published under a pseudo name, but that was no longer satisfying. Erik wanted his surname to be known, and his music to be performed in concert halls and opera houses. The

Opera Ghost yearned for a legacy, with recognition and acceptance from the real world.

Suddenly, drawing a hand to his face, Erik felt dampness on his cheek and discovered that he had been crying. He ripped the mask away from his face to wipe his eyes…then just stood there, holding the mask in his hands like a foreign object.

"What the hell is happening to me?" he groaned, glaring bleary-eyed at the mask.

"Am I going mad?" he questioned, listening to the solitary voice that echoed back.

Above him, the real world pulsated with the music of life and the dreams of beautiful people. They would fall in love, marry, and have children…while he would remain nothing but a ghost, a dark creature who engendered fear, or even worse, indifference. The suffocating darkness was slowly eating his soul and transforming him into a phantom, a man without a future or a past. He was growing old without having ever lived!

"Am I really only thirty-one?" he sighed, "I feel like fifty!"

His work was undiscovered. His talent had been wasted on magic tricks and childish pranks. He deserved more. He deserved better. He deserved to live like other men!

Baring his teeth, Erik growled in the back of his throat and suddenly lunged at the bookcase. Violently, he raked his arm across the shelf, knocking manuscripts and loose paper to the floor. He watched as clouds of dust and mildew wafted upward from the pile.

For some moments he stood scowling at the mess, torn between destruction and creation. Panting through his teeth, he clenched his fists as the veins of his neck bulged.

He might have destroyed it all, heaving every last shred of paper into the lake, where the ink of his music would have bled into the dark water and been no more…but gradually his expression softened as the anger slowly abated. Dropping to his knees with a weary exhalation of breath, he slowly began setting his music back in order.

Chapter 6
Night Visions

Erik slept only a few hours when he awoke in a sweat, the sheets sticking to his skin and his eyes sore and scratchy. Cracking one eye open, he groaned, wondering what time it was, and not really caring whether it was night or day. Too weary to look up at the clock, he rolled back over onto his stomach, determined to sleep for another hour or two.

Disengaging his body from the bedding by yanking the sheet out from under his weight, he swiped the pillow off with his arm and dropped his head on the bed. He squinted his eyes closed and stretched his legs until his toes hung over the end of the mattress.

As he tried to slip back into the silent seduction of sleep, a sound, a voice, echoed down into his chambers. It was very faint, but it was enough to rouse him from his stupor; a stupor not brought on by brandy, but from playing the organ too long, following weeks of inadequate rest.

He lay still with his eyes half-open, trying to determine if it had indeed been a scream, or was Carlotta screeching scales up in her frilly dressing room again? The underground acoustics were somewhat deceptive, and as Erik had discovered during his earliest days in the grotto, sounds from the opera house could be distorted by the network of grates, pipes, and corridors.

Depending on the singer's location, a soprano might sound like a squealing cat, or a cat might sound like a screaming woman…but this was no cat.

He pulled himself upright in the bed and listened, his eyes focused and his senses alert. Shaking his head, for a moment he considered the possibility that what he had heard was nothing more than a rehearsal; or perhaps he had been dreaming after all. Waiting to see if the sound would resurface, he reached down to the floor and retrieved his pillow, now desperate for sleep…but out of the darkness it came again; and this time the sound pierced his ears with its urgency.

The hair on the back of his neck bristled, and his pulse raced as the location of the scream registered in his brain. That ghastly sound was coming from the dormitories!

In an instant, he shot his lanky form up out of the four poster bed and yanked on his trousers, a shirt, his warmest cloak, his boots, and his gloves. As a final measure against the damp chill, he placed a black fedora on his head, tipping the wide brim over his left brow. Concerned that the child was in peril, Erik propelled his boat across the lake, moored it, and reached the stairway in record time, bounding up the stone steps recklessly, his cloak flaring out like black wings.

As he journeyed to the surface, he feared that he was taking leave of his senses. Why in Hades should he venture up to the cold and damp corridors, just to bother about a child; a child he had absolutely no connection with? He chuckled to himself at the absurdity of his actions, having no idea what was drawing him upward, or why he even gave a damn about the strange little girl. Even if the girl were in some kind of trouble, what the hell was he supposed to do about it?

Pausing briefly, Erik snapped his head around to look behind him. Had he heard something in the passage? Footsteps, perhaps?

Peering over his shoulder, down the stairs and across the lake as his eyes adjusted to the thick darkness of the opera's underbelly, he saw and heard nothing. He grunted and grumbled to himself as he continued his trek up the stairs, winding his way upward without the aid of a torch or lamp. Again he paused, listening, and then moved on, and with no time to investigate he trudged ahead, his boots barely making a sound on the old stone.

"I'll look into this business later," he muttered irritably, grabbing a hissing torch from the wall as he reached the first landing.

His lanky arms and legs were accustomed to the climb as he mounted another staircase. Higher and higher up into the opera house the stairs led him; through the fourth and third level cellars, all the way up to the stables and breezeway.

The child's faint screams continued as he headed down the long corridor, which seemed to stretch eternally before him as his torch illuminated the murky darkness. At last, he reached the hidden entrance to the mirror chamber where, out of breath, sweating and panting, he stepped inside.

Erik let out a long breath, relieved to find that Christine was not alone, and that she was safe in Madame Giry's arms. He could not imagine what had frightened her so, and listened for some clue…but Madame Giry spoke in hushed tones as Christine buried her face in the woman's shawl. After a quarter of an hour, Christine finally stopped crying, and Erik pressed his ear to a gap between the mirror and the frame, trying to make out their quiet conversation.

"Darling, darling girl," Madame comforted the child, "you've had another nightmare…but it's all right now. I'm here."

Madame rocked Christine in her arms until the child fell asleep, and Erik watched in fascination as the woman tucked her beneath the covers, then lingered at her bedside. Indeed, Madame might have been the child's true mother, he thought, cupping his gloved hand over his mouth. He had never seen anything as beautiful as the sleeping girl and the deep affection of Madame.

He turned away as a lump formed in his throat. Females were a mystery to him, and the world of women was one of secrets. For him there had never been a mother, or wife, or children. He would always be on the outside looking in, and witnessing this little scene through the mirror hurt him more than he could express. Straightening his back, Erik leaned against the chamber wall, waiting for his gloomy thoughts to pass. After Madame had returned to her own quarters, he remained in the chamber and watched in silence until he could be sure that Christine was sleeping peacefully.

The poor child had apparently been having nightmares, something he was painfully familiar with. He presumed the dreams to have been brought on by her father's death, but weeks had passed and he found it remarkable that she was still mourning his passing.

The death of Erik's father had been an insignificant event in Erik's life. He had barely flinched when Mademoiselle Jacqueline entered his room one morning and told him. He hadn't cried, nor had he felt any real sense of loss for a man who had become more of a figure-head than a human being. Only days later had the gravity of his father's death struck him; and yet even then he had restrained himself from mourning or expressing grief, lest he receive the wrath of his mother's disapproval.

Instead, he had sat cross-legged on the floor of his room, composing sheet after sheet of music until his fingertips were black, with a pile of new compositions surrounding him. Hours later, he had calmly pinned those sheets on his walls until one wall had been thickly papered in written music, with barely a hint of plaster visible between the pages. Afterward, he had seated himself on the bed and folded his hands in his lap. Looking up curiously at his notations, he wondered what had compelled him to make such a mess. His mother would be furious!

His father's funeral had come and gone with little pomp and circumstance, and after his burial, the only change in the household was that his mother rarely left her room. Months would go by without a single word from her, and Erik was certain that, had it not been for the kindness of Mademoiselle Jacqueline, he would have starved to death, with no one the wiser.

Sighing heavily, Erik crouched down on his haunches and placed his palms on the mirror as Christine slept. To his way of thinking there was nothing either lewd or sinister about his watching her, and he even entertained the idea of singing to the sleeping child right then and there. From his observations, young Christine responded to music in the very same way that he had as a child, and as Erik continued to watch her sleep, memories of his own childhood and events he had not thought about in years, took on new meaning.

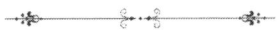

During the first year of his life beneath the opera house, Erik had managed to escape the cellars for one glorious day. Hiding out among the bales of hay and sacks of feed, he had managed to stow away in the wagon which brought the daily transport of goods to the opera house stables. He was desperate for fresh air and adventure, so he had jumped, unnoticed, into the back of the wagon as it prepared to leave the grounds.

It had been a bumpy but pleasurable ride as Erik lay in the hay, his eyes fixed on the cumulous clouds, and his nose filled with the scents of spring. In that sublime moment he had almost felt like a normal boy, feeling the fresh air on his face as the wagon had lurched and bumped its way to an unknown destination. He had not given a thought to where the wagon was headed, and had planned to simply jump out wherever it stopped.

In some ways, Erik loved the opera house, but he had also grown to hate the place. It was safe enough, and the Giry girl had been good to him; bringing food and keeping his whereabouts secret...but he had become sick of the dark and dampness, and sick of being alone day after day. Sometimes he had even missed the sounds and smells of the gypsy camps; the aroma of roasting meat and the music of fiddles and guitars.

As the city had passed by, Erik had scanned the massive buildings and listened to the voices of people and trotting horses. Following the rain showers earlier that morning, the chestnut trees had given off their scent, and Erik had breathed deeply of the sweet smelling blossoms.

Flattening himself on the wagon's bed, he had held his breath as the horses finally slowed their pace. He had then cautiously looked over the rail and pulled the hood of his cloak down low over his face. Striking a defensive posture, the moment the back end had been opened and pitch forks began stabbing at the bales of hay, Erik had lunged off the side of the wagon, then dived to the ground and rolled underneath its belly. Watching for an opportunity to bolt, he had warily kept track of gentlemen's legs and ladies skirts passing by, lying on the ground until the sidewalk had cleared of people.

He poked his head out just enough to see across the street, took a deep breath, and with a determined grunt, he had scooted out from behind the wagon wheel. Running as fast as he could to the other side of the street, he had managed to slip unseen into an alleyway, crouching behind some oak barrels. From that hiding place, Erik had been able to view the crowded market as Parisians were engaged in daily commerce; buying and selling produce, seafood, and dry goods. He had remained hidden in the alleyway for over an hour, waiting until the streets and market had cleared of customers and merchants. It had been rather pleasant listening to the snippets of conversation while sniffing the aromas of cooking from nearby bistros.

Finally, as the shadows in the market lengthened and lamps were lit along the Rue de l' Arcade, he heard distant church bells marking the hour and knew he must make his move, yet he had no idea where he was going or what he would do when he got there. He had planned to wait until dark, when he could move about the city more freely, and then he would be back at the market by dawn, where he could jump onto the wagon going back to the opera house.

Creeping out of the alley, Erik had breathed a sigh of relief as the streets had quickly emptied of people who were heading for their homes or apartments, or dining in one of the many bistros and cafes of that district. With his own stomach growling, he had managed to snatch an apple and a small loaf of bread from a merchant whose back was turned while he swept the sidewalk, then stopped to dump a bucket of rotting fruit into the ditch.

After Erik had stashed his meal in the pocket of his cloak, he had quickly stolen a drink from a fountain, whose water trickled from cherubs set atop a massive marble column base. Rinsing his hands and drying them on his trousers, he had listened as cathedral bells began to clang from somewhere beyond the market square...and then, the most amazing sounds he had ever heard stopped him cold.

He had listened in awe until the lamplighter had come too close for comfort. Avoiding the man's curious scowl, Erik had darted back into the shadows, waited until the lamplighter had moved onto the next street, and then crept back out onto the sidewalk, careful to remain near a building at all times. In this way, he slowly crept in the direction of the cathedral, energized by that extraordinary music.

Passing government buildings and entering the eighth arrondissement, Erik had remained completely out of sight as markets and shops disappeared from view in favor of wide boulevards lined with grand mansions and palatial hotels.

Admiring the architecture of that prosperous district, and making a mental note to sketch the facades and fountains upon his return to the opera house, his eyes had fallen on the church la Madeline, whose massive front steps were crowded with parishioners. The centerpiece of the Rue Royal, la Madeline's pediment, was supported by statuesque Corinthian columns, carved with a relief of what Erik had supposed to be saints or historical figures. The doors had stood wide open, and that glorious music had been a siren song to Erik, who had managed to make his way through the balustrades, gardens and fountain square.

Avoiding eye contact, he had darted his way through the crowd of people who were apparently leaving the Sunday evening mass. He slumped his shoulders and had tried to appear as inconspicuous as possible, moving through the parishioners with his masked face well-hidden underneath the hood. Ducking inside an archway, he had waited until he was certain that no one had taken notice, then dashed inside the doorway and flattened himself against the wall, plotting his next move.

His eyes took in the beauty of the church's candlelit, gold-leafed interior; but it was not immediately apparent where the music was coming from. Continuing his assessment of the sanctuary, he had discovered that the entire front wall was lined with magnificent golden pipes of many lengths and widths. They appeared to have been arranged in a particular pattern; with the shortest ones in the front and the tallest reaching all the way up to the ceiling. There could be no doubt that these pipes were transmitting the sound, but Erik had wondered…where was the musician…and how was the music being played?

Moving cautiously into the sanctuary, he dropped to the floor and crawled underneath a pew. It was his first time inside a church, and Erik thought that there was little difference between the church's grand interior and the opera's lavish decor. Both featured Neo-Classic design, candles, and massive sculptures, and both glittered with gold and marble surfaces.

Lying on his back, he listened as the extraordinary music literally shook the walls. It was informed by the sounds of bells and soaring trumpets, and it rumbled with an ear-shattering lower register that resonated in his belly.

The sound fluting up out through those pipes was powerful, exciting and awe-inspiring; and as Erik listened, the underside of his mask became moist with unexpected tears. He recognized the work of his favorite composers, but had never heard Mozart or Beethoven played with such audacity and grandeur! Turning to face the rear of the sanctuary, he propped himself up on his elbows and poked his head out from under the pew. He craned his neck and gazed up at what appeared to be a balcony, where he could see even more pipes of graduated sizes.

A quick observation told him that, with the exception of a few people remaining behind to pray, most of the parishioners had left. Erik had seen a priest attending to some sort of religious ceremony up at the front, but he was not about to let that stop him.

Cautiously unfolding himself from his hiding place, without a sound he had emerged out from under the pews and crept across the marble floor to the very back of the church, searching for an entrance to the balcony. Eyeing a door to the right of the main entrance, he had read the words, "Organ and Choir Loft."

Erik had hesitated a moment before trying the door. Holding his breath and puffing out his chest, he reminded himself that he had survived two hellish years with the gypsies.

"I may be only a boy, but I am certainly no child," he had muttered to himself.

Not only had he survived, but he had escaped, and had been managing on his own beneath the opera house; with no parents, no brothers or sisters!

He was surviving, and compared to the rubbish he'd already lived through, sneaking into a church was a small matter. If he were pursued, he would outrun or defend himself against anyone who dared to interfere. There was nothing to stop him now. He was going to turn that knob and open the door.

Clasping his fingers around the knob, Erik had easily opened the door and pushed inward, careful not to make a sound. A staircase was directly ahead, and he had hugged the wall with his body, creeping upward, and having no idea who or what awaited him in the loft. Nothing could have prepared him for the remarkable sight that had met his eyes when he reached the top of those stairs. From floor to ceiling, gleaming silver pipes occupied the entire facing wall, but as he had suspected, the pipes alone were not responsible for the music.

A balding, elderly gentleman sat with his back to Erik, attired in some sort of priest's robe and cap, with the lamp light creating a halo of the fringe of his white hair. He was sitting at an instrument that was far more complex than a piano, with multi-tiered keyboards and rows of ivory and brown knobs, which the man had then pulled and pushed, creating a variety of sounds. The pedals beneath the instrument were many, and Erik had watched breathlessly as the man rode those pedals with his feet, like a dancer.

The gentleman's entire body appeared to be engaged as the music source was produced through an air chamber...or some sort of bellows, visible in the underside of the instrument's console, where one foot continuously pumped out that sonorous music. The old man's reedy arms and gnarled fingers had never stopped moving, and his back had undulated and swayed, with his head lolling from side to side as if he hadn't a care in the world.

Erik had felt tears wetting the underside of his mask as he worshipped that music, wishing to lay his hands on the keyboard and longing to feel the power of its breath at his fingertips. He felt a sense of destiny, and the fine hairs on his arms had bristled as he grasped the balustrade and wept. In that moment, Erik had known that he would find some way to play such an instrument, even if it meant exposing himself to danger.

Lowering his head and closing his eyes, he sat down on the steps, and there he had remained for the better part of the evening. Wishing never to leave, he had listened whilst the gentleman played on, oblivious of the cloaked boy's presence.

Erik gazed through the mirror at Christine with the same sense of wonder that he had experienced on the occasion of hearing that church organ. Hearing her sing had brought back the joy of that moment in a way that only music could, and now that the ball was over and his finances secure, he was planning to devote his energies to the little orphan girl. He was not at all certain how to go about his plans for her, but given her unusual love for music, he wondered how she might respond to hearing his own work. It would be wonderful if someone, even one person in the world, could listen to his compositions; but even as the thought occurred to him, Erik dismissed it as absurd and turned his back on the mirror, fearing that he had made a mistake in coming.

More than mere glass stood between himself and friendship with an innocent child. His face was the true barrier that separated Erik from the rest of humankind, and as he lifted his chin, smirking angrily at his reflection, he realized in horror that, in his hasty ascent to the mirror, he had forgotten to wear the mask! His hand flew up to the right side of his face, and he spread his fingers across the disfigured flesh and bone.

"Oh, Christ!" he swore. "How could I have been such a bloody imbecile?"

The mask had become a second skin and there were times when he barely felt its persistent weight, but he never slept in it. Fearful that something dreadful had happened to Christine, he had failed to put the damn thing on!

"Damn it!" he spat, slamming his gloved fist into the wall. "What if someone had seen me?"

The secrecy of his home had been safeguarded years ago. Trap doors, mechanical devices, and all manner of obstacles riddled the journey to his realm; but with his comings and goings in preparation for the Bal Masque, Erik had sensed that he was being watched. He'd heard footsteps on a few occasions, and questioned whether he had also heard them earlier on his way up to Christine's mirror.

No one but Erik knew the intricacies of the deepest tunnels and chambers beneath the opera house, but what if some wretch had been fool enough to trail him? The mere possibility of confrontation fired up his blood and aroused his aggressive tendencies. Wide awake now and full of restless energy, he doubted that he would be able go back to sleep. He was in a poor frame of mind to compose, and in no mood for another boring book. He needed exercise and a bit of excitement, so why not have a look around to see who might be lurking? A little distraction could prove entertaining.

"Well, Monsieur, if you're out there…" he rasped, stroking his chin.

Glad for a diversion, Erik placed his hand on the backside of the mirror in a gesture of goodbye to Christine, who now appeared to be sleeping soundly. He tripped the chamber's closing mechanism, slipped out into the corridor and began his descent, this time deliberately taking an alternate route.

Certain that he had heard faint footsteps about a quarter of a mile behind him, Erik paused. His lips curved into a sardonic smile and his eyes flashed coldly as he remarked, "I am ready for you, Monsieur."

He quickly turned to the left and descended the stone stairway, plunging deeper toward the basement's fifth level. Feeling for a niche in the wall, he wrapped his black cloak around his body, slumped down onto the floor and waited. After half an hour, he saw a faint light flickering off the stone walls at the top of the stairway, signaling that an intruder had indeed entered his realm. He paused when he heard the man's boots click, then pulled himself out of the niche just enough to get a better look. This this poor soul was a rat catcher, dressed in pauper's clothing, with no hat to cover his balding head. In one hand he carried a torch, while the other grasped a large burlap sack that was slung across his shoulder and presently squirming with squealing rats.

Erik had always found the rat-catching business distasteful, but the fellow could sell the rats for a price and perhaps buy himself a meal. Disappointed, he resolved to leave the poor wretch alone and return to his bed.

Waiting until the man was out of sight, he then crawled out of his niche, stealthily winding down the stairs toward the lake…however, just as he rounded the corner, he caught a hint of movement out of his left eye. Shrinking back against the wall, he peered into the darkness, certain that someone was there. His breathing and pulse accelerated as his taste for danger heightened.

Erik observed that the fool obviously had no idea who he was dealing with as he lumbered down the stairs with an oafish gate, taking little precaution for his miserable life! Lifting a length of coiled cat gut from the inner lining of his cloak, Erik pulled it taut, and checked the loop.

As sleek and soundless as a panther, he prowled against the black mildewed wall toward his prey, the Punjab lasso ready to do his will. When the glow of the intruder's torch flickered on the opposite wall, Erik lunged out at him, poised to wrap the lasso around the bastard's neck! He was capable of applying deadly force but had no inclination to kill the man…that is not yet. Erik merely wished to toy with the fool, to scare away him from ever entering his hidden sanctuary again.

Fortunately for the fellow, just as the idiot held his torch up over his head, Erik got a good look at his pockmarked face and recognized him! It was Joseph Buquet, the newly hired chief sceneshifter. He was an ignorant, surly sort, but well liked by the company for his bawdy humor and loyalty to the house. Erik then came to the conclusion that he had no cause to kill the man in cold blood. Buquet had obviously followed the rat catcher that night, and had likely done so before, but Erik elected not to touch a hair on his head, certain that he would never return after he was finished with his sport.

"Good evening, Monsieur!" Erik announced boldly with a toothy grin, watching in amusement as Buquet's face went tombstone white. Buquet dropped the torch, turned around and ran up the staircase, screaming like a woman! Erik waited until the brute was out of sight, then reared his head back and laughed smugly. The Opera Ghost's face had done the job, to be sure. But suddenly, remembering himself, he regretted his actions. Given that the only other soul connected with the opera to have seen his unmasked face was Madame Giry, now he was in a bit of a predicament. He would need to watch Buquet carefully from here on out, and if the man dared to interfere or make trouble again, he'd take care of him.

As he poled back to his shores, Erik made a mental note to test his security devices. Mooring the boat to the rocky outcropping, he stepped up onto the platform and leaned the pole against the cave entrance. It had been an eventful evening, and he was finally ready for sleep.

Quickly disrobing, he washed up and sauntered down to the library for a nightcap. With his glass of brandy in hand, he walked up the stone steps to his bedchamber, set the glass on the nightstand, then crawled back into bed, folding his arms behind his head on the pillow. Staring up at the lake's luminous reflection on the grotto's vaulted ceiling, his thoughts turned again to the little girl. What a vulnerable and strange child she was, he mused to himself. Oddly enough, something about the girl had evoked memories of his own desolate childhood, and he did not like seeing her frightened or unhappy.

Her dance instruction had apparently begun, and he'd heard from Madame Giry that she was languishing, showing little interest, and having no desire to learn. She had been isolating herself, refusing to socialize with the other children and often wandered the halls alone. Giry was concerned that, unable or unwilling to cope with her father's death, the girl was slipping away. But no one seemed to know what to do for her.

Erik wondered how much longer the girl could continue in her current state. Her nightmares were clearly of an extreme nature, and he worried about her mental health.

"Just a few more weeks, Christine…just a little more time and your Angel of Music will come to you."

Chapter 7
Saying Goodbye

Winter had at last released France from its frosty grip, and springtime came to Paris in a profusion of flowers. Trees blossomed extravagantly, flocking the cobbled streets with white horse-chestnut and lavender plum blossoms. The fragrance of flowers in bloom was intoxicating, with wisteria vines hanging from balconies and lilac trees thick with purple. The Champs-Elysées rang with coaches and tourists, while lakes and ponds were crowded with rowboats. Lovers strolled hand in hand beneath shady trees, and the music of song-birds wheeled overhead.

Parisian women showed off their spring finery at sidewalk cafes and along the boulevards, while exclusive boutiques bustled with shoppers as people emerged in great numbers from their homes and chateaus, delighting in April's milder temperatures.

It seemed that the whole city had been asleep for months and was now awakening, stretching, and stepping out into the sun! The Paris Opera House was in preparation for its first opera of the season, Mozart's delightful fantasy, *The Magic Flute*. Set production was in full swing as gigantic trees were being constructed from plaster-of-paris, metal screen, and copper wire. The Queen's dark palace stood at center stage, with final coats of paint being applied by stagehands. The backdrops were hung, the pulleys and cable in the process of being tested, and the workshop was a veritable kaleidoscope of fabrics, trims, and costumes in various stages of design.

Rehearsals had been underway for three months, and with the gala night only weeks away, near panic had broken out in the ranks as every possible mishap and blunder had threatened to delay the opening. The Opera Ghost had been relatively quiet following the Bal Masque; but when production on *The Magic Flute* ensued, he had emerged out of hiding and was soon up to his old tricks again.

Notes had been passed from Madame Giry to Poligny and Debienne, announcing that O.G. was not pleased with the casting. Not only was he unhappy with the news that Carlotta had been cast in the role of the beautiful young princess, Pamina, he'd even had the gall to suggest that the show's opening would be delayed if Mademoiselle Simonette was not given the role. Mademoiselle Simonette possessed a pure, lyrical tonality and Carlotta was predictably spiteful, and insanely jealous, of her younger and prettier rival.

In addition to his displeasure over the casting of Carlotta as Pamina, the Opera Ghost was equally displeased with Signor Piangi in the role of Tamino; the handsome prince who falls in love with the princess after seeing her photograph. Meg Giry, who was always well-informed when it came to information about the Opera Ghost, told everyone that she had heard from Jammes that O.G. felt Piangi too stout to play a handsome prince. He thought Piangi better suited to the comical role of the flamboyant bird catcher, Papageno, a role that Piangi clearly felt was beneath him. O.G. had also demanded that Carlotta be cast as the Evil Queen, and that she be dressed entirely in dark blue! She had strutted about the stage, fuming that 'I looked horrible in dark blue' and had threatened to quit the opera outright!

Meg and I had watched from backstage, biting our cheeks to keep from laughing as Carlotta's face turned a deep shade of red. Throwing her score down onto the stage, the woman had cursed in Italian and stomped off with her sycophants following closely behind, muttering their outrage at the diva's mistreatment. She had remained locked in her dressing room for hours, with the sound of her curses leaking out into the hallways. In the end, however, the managers had relented, and O.G. had had his way.

The lovely Mademoiselle Simonette was immediately cast as Pamina, stirring up Carlotta's insufferable bad humors for days on end. She had been heard complaining about her costumes; had made snide comments about Simonette behind her back; and had said horrible things about the Opera Ghost, daring him to speak to her face to face!

Apparently he *had* heard her, because now, every rehearsal found Carlotta embroiled in yet another catastrophe. Her head-dress would come up missing, her score and libretto would be discovered in the trash, and dead mice or cockroaches would mysteriously appear in her make-up case. It was apparent that the Opera Ghost had declared war on the singer, and it was also rumored that he took great delight in watching her squirm.

To make matters worse, the ballet rats were constantly whispering to each other about shadows that lurked backstage, claiming to have heard strange voices materializing in the theater. Others reported a cloaked figure prowling up in the catwalks, whilst Joseph Buquet, the chief sceneshifter, entertained the dancers and chorus girls with stories about the ghost, vividly describing his grotesque face. The chorus girls shrieked with fear and delight as he tried to convince everyone that he had actually seen the ghost for himself, and as the date for the gala night neared, these stories escalated, with none of us daring to walk through the opera's backstage unaccompanied.

Meg and I had both completed our first course of training for the corps de ballet, but she was much further along than me in her exercises, positions, and choreographed dance.

She had been selected as a featured dancer in the children's ballet, while I still hung behind the flies watching her graceful Pirouette, Developpe', and Pas de Bourree. I admired her grace and beauty, and believed myself lacking in true talent for dance, but she always encouraged me to continue training. Despite my uncooperative feet, I rehearsed before my mirror each day, but I had little interest in dance...I had little interest in anything.

Unlike all of Paris, the winter chill had not left my heart, and at all times, no matter what I did or where we went, the pain of losing my father would not let go. Consequently, adjusting to life at the opera house was difficult as I tried to find my place in a world of more than a thousand strangers.

Everyone in the opera house was aware of my orphan status; that I had been taken in by the kindness of Madame Giry. From the beginning, I had been made to understand that I was not wanted or needed in the corps de ballet. In the eyes of the older girls, neither I nor the other orphan girls were their equals, so whenever adults were absent, often on my way to the dining hall, or when I was alone in the corridors, the older girls bullied me. They insulted my clothing and called me horrid names, speaking ill of my frizzy hair, and teasing me for my pale skin. Remarking that I looked like a rag doll, they said that I was bug-eyed...and even worse comments were flung at me in those early months.

Mademoiselle Marie explained their behavior as the pecking order in the dormitory, and she informed me that some of the girls were jealous that an orphan had been given a private room, while other young ladies from better families were expected to share their quarters. Meg tried to convince me not to pay attention to their rude behavior, and whenever she witnessed the bullying for herself, she was quick to defend me, defusing awkward encounters with nothing more than her affability and her position as the ballet mistress's daughter. I made every attempt to keep to myself, hanging always on Meg, who was my protector and only friend.

One evening when rehearsals had gone over-time, Meg and I had left the stage with our dance shoes and bags in hand, wearily making our way back to the dormitory wing. A girl called Claire and four of the older girls had lagged behind, giggling and shouting the usual names at me: "bug-eyes," "rag-doll," and the name I detested most of all, "stork-legs."

Claire was the ring leader, who instigated a great deal of mischief, and though only one year older than Meg, she was mean-spirited and intimidating. Younger girls easily fell under her influence, and students who would not have ordinarily teased other children became the school's worst bullies. Claire had been a thorn in Madame Giry's side since the day her politician father had enrolled her in the academy; and when no one was around but Meg and me, Madame would confide that Mademoiselle Claire's only talent was getting into trouble. It was common knowledge among all the directors and instructors that her father was a man of influence, whose daughter must be handled properly or his financial support would be suspended. Therefore, every attempt had been made to accommodate the young lady, who, although she did not deserve them, was often given privileges not enjoyed by her peers. She, in turn, bought special favors from the other girls, promising trinkets and treats in reward for their loyalty.

For a girl who had grown up without playmates, these behaviors and social groups were all new to me, and I could not comprehend such meanness or understand why I had become the target of cruelty. It was true, funds provided by the opera's patrons were not enough to outfit me in stylish clothing, and my dresses were plainer than those of the other girls...but I was grateful, nonetheless. Every so often, Madame treated me to a new dress or cloak, but most of my clothes were handed down from the older girls who had outgrown them. It was also true that my legs were thin and my face was pale, but I was taller than most girls my own age, and I had inherited my family's Scandinavian complexion. The name-calling and teasing would leave me in tears, but Meg, Madame, and Marie watched over me.

That night as we headed to the dormitories, we heard Claire calling after us, and Meg looped her arm through mine, whispering in my ear, "Just ignore them, Christine, they are only jealous."

We turned down the torch lit hall to our rooms, while the girls remained near the stairs, watching and murmuring amongst themselves as we arrived at Meg's apartment door. Hitching the strap of her bag up onto her shoulder, Meg kissed me on the cheek and unlocked the door.

"I think I'll stay with Mama tonight, Christine. If I sleep in your room like always, neither of us shall have any sleep!" she giggled and yawned.

With an early morning rehearsal only hours away, I nodded my head in agreement, returned her kiss, and we said our goodnights. Looking back over my shoulder, I waited to be certain that Claire and her friends were out of sight, and then dragging my feet down the hall, I arrived at my own door. Upon entering my room, the physical exhaustion of the long rehearsal caught up to me, and I dropped my bag and dance shoes in the chair, then lifted the chimney off the lamp, struck a match, and lit the wick. I watched the familiar rosy glow illuminate my pink plaster walls, sat down on the bed and pulled off my shoes, wondering when

Madame would come to tuck me in. Shuffling in my stocking feet across the carpet, I rummaged in my bureau for my hairbrush and prepared to visit the washroom for my evening toilet. However, there was a knock on my door, and supposing it was Madame, I was shocked when upon opening it, Claire and two of her playmates pushed their way right past me and sashayed into my room!

Claire did not possess the typical physique of a ballerina, but was a rather large-boned and plank-faced girl, whose only pretty feature was her waist length blonde hair, which was presently tied back in a ribbon. Whenever she was in the presence of boys, she could be seen flipping her hair about, and we all knew that her hair was a point of great pride for a girl who was otherwise quite plain. While Meg and many of the other students appeared to float across a room when they walked, Claire was heavy footed and clumsy, and I stood aside as she appraised my room with a most unattractive scowl.

"My, what a charming room," she said, unsmiling. "Furnished with castoffs, I see."

Not knowing what else to do, I stood, the silent fool, as she and her friends insulted me. I did not generally invite other children into my room. Only Meg and Madame had seen my quarters, and this intrusion immediately set me on edge.

"Madame and the patrons have been very generous," I spoke shyly, staring down at my feet.

Backing up against the mirror, I watched warily as Claire and her friends wandered through my room, touching my things and commenting between themselves. I could not imagine what they intended, but was too timid to ask them to leave. Instead, I nervously pointed out that Madame would be arriving at any moment to say goodnight, but this generated only a mild response.

Opening a bureau drawer, Claire continued her inspection of my belongings as I tried to muster the courage to ask her to stop. Finally, I recoiled in fear when she spotted my father's violin in the corner, behind the damask chair.

Without even thinking, I lunged next to Claire as she bent down and picked up the case.

"What is this?" she asked, as the other two crowded behind her.

"Well, it's…it's my father's," I stammered, heat flushing into my cheeks as she fumbled with the fasteners.

"Let's have a look," Claire suggested to her friends, only glancing briefly over her shoulder at me.

I clenched my fists at my side, took another step forward and raised my voice. "Please, don't!" I cried out, "It is very old."

It seemed to me that the more I spoke out, the more bold and nasty Claire became. With a smile that was more or less a sneer, she roughly handled the violin case, and I could not help but gasp when she flipped open the fasteners. Whilst I stared in disbelief, she jerked the violin from the case and finally, sucking in my breath, I'd had enough.

"Please put that down!" I insisted, rushing toward the bed, ready to remove the violin from her hands, with force if necessary. Laughing, the other two girls stood in my way and blocked me bodily from interfering with Claire's harsh treatment of my father's violin.

"Claire, please, please be careful!" I repeated, with sweat beading up on my forehead as unwanted tears stung my eyes.

"Oh, don't worry," she spoke in a mocking tone as she gripped the violin roughly by the neck and waved it around, "I shall be ever so careful."

Doubting her words, and realizing her true intention, I gritted my teeth and forced my way around Claire's playmates, but by then…it was too late. I watched, horrified, as she allowed the violin to slowly slip from her hand right before my eyes. It hit the floorboards face down with a sickening crack, and pushing the girls out of my way, I fell to my knees. Carefully lifting the violin, I could see that the bridge and tailpiece had broken off from the belly, leaving the strings to dangle loosely from the pegs.

"Oh, dear," she said, spreading out her arms open-palmed, "how could I have been so clumsy?"

My hands shook as I shouted angrily, "You broke it on purpose!"

I was no longer interested in hiding my outrage. She had deliberately broken my most cherished possession, but merely stood there with a smug look on her face as I sobbed openly. The violin had been my Grandfather's, and before him it had belonged to his father. Passed down through the Daaé family, it had been more than an heirloom, and had survived a house fire and two wars. In only a moment, this girl had deliberately broken an instrument whose varnish and strings still resonated with the fingerprints of not only my father, but generations of musicians before him. To me, the violin was an enchanted storyteller, and I hated her for even daring to touch it!

Suddenly, the door flew open and Madame Giry loomed larger than her actual size in the doorway. Her lips were drawn in a taut line and her eyes flashed intensely from Claire to her friends, and then down to where I sat crumpled on the floor, embracing my father's violin as if it were a baby in my arms.

"Christine?" she groaned my name as she flew to my side and knelt on the floor next to me, "What has happened, darling?"

Glaring up at Claire through my tears, I accused with anger, "She broke it on purpose!"

With her face blanching, and a poor attempt at a smile, Claire held out her hands and protested, "No, no, Madame, it was an accident. I swear it!"

"I see, an accident," Madame spoke, her voice dangerously low, the consonants clipped and measured. "Well, then, suppose you tell me how you *accidentally* broke this child's most prized treasure?"

Placing her arm around my shoulder, Madame examined the violin as Claire hesitated, her haughty posture shrinking before my eyes.

"Well, I only wanted to see it," she whined, her two friends hanging back in the room's violet shadows, not saying a word.

Directing her full attention at me, Madame lowered her voice and spoke very calmly, "We shall have it repaired, Christine. Maestro Reyer will know where to send it. Do not cry, darling, all is not lost."

Slowly rising to her feet, Madame whirled around to face Claire, grabbed hold of the girl's shoulder, and escorted her and her playmates toward the door, saying through clenched teeth, "You should be ashamed of yourself, Claire! A girl whose parents give her all that money can afford…and you do this to a child who has lost everything. You are a spiteful little wretch and I shall personally see that your father and everyone connected with the opera house learn the truth!"

"Madame I didn't..." Claire began to voice a retort, but Madame Giry stopped her with a hard glare. The girl snapped her mouth shut as Madame opened the door, and with her face turning red, Claire started to cry, her eyes puffing up as she sniffed and snorted into a handkerchief.

"You young ladies will come with me now!" she ordered Claire's cohorts.

Turning to address me, she softened her voice and said, "Christine, I shall be back to hear your prayers momentarily."

The violin incident was then well-publicized throughout the opera house, with the end result being Claire's suspension from dancing in *The Magic Flute*. Her father had offered to pay for the expensive repairs, and to my relief, when the violin was returned to me, one could hardly see where the damage had been done. Bee's wax and varnish touch-ups had been applied to the few scratches incurred by the crash to the floor, and the bridge and tailpiece had been replaced by near replicas of my father's model.

It seemed to me that, following the incident, I was treated differently by my peers. Whereas, before, I had been either ignored or teased by the other girls, they now included me in their circle of friends, inviting me to birthday parties or outings and even sleepovers. I was pleased that the social tensions had lessened somewhat, and Claire never bothered me again.

For a while things were relatively quiet in the dormitory wing, until a few weeks later, when Claire awoke one morning to find her blonde tresses cut off! The story was told that, upon opening her eyes, she shrieked in horror at the shorn locks that were spread across her pillow and strewn about on the floor. Whoever had done the job had left her with chin length hair, as short as a boy's bowl cut. No scissors were found in her room, and none of her roommates had seen or heard a thing that night, but since mysterious incidents were often attributed to the Opera

Ghost, the hair disaster became known as his most audacious crime, with some believing him justified in his actions.

As angry as I had been with Claire for what she had done to my father's violin, I felt sorry for the poor girl, who went about the opera house with her head covered by a bonnet, behaving like a bird whose feathers had been plucked. Without her golden mane she seemed to physically shrink, and I could not help wondering who had been so cruel as to leave her in such a state. Unlike Meg, I was not grateful to the Opera Ghost for taking his vengeance against her, and was rather relieved when her hair eventually began to grow back.

Five months had now passed since my father's death, and even when encompassed by the excitement of the opera house, I was desperately lonely. Madame Giry thought up countless ways to take my mind off my father, but they only temporarily eased my loneliness. She took me to beautiful shops and purchased brand new dresses, cloaks, and hats for my wardrobe. She had furnished my room with a rose embroidered coverlet, and a gold leaf vanity that we placed beside the mirror. She had also purchased an engraved cedar wardrobe which stood next to the dressing screen in the opposite corner. The wardrobe had been filled with the most beautiful clothes, hats and shoes I had ever seen, and when I asked Madame where they had all come from, she informed me cheerfully that I had acquired a benefactor who was now paying for my education and personal needs.

Each month I found a new dress or a new doll wrapped up with ribbon, and a note attached, reading: For Christine, from her benefactor, Monsieur E. Though I asked her repeatedly the identity of this kind person, Madame replied that he wished to remain anonymous. Wishing to express my appreciation to this gentleman after several months of receiving his lovely gifts, I asked Madame if I might create a thank you card for him. Using parchment and paints, I decorated a card with flowers, and in my childish cursive, wrote:

Dear Monsieur Benefactor,
Thank you for the lovely gifts.
Your friend, Christine Yvette Daaé

Each time he left a new gift for me, I made a similar card, and Madame always promised to deliver them to him personally.

I did take pleasure in all his beautiful gifts, but even that small pleasure could not take my mind off my father, and it seemed that nothing could. How I had wished that those gifts had come from my father, and not a complete stranger, whose name I did not know.

One night, alone in my room, I lit a candle for my father and knelt down on my knees to pray. The room was as quiet as a tomb, the candle casting eerie shadows across every surface. My collection of dolls sitting atop the wardrobe seemed to stare at me with lifeless glass eyes, and I rubbed my arms as chills spread over my body. The candle wavered, and as I looked at my face in the mirror, for the first time I noticed the dark circles under my eyes.

"I do have bug-eyes." I whispered sadly.

My thoughts then turned to memories from the previous summer when my father, Raoul de Chagny and I had spent the day at Madame Valleria's beach house. Father's handmade kite had soared above us under an azure sky, as Raoul and I collected sea shells that had washed in along the shore. But like so many of my happy childhood memories, the border between reality and dreams had begun to blur, and I wondered, had we really known days like that? Days when I had been perfectly happy? What had it felt like to be truly happy? I could no longer remember.

Closing my eyes, I stretched my arms out before me, reaching toward the girl in the mirror, whom I no longer knew. My face was pale and I looked thinner than when I had first arrived at the opera house.

"What is wrong with me?" I asked the girl in the mirror.

I was suddenly completely overcome by fresh grief, and was desperate to leave my room. I felt the walls closing in around me, and it was as if there was no air. The ceiling seemed to thwart my efforts to pray and I needed to be closer to God and to my father, so picking up the candle from my bureau, I stepped into my slippers and carefully opened the door. Peeking down the darkened hallway and seeing that no one was about, I left my room, crept upstairs and out into the corridor toward the backstage. Enveloped by purple and gray shadows, my candle flickered and sputtered in the persistent draft as I creaked the door open to *Jacob's Ladder*, the winding staircase that climbed all the way up to the opera's roof. Meg had taken me there a few days after my arrival at the opera house, and since then I had frequented its starry summit many times when I needed to sneak away, to read and to escape from the noise of the dormitories.

Gathering up the hem of my robe, I climbed the stairs until I reached the pine-scented underside of the roof, then crept across the wide wooden planks to arrive at a narrow door.

A blast of fresh spring air immediately extinguished my candle when the door opened, and although I could see a bright dusting of stars overhead, there was no moon that night. The colossal statue of Apollo was a mere shadow that loomed above me, stretching his harp out over the edge of the roof against a sparkling backdrop of the darkening sky. I pulled my robe more tightly around me as a stiff evening breeze blew through the velvet fabric. How small I felt looking down at the vast expanse of Paris...as if I were completely alone in the world!

Madame Giry and others had tried their best to help me adjust, but it seemed that nothing could assuage my sense of isolation. Unable to hold back the tears, I let them flow. With a physical ache squeezing my insides, I wept into my hands until my face hurt and I could cry no more. I knelt beneath Apollo, lifting my eyes the entire length of his extraordinary height to the canopy of stars overhead.

"Dear Father in heaven," I cried, "if my papa can't come back, don't make me stay here. I don't want to!"

For some minutes I cried aloud, watching and listening, waiting for a reply...but God was silent. The sky above had darkened to indigo blue, the stars held no warmth, and like millions of indifferent observers, they looked down upon me without compassion. Folding my hands tightly against my chest, I continued to pray.

"Father taught me that the dead awake in your presence with the angels. My mother is with you, and so is Papa...even my grandparents are there. Father used to say that heaven is a good place. Please take me there, so I can be with them!" I cried.

I reached my arms heavenward, searching the stars for evidence of God's existence, and was surprised when I felt a drop of water land on my face. Drawing my hand to my cheek, I pressed it between my fingers, wondering how a raindrop had come from a cloudless sky.

Slowly, I stood to my feet as a peculiar feeling of numbness crept over me. I wandered to the roof's edge, peering over the barrier and down the sides of the opera house. It would have been so simple to just let go. All my loved ones were gone and I had no one. How easy it would have been just to fly away...to close my eyes, step up onto the concrete railing, and let myself go. Raising my slippered foot up onto the rail, I suddenly lurched backward as a strange 'whooshing' sound passed over my head. Had I only imagined it, I wondered? Was something up there with me?

"What was that?" I spoke out loud.

Confused and frightened, I waited for a few moments, hearing only the breeze. Yet seconds ago, I thought that I had heard a flapping sound, like the wings of a great bird. Stepping up closer to the statue, I wiped my face and peered up at Apollo through the darkness, seeing nothing but his bleak, gigantic form.

"There must be bats up here," I whispered with an odd sense of relief.

I began to feel a chill as the breeze picked up, and I shivered with its dampness. My hair whipped in the wind, with loose tendrils slapping and stinging my cheek. Deciding that it was too cold to stay there any longer, I looked up once again at the silent stars and tiptoed across the roof, opened the door, and began my lonely descent back to my bedroom.

On that same moonless night, upon opening the door to the mirror chamber, Erik had observed as Christine sat on the edge of the bed. There had been something peculiar about her eyes that had made him immediately apprehensive. She had been sitting quietly in the dark, but then had slowly risen from her bed, taken up a lamp and walked out into the darkened corridor. Erik hadn't been able to imagine where she was going unaccompanied at that time of night, but he had known instinctively that she must not be alone.

Closing the chamber door behind him, he had decided to take a great risk and had felt around the mirror's inside edge for the hidden latches. Once he had released the locks, he flattened his hands on the glass and applied pressure, but the rusted hinges made a miserable grinding sound, and refused to budge.

Erik had leaned his body against the mirror and pushed harder until it had slowly swung inward on its rusted pivots. Stepping down into her bedroom, he had closed the mirror, padded across the floor and opened her door. The glow of her lamp was still visible from down the hall as he had cautiously followed its arc of light. He had then remained several paces behind in the shadows until he was certain of her destination. Once he had ascertained that she was heading for the roof, he had taken a lesser known route and had managed to reach the roof top a few minutes before her.

Moving swiftly to Apollo's Lyre as Christine had wound her way up the stairs, Erik had crawled up onto its massive stone base and climbed the great god. He pulled himself up onto the statue's right arm and then hitching his long legs and body up onto the figure's broad shoulder, he had braced one arm around its neck and silently waited, tugging his cloak tightly against the brisk wind.

Finally the door opened and the girl had tiptoed quietly across the roof surface, kneeling below Apollo's Lyre. At first she had been silent, but as Erik watched, squinting his eyes against the wind, Christine's head had drooped into her hands and her thin shoulders had begun to shake. Having never seen such a display of sorrow, Erik had bitten down on his lower lip, watching as she had rocked back and forth on her knees, her arms crossed over her chest. Sobbing soundlessly, she had then buried her face in her hands, uttering her prayers in the language of a broken heart.

Observing Christine from his perch on Apollo, Erik had understood all too well a suffering and loneliness that seemed to nearly equal his own...and as she wept below him, lifting her face into the roof's reflective light and holding out her arms in prayer, he had felt his guts wrenching for her, recalling his own childhood.

Despite a heroic effort to maintain his composure, he had not been able to prevent his own messy tears, and he had awkwardly pulled off his mask with his free hand to wipe his eyes and nose.

Holding his breath, Erik had prayed that she would not look up to see him spying from the god's shoulder, and when for some moments she did not stir, he had let out his breath slowly. Although she had indeed looked up, her vision had seemed to focus beyond Apollo and up to the canvas of stars overhead. Reflectively, Erik had done the same, his eyes marking the seasonal constellations, drawing out their symbolic patterns from the vast flecks of light.

Movement below had then jolted his attention back down to Christine, and Erik ground his teeth as she rose up from her kneeling position, her body oddly stiff and her expression vacant. Disbelieving his own eyes, he had stared, horrified, as she had moved dangerously close to the roof's edge.

"What the devil is this?" Erik had sworn under his breath. "What is the child doing?"

Seeing that Christine intended to step up onto the barrier, he had reacted instinctively, unfurling his cloak with the noisy flapping of heavy wool, ready to jump down and grab her. With his pulse pounding, Erik's leg muscles had become taut as he prepared to dislodge himself from his hiding place, thinking it better to be found out prematurely than to let this poor child injure herself...or even worse, fall to her death. He had shuddered at the image of her frail body tumbling down the side of the opera house, but had breathed a sigh of relief when the child appeared to have heard something. She had stepped away from the edge just in time to make a rescue unnecessary, and pulling the collar high up around his neck, Erik had frozen in place, forcing his body to relax and his breathing to slow. Her eyes had scanned the length of the statue, but shrouded in his black cloak, his figure had blended into the shadows, and she had thankfully mistaken his movements for bats.

Erik had almost chuckled at being mistaken for bats, given that he had often made the comparison himself. Quickly replacing the mask on his face, he had waited until Christine left the rooftop, and when he had felt assured that she was on her way back to her room, he had soundlessly slipped down from the statue and ran for the door. Bounding down the stairs two at a time, he had kept enough distance between himself and Christine so that she wouldn't hear. Once back down on the main level, he had raced to the breezeway behind the dorms and to the mirror chamber, opening it just as she had entered her room.

Out of breath, he had watched as at last she climbed safely into her bed. With a chilly draft blowing in from the breezeway, he had drawn his cloak tightly about his body and had slunk down to the floor behind the mirror, listening as Christine sang the gypsy love song. Lying on her side, her lips moving and her eyes closed, the child had gradually drifted off. Erik tried to get comfortable and had pulled his knees up to his chest, leaned his head against the stone wall, and had then quickly fallen asleep.

The next morning Erik squinted his eyes open, moaning with considerable physical discomfort, his arms and legs tingling with numbness. Anxious about leaving Christine alone in the state he found her last night, he had slept in an awkward position behind the mirror, only to awaken stiff and cold, feeling less than elegant! The taste of last night's supper coated his tongue, and he desperately wished for a swallow of water. Slowly unfolding his long frame, he stretched to his feet, with his hindquarters and back aching miserably. Shaking out his legs, he yawned and stretched his arms above his head, flexing with a groan. Adjusting his clothing as best he could, he glanced through the mirror just as Christine began to awaken.

The next morning I awoke disheartened and weary, rising listlessly from the bed. Pulling my dressing gown on, I hung my clothes in the wardrobe, cleared the clutter from the vanity, and stacked my school books neatly into the shelves. As I was in the process of making the bed, Madame Giry entered my room and sat down, motioning for me to sit beside her.

With her hair pulled back in a tight braid and worry creasing her high forehead, Madame fluffed her practice skirt and leveled her eyes to mine. "Christine, my dear," she began in a somber tone, "I would like to speak with you about something important."

"Yes, Madame?" I asked politely.

I was confused by her grave expression as she patted my knee with her slender white hand.

"Dear, your instructors and I are concerned that you are not progressing as you should be. It has been over five months since your father passed away, Christine, and you still grieve for him in a manner that is, well…troubling to those who love you."

I did not say a word, but listened with my eyes downcast. I had apparently disappointed her in the same way I seemed to disappoint everyone. I had tried to do well in my studies, but there always seemed to be an invisible barrier between me and the rest of the world. Regardless of what I did, I could not think of the opera house as my home; to me it was just a fancy building. My only real home had been with my father; traveling throughout the countryside in our little wagon, camping at the seashore, and reading beside the hearth in our Swedish boardinghouse. Father had been my home…but he was gone now and nothing could bring him back, not even my faithful prayers each night, and not even his promise to send the Angel of Music. Besides, I was beginning to believe he had lied to me, that the whole world had lied to me, and that the opera house was merely a part of that lie.

The stage and rehearsal halls were full of music and dance nearly twenty-four hours a day, but the music held no joy for me, and I only did my lessons because I had been told that I must. Blinking back tears, I gazed up again at Madame Giry's face, taking note that her eyes were shadowed with concern. She had wanted me to think of her as a mother, but my mother was Katrine Daaé, and this woman, though very good to me, could never be my mother. I suppose I loved her after a fashion, in the same way I had loved Madame Valleria...but neither of these ladies would ever be a real mother to me. As far as I was concerned, I had no real mother or father. I was an orphan and that would never change.

Madame's eyes softened as she reached for a handkerchief in her skirt pocket and dabbed my eyes and cheeks. Folding the handkerchief in her hand, she placed her arm around my shoulder and drew me closer. Despite my anger, I let her hold me and listened politely as she spoke.

"Christine, it is time to stop grieving and to begin living the life your father wanted you to have," Madame advised quietly.

I stared up at her, surprised by words I had not expected.

Taking my hand in hers, Madame continued and said, "Gustave arranged for your instruction in dance and in all the performing arts so that one day you might perform as a principal singer."

I merely stared at her, saying nothing, and when I did not reply, she cleared her throat and rubbed her chin thoughtfully.

"Christine, do you know what is meant by the term 'prodigy'?" she asked me.

I thought perhaps I had heard the word before, but its meaning was unclear.

"No, Madame," I answered shaking my head.

One corner of her mouth turned upward, and I watched a glint appear in Madame's hazel eyes as she explained.

"A prodigy is a person...usually a child, gifted with extraordinary talent surpassing their age and experience. In your case, my dear, you are a vocally musical prodigy, while other children in the academy are gifted dancers."

Again, I could offer no reply and merely stared up at her. Chuckling under her breath, Madame gave my hand a squeeze and smiled.

"Christine, do you know what I am trying to say?" she asked again.

I shook my head and thought back on the many times Papa had accompanied me on his violin. It was true that the people had clapped and cheered loudly, and one time he had even insisted that it was me they came to hear, and not his violin. Well, naturally I did not believe him, because everyone knew that my father was the greatest violinist in all the world. Why, people had lined up to hear his music, and I had only sung with him because he had asked me to.

Looking back, I suddenly recalled one or two occasions when people in the crowd had shouted, "Let the little girl sing!" And there were also those times when Madame Valleria had said I sang like an angel...but I did not see that my voice was all that special.

Gazing at Madame in confusion, I muttered, "I am sorry, Madame. I am trying to understand."

With a bright smile and watering eyes, Madame threw her arms around me, and I could hear the warm laugh in her voice as she exclaimed, "Christine Yvette Daaé, did no one ever tell you that you have a special gift, and that your voice is as mature and beautiful as a young woman well-past her adolescence? You are a prodigy, my dear...and your father left you in my care so that you might receive the proper training. However, I must tell you that, even without formal training, darling girl, why...your voice surpasses the talent of generations of singers who have performed in this very opera house!"

Taken aback, I found this difficult to believe! With my own ears I had heard the opera's most notable performers, and in comparison to those women, my voice sounded rather ordinary.

"But Madame, I am only ten years old!" I protested.

"Yes, you are, and at only ten, you possess a voice that even La Carlotta would covet for her own. I'll grant you...your voice is undeveloped, but in time you will develop the proper technique...that is...if you wish to."

Pausing thoughtfully, Madame seemed to be waiting for a verbal response from me, but words failed me and folding my hands in my lap, I kept my thoughts to myself as Madame resumed.

"Christine, it is, of course, your choice...a decision that only you can make, but I happen to know that your father believed in you, and having heard you sing on the opera stage, I believe in you too!"

Again, Madame seemed to be waiting for me to say something, but what could I say? It was all so strange having these important decisions thrust at me, when I felt so utterly incapable of knowing my own mind. After some moments of staring down at my hands, I lifted my eyes briefly and politely replied, "Thank you, Madame."

Christine, it matters little that I believe in you, or even that your father believed your gifts. What is important now is that you must believe in yourself! You must carry on with your life! It is time to let go, my dear child. You have grieved long enough."

Madame ended her statement, leveling her gaze to mine, with her voice in its deepest and most gentle register. I still did not answer, fidgeting with my dressing gown tie as I hummed absently to myself. I did not want to hear any more of what she had to say. Patiently, she cupped my cheek with her hand and continued, while I avoided her insistent eyes.

"You have isolated yourself from the other girls, Christine, and keep to your books and your daydreams…and you have grown pale, my dear. I am worried about your health."

Madame tried to put her arm around me again, but I twisted away, tears beginning to sting the corners of my eyes as she went on.

"Christine, your father would not want to see you like this. You must know that. Honor his memory, yes, but do so by living the life he wanted for you, and not by mourning his loss every single day!"

She had spoken firmly, but not without compassion, and this time when she placed her arm around me, I did not pull away.

"Christine, I think it is time that you visit your father's grave again," Madame suggested with a whisper.

My father's lonely grave was the last place on earth I wanted to visit, and I stiffened at the mere suggestion of seeing that awful place again. I had not been to the cemetery since the day of his burial, and I could not bear to think of him all alone in that frozen wasteland of the dead.

"No! I hate that horrible place!" I cried out, burying my face in Madame's shawl. "I can't ever go back there again, Madame; please don't make me! I won't go! I swear I won't!"

In her patient way, Madame allowed me to have my tantrum and waited for me to calm down. I sniffled loudly and wiped my nose with her handkerchief as she stroked my hair.

"Christine, dear," she soothed, gently lifting my chin. "No one will force you to go; the choice is yours…but I believe it is time for you to say a final goodbye."

"But I don't want to say goodbye!" I cried stubbornly, flinging my arms around her. "Oh, Madame…why did he have to die?"

She held me in her arms and let me sob until my tears wet the soft fringe of her shawl. With one soft hand she stroked the back of my head, rocking me gently. With a deep sigh and the sound of sorrow in her voice, Madame whispered against my ear.

"No one knows why we must die, my dear, but all things living must one day be no more on this earth. Yet the people we love, Christine, will always be with us, because like a treasure chest, our hearts will hold their memory forever. Nothing will ever take those treasured memories away from you. It is right that you never forget your father, but you must stop grieving for him every day. If you don't, you will never live your life as he would have wanted. Do you believe it makes him happy to look down from heaven and see his daughter so sad and lonely…crying all the time, when she should be learning and enjoying everything the opera house has to offer?"

Allowing her words to take root in my heart, I lifted my head from Madame's shawl and looked up at her in surprise. I had never thought of it that way; that Father might be disappointed in me…or that he might want me to be happy without him. He had always kept me so close, and we were so much a part of each other that it was as if half of me had been buried in the ground with him. I knew Madame to be a wise woman, who had shown me nothing but kindness, but what would it mean to say goodbye? Must I discontinue my nightly prayers and forget his promises? I had grown weary of sadness, and I wanted to make him proud…but to say goodbye? Forever?

For several minutes I sat silently with my hands folded in my lap, considering her words, then finally looking up at her, I nodded my head.

"All right, Madame, I'll go." I agreed.

Chapter 8
The Angel of Music

As he listened in on Christine's conversation with Madame Giry from behind the mirror, Erik was flabbergasted that the child seemed totally unaware of her talent. Louise was correct in her assertion that Christine was a child prodigy, and he could not imagine why her father had not simply sat her down and told her so. Clearly, he must have known that her talent far outshone his skills as a violinist, and even Christine had attested to the crowds shouting for her. To his way of thinking, with the correct instruction and the natural maturing of her voice, this child could someday perform in the world's finest concert halls, but she was too pure to remain at the opera house, which would only spoil her with false admiration.

What Christine Daaé needed was discipline and careful guidance in her technique.

"What she needs is me," he muttered, surprised to hear the words actually coming from his own mouth.

Contemplating his plans for Christine, Erik scuffed his boots on the stone floor. The time to contact her had come, even if it must be done through indirect means. He would never be able to accomplish a thing without opening up some form of communication with her; and although he had been waiting for the right moment, after the odd behavior he had witnessed on the previous night, he was inclined to act quickly...but how, he wondered?

Like rehearsing for a play, in his mind he had lived out a variety of scenarios. He had been musing about what he should say to her and how he would go about projecting an angelic, fatherly character. But now that the magnitude of devising an actual plan was upon him, he felt apprehensive and unprepared.

What did he know of children? What if he frightened her? What if she wouldn't believe him? She had been pre-eminent in his thoughts for weeks, but now as he watched her through the mirror, the whole scheme seemed ridiculous!

"Even if I can convince her that I am her dead father, or at the very least, some sort of guardian angel…what did she call it? Ah, yes, the Angel of Music…what then?" he argued with himself, chewing on his lower lip. "I must be taking leave of my senses to even attempt this!"

Backing away from the mirror, Erik stomped out into the corridor, paced in long, heavy-footed strides, then turned on his heel and continued pacing in the opposite direction. He puffed ragged breaths across his tongue as he rubbed his hands together, mulling over his plans for their first meeting. What if he were to sing for her now? He could wait for Madame Giry to leave, and then begin by singing the child's favorite gypsy song. Or perhaps he should speak to her first, by simply introducing himself as her father's Angel of Music. Perhaps in the case of children, a direct approach was best.

Scoffing to himself, Erik chuckled darkly and commented, "No, that is utterly absurd! I would most certainly scare the poor girl half to death!"

Watching over his shoulder for intruders in the corridor, he spoke aloud, "Oh, for Christ's sake, how in the hell does one portray an angel?"

Erik stepped again inside the mirror chamber and watched as Madame Giry left Christine's room, leaving the child to sit quietly on the bed, her eyes still glimmering with tears. Wouldn't this be the ideal time to break the silence between them, before she left to visit her father's grave? Hearing the voice of her father's angel might be a comfort to her as she said those final goodbyes.

"Just open your mouth and sing!" he whispered to himself through clenched teeth.

Squaring his shoulders, Erik positioned himself close enough to fog the mirror with his breath. His heart hammered, his forehead was sweating, and his hands would not stop shaking. He nervously smoothed back his hair, adjusted the fit of his mask, and opened his mouth to sing…but he couldn't get control of his pulse, never mind singing anything remotely angelic! He was far too tired after a miserable night crouched behind the mirror. His mouth was uncomfortably dry, and he needed more time to prepare. Frustrated, he slunk back out into the corridor to catch his breath and leaned against the stone wall, his arms crossed over his chest.

"Damn!" he swore, "I have no idea how to go about this!"

It had been so many years since anyone but basement rats had heard him sing, and the whole concept of a ghost or an angel had begun to sound preposterous! But he was a man of two minds, torn between his need for human companionship and his fear of people. If she could learn to accept him, perhaps even come to care for him in some way, he would have someone to talk to…someone who would know of his existence. Instinctively he sensed that she might be his last chance, his only chance for happiness. Wasn't that what he had been feeling in her presence, or even when she merely came to mind? Hadn't that odd sense of happiness driven him to buy gifts for the girl; to see her smile, and then to collect the cards she had made for him?

With a slow smile, Erik contemplated Christine's growing importance in his life. When he had learned of the injustice and bullying perpetrated against Christine Daaé, he had flown into a rage, vowing swift revenge. Thereafter, sniggering each time he caught sight of Mademoiselle Claire in one of her hideous bonnets, Erik had felt completely justified in his actions; for in his estimation, she deserved far worse than the harmless little trim he had given her.

He had been relieved when Christine had seemed to recover quickly from the unfortunate violin incident, going about her life in the opera house with no further harassment.

It had been gratifying to see her dressed in the stylish clothing his funds had provided, and to watch her pensive face light up with each new doll or book. Finding himself enjoying his role as her protector, he had been dreaming up greater extravagances against Madame Giry's gentle scolding that he must not spoil the child.

Nowadays, even as he composed music and went about his daily activities, Christine was often in his thoughts, and he had been anxiously anticipating the day when he would finally breach the silence of the mirror. He knew it was probably insane, and had no idea where it would ultimately take him or how the child would fit into his world, but he felt compelled to do it. Erik was desperate for a musical bond with someone, *and who better than an innocent and trusting child?* he asked himself.

What did he have to fear from her? How could a little girl like Christine be a threat to him from behind the mirror? True, he was uncertain of the correct approach, but the longer he watched, the more desperate he was becoming to communicate with her. She was just sitting there, alone and frightened, about to say goodbye to her father, a thing she clearly did not want to do. She had been content to hold onto Daaé's memory; even clinging to the belief that he might someday soon, magically return from the dead.

Stooping down on his haunches, Erik flipped the cloak from his shoulders and drug a knuckle across his mouth, undecided and wavering on his intentions. However, as his mind began to clear, another idea took shape; a different method of introduction, and perhaps a better way to approach this child.

"Her father played the violin," he whispered, stretching back up to his feet with his eyes fixed on the mirror. "The violin," he repeated, narrowing his eyes. Chuckling to himself, he spotted Daaé's old violin in Christine's room, and suddenly, he knew exactly how he would begin their association!

"Damn!" he swore again, "I should have thought of it before! What better place to raise up a man's ghost than a cemetery?"

Throwing on his cloak, he backed away from the mirror and quickly closed the chamber door behind him. Erik stormed down the breezeway with his cloak flapping noisily, then raced down the stairs to his boat, his plan evolving as he poled away from the platform. He would first collect his own violin, wait near the carriage house, and then follow Christine to her father's grave!

I sat in silence, gazing out the cab window as the carriage rolled up the steep hill to the cemetery. The day was bright, and the sky a clear shade of periwinkle blue. Morning breezes sent clouds sailing across the horizon, and the sun shone vividly through lime-colored leaves. I had not taken that journey for many months, and as we passed through the countryside, I contemplated the difference between Papa's winter afternoon burial and this second visitation. There was no sign of snow or barren trees now, only the serenity of spring stretching out before us in every direction.

My hands began to shake dreadfully as we approached the large iron gate, and reaching over to steady them, Madame nodded her head with a faint smile. The coachman eased the horses to a halt, dismounted his seat, then assisted me down from the running board. After pulling up the rear window shade, Madame removed a small book from her bag, opened to a marked page, and said, "I shall wait here in the carriage, my dear. Take all the time you need."

As I stepped down onto the manicured lawn, I felt the warm ground beneath my shoes, springy with grass and purple crocus that bobbed in the breeze. I stared up at the huge gate, listening to its hinges grind as the coachman pulled it open. Walking through the avenue of monuments, I was expecting to feel the same dread that Papa's burial had cast over me months ago, but somehow I did not.

All throughout the memorial to the dead, I saw signs of plant life reaching up greedily from beneath the ground. Ivy crept over the stone statuary, while ferns and wildflowers grew between the gravestones. Wild roses and wisteria vines clung to the mausoleum walls, and the trees which had appeared so sinister winter last were now carpeted with bright yellow-green lichen. Arching over the grounds, their graceful branches gently swayed as I inhaled the organic aromas of earth and grass and flowers. I let my fingers touch the translucent new growth of boxwood and lilac, and my senses were overwhelmed by beauty.

The graveyard had become a garden, where every manner of plant and tree flourished above the abode of the dead, who were unaware that another winter had come and gone. I found comfort in knowing that they were no longer prisoners of the earth, subject to pain and heartache among the living. According to my faith, their souls had been set free in a world of even greater beauty than these trees and flowers, and I felt the peace of God settle over me as the warm sun at last began to heal my broken heart.

I knew now that father was in a better place, that he was in the presence of God, my mother and all those who had gone before him. He was in the presence of the music of angels, to which now his own violin and voice had been added. Theirs was a music that would never fade, but would fill the expanse of eternity, and I was beginning to see that Madame Giry had given wise counsel. Father *would* have wanted me to carry on without him. He had secured my future with the opera house, and in that moment of clarity, I made up my mind that I would not disappoint him. Father's own strength was within me to achieve his dream for my life; therefore, if he wanted me to study the arts, and if he believed me capable of becoming a great singer...I must somehow make his dreams my own!

Gazing up at the blue sky, I resolved that, upon my return to the opera house, I would work harder than any other student and I would make my father proud.

With this new resolve taking shape in my heart, I moved through the long corridor of angels and saints and located my father's grave near the foot of the great elm. The icy pale gray of last winter had given these figures evil countenances; but now in the brilliance of spring, they appeared like friendly protectors, watching over the souls who slept beneath their shadows.

I knelt down in the shade of the elm, closed my eyes, and prepared to tell my father goodbye...but the moment I folded my hands in prayer, a soft sound of music arrested my breath!

Like a melody in the mere sighing of the breeze, I heard something like the whirring of hummingbird wings. Cracking one eye open, I could see no birds, and I instinctively cupped my hand to my ear.

"What was that?" I questioned, straining to listen.

Hearing nothing more, I bowed my head and continued my prayer, but suddenly I heard it again, and this time the sound was distinct and clear! It was a violin! Through the trees it floated, then echoed behind me in the marble mausoleum! My eyes sprang open and I rose to my feet as its mellow strings thrummed in my ears, soft and velvety like the buzzing of bees. With the melody climbing higher into the instrument's brightest voice…it rose and fell, and I could hear the invisible bow vibrating across the strings. Languid vibrato drove me to ecstasies unknown to mortals, and that music seeped into my mind…making the hair bristle on the back of my neck, with every inch of my skin tingling.

My heart was beating erratically as the violin called to me…and then I knew! Father was there…I would have known his violin anywhere! He was playing *The Bleeding Rose* as I had never heard him play before, and as I listened in ecstasy, the music began to bind his spirit to mine.

"Papa!" I cried, "I hear you!"

Dropping to my knees beside the grave, I fell forward and collapsed face down on the turf, embracing the place where he lay. Tears coursed down my cheeks, unabated, as the sound of my sobbing merged with the musical violin, and then I understood what I must do.

This could only mean that Father did not want me to say goodbye! It was a sign that he was still with me, watching over me and protecting me!

Oh, I could not let go of him now, and I would never let go or say goodbye! He had found a way! My father had come back to me and I would cling to his music and to his memory, knowing that he would never leave me again! I lay across his grave for what seemed like hours, his violin playing on and on until, as magically as it had begun, it slowly faded into the cemetery's cool green shadows.

After his morning performance at the cemetery, Erik had returned to the lakeside grotto where he had undressed, bathed in the tub, pulled on his dark green robe and had eaten a light lunch, accompanied by a cup of hot tea.

Following the meal, he then sat down at the organ to work on the *Don Juan* duet. Laboring over the opera with his usual frustration, he furiously filled page after page with notations and then added those pages to a growing pile of crumpled manuscript paper on the floor. He withdrew his hands from the keyboard, folded them in his lap and closed his eyes, as his mind wandered elsewhere. Unable to concentrate on his task, and sucking in a sharp breath, he placed one hand on the manuals and let his fingers drift absently from key to key. With no intention of writing a particular theme or motif, he noticed that a new and entirely different composition was unexpectedly beginning to emerge.

In the beginning, it was a simple melody in the key of C sharp minor, but the sound of it physically lifted him from his seat at the organ, and walking down to the water's edge, he began to hum the tune. The new melody began to take on structure, and closing his eyes, Erik slowly conceived the piece. Hearing violins and cellos in his mind, with basses and strings underscoring a variation on the primary theme, he reached his arms outward over the lake. Inclining his face upward, he found himself thoroughly imbued with the mystery of this new aria's conception.

"Yes!" he spoke breathlessly, surprised by his own ingenuity. "Yes...I hear it!"

With the enthusiasm of a child, Erik continued to direct the imaginary orchestra, his arms weaving lavishly before him, his entire body an expression of music, not born of the lust and violence of *Don Juan*; but of something new. Each instrument played accurately in his head, while a symphonic choir sang rich harmonies in arpeggio voices that filled him with peace.

Suddenly, dropping his arms to his sides, he ran to the organ like a man possessed, then lifted the heavy *Don Juan* manuscript up from the organ and cast it down onto the floor. Muttering to himself excitedly, he laid a stack of fresh manuscript paper across the keyboard and dipped his pen in the ink pot, grinning to himself as line upon line of music appeared on the page.

He could not write it fast enough, so overpowering was this music's becoming, and time seemed suspended as he sat hunched over the organ, intermittently singing and writing. In less than two hours, the score had been roughed out, and he tightened the ink pot lid, set down his pen, and arranged the sheets of music on his easel.

He stretched his fingers wide across the keyboard, his head bowed and his eyes closed, then paused to relax, drawing a deep breath. Placing one foot on a pedal and the other priming the pump, his entire body began to move majestically; his arms and legs utterly engaged in the process. The angelic melody emphasized the organ's tender tones, as a counter melody emerged in ascending chords. The music swelled and expanded, filling his subterranean world with the beginnings of a new opera.

Music had always been Erik's refuge. He had loved through it, hated through it, and had used his genius to unleash the savagery of *Don Juan*. He had throttled his senses with music that bore little resemblance to the works he had loved as a child. Symphonies and concertos of faith and romance had been the apex of his early childhood training, and he fondly recalled the all too brief years of playing Handel, Beethoven, and Bach on his mother's grand piano. But as an adult, he had lost touch with those noble works, rejecting the higher ideals of that music and choosing, instead, to write of man's darker passions.

Frequently, he had asked himself how he had survived all those years in the basement. What had kept him going? What had driven him to preserve his life? The answer was always the same. It was his music. Music was his soul, and his soul was his music. He had no woman in his life, no family, but he had always had his music.

Music was his love and his true religion. Music did not judge him or reject his deformity, but it empowered him beyond other men. Music had given an invisible man a voice…so he lived it, breathed it, and drank it like a man dying of thirst. Music was the center of his world, and without it he would have died.

Returning to the new piece, Erik bent his head down and again closed his eyes. His fingers glided across the black and ivory keys with breathtaking speed and dexterity. He felt this music saturating him, illuminating his thoughts with a serenity he had never known.

After several minutes of playing, he then brought his hands to rest on the keyboard and sat motionless, fully absorbed in his thoughts. With a deep intake of breath, a face and name crystallized in his mind, and he spoke the name aloud…"Christine," he rasped, "you are the inspiration for this extraordinary music!"

Sitting upright with his hands clasped in an attitude of

meditation, Erik reflected on that very morning at the cemetery when he had hidden in the mausoleum and played the violin. He remembered Christine's enraptured expression, the joy he had seen in her eyes, and the manner in which she had responded to his music when the violin had taken on a life of its own.

Apart from Louise, Christine was the first person to have heard his music in twenty years, and he was intoxicated by its power to make her cry or to bring a smile to her otherwise solemn features.

He was surprised by the revelation that Christine Daaé had inspired this new composition, and as he again resumed the primary theme, he began to see that she just might be the key to the fulfillment of his ambitions.

Chapter 9
Mementos

Upon her return from the cemetery, Louise Madeline Giry sat staring at a stack of yellowed postcards that had been tied with satin ribbon. Framed photographs were scattered across her desk; images of her husband, little Meg, and of other family members that were the centerpiece of her personal decor. The seasons of her life were displayed on the desk, hung on the walls, and had been strewn throughout the cluttered and disorganized room.

Her first pair of satin pointe-shoes lay across a pile of embroidery patterns, their pink ribbons reminding one of wilted roses; brown and frayed with age. A collection of Chinese fans was displayed above the headboard, softly lit by a glowing lamp that illuminated her cherished memories.

Surrounded by all the things she loved, Louise held in her hand a telegram which had arrived that morning, bearing news she did not want to hear. Slowly, she arose from her chair and walked over to the chaise lounge, lowered herself onto the violet cushions and again read the post in her hand. It required immediate attention, so tomorrow would find her making plans for a journey she dreaded. In two days time she would take the carriage to the depot, and then board the train for Lyon. She prayed that this visit would not be a long one, hoping that she would back in two or three weeks at the most.

Glancing around the room, Louise caught her refection in the vanity mirror and noticed that a few more silver hairs glinted from her thick auburn braid. She knitted her brows together in a frown, contemplating the all too swift passing of time. It seemed only a few springs ago that she had been a young woman, preparing for life on the stage. Now she was almost thirty years of age, already showing the prematurely graying hair inherited from her mother's side of the family. By the time her mother was in her late thirties, her hair had been almost completely silver, but Louise had made up her mind long ago that she would never let her hair go gray. Actresses and performers had long utilized the wonders of henna dyes, and Louise had been giving her hair monthly treatments since her twenty-fifth birthday.

"I'll have to give it another rinse before the trip," she commented to herself.

Louise set the letter down on a side table beside the chaise, arose and walked over to the mirror, unpinning her braid. Slowly she unbound it and let her hair fall freely to her waist. Loosening the tie of her black Japanese kimono, she pulled the silk garment off her shoulders and let it drop to the floor, then appraised her naked body, taking a step backward with a tilt of her head.

With her fingers trailing down from her narrow waist to her hips, and thinking back on her life with bittersweet introspection, she wondered if she would ever know the love of a man again. From her girlhood, Louise Madeline had been one of the most promising talents the conservatory had ever sponsored. They had been grooming her as the prima ballerina of the company until, at seventeen years of age, she had fallen in love with Anton Giry, and had given up her aspirations for the stage when her untimely pregnancy forced a quick wedding, an event which had caused a deep rift in her family.

Louise fanned her fingers over her well-toned belly, proud that a routine of dance over the years had helped to maintain her figure. Still absorbed by memories and regrets, she gazed at the mirror, wistfully thinking of her youth.

She had married Anton Giry knowing that he was handsome, charming...and in her father's eyes, completely unsuitable. Despite the miscarriage of their first child, her husband's extramarital affairs, and his mounting gambling debts, Louise and Anton had managed to keep their marriage intact for several years; however, when Meg was born he quickly tired of the growing responsibilities that came with being a husband and father. Eight years had passed since he deserted his family to pursue other interests in America, leaving them with little contact or financial assistance.

Prior to her passing, Louise's mother had made certain that her daughter and grandchild would receive a monthly stipend from the estate, but Louise had never been permitted to return to the family home, and her father had refused to see either her or her daughter.

Another family crisis had shred any hope she'd had of returning to the stage, but Louise was a strong woman, now managing to support herself and Meg with her position as ballet mistress at the opera. She had not been entirely without male companionship, and had taken occasional lovers over the years, but she preferred her unattached, less complicated single status.

Despite her husband's philandering ways, a part of Louise was now, and would always be, still in love with him...but it was best for everyone that he remained in America and out of Meg's life. Now and again she regretted the events that had altered her chosen path, but generally, Louise had accepted her lot in life and had learned to take the good with the bad.

"That was not to be," she whispered, seating herself on the vanity stool.

Lifting a brush from an open drawer, Louise leaned close to the mirror and appraised the first sign of crows-feet. She was aware that few considered her a beautiful woman; her sister having been the true beauty of the family...nevertheless, Louise had learned to make the most of her plain features and prided herself on employing oriental techniques in her beauty regime. She stared at her reflection and brushed out her hair, her thoughts turning again to the unpleasant task that awaited. She was being summoned away from her beloved opera house, and would be forced to miss the opening gala of *The Magic Flute*. Tomorrow she would make arrangements for her assistant, Mademoiselle Suzanne, to take over her duties while she was gone.

She had been training Suzanne for three years and was confident that the woman was fully capable of taking over for a few weeks, but Louise hated to miss the excitement of a grand gala. She had trained the finest company of her career, and had been pleased by the the management team's words of approval. Even the highly critical Erik had sent her a note complimenting her on the dancers, stating that they were the most accomplished company the opera house had ever produced.

Compliments from the Opera Ghost were rare indeed, and Louise took pride in his praise whenever it was offered. She made a mental note that, before leaving, she must inform Erik of her travel plans. She was uncertain how he would manage in her absence, but she expected the resourceful man to keep himself occupied. Louise smiled just thinking about his recent teasing of Carlotta, but to her shame, she found it quite amusing to see him put the woman in her place.

Setting the brush back inside the drawer, Louise sniggered at the image of Carlotta's wardrobe squirming with rats. It had been a nasty trick, and Louise had scolded Erik for doing it whilst secretly enjoying the diva's priceless reaction.

"Oh dear, that was mean of him!" Louise chuckled, scooping her kimono up off the floor and tossing it on over her shoulders. Erik never ceased to surprise her with his inventiveness and audacity where Carlotta and the managers were concerned, but more recently she had been surprised by the tenderness he had shown Christine as Monsieur E.

Over the years, Meg had been the only child Erik had remotely shown an interest in, but though he had given her daughter a few presents, he rarely even mentioned the girl in their correspondence. Christine had apparently brought out a different side of him, and Louise sensed that he genuinely cared for the child and was concerned for her welfare.

Based on some of the music she had heard him play, she had always suspected that compassion and kindness were buried deep inside the man and wondered why Christine had been the one to draw it out. There had been a time when Louise had fantasized about a deeper friendship with him, but then Anton had come into her life with his dark good looks, and Louise had quickly fallen under his spell. She and Erik had, instead, become associates, and he had come to rely on her loyalty and discretion.

Standing up from the stool, Louise tied the sash around her waist, worrying about how Christine would do without her. She was concerned about leaving her for even a few days, let alone a few weeks...but it could not be helped. Marie would look after Meg and Christine in her absence.

Fully aware that this trip to Lyon would not be the last, Louise began to make a mental list of the items she would need for the journey. Stooping down, she pulled a suitcase out from under her bed and set it on top of the mauve satin spread. She opened the clasps and packed the well-traveled case with skirts, frocks, corsets, and other items she would need for her trip. Gathering her hat-boxes, she chose several bonnets, stacking them one on top of the other, but her heart grew heavier as she contemplated what the next few days might bring. With her packing only half-finished, Louise picked up the telegram from the side table and read the first line of the message again:

> *Urgent:*
> *Madame, your immediate assistance is requested...*

Louise Giry let the letter fall from her hand, laid down on the chaise and prepared to nap before the afternoon rehearsal.

Chapter 10
The Voice

From the moment I rejoined Madame Giry outside the cemetery gates, I decided to tell no one of what had happened at my father's grave. It would remain my secret, but I could barely contain my joy as we traveled back to the city. The journey to the opera house seemed to take forever, and as Madame made conversation, I listened politely...but my thoughts were only of him. I was filled with anticipation and could not wait to be alone in my room where I could relive each moment of that divine visitation. I wondered if he would come again...and if so, how long would I have to wait until his next visitation? Had it all been a dream? But despite these questions, I knew for certain that it had been real! Father had played the violin for me...I had not dreamt it!

As the horses trotted up to the carriage house, I could still hear that music in my mind and I could feel it warming my heart! Somehow, knowing that I could not go on without his guidance, my father had reached beyond the grave and answered my prayers, and now we would be together always!

We arrived at the opera house in time for a late lunch, followed by a long afternoon of rehearsals. With *The Magic Flute* opening in one week, this would be the first in a number of intense and chaotic dress rehearsals, so the backstage was in near panic as costumes were distributed among the demanding and noisy cast of over one hundred.

Poor Marie was barely visible behind the pile of costumes that needed to be refitted or repaired, and her assistants were little help as gowns, trousers, and head-dresses were given to their wearers and checked off a very long list. The opera house cast had never been known for its patience, and the tired cast members were already feeling the pressure of opening night.

Dressed in her prettiest practice skirt that afternoon, Meg reminded me of a butterfly as she cheerfully danced about on pointe, assuming dance positions wherever she went. With a beaming smile and her eyes wide with excitement, she whispered her criticisms or compliments in my ear as the ladies tried on their costumes.

The two of us had become very close, and I had briefly contemplated telling her about my morning encounter at Father's grave, but Meg was hopeless when it came to keeping secrets, so I decided to keep the visitation to myself. Buquet and the sceneshifters lowered a blue-green scrim from high up in the catwalks, causing the pulleys and counterweights to sway and squeak above our heads as we devoured our snacks. The sights and sounds of the backstage were thrilling, and for the first time since before Father's death, I began to believe in his dreams for my life, especially now that he would be there to see them through. With his return, I was beginning to envision myself in the midst of it all; costume fittings, rehearsals, voice lessons, and dance! Suddenly, music had begun to call me again from a secret place I thought had been buried in Father's grave. The sounds of the orchestra warming up...of hammers and saws, of tenors vocalizing and sopranos singing cadenzas sent chills down my arms, and for the first time I felt as if I, too, might someday belong to that world.

Meg giggled and led the way as we dodged around the adult actors and backstage crew. The two of us ran for the dance studio where Madame was rehearsing the principal dancers. Dressed in her black rehearsal ensemble and wearing an appropriately stern expression, Madame Giry drilled the dancers, who gracefully followed her expert instruction, dancing in front of the wall of mirrors.

"Four, five, six, seven, eight! Attitude, ladies and gentlemen! Arabesque!" she ordered, tapping her cane with each change of position.

"Changement de pieds! Developp`e, Jammes! Stretch that leg! Arms higher! One and two and three...Fouette, Giselle! More extension on the left arm...and turn out the leg!"

I was always fascinated as, before my own eyes, Madame seemed to transform into a different person when she taught classes. She exercised a firm hand and never permitted laziness from her dancers, appearing to be cross and short-tempered when they did not measure up to her expectations. Some of the girls had even made up unflattering names for her, mocking behind her back...but I knew a different Louise Giry from the strict ballet mistress who now tapped her cane and barked out orders. The Madame Giry I knew was patient and gentle, and I was beginning to learn that she was also very wise.

Observing her as she continued her instruction, I noticed that her eyes and mouth were hard-set in an expression of concentration, but I had also seen her features soft and pensive in the evening lamplight when she read a book or stitched her embroidery.

I stretched and yawned as the class continued, growing bored while Meg's full attention was riveted on the dancers, who were skilled in steps and movement that our own growing bodies could not yet achieve. I could see the yearning in her eyes as she observed those dancers in awe. Unlike me, Meg often sat and watched the principals rehearse for hours at a time, but deciding to see what was happening in the theater, I quietly snuck away from the studio. Entering through a back door, I slipped into a back row seat as the costumes were being paraded across the stage for management's approval. Monsieurs Debienne and Poligny applauded from the first balcony as Mademoiselle Simonette stepped onto the stage in her shimmering costume for the third act. It was an ethereal gown of floating aqua, embellished with sparkling crystal beads across the bodice. She wore a delicate crown of pink roses and ivy atop her waist length blond wig, and her cheeks flushed prettily as she garnered male attention from the wings. Whistles and cheers rained down from the catwalks, and the female members of the cast murmured and sighed as Simonette curtsied, then glided off the stage with a fluttering of her skirts and petticoat.

One at a time, the lead singers and actors paraded before the managers, with Marie taking careful notes on adjustments and alterations to be made. When it was Piangi's turn, he scowled, making no effort to hide his displeasure with the comedic and voluminous red feathered costume of the bird catcher Papageno…but it was La Carlotta's stunning indigo blue and silver Queen of the Night gown which drew every gaze as she proudly waltzed to center stage.

The stately young woman was dazzling in an off-the-shoulder gown of dark blue jeweled chiffon, cut daringly low across her bosom. The flowing butterfly sleeves nearly brushed the floor, and a tall crown of silver spires, crystal stars, and glittering beads adorned her head, with her wavy red hair falling freely across her shoulders and down her back. Though she was not to be the star of this opera, she was obviously quite pleased by her costume, and to Madame Marie's relief, for once the diva voiced no complaints.

Coming up alongside me, Meg sat down, looped her arm through mine and leaned closely to whisper in my ear, "Christine, I have just heard the most delicious gossip, and I must tell you!"

While everyone cheered, Carlotta curtsied on the stage, and Meg excitedly drew me up from my seat, down the aisle and through a door to our backstage hideout behind the mats.

"Christine," she whispered, with her blue eyes flashing mischievously, "Did you know that they are saying that the man who came to the Bal Masque dressed as the Persian Prince may have really been the Opera Ghost?"

"The Persian Prince?" I asked, my curiosity piqued. I had been fascinated, yet at the same time, oddly apprehensive at the Persian's appearance at the ball. In my opinion, he certainly did not fit descriptions of the Opera Ghost, but no one had yet been able to identify the tall Persian among the invited guests and dignitaries, and he was certainly not a member of the opera house staff.

It had been rumored that Madame Debienne had urged her husband to have the fellow arrested, but it seemed he had simply vanished after the ball, and no one had seen or heard from him since. The tall Persian had, in fact, become a sort of legend, and the story of how the necklace had been returned to Debienne's office had even made the papers.

"But, Meg, the Persian…well, he was handsome, but I thought the Opera Ghost was supposed to be ugly," I argued.

"How do we know?" Meg put in, her cheeks flushing scarlet as her excitement mounted. "He was wearing a mask like everyone else, Christine…so it really could have been him! They say he can change into any shape or form, and Buquet says he is truly a horrible ghost with evil eyes!"

"Meg, don't be silly," I replied without thinking, "there are no such things as ghosts!"

The moment the words left my mouth, I could feel my own cheeks turning red. I had spoken in my haste, knowing full well that I did not believe my own words…for had I not heard my father's ghost playing the violin that very morning?

"But Buquet has seen him, Christine!" Meg insisted, tugging my arm playfully. "And I'll tell you the scariest secret of all," she whispered in my ear. "Buquet says that he lives in a dungeon, right here underneath the opera house!"

Sucking in my breath, with my gaze darting around I suddenly had an uncanny feeling that someone's eyes were bearing down on me. I lifted my chin and peered overhead to the pulleys and counterweights…and there, leaning over the flywheel with a wine bottle grasped in his ruddy hand, was Joseph Buquet, who appeared to be looking down on us. Grabbing Meg's hand, I pulled her into the scenery bay and cupped my hand over her ear.

"That's not true!" I retorted, "Joseph is only trying to scare us!"

"But, Chris…"

Just then, we were interrupted when the orchestra began to rehearse the overture, and we were all called to silence by the directors and by Maestro Reyer's baton…as the sights and sounds of *The Magic Flute* filled my senses. There were many stops and starts, with Carlotta flying off into one of her famous tantrums when a dancer tripped on the train of her gown…but overall, Poligny and Debienne were pleased when the entire cast proudly sang the final chorus of the third act.

Having now seen the opera in its entirety for the first time, I loved the romantic and magical story, and began to dream of one day playing the role of the princess Pamina myself. However, it had been a long day, and I was relieved when rehearsal ended and we all retired to the dining hall for a warm supper of roast chicken with potatoes and vegetables. Following the meal, with the cast having had its fill of wine, the conversation grew bawdy and loud;

and Meg and I giggled at the flirtatious behavior between the adult men and women.

Having been raised by a widower, I knew little of the coupling of adults, but was entranced by the romances that had been budding throughout rehearsals. In the opera house it was not at all unusual to catch a furtive kiss behind a fly, or an embrace in the wardrobe workshop. Romantic love was a sweet mystery to my young mind, but like any girl my age, I had dreamed of one day being kissed, and had often entertained images of Father kissing my mother. I was certain that they had been a romantic pair, and I used to imagine them as a happy young couple...but suddenly, after the large meal and all the excitement, I became dizzy with exhaustion and a million questions, wanting only the quiet of my room. It seemed an eternity to Meg and me before we finally followed Madame back downstairs to the dormitory wing. Saying our 'goodnights' at Madame Giry's apartment door, I made my way down the narrow hall and opened the door to my own room with a sigh of relief. Undressing behind the screen, I changed into my nightgown and robe, readying myself for bed. I stepped over to the night table, lit my white prayer candle, then knelt down in the center of the floor, just so that I could see the reflection of my candle in the mirror. A little girl's face looked back at me from the glass...the same little girl who had visited her father's grave that morning, but something had changed with my father's visitation...the whole world had changed!

Folding my hands in my lap, I closed my eyes, offering my thanks to God and begging my father to visit me again. The room was like a quiet cocoon, and I could even hear the faint sound of the candle flame flickering as everything became eerily still.

"Father," I breathed, looking all around me, half-expecting him to walk right through the walls.

I then began to hum *The Bleeding Rose*, closing my eyes and trying to conjure his face from memory...but I could not recall the exact shape of his mouth, or the correct shape of his face. Pulling the locket from inside my nightgown, I clicked it open and gazed at his likeness, bleary-eyed, with my heart begging for his return.

"Father, please hear me!" I cried, as the locket blurred in my vision.

For some moments I waited in the silence of my room, grasping the locket desperately to my chest. When he failed to appear as he had done in the cemetery that morning, I hung my head and sniffed back the tears, my heart breaking yet again. But all at once, shivers spread from the top of my head down to the tips of my toes, as from somewhere outside my room I heard the violin! Swallowing hard, I sucked in my breath, then stopped breathing altogether! He was there! At first the violin sounded very far away…but he drew closer and closer until I could have sworn that he was right there in the room with me…yet I saw nothing!

"Papa!" I cried out, jumping to my feet.

I drifted closer to the mirror, singing the words as he played the melody on his violin:

> *An angel sent from heaven*
> *Came to a garden fair…*

As I began to sing with more confidence, I lifted my shoulders and chin, trying to perform my best for him. In the beginning only the violin responded, with the bow arching across the instrument in rapturous strokes. The strings vibrated with low earthy intonation, then swept upward into ethereal bliss, making my soul soar higher with every stroke. I could not remember my father ever playing with such abandon, and just as I thought I had reached the height of happiness…he began to sing!

From inside my mirror I heard an impossibly beguiling voice; a man's voice that sounded nothing like my father's voice when he was alive. The voice was ephemeral and commanding in its lower resonance, but hypnotic and angelic in its upper range. This was the voice of a mystic being, and no ordinary man…and I knew without a shred of doubt that I had heard the voice of my father's spirit!

Tears coursed down my cheeks as his voice amplified in power, electrifying the room with a splendor I was certain human ears had never heard. My mind colored with images of my father's face, his hands, the comfort of his arms, and suddenly I felt afresh the sadness of losing him. The voice then began to sing with profound sorrow, and I clung to its anguish, for somehow it was more sacred to me than a prayer. Like a chalice of tears, the suffering of the whole world was cupped within his voice, and the heartache it sang seemed to become one with my own. Stunned and confused by these strange happenings, I wondered, what kind of creature could make me feel joy and sorrow in equal measure? But ignoring my questioning mind, I began to sing *The Bleeding Rose,* as his voice complimented mine in harmony:

> *She cast it to the ground*
> *And then she did dispose*
> *Choosing the pale lily…*
> *Instead of the bleeding rose.*

He sang for me until I sagged down onto the floor like a ragdoll, weeping tears of joy and exhaustion…but suddenly, the room fell silent again. Candles guttered and the wind moaned outside my window, but the voice had vanished. The silence that followed was harsh and cruel, and I crawled to the mirror, pleading with him, "Papa, please don't go!"

I was tethered to the mirror, and as if all the oxygen had been suctioned out of the room, I held my breath, unable to move, his sudden withdrawal seeming to crack my soul in half. I had now heard the violin and his voice with my own ears…and it was not enough to have heard him sing for those few precious moments. I needed to hear him always…in my sleep, in my waking hours, every day and every night! As I leaned against the mirror's cold glass, the minutes passed slowly in a vacuum of silence, and I came to the sad conclusion that I must not have been worthy of the few crumbs he had already given me. Perhaps God had deemed me a disobedient child, undeserving of her father's love, and perhaps that is why he had been taken from me in the first place. But then, why come back to me at all? Why shed joy in my heart only to rip it away, I questioned to myself.

"Please…please, Papa!"

"Christine, don't cry," a voice spoke into my right ear.

Turning my head, I looked to my right, but there was no one there! Hearing my name on his lips was the most beautiful sound I had ever heard, and I reached out my arms to embrace him, my lips quivering and my eyes searching the room.

"Christine!" he repeated, but this time the voice was in my left ear!

Dizzy with confusion, I spun around on my toes and questioned breathlessly, "Father, where are you?"

There was a pause, and then came this surprising answer, "Christine, I am not your father."

Rubbing my eyes with my sleeve, I could not believe my own ears. My heart sank like a stone and I nearly lost my balance, struggling to understand his words. It was true, the voice did not sound like my father, but I reasoned that he would sound different as a spirit than he had as man.

"If you are not the spirit of my father...then who are you?" I stammered, glaring at the mirror and recognizing fear in my own eyes.

His soft whisper chilled me to the bone as it resonated through the glass, "Do not fear me, child."

"But...but who are you?" I repeated.

Again his voice seemed to float through the mirror as he whispered into my ear, "I assure you, my dear, I wish you no harm."

Touching the glass cautiously, I moved closer, and with the need to know his identity overshadowing my misgivings, I continued to question him.

"But I heard the violin...that's my father's song you were playing," I asserted, tugging absently on my braid.

"Christine, it was your father who sent me...so there is nothing to fear. Do you remember the promise he made before he died?" the voice inquired.

I did not wish to be reminded of that day, and turned my back on the mirror, squeezing my eyes closed as he explained.

"Your father promised to send the Angel of Music, Christine, and I, my child...I am that angel."

Lifting my chin, I slowly rotated my body around to face the mirror again, stunned by this revelation. The Angel of Music and

Little Lotte were make-believe characters from a story my father had told me many times, but I had never envisioned an angel who played the violin or spoke with a man's voice. Nevertheless, I had heard the violin with my own ears and someone was indeed talking to me right there in my room. I could hear his voice clearly, but I could not see him with my eyes, so therefore, if it was not my father or a ghost…then it must be an angel!

"You are not disappointed, are you?" he asked.

Shaking my head, I hesitated for a moment, and then answered him with a slight wavering of my voice, "No, no…well, maybe a little."

I recalled the promise of the angel, but at the time I'd had no desire to be visited by an angel in the stead of my father…yet now, faced with this unseen visitor, how could I be disappointed? He sang with the voice of an angel from heaven, and although I could not see him, like all angels, I knew he must be very beautiful.

Approaching the mirror shyly, I reached out and let my index finger barely graze the glass.

"I'm not disappointed," I contradicted myself, wishing not to hurt his feelings. "Then you are my true Angel of Music?" I asked.

"Yes, I am true your Angel of Music, and your father sent me to watch over you, as your guardian and your teacher," the voice declared.

I raised my eyebrows and wondered at his words. Was it possible for an angel to teach a human child?

"My teacher?" I questioned. "What shall you teach me?"

"I shall teach you to sing, and you shall become a great soprano, Christine," he said softly, his voice thrumming pleasantly in my ears.

"Oh, you mean like La Carlotta?" I questioned.

I thought I heard him laugh a little, and this surprised me as he answered, "Well, not exactly…you will be a much better singer than Carlotta ever was in her prime!"

I could not imagine that there could be a better singer than Carlotta, and peering directly into the mirror's reflection of my eyes, I wrapped my braid around my fingers with a million questions racing through my mind.

"Do you live in the mirror, Angel?" I questioned, placing my palms flat on the glass and spreading my fingers wide. Opening my mouth I leaned forward and fogged the mirror with my breath.

This time his answer came from behind me as he spoke with a funny catch in his voice, "Sometimes I live in the mirror, Christine, but I am everywhere."

Spinning around on my toes, my mouth opened wider as the voice seemed to be moving all around my room.

"Everywhere, and anywhere you need me!" he exclaimed, his voice gaining in volume.

I sought out the voice! I followed the sound across the floor and seated myself on the bed, scooping a doll into my arms.

"Then you are mine, and you will never leave me?" I sought affirmation, cradling the doll like a real baby.

"No, my dear, I shall never leave you," came his answer.

Rocking the doll gently, I looked up and pressed him further, "Promise me that you won't leave me like Grandpapa, Grandmama, Madame Valleria...and my papa did."

He said nothing, and I sat up straight, grasping the doll tightly in my lap. "Angel, are you still here?" I asked.

The tone of his voice was comforting and sweet as he affirmed, "I will be here whenever you need me."

"You didn't say promise. Say you promise never to leave me, and I will believe you!" I spoke more emphatically, "Say you promise!"

"I promise, Christine. I shall never leave you...but it is late, child," he added, "and you must sleep now."

"But I'm not tired at all!" I protested, rubbing my eyes with a yawn as the doll slipped from my fingers and dropped onto the rug.

"I can see that you are very tired," he answered quietly. "Now blow out the candle and get into bed."

I did not question his authority and obeyed him immediately. Leaning over, I blew out my prayer candle, then crawled beneath the blankets, smiling up at the ceiling.

"Can you see me now, Angel?" I asked, tugging the blankets closer.

Very faintly he replied, "Yes, child, I can see you."

"Will I ever see you...I mean, what you look like?" I asked hopefully, imagining his white wings and golden hair.

There was no answer so I lay there, waiting, as he had again fallen silent. I began to wonder if he had left me again, and I called out, "Angel, are you still there?"

There was another long stretch of quiet between us, and then..."I am still here." I heard him say. I sighed deeply, relieved that he had not gone.

"Tomorrow night, Christine, we shall begin your lessons here in this room. You will be a great singer one day, for that is your destiny, child."

He had pronounced this with an authority that I dared not question.

"But now, you must sleep, close your eyes." he said softly.

The sound of his voice seemed to make me sleepier as my heavy eyelids blocked out the lamp. A comforting haze enveloped my mind as the angel began to hum an unfamiliar tune.

"Angel?" I muttered, drowsily lifting my head from the pillow, "Do you have a real name?"

Breaking off his vocalization, he replied, "Yes, Christine, and perhaps you shall know it one day. Now sleep, child," he told me.

Obeying his voice, I let my head drop back onto the pillow, a pleasant heaviness descending on my whole body.

His voice was very far away as he remarked, "That's a good girl."

"But why can't you tell me now?" I questioned with a yawn, turning over onto my side and clasping my hands together under my chin.

"Hush now and go to sleep, Christine," he sang with a lovely melody.

"Angel," I asked once more, hardly able to move my lips, "Will you stay and sing to me until I fall asleep?"

There was another long pause before he finally answered, "Yes, Christine, I will stay."

I opened my eyes one last time, briefly observing the lamp's reflection in the mirror, and my mind filed with images of a beautiful golden angel as my dreams closed around his voice.

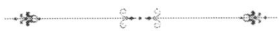

The following evening, as Erik stood in the dark breezeway, leaning against the stone wall, he vacillated between entering the mirror chamber or heading back to his boat. Christine would be standing in full view on the other side, waiting for him to begin her vocal instruction. He had at last communicated with her and a bond had formed between them that he had not anticipated. With a quick opening of the chamber he would now become her teacher...but after last night's success, why was he suddenly plagued by doubts?

"Just open the bloody chamber, Erik," he mocked as something nagged at him.

"What am I doing here?" he mouthed.

The day leading up to this moment had dragged on tediously, and he had talked himself out of coming back up to the dormitory several times, only to convince himself that he was doing the right thing. No matter how hard he fought the absurd notion of becoming the child's teacher, he could not deny the significance of how she had made him feel with her trusting and childish questions. She actually believed that he was the Angel of Music. His scheme was working! There had been a few moments during last night's encounter when he had considered leaving the chamber, never to return...but now here he was again, being drawn to her, waiting to shape the sound of her voice.

"What harm can there be in teaching her?" he whispered.

Turning to face the wall, he flattened his hands against the cold stone surface. A warning light began to flash in his mind, telling him that something was amiss, but last night had been one of the most satisfying moments he had ever known, so he chose to ignore the warning. Watching the girl, singing with her and playing the violin for her had made him feel valued. She believed that he was her Angel, and it was marvelous to be thought of as something beautiful for a change. They had talked together like other human beings did. She had asked questions, and he had answered. Conversation was an activity enjoyed by normal people every day, and likely taken for granted; but Erik had cherished every spoken word, as if each was a note of music that had passed between them.

Leaning in closer, he pressed his forehead hard against the rough brick wall and squeezed his eyes shut. Christine Daaé was gifted with musical sensitivity and a vivid imagination. He had watched other talented children come and go through the conservatory, but this child outshone them all. She possessed a singular gift of natural ability. Her natural instincts had obviously been nurtured by her father, but there was so much more Erik could teach her. It would be a challenge to teach discipline and technique to one so young, but he feared that if left to the conservatory she would never reach her full potential.

"And that would rob the world of greatness," he commented, striking his gloved fist on the wall and then backing up into the breezeway.

Erik straightened his spine, squared his shoulders, then drew a sharp breath through his teeth. He raised his chin and stared at the chamber entrance, trying to decide if he should open it or simply run back to the canals. Turning his head in the direction of the stables, he contemplated abandoning the whole idea...but after moments of inner deliberation, he puffed out his cheeks with a groan and silenced the opposing thoughts in his head, as he turned around and opened the chamber door.

He could wait no longer to submerge himself in the work of drawing out that magical voice. He must instruct her! He must know her thoughts, and listen to the sound of her voice improving under his guidance. Now that he had made first contact, he found himself craving her company, for she had unexpectedly brought variety to his otherwise monotonous life.

Stepping inside the chamber, Erik approached the mirror with a mixture of excitement and trepidation. Christine was sitting on the edge of the bed with her hands folded in her lap in an attitude of prayer. Her prayer candle flickered softly on the night table, its light casting a glow on her somber features. She was wearing her nightgown and robe, and her hair hung down in two thick braids. Erik was fascinated by the underlying sorrow of her eyes that seemed to recall his own childhood. From observing her in the cemetery, at rehearsals and through the mirror, he had learned that music alone made the child truly happy, and given that it was the only happiness he had ever known, he, of all people, understood that kind of happiness.

Moving close to the mirror, Erik placed his hands on the frame and spoke her name just above a whisper, "Christine."

His stomach jumped when her thin lips curved into a smile and color bloomed into her pale cheeks. She inclined her chin with her brown eyes sparkling, and Erik could not help but crack a smile himself.

"Angel?" she spoke shyly, "Is it you?"

He was not certain he would ever adjust to being called "Angel"…and it was not just hearing the word that moved him, but the way she said it. The name she had given him implied trust, and as he caught his own masked reflection in the glass he felt anything but trustworthy…but he could not leave her.

Tilting his head back, Erik stroked the mirror and answered, "Yes, I am here, Christine."

Dangling her legs over the side of the mattress, Christine reached for her doll, stroking its life-like hair with her fingertips.

"I've been waiting for you, Angel," she spoke softly.

Trying not to sound harsh, Erik invested his voice with an air of authority and informed her, "I am here to begin your lessons, Mademoiselle Daaé."

She immediately responded, set the doll down on the bed beside her, then straightened her shoulders. Chuckling softly, Erik rubbed his chin, wondering how to begin her instruction. Without being seen, he must communicate the very physical nature of singing with his voice alone. He must be gentle and patient and he must not rush the child, but encourage and strengthen her lagging confidence.

"Christine, my dear," he began in his melodious speaking voice. "Are you ready?"

Nodding her head, she affirmed, "I'm ready, Angel."

"Very well, come to the mirror so that you may clearly see your reflection," he instructed.

Christine rose up from the bed, then padded across the rug with an expectant smile flashing across her features.

Swallowing hard, Erik clasped his gloved hands together tightly and inhaled a deep breath.

"You were born to be a performer, Christine. I have heard you sing many times, and you have been endowed with a rare gift."

The child stared at the mirror blankly, absently twisting her braid.

He waited, but when she said nothing, he went on, "Those who have been thusly gifted must learn discipline and technique in order to rise to their full potential."

"You think I have talent, Angel?" she questioned, tilting her head to the side.

Erik could hardly believe that she had no idea just how talented she was, and he found her humility endearing. Other children of her caliber often believed themselves superior, which in his opinion made them egotistical and unattractive performers. He had seen many such children in the opera's halls, and was certain that La Carlotta had fit that description in her formative years. In any case, Erik was appalled that Christine's father had been negligent in telling her the truth; that she was indeed the prodigy, and he merely her accompanist!

"Christine, did your father never tell you this?" Erik asked with just a hint of a sneer in his otherwise buttery voice.

Blinking her eyes, Christine scuffed her left foot on the carpet and answered shyly, "Papa used to say that the people loved to hear me sing."

"I should think so, Christine, because you have a gift, and if you allow me to guide you, and if you promise to practice and study according to my instruction, you shall be a great singer one day," Erik informed her, scrutinizing her reaction as she absorbed his words. "Do you believe me, Christine?" he asked.

She did not answer at first, her eyes downcast and her expression pensive. Erik let the silence draw out between them, watching as she thought over his question.

Finally, raising her eyes to the mirror, Christine nodded her head. "You're an angel...and if you tell me something, then it must be true...because everyone knows that angels cannot lie," she replied.

With his mouth gaping open, Erik pulled away from the mirror, taken aback by her statement. He had never come across anyone so trusting; not even Louise Giry who, in her own way, had also been a trusting young girl. It occurred to Erik that Christine had probably never told a single lie in her life, and he could not imagine being free from guile or suspicion of another's motives. Shaking his head and setting his mind on this evening's first lesson, Erik removed his gloves, then tucked them into his cloak pocket. He swung the cloak off his shoulders and let it drop to the floor.

"The first thing we must do is address your posture," he began, noticing that the girl had a tendency to slouch, which crunched her ribcage and made her belly distend unnaturally.

"Now, it's very important that you stand up straight, Christine. Shoulders back, tuck in your tummy, and hold your chin up!" he commanded, his own body mimicking his instruction as she tried to comply.

"Now, place your hands on your upper abdomen, just beneath your ribcage, and inhale until that part of your stomach pushes outward."

Sucking in his cheeks, Erik tried not to chuckle as the girl over-exaggerated every move, her face and body contorting with the effort, and her little dark brows knitting together in a scowl.

"Do you feel the movement beneath your hands, Christine? Now, when you exhale, your hands should move inward, toward your body. Do you feel it, my dear?"

She nodded yes, and Erik continued, "That is your diaphragm. You must learn to breathe properly, with support from your diaphragm before your singing lessons can begin. Now, inhale deeply through your nose, then exhale through your mouth, slowly, until you feel the action of your diaphragm. Do not allow the breath to remain shallow in your throat."

Erik could see that Christine was becoming dizzy, and was impressed that she had not complained. She clearly took their work seriously and seemed very eager to learn. Intending to encourage her, he stepped closer to the mirror, locked his eyes on hers and continued his instruction.

"That is very good, Christine. I am pleased with you. With time and more practice you shall learn the difference between the diaphragmatic breathing technique and breathing through your throat and chest. You shall also learn that breathing correctly affords the voice tremendous power and control. Do you have any questions before we continue?"

Christine shifted her weight from one foot to the other, then spoke quietly, "Is that all, Angel?"

Chuckling aloud, Erik answered, "No, Christine. We have scarcely even begun!"

"Oh, I'm glad," she said with a smile.

Erik was struck by how little she actually knew about singing, and yet even at her age, the mature tonal quality she produced was astounding. He was anxious to move beyond the rudimentary and could barely contain his excitement as he proceeded.

"Now, before we go on, Christine, I want you to relax your body. Gently shake out your arms and shoulders, and move your head from side to side."

He watched in amusement as, without question, she did exactly what he said. Standing before the mirror, she was utterly under his control and he relished the rapport they were developing through the glass.

"Like this, Angel?" Christine asked, still following his commands.

"Good girl." he praised her, "Now, shall we move on?"

With her cheeks flushing and her eyes bright, Christine replied, "Oh, please yes, Angel! I like this very much!"

Erik was enjoying himself as well, and this revelation surprised him. It wasn't so difficult after all, teaching a child…nothing to it really, he congratulated himself. Removing his cuff fasteners and dropping them into his trouser pocket, Erik rolled up one shirt sleeve to the elbows, and then the other. Placing the palm of his hand on the mirror, he leaned his weight against it and prepared to engage her further.

"Christine, now that you have learned the function of your diaphragm, I shall teach you to sing while supporting your voice with that most remarkable muscle," he suggested, as Christine gazed into the mirror and nodded her head enthusiastically.

He then described the correct placement of her tongue and lips, and taught her how to form vowel sounds with the proper shaping of her throat. The girl mimicked every verbal instruction he gave her, without even once complaining or interrupting.

Shoving both hands into his trouser pockets, Erik smirked, pleased with how smoothly the lesson was progressing.

"Now that you know how to place the sound in your mouth," he resumed confidently, "I am going to assign you a note and I want you to sing, using your diaphragm to support your voice. Once again, place your hands on your upper abdomen and practice breathing, feeling your tummy rise and fall as you inhale and exhale. I shall sing the note and you shall sing after me...and I want you to hold the note for as long as you can. Do you understand, my dear?"

"Yes. I think so," she answered.

"Good, now let's give it a try. Sing E major with me, Christine."

Erik sang the correct note, and although Christine sang the pitch perfectly, her voice faltered with a gasp for air, while Erik's own voice sustained the note.

Growling in the back of his throat, he corrected her, saying, "No, that is not quite right; your breath is still too shallow. This time, use your diaphragm to support the voice. Again!" he commanded.

Raising her chin, her eyes opening wide, Christine drew in her breath as Erik reprised the E, but once more, her voice gave out while his floated on the note effortlessly.

Without meaning to, he cut her off, his voice irritable as he snapped, "No, Christine, that is not correct! Try it again as I showed you!"

Immediately the child's face fell, with her brown eyes watering as she lowered her chin. Slumping her shoulders, her arms drooped to her sides. Erik felt like a beast for shouting at her, but he could not understand why she failed to grasp such an elementary concept. He had not expected such sensitivity to his reasonable critique, and he backed away from the mirror, wondering what to do next...as he had apparently hurt her feelings.

Erik was shocked when she flicked her dewy eyes back up to the mirror and said in a thin little voice, "I am sorry I did it wrong. Would you please *show* me, Angel?"

It was such a simple request, but one he could not grant. Of course, if she could see him perform the exercise, she might understand what he wanted of her...but that was out of the question.

"What the devil shall I do with her now?" Erik asked himself, rubbing a knuckle hard across his mouth.

Clearing his throat, he stepped up to the mirror and watched as a single tear slipped down her cheek.

"My dear child, please forgive my impatience." he apologized awkwardly. "You are doing very well, and I am quite pleased with your progress."

As if she could see him through the mirror, Christine's lips turned up slightly, not in a complete smile, but it was an indication that his comment had had the desired effect. Her emotions were transparently reflected in her every feature, and Erik found himself charmed by her. Sucking in his breath, he straightened his spine and continued his tutelage, taking care to gentle his voice.

"This time when you sing the note, pretend that you are pressing your voice downward through your body, and feel it in your belly. I shall keep singing, and if you get it wrong...we'll simply start again."

Nodding her consent, Christine raised her chin, and after a few stops and starts, she finally sang the note, supported and powered by her diaphragm.

Erik startled her when he enthusiastically shouted, "That is correct, Christine! No, do not stop...hold out that note with me!"

He sang with her, and when she finally ran out of breath he encouraged her to sing again, teaching her to hear the difference in her voice. Once she had perfected the E he gave her a simple scale to sing, listening with his eyes closed as the tonal quality of her voice immediately improved.

The hour passed quickly for both student and teacher. Once she had overcome the fear of failure, she had been a quick learner, but he could see by her yawning between vocalizations that she was tired.

"You did well, my child. Your Angel is pleased," he praised her.

Christine's cheeks flushed, and although she continued to yawn and stretch, she remained standing before the mirror.

"Is the lesson over, Angel?" she asked, the veins of her eyes reddening as she reached up to rub them.

"For tonight," he affirmed. "Tomorrow night you will repeat your exercises, then I shall assign you more challenging scales."

Erik was himself exhausted, craving a brandy and his bed. It would be delicate work perfecting the child's voice, but he was already looking forward to tomorrow night's session. Stooping down, he lifted his cloak from the floor and brushed off the debris. He threw it on over his shoulders, reached in his pockets and pulled out his gloves, preparing to say goodnight, but her little voice again chirped at him through the mirror, "Angel, when may I sing a real song?" Christine asked, twisting her braid, with one foot wrapped behind the other.

"That will come later," he answered, tugging a glove onto his right hand. "You must first learn the fundamentals."

"What are fundamentals, Angel?" she questioned.

He couldn't help a chuckle and covered his mouth with his hand before answering, "The fundamentals are everything you must learn first. Afterward, I will give you real music to sing."

"Oh," she replied, "Angel, must you leave now?" she asked.

Erik was touched by her desire to have him stay longer, but there was nothing to sit on behind the mirror and his legs were growing stiff with the breezeway's chill. Looking at her through the glass, he began to feel like a heel, as she clearly seemed to be enjoying his company.

"What would be the harm in a few more minutes?" he questioned himself.

"I will stay a while longer, Christine, if you like," he said.

"Oh, please!" she replied, smiling, "Would you sing for me?"

Narrowing his eyes, he folded his hands across his chest and answered, "Yes, Christine, but first you must get into your bed."

Without saying a word, Christine turned around, folded down her bedding, and crawled beneath the covers. Lying on her side facing the mirror, she asked, "Angel, when will you tell me your real name?"

Erik was delighted by the sound of her childish voice, soft in the darkness.

"When you are ready to learn it, my dear," he replied.

"But when will I be ready?" she asked again.

"When it is time," he answered patiently, knowing that she would never hear it. Suddenly, his mood shifted from the enjoyment of having taught her, to one of irritation. She would never know his name, would never see his face, and someday she would outgrow him.

"Angel," she asked, "Do you live in heaven?"

Had she not been a mere child, Erik's immediate response would have been a sarcastic and bitter retort, but her question required some thought. He took his time, reaching behind his head to remove the mask.

"My world is very different from yours," he answered truthfully, dangling the mask from his hand. Pulling a handkerchief from his pocket, he wiped the moisture from his right brow and cheek, grimacing with the sensitivity of his skin. Giving the inside of the mask a few swipes with the cloth, he tied it back on and fit it snugly over his features, then adjusted the wig with his fingertips.

"Is your world pretty?" she persisted.

"It is my home," he replied, wondering if all children asked so many questions. He thought of how ridiculous his home was; a veritable dungeon beneath the ground, which would one day become his grave. But the girl need never know, for neither she nor any other soul would ever see his hiding place.

Christine changed positions in her bed and then inquired sleepily, "Have you ever seen God?"

Cocking his head backward, Erik chuckled to himself, having no idea how to answer the question. The girl had been brought up with religious nonsense, and he must be cautious. He would attempt to remain sensitive to her beliefs, but he had given up on God and religion years ago.

"No, Christine, I have never seen Him," he spoke darkly. "Perhaps I will one day."

Yes, and when you do, it will be when he casts you into hell! a voice mocked in his head. Ignoring his detractor, Erik turned around and leaned his back against the mirror, his arms folded across his chest as her questions continued.

"Have you seen my father?" Christine asked, propping her head up with her elbow.

Having no wish to lie to the girl, Erik formulated an answer carefully, turning his head to the side so that his voice would carry through the gaps around the frame. "Your father has quite a reputation, my dear. He is known to be a good man who loved his daughter very much."

The thought suddenly occurred to him that Gustave Daaé's reason for not promoting her talent may have been honorable after all. From what he gathered through his investigation of Daaé, the man had doted on the girl and had had no life of his own. Christine had been the center of his world, as he had been hers. Perhaps Erik had been too quick in condemning the man without knowing his true motives. Turning around, he looked again at Christine, who was clearly falling asleep. Erik reconsidered Daaé's point of view. Who could blame the man for wanting to protect her and to keep her safe? Even if Daaé had managed the right connections for her, she might have been snapped up by some unscrupulous impresario. Erik had only known Christine for a short time, and already he had begun to foster protective instincts in her regard, so perhaps there was something about the girl that warranted protection by all the men in her life.

Now half-asleep, with her cheek pressed into the pillow, to Erik the girl looked the picture of innocence.

"Christine, that is enough questions for tonight. Hush now and let me sing you to sleep," he said gently, anxious to return to his organ and a nightcap.

Fluttering her eyes open, with her voice muted by drowsiness, she replied, "Oh, Angel…yes, please!"

"Close your eyes," he whispered as his mind was suddenly invaded by memories of his mother's voice. Clearing his throat, he forced those memories into the recesses of his past where they would coil like serpents in the dark, until he called them forth again. For now, he chose not to remember.

Christine closed her eyes as Erik began to sing softly from the backside of the mirror. He sang one of his early compositions, a piece he had written when he was just a boy. He watched with interest as Christine's face softened and relaxed with the sound of his voice. How peaceful she looked with all of the sadness gone from her face…and how easily his voice seemed to wrap around her. He sang in his sweetest falsetto; smoothing out the vibrato and allowing the upper timbre of his voice to resonate like an oboe. He could see by her even breaths and her little fingers opening like the petals of a flower, that she had fallen asleep.

Backing away from the mirror, Erik fastened his cloak collar and prepared to leave the chamber, but was stopped abruptly at the doorway when Christine's voice immobilized him.

"Angel," she murmured sleepily in the dark, "I love you."

Immediately, the floor seemed to drop out from under his feet as he felt the air being squeezed out of his lungs. Nothing could have prepared him for those words, and sucking in his breath, Erik staggered sideways as if suffering a sharp blow. For some time he stood slumped against the wall, unable to move, not knowing how to respond, and hardly believing what he had heard her say. In all his thirty-one years, no one had ever said those words to him. No one…not ever, and now this child with her large brown eyes and angelic voice had spoken the three simple words he had been denied his entire life. Sinking down to his knees, he tried to speak, but his throat became constricted and his tongue went dry. Drooping his head down into his hands, he finally managed to clear his throat, and forced a reply, "Good night, my dear."

As Christine came to mean more to him each day, Erik's solitude began to wane; and before he had realized it, weeks had gone by; weeks of teaching her, weeks of listening to the quality and power of her voice improve, and weeks of his affection for her growing day by day. Through his efforts to transform Christine's naturally gifted voice from shy and uncertain into a fuller and more confident instrument, Christine Daaé had given him purpose…

…and so it began.

Chapter 11
Interlude

Four and a half weeks after Madame had left on her trip to Lyon, she had arrived back at the Paris depot on a late Monday evening. Given the lateness of the hour, Louise had made her own way back to the opera house, where she had been reunited with her daughter and had slept in her own bed with Meg curled up beside her. Meg had informed Louise of the opera house dramas and intrigues that had occurred while she was gone, and as the conversation had moved on to other topics, Meg had also informed her mother of Christine's decision to stay permanently in her own room, rather than moving into the Giry's apartment as expected. Meg had expressed her disappointment that her best friend would not be sharing her room after all, and had been somewhat confused as to why Christine had so suddenly changed her mind when the arrangements had been made even before her mother's departure. Finally, after talking late into the night about these, and many other issues, Louise and Meg had fallen asleep just before the one o'clock hour.

The morning after her return to Paris, Louise approached Christine's bedroom door just as the girl was performing her daily vocal exercises. It was not at all uncommon for young vocal students to be heard warming up or practicing in the dormitory wing, but this was the first time Louise had heard Christine's voice carrying all the way out into the hall, and she was surprised by its power and maturity. She stood outside in the corridor and listened, utterly dumbfounded by the obvious improvement in Christine's voice; and it wasn't just her voice that was different…there was something profoundly different in her spirit.

Pressing her ear to the door, she was quite content just to listen, convinced that the girl had not achieved such heights on her own…something extraordinary had happened in her absence! As Christine ended her vocalise, Louise paused a moment before knocking lightly.

"Christine, may I come in?" she asked.

Flinging the door open, her eyes bright and her face flushed, Christine exclaimed, "Oh, Madame, you are back! I am so happy to see you!"

The girl flung herself into the older woman's arms with an embrace that pleasantly surprised Louise, making her realize how much she had missed the child. Noticing the marked change in both Christine's demeanor and appearance, she felt a welcome sense of relief. How good it was to see the girl behaving like a normal child; and after hearing her sing, Madame had a fair indication of exactly who was responsible for the vocal transformation.

"Christine, I missed you while I was away…and my goodness, you sound wonderful!" Louise praised, watching as Christine blushed with a shy smile.

"Thank you, Madame. I have been…that is, he…well, I have been working hard," Christine stammered, averting Madame Giry's intense hazel eyes.

Tilting the girl's chin upward with her thumb, Louise leveled her gaze to Christine's and said with a smile, "Well, my dear, we must have a long talk, and you must tell me all about your new teacher…and about the opera, and everything else that happened while I was away!"

Christine's lips parted just as she was about to speak, but looking up at Madame's face, she noticed the dark circles under her eyes. Her naturally beautiful complexion was haggard, and even with the hint of lipstick and rouge she wore, it seemed to Christine that Madame looked thinner than before she had left.

Drawing her brows together, Christine inquired, "Madame, are you ill?"

Louise was taken aback by the girl's question, for she had scarcely even had time to glance in a mirror since her return. She had not even begun to unpack, and had thrown on her lipstick in a hurry.

Pausing, her eyes fell on Christine's full-length mirror, and she was aghast at what she saw. She certainly did look ill, though illness was not responsible for her shabby appearance. Her journey had been far more traumatic than past visits, and the emotional upheaval she had endured in Lyon had drained her. She was happy to be back in her beloved opera house, but it would take time to recover from the distress she had experienced during her time away.

Scrutinizing her pale reflection, she drew her hands to her face and pinched some color into her cheeks, scowling when there was little improvement. Turning away from the mirror with a sigh, Louise forced a smile as she cleared her throat and placed her hands gently on Christine's shoulders, anxious to hear about Erik's entrance into the girl's life. While away, she had harbored concerns about his tutoring techniques and was curious about how their first meeting had gone. He had promised not to show his face to the girl; and therefore, given the extraordinary nature of the situation, Louise wondered how on earth he had accomplished the singing lessons!

"No, Christine, I am not ill…just tired from the train ride," she fibbed. "Perhaps all I need is a little fresh air!"

"Yes, Madame," Christine replied, concern still evident in her unchanged expression. Taking hold of Christine's hands, Louise gaily raised the pitch of her voice.

"I have a grand idea, Christine!" she exclaimed. "Why don't we take the carriage to the park and have a nice stroll in the sunshine? Suzanne is tutoring Meg this morning, and you and I might spend a little time alone together! Would you like that?"

Nodding her head, Christine offered a pretty smile and answered, "Yes, Madame, I would like that very much."

Earlier that morning, Christine had gazed out the windows at the birds scattering about on the lawn. While she had come to appreciate her life in the opera house, there were still times when the dark corridors and damp stone began to close in around her. She had been raised in the countryside and had spent her earliest childhood out of doors with her father; but life in the opera house now meant that most of her days were occupied indoors. Madame's invitation for a walk was a lovely gesture, and Christine was bursting to tell someone about her Angel!

Madame helped Christine change into a pretty spring frock and ribbon-trimmed straw bonnet; a fetching ensemble which had been purchased through Monsieur E's generosity. The blue of the dress brought out the peachy tones of Christine's complexion, and Madame was delighted to see her looking so healthy. Among all of the opera's lovely young women, it was easy to overlook Christine's fragile beauty. Her pale complexion and sad brown eyes frequently set her apart from the other girls. She was tall for her age; her willowy frame, slender arms and legs awkward at times. Louise had watched many young ladies transition from girlhood to womanhood, and in her opinion there was little doubt that Christine would be extraordinarily beautiful. She and Christine observed one another in the glass as Louise tied Christine's sash.

"Do you like your new bonnet and frock, Christine?" Madame questioned, forming the wide blue ribbon into a perfect bow.

With her eyes flashing golden in the mirror, Christine smiled and said, "Oh, yes, Madame. Never have I seen such beautiful clothes!"

"We mustn't neglect to thank him," Louise murmured, smoothing the lace of Christine's skirt.

Gazing at her reflection, Christine thought she looked just like a girl from a wealthy family; someone like Claire, who had always had the prettiest clothes of anyone in the academy. Christine smiled demurely, admiring the freshness of her starched new pinafore. She sniffed the fine cotton sleeves, loving the stiff new petticoats beneath her skirts. She was thankful that her benefactor had cared enough to have provided such pretty things, and pictured Monsieur E. as an elderly gentleman quite like Maestro Reyer; with silver hair and a great curling mustache. She could not imagine why he had chosen her from among all the other, more deserving girls who lived and trained beneath the opera's roof, but his generosity had made her life far more pleasant, and she had hopes of meeting him in person one day.

With Madame adjusting her bonnet, Christine assured her, "Oh no, Madame, I shan't forget to write him this very evening!"

The carriage ride was pleasant as Christine absorbed the sights and sounds of late spring. She considered Paris the most beautiful city in the world, especially when it wore its brightest spring colors. Music could be heard all over the city as musicians entertained in the outdoor cafes, city squares, and public courtyards.

Listening to the distant strains of a small orchestra, Christine's thoughts turned to her father as the carriage made its way down the boulevard. Her father, it seemed, had never cared for France, and had often spoken of returning to Sweden, but she had fallen in love with Paris from the moment they had first arrived in the early autumn of her seventh year. Christine had felt quite at home in their tiny flat with its leaky ceiling and musty smells; and she had still missed the apartment even after Madame Valleria had settled them into a more respectable district.

Having never understood her father's dislike of the city, Christine thought that perhaps his reticence had been due to his dismissal after the one year probationary period with the opera's orchestra; an experience he had briefly mentioned but never fully explained. She often wondered why he had never played first chair, and had always believed that his talents and skills had been wasted.

She had always known that he felt out of place in Paris, thinking himself more suited to a quiet life in the country outside Sigtuna, where he had been born and raised, and where she had spent the first seven years of her childhood.

Happy to be taking a carriage ride with Madame that morning, and enchanted by the blossoms swaying in the morning breeze, as they traveled away from the opera district, Christine decided that she would never want to live anywhere else but Paris.

After they had been dropped off at the park, they stopped to purchase peanuts from a street vendor. Tucking the bag of nuts in the picnic basket, Louise opened her parasol, and together they walked along a flowered path that encircled a beautiful reflective green pond. Magnificent swans could be seen preening their feathers, gliding like white-gowned ballerinas across the silky water. Their long necks were arched gracefully as they unfurled lustrous wings in the tree-dappled shade, while tiny feather motes floated above the lake in sheaths of yellow sunlight. The branches of a weeping willow trailed lazily into the pond, catching up all manner of leaves and debris in their tangles. Visitors tossed breadcrumbs for the noisy geese and ducks, which also populated the pond, and children squealed with delight in the park's designated play areas. Madame and Christine strolled around the pond several times before settling near a park bench to feed a bushy-tailed squirrel.

Setting her basket down on the bench, Louise spread their tablecloth out on the grassy turf, and the two sat down where they could watch the water fowl.

Louise lifted her eyes, gazed up through the lace of her parasol and sighed, "It is a perfectly lovely day."

Nodding her head in agreement, Christine tossed the peanuts onto the grass and watched in fascination as the squirrel shed the nut of its shell, then filled its chubby cheeks.

"It is beautiful here, Madame. Thank you for bringing me," Christine said happily.

With the sun having moved behind a giant ash tree, Louise closed up her parasol and set it down on the blanket. Smoothing the folds of her skirt, she took pleasure in Christine's carefree expression as the child watched the squirrel's delightful antics. The dappled sunshine lit her dark braids with ribbons of gold, and sitting beneath the trees in a halo of light, Christine did indeed look like a dark-haired angel. Louise watched her with a mother's pride, thinking that the dress she had purchased on behalf of Monsieur E. suited Christine very well.

"And now, Christine," she interrupted her own thoughts, "you must tell me all about your new teacher."

Turning her attention away from the squirrel, Christine looked up at Louise and hesitated, uncertain of whether or not she should tell Madame anything at all. She had first thought that he must remain a secret, but strangely, Madame Giry seemed to already know of him. Christine pressed her lips together, and narrowing her eyes, she thought of all that Madame had done for her. Christine had come to trust and care for her, as she had once cared for Madame Valleria, and she feared that if she did not soon tell someone the truth, she would simply explode!

158

Turning her whole body to face her guardian, Christine's cheeks blushed bright pink as she whispered under her breath, "He is wonderful, Madame. He is very strict, but also kind and gentle."

For some moments, Madame scrutinized her charge with a peculiar expression, then smiled faintly, placing her arm around Christine's shoulder affectionately.

"I can tell by your progress, my dear, that he is a very great teacher; therefore, you must follow his instructions to the letter, and work very hard to please him," Louise advised.

Christine nodded her head in agreement, but remained silent. Opening and closing her mouth several times, she tried to ask a question; but finally settled back against the bench with her hands folded in her lap.

"Child, what is your teacher's name?" Louise asked, drawing Christine back into their discussion.

"Madame, he says I am not to know his name," she answered sadly. This was what she wanted to know about him most of all, and yet he had repeatedly refused to tell her his real name.

"I suppose that is wise," Louise replied mysteriously, adding with a tilt of her chin, "How often are your lessons, dear?"

"Mostly every night before I go to bed," Christine answered wistfully, "except for performance nights…then he comes in the morning."

Madame tilted back the rim of Christine's straw bonnet until she could see her eyes and remarked, "Then we must see to it that your lessons are not disturbed."

Clearing her throat, Christine sat up straight, and finally getting the courage to ask her question, she exclaimed, "Madame, how do you know of him? I haven't even told Meg!"

Chuckling softly, Louise glanced in the direction of the pond and replied, "Why, Christine, when it comes to my girls, there is very little I do not know!"

This seemed to satisfy Christine, who nodded her head with a smile. It was understood by all the girls, that Madame knew about everything and everyone in the opera house. Some even suspected that she could read minds! Girls often found themselves admonished for bad behavior when there was no possible way Madame could have actually seen their mischief. It was commonly believed that Madame Giry even had spies who kept watch over the corps de ballet in her absence. Everything was reported, and very little went unnoticed by the ballet mistress with the strange cat-eyes.

"Then, it is all right? I mean...you approve?" Christine queried, following Madame's gaze across the pond.

"Of course I do, Christine. Receiving the proper training is exactly why your father sent you here."

Letting out her breath, and greatly relieved, Christine relaxed her shoulders and remarked, "Yes, Madame...Father is the one who sent him to me...and he is so wonderful!"

"I'm pleased that you find him suitable, Christine. His knowledge of music is nothing short of genius," Louise muttered wearily. Shading her eyes with her hand as the sun broke through the trees in full force, Louise slid closer to Christine and patted her knee.

"My dear, I'm still dreadfully tired from the train ride. Perhaps you wouldn't mind if I closed my eyes for a few moments, and then we'll have our picnic?"

Lifting the picnic basket lid, Christine retrieved a few slices of stale bread.

"No, Madame, I don't mind. I shall feed the ducks and geese while you rest!" she said cheerfully.

"Very well, darling, but do not wander off too far."

As Christine rose up from the bench and skipped off toward the pond, Louise reached down and fetched her parasol. Snapping it open, she lay back on the blanket and closed her eyes, speculating about what had happened at the opera house during her absence. The moment she had returned from the depot, Meg had happily told her about *The Magic Flute* gala performance. Describing the beautiful costumes and the magical set, she had gone into graphic detail about Carlotta's quarrel with Mademoiselle Simonette, which had, in turn, incurred the wrath of the Opera Ghost. According to Meg, upon storming into

Simonette's dressing room and seeing it simply blooming with roses, Carlotta had vindictively dumped a fresh bouquet to the floor and stomped the flowers with her jeweled shoes.

At the conclusion of the following night's performance while taking her bows, Carlotta had received a flower box wrapped luxuriously with black satin ribbon. There was no card attached to identify the giver, so she had naturally presumed them to be from an admirer and showed off the box to everyone on stage. With cast and crew watching, the diva had excitedly untied the ribbon, pulled off the box top, parted the tissue…then nearly fainted when she saw dozens of dried up roses nestled in the tissue! A card tucked into the flowers had read:

> *Fondest greetings, my dear Carlotta. A word of advice:*
> *A woman receives as she gives.*
>
> *O.G.*

Lying under the shade of the parasol, Louise laughed aloud, thinking of Erik's audacity as she imagined the indignant look on Carlotta's face. Apparently, the woman had shrieked upon reading the note, demanding that the mangers call for an immediate investigation by the authorities. Of course, nothing had been done about the incident, and Carlotta had eventually found other excuses for her tantrums.

According to Meg's amusing account, the gala grand opening of *The Magic Flute* had come and gone in a flurry of success and applause. Life at the opera house had then resumed its customary chaotic pace as the cast and crew began a short break before mounting the next production.

Squinting her eyes, Louise sat up and gazed over to the pond, where she could see Christine squatting near the water's edge, tossing breadcrumbs to the geese. Satisfied that she was still within earshot, Louise resumed her musing and closed her eyes. Meg had also spoken at length about her friendship with Christine, and about how they had become as close as sisters. Louise could not have been more pleased, because that was exactly what she had hoped for; two fatherless girls forging a close bond.

She had sensed that they would be good for each other, and now it seemed the three of them were, at last, becoming a family. Letting her head droop lazily back down onto the blanket, she smiled as the warmth of the sun seeped into her bones. With her thoughts drifting hazily, her mind and body began to relax in a much needed respite.

Careful not to soil the hem of her skirt and petticoats, Christine knelt beside the pond, admiring the luminous swans. Had she been with her father on such an outing, she would have removed her black stockings and shoes and waded barefoot in the shallows...but Parisian girls did not behave in such a casual manner in public parks. As Madame Valleria had said, "It is not proper for young ladies to display their bare legs and feet when gentlemen are present."

Just the same, she longed to feel the cool water splashing across her toes, but for now would enjoy its calming reflections. Madame Giry had promised to take Christine and Meg to the countryside where they could wade in the river; and as she considered the delights of such a day, she spotted a flock of ducklings swimming near a cluster of reeds. She thought them the sweetest little creatures she had ever seen! Their soft yellow down and adorable little orange beaks made her want to pick one up and tuck it safely inside her pocket to keep as a pet, but of course, pets were out of the question at the opera house.

Hearing a great splash and squawking in the water, Christine raised her head and moved closer to the reeds for a better look. A dozen or so mature ducks had surrounded a little gray duckling that looked scrawny and sick compared to the rest of the flock. Its down was dull, with no luster or sheen, and grayish feathers poked out all over its awkward little body. Its ugly black beak appeared too large for the little head, and the poor thing was paddling furiously, trying to get away from the larger ducks.

Christine was horrified when the mature ducks began to peck viciously at the little duckling. First one, and then another struck at him, until the little thing was surrounded by dozens of pecking beaks. It squawked miserably, paddling its little legs beneath the water in a desperate attempt to flee the assault, but it was simply too small.

Certain that the other ducks were going to kill it, Christine screamed out loud, "Someone, stop them! They're going to kill him!" she cried. "No! Leave him alone, you little beasts!"

Louise was startled awake by Christine's outcry and bolted up from the blanket, rushing to the edge of the pond where the child was thrashing at the water. Fearful that she had been harmed, Madame swooped down, her motherly instincts fully engaged as she heard the sound of Christine's voice.

"What is it, darling?" Louise asked, "What has happened?"

With her brown eyes full of tears and her nose red, Christine pointed at a growth of reeds and stammered, "Those beastly ducks are going to kill that little one! Please, Madame, make them stop!"

Following Christine's terrified gaze, Louise caught sight of the little duckling, surrounded by at least a dozen pecking beaks. Calmly stooping down, she picked up a large twig and flung it into the midst of the fray. The mature ducks immediately scattered and squawked away, leaving the solitary little creature dazed, but not badly hurt. Grasping Madame Giry's hand, Christine threw herself into her guardian's embrace.

"Why must they be so cruel...just because he's not as pretty as those other baby ducks?" she asked, her brown eyes intense and her shoulders shaking.

Moved by the child's compassionate nature, Louise patted Christine's back, then knelt down on the grass, taking hold of her hands.

"Christine," she explained, "that little one is not a duck at all, my dear...but a swan hatchling!"

With her eyes widening, Christine sniffed and glanced over her shoulder at the solitary baby bird, now paddling across the pond.

"A hatchling swan, Madame?"

"Yes, dear, a swan. And he is not really hurt, Christine, only frightened. He will join his own kind on the swan's island in the center of the pond and all will be well!" Louise comforted her, as

Christine dried her eyes with a handkerchief.

"But, Madame, why were they so mean to him?" she asked.

Louise gently squeezed the child's hands, then rose to her feet, guiding the girl on the path around the pond.

"The ducks rejected him because he is not of their kind," she calmly explained. She led Christine to the other side of the pond where they could have a better view of the swans on their island, then continued, "The ways of nature are very mysterious, my darling girl. Sometimes, what appears ugly on the outside hides that which is most beautiful on the inside. Swan chicks hatch looking like that little one there, but as they mature, their gray feathers are replaced by white plumage and their scrawny necks grow long and graceful, until they transform into the majestic creatures you see floating on the water."

The sun had moved higher up in the sky, and the swan island was flooded with light, making the white birds even more spectacular as they preened and sunned themselves. A mother swan floated toward the island with her brood tucked under her wing feathers, their little brown and gray heads protruding like odd appendages.

"Is it magic, Madame?" Christine asked, wide-eyed and sniffling.

"Yes. I expect it is a kind of magic, my dear," Madame replied. "God's magic."

With the trauma over and the swan chick restored to his family on the island, Christine seemed satisfied that the little fellow was safe. As the two of them watched the hatchlings eating breadcrumbs off the water, an adult trumpet swan glided out from under the willows and unfurled its magnificent wings in an arc of light.

The sun shone through droplets of water as the male swan splashed and beat its wings on the pond's emerald surface, and Christine opened her mouth in awe as its feathers glistened like diamonds, reflecting all the colors of a rainbow.

"Oh, Madame, look!" Christine exclaimed. "More of God's magic!"

Smiling down at the girl, Louise's eyes began to mist. Her little charge was indeed a special child, whose tender heart was itself a gift from God.

"Yes it is, my dear," Louise whispered under her breath. "God's magic indeed."

The two of them stood silent and breathless for some moments as the swan performed his mating dance; and before long, Christine forgot about the little hatchling that had been attacked. Overcome by the beauty before her eyes, she forgave nature for its earlier cruelty, and was ready for more adventures.

"Madame, may we soon visit the countryside?" Christine asked, tugging on Louise's dress sleeve.

Relieved that the girl was smiling again, Louise placed a hand on her shoulder and said, "Yes, we shall, Christine, but next time let's bring Meg along!"

"Oh, yes, Madame, and Marie, too?" Christine suggested, following Madame down the path with a little skip in her step.

Enjoying Christine's enthusiasm, Louise answered, "Of course we shall bring Marie!"As Christine chattered about swans and geese and squirrels, Louise set out the picnic lunch, and the two enjoyed their meal on a day that neither would ever forget.

Chapter 12
Heart Sounds—1874

In the final days of the spring of eighteen-seventy-four, an influenza outbreak raged through Paris, its outlying cities and villages. Schools and universities closed, businesses reported heavy absenteeism, and hospitals were filled to capacity with patients suffering from complications of the deadly virus. The old and the young were the most vulnerable, and funerals were held in churches and chapels throughout the city as the infirm began to perish in large numbers. Restaurants and cafes were nearly empty, with the parks and shops deserted as citizens remained in their homes to avoid infection. Dance halls and concert venues had canceled all upcoming entertainments, and The Paris Opera had also been forced to close its doors at the peak of the outbreak.

Of the more than five hundred cast, crew, and staff who made up the opera's company, thirty-five percent had come down with some degree of the illness. Poligny's wife had been recovering in her villa just outside Paris, and two of Debienne's children had also been ill with a milder form of the sickness. Several members of the corps de ballet had been sent home to relatives when they began exhibiting symptoms, but had fortunately recovered in only a matter of weeks.

Strict measures were then undertaken within the opera house to prevent further spread of the illness. Food was no longer shared, residents were instructed to wash their hands repeatedly, and Madame Giry made certain that, at the first sign of a cough or fever, those who had been infected were isolated from other residents.

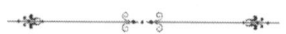

With the opera's backstage and workshops now nearly deserted, Meg and I took advantage of the influenza outbreak by turning those fascinating environs into our own personal playground. We spent our free time exploring the closets, lofts and many rooms of the opera house in games of hide and seek. For the two of us it was like a holiday, and although Madame had made certain we would not fall behind in our studies, she permitted us to wander about as long as we did not break any of the opera house rules.

We were not permitted up in the catwalks or in the dressing rooms, and we were absolutely forbidden from going down into the cellars. Most of our time was spent in the workshop bay, where we sculpted small figures with clay, or worked on paper-mache masks. Meg was fond of shaping animal masks, while I had formed mine into eccentric human faces...or at least I had tried to. Neither of us was very good at the craft, but it took our minds off the crisis in our city and therefore, Madame encouraged our creativity.

When we were not studying or practicing dance with Madame, Meg and I played in the wardrobe room, trying on old costumes and performing our own little operas. Meg was always the handsome hero, and I, the damsel who required rescuing from the villain. We used a mannequin for our villain, dressing him up in the white death mask, long black coat and tricorne hat that had been used in *Don Giovani*. Running about the wardrobes, shrieking and singing, we ducked in and out of closets and storage cabinets as our make-believe villain pursued us.

One evening, three weeks into the outbreak, Madame read stories to Meg and me in her cozy fire lit room, as I fashioned several new cards for my benefactor, who had recently given me a paint set of bright water colors and brushes. Meg was snuggled beside Madame on the chaise lounge, while I lay on the floor painting swan pictures. Feeling a little tired, I pulled one of Madame's quilts over my legs and continued my project, wondering why my body was sore. Assuming that I was a little more tired than usual from following Meg around all day, I remembered also that I had not eaten much at supper, so perhaps I was feeling poorly from not having enough food in my tummy.

Oh well, I thought to myself, *I'll eat a good breakfast tomorrow morning.*

As Madame read aloud from a book of Hans Christian Anderson's tales, I found myself yawning repeatedly, my eyelids becoming heavy and hot. Fighting to keep them open, I rested my head on my arm, listening to Madame's pleasant voice, which had begun to sound very far away. I had enjoyed Madame's storytelling, but at the same time I could not help thinking that Father was a much more skilled raconteur. There were still moments when I missed him desperately; but having my Angel was almost the same as having Father back.

Despite the influenza outbreak, each night my Angel had still come to my mirror and I could hardly wait for tonight's session. Gradually, Madame's story-telling receded farther back into my conscious thoughts as thoughts of my Angel moved to the forefront. After an hour of drowsing on the floor, I glanced up at the mantel and was shocked to see that it was nearly seven o'clock, and almost time for my voice lesson!

Forcing myself up onto my knees, I gathered my paper and paints and placed them safely in my satchel as Madame continued to read to Meg. Standing up on shaky legs, I tiptoed over to the chaise, bent down and kissed Madame's cheek, whispering in her ear, "I must do my vocal exercises, Madame."

Madame wedged her thumb between the pages of her book, closed it and replied, "Of course, dear. I shall come tuck you in afterward."

Lying beside her mother, Meg cracked one eye open and said with a sleepy smile, "Goodnight, Christine."

"Goodnight, Meg," I answered, as I picked up my brushes and water jar. Madame continued her reading of *The Red Shoes*, as I tiptoed into the pantry and rinsed my paint brushes, watching the yellows, reds, and blues marble in the basin. Setting the empty jar on the sideboard, I returned quietly to the parlor and collected my satchel, then waved and turned toward the door.

As I walked down the corridor to my room, my feet seemed to drag and the glare of the torches hurt my eyes. Upon opening the door, it was all I could do to keep myself from immediately flopping down on the bed; but the knowledge that my Angel would be arriving at any moment kept me on my feet. Stepping behind the wardrobe screen, I undressed, changed into my night clothes, then selected my heavier robe in place of the cotton one I usually wore. The stove glowed with heat in the corner, but I still felt cold and pulled the robe tightly around me. I lit my candle, then knelt down on the floor and began my prayers.

My throat was a little sore, so I hurried through my list of people to bless and hoped that my Angel would not be cross with my scratchy voice. After completing my nightly ritual, I sat on the edge of the bed and waited for him to call my name…but when he had still not arrived at ten minutes after seven, I grew sleepy and laid down to rest. Shivering, I pulled the blankets around my body, wondering why the room was so cold.

Erik sat slumped over the organ, his fingers stained black and his knuckles sore from a particularly lengthy session. With only a few candles remaining lit across the console, the room was dark, and he had not bothered to glance at a clock for hours. His brandy glass sat empty, and his stomach rumbled as he realized he had not even stopped for supper; but as always, when there was music to be written he couldn't be bothered with the mundane.

Lifting his head, he set down his pen and ran a hand across the unmasked side of his face, realizing that he hadn't shaved. He sighed heavily, straightened his back and tore his eyes away from the half-written manuscript, curious about the hour.

"Surely it can't be much later than six," he muttered to himself, fishing for his pocket-watch and checking the time. Blinking his eyes, he jumped up from the bench and cursed as he snapped it closed, "Bloody hell, seven-twenty! I'm late for Christine!"

For an entire glorious year he had been teaching the child,

and each evening her lesson was the highlight of his day. Shaking his head, he cursed under his breath and stomped down from the organ, dashing throughout the grotto in a huff to grab his cloak, his violin, and some sheets of music. He could scarcely believe that he had overworked himself to the point of nearly missing her session, and tossed his cloak into the boat with an impatient grunt. Dropping the violin and music on the cushions, he shoved off from the shore, still cursing and feeling ill-prepared.

There had been no time to select a piece for her to work on, and he would have to sort through the mess of manuscripts later. Guiding his boat beneath the portcullis, Erik poled through the green canals. In a record twenty minutes later, with the violin tucked under his arm and the music clasped tightly in his hand, he tore up the long staircase like a madman, grumbling angrily as he headed for the back of the dormitory wing. The poor child had been kept waiting for nearly thirty minutes, and he felt like a heel for all the times he had scolded her in the event of her own tardiness. Finally entering the mirror chamber, he was disappointed to see that Christine was fast asleep in bed, with her favorite doll nestled in her arms.

"Damn!" he cursed, setting the violin on his stool and placing his stack of music on the easel. Moving closer to the mirror, he set about removing his gloves and wondered if he should wake her or let her sleep. However, as he observed her more carefully, he saw that she was shaking, and immediately the hair on the back of his neck bristled.

Erik slipped back out into the corridor and dispatched his torch into the wall-bracket, then entered the chamber again, this time closing the door behind him. From the darkness of the chamber, looking through the mirror into her candlelit room, he could plainly see that her face appeared flushed with beads of sweat. Needing a closer look, he squinted his eyes, drawing his face so close to the mirror that his breath fogged the glass.

"Damn!" he swore again, wiping the smudge with his coat sleeve.

Erik scrutinized her entire form, his eyes sweeping down to her legs that were clearly trembling beneath the blankets. With an explosion of air across his lips, he lunged toward the mirror and shouted, "Damn it to hell! The girl is ill!"

He clenched his fists and ground his teeth, wanting to go for help...but how could he go about getting help for her from behind that damned mirror? He could see that her condition was worsening as her breathing appeared labored, and he was growing more agitated by the moment.

"Christine!" he shouted through the mirror. "Christine, wake up, child!"

The sound of his voice had always been enough to rouse her from her deepest dreams, but this time she did not move, and Erik panicked when she failed to respond.

"Christine!" he shouted again, pounding his fist on the mirror.

Clenching his jaw, Erik realized that he had no choice but to intervene and go for help. He was well aware of the risk he was taking, but it was clear that she had taken ill with influenza and was raging with fever. He snapped into action, felt around the mirror's inside edge and flipped the hidden latches. He pushed on the back of the mirror and flinched when the hinges ground with an ugly screech. He made a mental note to work on the device after Christine had recovered. Stepping through the opening, with a gust of air blowing out behind him, Erik raced to Christine's bedside, ripped off his cloak and let it drop to the floor. He bent over her bed and placed his hand on her forehead, biting down on his lower lip as he exclaimed, "My God, she's burning up!"

With not a minute to lose, he backed away from the bed, cautiously opened Christine's door and peered out into the hallway, where muffled voices could be heard from the few rooms that were still being occupied. Seeing that the hallway was deserted, he looked back on Christine and muttered softly, "I shall take care of you, Christine."

He closed Christine's door behind him and charged like a madman down the hall to Madame's blue door, then knocked.

With the blood pounding in his ears, he spoke urgently, "Madame, open the door!"

When she did not immediately answer, he clenched his hand into a fist, pounded on the door and commanded with a shout, "Madame Louise, it is Erik, open the damn door now!"

Having draped a shawl around her shoulders and carrying the

book in her hand, Madame Giry opened the door, shocked to see Erik's tall masked form in front of her. She had only met him face to face on rare occasions, but never in the dormitory. He looked dreadful; his mouth was a hard slash across his face, the exposed side of his complexion was pale, and the eye behind his mask was bulging. She knew immediately that something was terribly wrong, but before she had the chance to speak a word, Erik grabbed her by the hand and yanked her out of her doorway, barking his orders, "Come with me, Louise!"

He pulled her down the hall and thrust open Christine's door, practically dragging Louise through its opening. The minute Madame saw the child shivering in her bed, she dropped her book the floor and her hands flew up to her face as she cried out, "Oh my God!"

Madame's panic was evident as her face turned white, and seeing her in that condition, Erik turned his body to face her directly, leaned down and grasped her shoulders, boring his eyes into hers with an intensity that she had never seen before from anyone.

"Now, listen to me, Louise!" he commanded, "get hold of yourself, woman! We must act quickly! I know what to do, but I need your help!"

Louise Giry had cared for many ill children in her days at the opera house, and some had even been dangerously ill; but Meg had always been a healthy child, never prone to the childhood diseases so common in other youngsters. It had become obvious soon after Christine had joined them however, that she had not been blessed with a strong constitution, for the girl seemed to succumb to every cold or virus that passed through the opera's ranks. Observing Christine's frail condition was not the same as watching one of the ballet girls fall ill; where one must remain calm and emotionally detached. This child was like a daughter to her, and she was terrified of losing her. Praying under her breath, Louise asked for St Michael's protection.

Taking notice of Louise's panicked expression, Erik took hold of her cheek with his hand and lowered his voice, enunciating every word through his teeth, "Do not look at Christine, Madame. Look at me and do as I say!"

Louise swallowed hard, nodded her head, blinked back the tears and answered, "Yes, of course, anything…just tell me what to do!"

Releasing his grip, Erik softened his voice and instructed, "Go to the kitchen and fill a wash basin with ice. Bring some towels and wash cloths, and a bottle of rubbing alcohol. I will stay here with Christine! Hurry, Louise," he added urgently.

Within a few minutes Madame returned with the items he had requested to find him sitting on the edge of the bed. He had pulled all the blankets off of Christine, leaving her to be covered only by the sheet. The child moaned and wheezed, but seemed completely unaware of his presence.

"Now, Madame," he instructed, "I must return to my rooms for some supplies. Arrange those towels around her, pour some of the alcohol into the ice basin and sponge her whole body until I return. This should bring her fever down."

Hardly believing her eyes, Madame Giry stared opened-mouth as, turning on his heel, Erik dashed across the floor, his dark form disappearing through the mirror…the exact mirror that had hung in this very room since she was a child. She had danced before it, dressed in front of it, had admired or critiqued her reflection in that same mirror, and the implication of its true purpose was simply astounding. She promised herself that she would question him later, but for now she was intent on nursing Christine back to health. She ignored the mirror, and trying not to think about its true purpose, she tucked towels under Christine's body, then rubbed her arms, legs, and torso with the ice and alcohol. She winced as the smell of the alcohol made her vaguely nauseous, reminding her of similar odors from her recent journey to Lyon. Christine whimpered as Madame dipped the washcloth and squeezed out the excess liquid, placing the cold cloth against her hot forehead.

What if this child dies? she worried with a shudder, perfectly aware of the list of fatalities posted daily in the paper. Scolding herself for her lack of faith, she continued her ministrations, massaging Christine's feet and legs and rinsing out the washcloth repeatedly. The child had come to mean so much to her, and she had been making plans that she must see to completion, as she had promised Gustave she would do.

"Why this…and why now?" she questioned aloud.

The minutes stretched into a dreadful half hour, and Madame began to panic again. Christine's breathing was ragged, her cheeks had lost their flushed appearance, and she had grown even more pale.

"Where is he?" Madame asked under her breath, trying to recall verses from the book of Psalms. The basin was nearly empty, and she needed to fetch more ice, but was afraid to leave the girl alone. Closing her eyes, she clasped Christine's hands between her own, rubbing them while reciting the verse over and over again.

At last, Erik burst through the mirror carrying a mysterious black leather case, which he hoisted up onto the bureau, then jerked open the latches. He pulled out vials of liquid in various colors and sizes, lining them up on the top of the bureau.

Having rarely seen him in the flesh, Louise stared at him completely mesmerized. Her meetings with him had always been limited by his insistence on privacy, and she had never seen him as he truly was; tall and imposing. She tried to look away as he set up his supplies, but continued to stare, wondering what in the world he was intending to do with those odd looking bottles.

"Madame!" he snapped, feeling her eyes on his back, "You will go to the kitchen for more ice, then please heat up a kettle and bring it back with you. Oh, and I shall also require a tea cup and spoon." he added.

Madame nodded her assent, rose up from Christine's bed and marched out the door.

Never taking his eyes from Christine, Erik removed his coat, his brocade vest, untied his cravat and yanked it off from around his neck. He unfastened his shirt collar, rolled up his sleeves to the elbows, then tossed his clothing onto the trunk at the foot of the bed. Dipping the washcloth into the water and alcohol, he leaned over Christine and spoke soothing words in his low hypnotic voice as he blotted her feverish brow.

"I am here, Christine…your Angel is here." he whispered.

Some time later, as Madame brought in the kettle and ice, Erik handed her the washcloth, turned back to the bureau and began digging inside his case. He removed an empty bottle, pulled out the cork with his teeth, then set it down on the bureau. Motioning for Madame to bring the kettle, he poured the jar half-full with the hot water. Next he emptied the contents of several foul smelling vials into the jar, mixing the ingredients with the spoon until they swirled into a dark brown fluid.

"I spent a good deal of time with the gypsies, Madame," Erik explained over his shoulder. Opening more vials and adding their contents to the jar, he continued his discourse, "Due to the instruction of a certain gentleman, I absorbed their culture's knowledge of herbs and learned to distill remedies from nature's own apothecary. These oils will strengthen her body and loosen the secretions in her chest. You see...I've been using this mixture to ward off illness for years," he concluded, glancing over his shoulder at Louise as he worked.

Raising an eyebrow at the dubious expression he recognized in her eyes, Erik could hardly blame her for doubting him. The woman had been told only snippets of information about his experiences with the gypsies, and even those accounts had been greatly sanitized for her delicacy. He softened his expression, and as he bit down on his lower lip, he felt a twinge of guilt for all the times he'd taken advantage of her kindness; ordering her about like some low-born servant. But he would make amends for his offenses another day. Presently he must tend to the child, so he cleared his throat and went back to his work, continuing to mix the oils as a pungent vapor wafted up from the jar.

Pouring some of the brown mixture into the teacup, Erik quietly remarked, "And now, Madame, we must get as much of this down her as possible."

He moved over to the bed and gently wrapped Christine in the sheet, then lifted her up and cradled her like a rag-doll in his arms as Madame removed the damp towels from the bed. With Christine's head tucked against his chest, Erik sat down on the damask chair, his hand stroking the side of her face.

"The fever is no higher, Madame; you did well," he said, settling Christine across his lap.

Louise stood motionless, her hands clasped behind her back, shocked by his gentle manner toward the child. To her knowledge,

Erik's only contact with children had been in the gypsy tents when they had hurled objects and laughed at him. He had no siblings, no family at all, so where on earth had this nurturing instinct come from, she wondered? In the way he held her, and in the calm of his voice, he might very well have been Christine's father, and Louise was simply dumbfounded by such an affectionate display from a man who was quite adept at wreaking havoc!

Wedging his index finger between Christine's lips, he pried open her teeth, then placed the spoon to her mouth, pouring in a little at a time as she gagged and retched down the fluid's bitterness. With the side of his thumb he gently massaged her neck, helping the potion to ease down her throat until she swallowed. He continued the same process until the cup was empty, and then instructed Madame to refill it, repeating the treatment several more times.

Looking over her shoulder as she glided toward the door, Louise stated, "I shall go for a change of sheets and some fresh towels."

Before opening the door, she observed the scene with a lump lodged in her throat. The child lay in his arms, completely unaware that something akin to fatherly affection shone in this dark man's eyes. Opening the door, Louise quickly dashed a tear from her eye, and closed it behind her as she walked out into the corridor.

Upon Louise's exit, Erik gazed down on Christine's face with more concern than he had let on in Louise's company. The child was so thin that he could feel each individual rib and the knobs of her spine beneath her gown. She felt so delicate…that he feared she might break in two should he even dare to move her. In teaching her through the mirror all those months, there had been a chasm of glass between them, and somehow that division had made her seem as unreal and magical to him, as he must have been to her. But this was a flesh and blood child whose life was in danger, and she was more precious to him than he had imagined anyone would ever be. Squeezing his eyes shut, he began to sing as he brushed the side of her face with his thumb.

Moments later, Erik lifted his head and cleared his throat as Louise emerged through the door, her arms full of bedding and towels. Walking briskly across the rug, she set her stack of linens on the trunk, then turned to the bureau and opened a drawer, pulling out a fresh nightgown.

"This is all we can do for the moment, I'm afraid," Erik advised under his breath, wiping his forehead with the back of his hand. "We must hope the oils do their magic quickly."

"No, Erik, we can do more than hope...we can pray for her," Louise rebuffed, draping the night gown over her arm.

Erik turned on her suddenly, his mouth a thin slit on his face and his eyes darkening as he sneered, "You pray to your God if you so desire, Madame...but I shall put my money on gypsy medicine!"

Already startled by the cynicism of his comment, Louise flinched when he commanded loudly, "Get the child changed, Madame! The fever is down and we must keep her warm!"

Just as Louise was recovering from this show of temper, in the next breath he lowered his head with a heavy sigh, addressing her in a gentle voice, "Louise, my apologies; my temper often gets the best of me."

Louise acknowledged his apology with a nod, musing to herself that men like Erik often used anger to mask fear. She could clearly see that he was distraught over Christine's weakened condition. Stripping off the wet sheets and blankets, Louise remade the bed with dry linens as Erik continued to cradle Christine in his arms, his expression stoic as he leaned his head back in the chair. Louise tucked in the corners and smoothed out the clean cotton sheets, then glanced over at Christine, who had stopped mumbling and now rested her head in the crook of Erik's arm. Louise fluffed the pillow, then arranged the quilt as Erik slowly stood up and laid Christine down on the bed.

Suddenly, resuming her customary authoritative air, Louise spoke sternly, "Turn your back, Monsieur, and I shall tend to her wet things."

Obeying Louise's instructions, Erik turned about, drug his feet to the other side of the room and rubbed his hands together over the stove. He hadn't realized how cold they were. Stuffing them into his pockets, he glanced up at Christine's plaster wall, decorated with childish paintings of swans on a lake, and what looked like a depiction of Meg in her dance costume. There were rough sketches of angels everywhere, and Erik sucked in his breath when his eyes fell across a drawing of a robed angel with large wings, yellow hair and a halo. In her childish script she had labeled that drawing, "The Angel Of Music." Shaking his head, he wondered, *is this how she sees me?*

As he backed away from the wall, he folded his arms across his chest and commented bitterly to himself that her image of him could not have been farther from the truth, and yet he was the one who had encouraged her to see him as something beautiful instead of who, and what, he truly was. Shaken from his dark introspection, Erik was grateful when Louise finally gave him permission to turn around.

He turned to see her standing beside the bed, her hands clasped at her waist and her chin erect. Raising an eyebrow, she said nothing as Erik lumbered across the rug and back to the bedside. Bending over Christine protectively, Louise pulled the quilt up to the girl's chin, tucking it in around her body as she remarked matter-of-factly, "Thank you, Erik. I'll take over from here."

Erik stiffened his back and stretched to his full height. He squared his shoulders and said firmly, but gently, "No, Louise. I insist you go back to your room and get some rest…it's bound to be a long night."

"No, Erik, I will stay with her now," Madame stood her ground, with her chin lifted haughtily and her eyes narrowed.

Chuckling darkly and invigorated by a challenge, Erik reached out and placed his hand on Madame's forearm with just a hint of pressure. Leveling his steely gaze to hers, he said almost too politely, "My dear, I am accustomed to less sleep than you are. You get some sleep and I shall stay with her through the night. I will come for you if you are needed," he dismissed her with a flick of his hand.

"*If* I'm needed?" Louise huffed back at him. "She is like a daughter to me; how dare you…!"

Louise was stopped mid-sentence as he said in a sultry voice, "Madame, you must trust me."

He softened his eyes, and his lower lip twitched as she

continued to glare at him. Nodding curtly, Louise glanced again at Christine, gathered her skirts and spun around to face the door. She knew that when he applied that certain tone of voice…he meant business. Opening the door to leave, she resolved to trust him for now, but there would be a confrontation once the crisis was over. She turned the doorknob and spoke crisply over her shoulder, "Goodnight, Monsieur."

"Goodnight, my dear," he replied in a subdued voice.

Following Madame Giry's departure, Erik pulled the damask chair up beside the bed, lifted a small book from his bag, and sank down into the chair; only to stare at the same page for ten minutes before realizing that he hadn't read a single word. *How strange*, he thought, drumming his fingers on the open page. Peering around the room, with almost a surreal sense of things, Erik had never felt more out of place. Everything in Christine's room was girlish and pink; and it all represented a world he had only observed from afar. He knew that he did not belong there, but there he was, nonetheless, in the mysterious world of females.

He leaned his head back and rubbed his chin, thinking about the strangeness of his close proximity with two females at one time. Despite his earlier confrontation with Louise, the truth was, he liked her! Had it not been for their precarious arrangement, he might have enjoyed conversation with her over a glass of wine; but given the delicate nature of their business relationship, he felt it best to keep their friendship at arm's length. In his view, though, Louise Giry was a grand woman who deserved a more worthy husband than the horse's ass who still seemed to hold her heart captive. Clenching his jaw, Erik reflected on Louise's romance with Anton Giry. If there was one thing he could not abide, it was a foolish man, and from the very first he had never approved of Giry. Unfortunately, however, Louise had not asked his permission to marry the fellow!

Erik glanced down at his book and made a concerted effort to focus on the text, but found his thoughts wandering back to

Christine. He scrutinized her sleeping form, and was concerned about her pale complexion and the faint but persistent rattle in her chest. Furrowing his brow he scraped his tongue across his upper teeth, and cautioned himself that she might not have the strength to fight the fever. He leaned forward in the chair and braced his forearms across his legs, determined to pull her through. "By God!" he whispered under his breath, "I have enough strength for us both, and I will never let her come to harm…even if it means being found out by the authorities!"

Erik was determined to do whatever he must to make her well; and if that entailed transporting her to a public hospital…then so be it! His loss of freedom would be a small price to pay for the well-being of this child.

With a sense of purpose, Erik returned to his reading material, but each little move or sound from Christine diverted his attention, and he kept looking up to assess her condition. The process was exhausting, and given that he had composed all day and had gone without supper, his eyes grew heavy. Finally, his head drooped forward, and after he had dozed for about an hour, the book slipped from his lap and landed with a thump on the rug. Snapping his head up, he awoke abruptly to the horrifying sound of the child struggling to breathe.

"Damn it!" he hissed.

The child's bronchial passages were now badly congested, and she was apparently too weak to cough on her own. Erik shot up out of the chair, threw back the blankets, lifted Christine into his arms, and sat down on the edge of the bed. Bending her face-down over his left arm, he massaged her back and shoulders with his right hand.

"Come, Christine, darling," he coaxed her, "cough for me!"

Her spine stiffened beneath his hand as she inhaled wheezing breaths, but she continued to suffer through a fit of non-productive coughs that left her face flushed and her forehead glistening. Using the side of his hand, Erik gently pummeled her upper back for several minutes, moving his fist down to the middle of her spine and then between her shoulder blades with the same attention. As he increased the pressure, her coughing deepened with a miserable rasp, causing her to arch her back. She began to make gurgling sounds in the back of her throat, and as her lips turned pale, Erik realized that she was choking! Fighting down his panic, he jumped up from the chair, pulled Christine to her feet and shouted, "Christine, breathe…breathe!"

When her eyes suddenly rolled back, he braced her firmly against his body, and wrapping his arms around her waist, he clasped his hands together just above her naval. Holding his breath and squinting his eyes closed, he squeezed upward with a thrust of his fists against her diaphragm, and immediately Christine's mouth opened wide with a gasping breath. She retched and moaned, coughing up thick green, infected sputum, which Erik then caught in his handkerchief and examined for signs of blood. Thankful that at least she did not have pneumonia, he balled up the handkerchief and dropped it onto the table. He then stooped down and tucked his hands under her knees, scooping her up into his arms.

"Good girl!" he sighed in relief. "Now, let's get some more of that infection out of you."

As Erik carried her over to the bed and sat down on the edge of the mattress, Christine continued to cough up more of the infection.

The coughing had persisted throughout the night, leaving Christine drenched in sweat…but finally, just before dawn, the gypsy oils relaxed her airways and she began to breathe more easily. She lay, exhausted, in Erik's arms, sleeping heavily under the influence of the remedy. Leaning his back against the wall, Erik cradled her head against his chest, gently stroking her damp face as he pulled the matted hair away from her eyes. He hummed softly and bent his head over her, gazing down on her face as her eyelids fluttered in sleep.

He soon dozed off with Christine in his arms, but he never lost awareness of her presence and awoke periodically to listen to her breathing. It struck him that this might be the last time he would have close contact with another person, for he knew that the mirror must never be breeched again. His world and hers might as well have been separated by a thousand mirrors; and as the morning dawned from Christine's rose colored window, Erik resigned himself to retreat back to the underground lake where he belonged. His only connection to this child must remain exclusively through music.

Madame Giry opened the door as Erik was preparing to dislodge Christine from his arms. Bearing a blank expression, she drew a handkerchief to her lips and took in Christine's improved appearance, watching as the child slept in Erik's arms.

Raising his chin, Erik acknowledged Louise with a nod, his voice threaded with exhaustion as he said, "I believe the child is out of danger…at least for now."

"Thank heavens!" Louise exclaimed, her lower eyelids rimming with tears. "Thank God in heaven, Erik." she repeated with a smile.

Gently disengaging his arms from beneath Christine's body while supporting her head with his hand, Erik settled her down in the bed and stretched to his feet. She moaned softly, then rolled over onto her side as Madame Giry seated herself on the edge of the bed. At a loss for words, Louise was stunned by the turn of events. Through an ordinary mirror, this man had emerged from his underground world and now, after all these years in hiding, he had taken on flesh; and she scarcely knew how to deal with him. She watched as he stood awkwardly with his hands in his pockets. He was completely out of his element, having previously shed his customary formal coat and cloak. His dress shirt was wrinkled and his dark wig sat slightly askew on his head. Louise felt that she should turn away as he adjusted the mask, but her eyes remained riveted on him as he gathered up his clothing and draped the cloak across his arm.

"She is still a very sick girl, Madame," Erik warned, brushing straw off the cloak with the back of his hand. "She must be given my remedy three times a day. She must take plenty of fluids, and you must watch for the return of the fever. If she worsens, Madame Giry, I trust that you will inform me immediately."

As Erik slowly moved toward the mirror, Louise straightened her back and lifted her eyes, clasping a handkerchief in her hand.

With a grave expression hardening her features, she stood to her feet, crossed her arms over her chest and addressed him coldly, "It would seem, my friend, that you have your own methods of watching over the child."

Pausing at the mirror with his back to her, Erik said nothing as a muscle twitched in his jaw.

"Erik," she pressed him, "we had an agreement that she was never to see you!"

He could hear a small measure of respect in Louise's tone of voice, but there was little friendliness. He decided that he was too tired for a confrontation and shrugged his shoulders. Clearing his throat, he kept his gaze straight ahead on the mirror and replied, "Ah...yes...we had an agreement."

"Yes, we certainly did!" Louise shot back, her chin held high as she added, "A lady expects a gentleman's eye contact when she speaks to him. Now, tell me about this trick mirror...is it merely another example of your wasted genius?"

Amused by her persistence, but insulted by her accusation, Erik slowly rotated his body around to face her, with one corner of his mouth turning upward in a smirk as he leveled his gaze to hers.

"You may choose to believe me or not, Madame, but I assure you...I did not devise this mechanism, for had I done so, it would function properly! he rebuffed. Continuing his defense, he took a step toward the bed and went on, "I have never used the mirror up until this evening...and only because Christine fell ill. I will hereafter, secure the damn thing against future entries!"

Considering his explanation, Louise scrutinized Erik's expression and decided that he was speaking the truth. Nodding her head, she resigned herself to discuss the matter later, as Erik was obviously exhausted. She softened her voice and dropped her arms to her sides, having decided to give him the benefit of the doubt.

"See that you never use that mirror again...except for emergencies," Madame spoke firmly.

With a nod of his head, Erik turned to go, but stopped short when Louise added under her breath, "Erik, thank you. I believe you saved her life."

Turning to face her again, he stepped back and swept his arm outward with a gallant bow, then quietly slipped through the mirror.

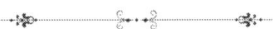

In time, the influenza ran its course, The Paris Opera Company returned to work with much bravado, and the city again bustled with its usual vitality. Many families, however, had lost loved ones, and that year's outbreak would not soon be forgotten.

Christine had been confined to her bed for several more weeks, and Erik had kept constant vigil over her as Louise and Meg had nursed her back to health. He had made good on his word to Madame Giry and had subsequently secured the mirror's swiveling device against further entry. The two-way properties, however, were kept intact. He continued to work on *Don Juan,* occupying his time until Christine's voice became strong enough to resume her training, and although the lessons had been temporarily suspended, he visited her mirror nearly every night; watching over her, talking with her…and never failing to sing her to sleep.

Chapter 13
Pieces of His Soul—1878

Throughout its illustrious history, The Paris Opera had occasionally grappled with financial adversity, making it necessary for managers and financiers to court wealthy patrons. Patrons were invaluable in their ability to draw influential friends and relatives, not only to view productions on a seasonal basis, but also to encourage generosity from the creme de le'creme of society.

Audience preferences were in constant fluctuation, and the trends in entertainment were known to change almost overnight. As the opera house prepared its third opera of the season, traditional operas that featured love stories and redemptive themes were suddenly no longer in vogue, making way for more dramatic and gritty productions. With the use of live animals, realistic violence, eye-popping spectacle, and political narrative, modern operas had become more relevant to the turbulent times.

The Paris Opera's production of *Romeo and Juliet* had been a complete flop; ticket sales had been dismal and the reviews even worse. In mid-production, the young and beautiful diva, Simonette, had abruptly abandoned the company to be married, which had left the more strident-voiced Carlotta to fill the role of Juliet. Juliet was a role she had been entirely unfit for, and according to the scathing reviews, she had transformed the romantic tragedy into a ridiculous farce!

Complicating the opera's shaky financial standings was Poligny's impending retirement, which would then leave his less savvy partner, Debienne, to sort out the unfolding crisis.

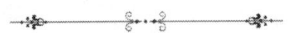

The Opera Ghost had been somewhat inactive since the influenza outbreak of eighteen-seventy-four. No one had any idea why he had suddenly lost interest in the opera's affairs, or why, in four year's time, he had surfaced only occasionally to tease Carlotta and to remind his managers of their financial obligations. Now, however, due to drastic changes in the opera's financial and artistic status, the Opera Ghost had resumed throwing his weight around.

Once again the chorus girls, who loved dashing about the cellars, claimed that they had heard the ghost's laughter, and when it had become clear that he was again asserting his will, gossip and stories began to spread like wildfire.

In a series of messages to the main office, O.G. had renewed his demands, offering friendly suggestions for the day to day management of 'his' theater. Word had spread that the ghost had also resumed his war with La Carlotta, and now each time she would do anything he disliked, the entire house knew about it through her incessant ravings. Naturally, no one had blamed the poor woman, whose nerves were constantly on edge as O.G.'s threats and pranks accelerated. Among his suggestions for operas and casting, O.G. had insisted that Christine Daaé was to be added to the roster of featured chorus girls.

At fifteen years of age, she was younger than most of the applicants, but recent correspondence from O.G. had opined that Christine's talent far outshone a number of the opera's more experienced females. Not wishing to be burdened by more backstage dramas, and having never forgotten the necklace incident, Debienne arranged for Christine to perform a series of grueling auditions and interviews. To his surprise, she had proven that she did indeed possess the talent O.G. had attributed to her; and consequently, that very season Debienne announced the girl as his own personal discovery!

With material for the new season under scrutiny, and mounting debt for the opera currently in production, Debienne had been forced to seek out the patronage of one of the oldest and most distinguished families in France, whose coat of arms dated back to the fourteenth century: the de Chagny's.

Following the death of his father, Count Philibert, Philippe

Georges Marie Comte de Chagny had been given sole custody and control over his father's estate. Moreover, as the eldest son, he had been appointed guardian over his two younger sisters and one younger brother, Raoul, who was twenty years his junior. Philippe was thirty-eight years of age, tall, slender, and rakishly handsome with gray eyes, a pencil mustache and wavy blond hair. He had served in the Royal Navy, was pursued by women, and was therefore envied by other men. Still unattached, Philippe was rarely seen without a beautiful woman on his arm, and the eligible women of Paris considered him quite the catch. He had been frequenting the opera for a number of years, but had only recently become aware of its dire financial status. When approached by Debienne at a local gambling establishment, the Comte had generously offered his influence and money to bolster the opera's economy. He had quickly become The Paris Opera's most extravagant patron, and in time, he had attracted Parisian society's renowned citizenry to the floundering opera house once again.

For his brother's nineteenth birthday, Philippe had made arrangements for Raoul to attend the current production of *Favola d'Orfeo*, an opera based on the Orpheus legend. The Comte Philippe and his brother had attracted much attention as they were escorted to their private box, which afforded them both a fine view of the stage. Philippe preferred the view from box five in the grand tier, but had been informed that box five was on reserve for a foreign dignitary. Philippe thought it quite odd that the occupant of box five always kept the curtain drawn throughout the performance, but that evening, as always, he was more interested in scoping out the theater for beautiful women than he was in watching the opera. As the eldest brother and Raoul's legal guardian, Philippe had taken it upon himself to find the boy a suitable wife, and as the brothers took their seats, the Comte pointed out two young ladies from a good family, hoping to spur his brother's interest in meeting the youngest of the Rousselot sisters.

Philippe had chosen to remain a bachelor, but he fancied his younger brother the sort of man who required the stability of marriage. Philippe had observed that Raoul's shy nature prevented him from courting young women on his own, and in Philippe's opinion, when it came to the opposite sex, the boy needed a bit of encouragement.

Years ago, The Comte de Chagny had discovered that one did not attend the opera to watch the performance; rather, one attended the opera to be seen, and he very much liked to be seen. That evening, as Philippe again chose to ignore the proceedings onstage in favor of peering through his glasses at a certain young lady's plunging neckline, his younger brother Raoul's attention was riveted on a group of young chorus girls who had just appeared on the set. Among them was a tall, slender girl with large brown eyes and an unusually pale complexion. Her waist-length chestnut hair fell across her shoulders in luxuriant curls, and as the stage lights cast a golden glow all around her, Raoul could not take his eyes off the girl. The violet goddess costume she wore complimented her flawless complexion, her graceful white neck, and her slender arms. Her tiny waist was jeweled by a golden belt, and her lips and cheeks were faintly stained the color of roses.

As he continued to observe her through his opera glasses, Raoul began to notice that there was something vaguely familiar about her doll-like features, but he couldn't quite place her. She moved differently from the other young ladies; each gesture slow and deliberate, and there was a shyness about her mannerisms as she found her place next to a group of older girls. Whereas, her more colorful companions seemed to pose and draw attention to themselves, the girl with the chestnut hair fell back behind her fellow cast members, as if trying not to stand out.

Dropping the opera glasses into the empty seat beside him, Raoul thumbed through his program and scanned the list of chorus girls. As his eyes fell on a familiar name, he snapped his head up and said with a sigh, "Well, I'll be…that is Christine Daaé!"

Raising the opera glasses again onto the bridge of his nose, he adjusted the focus for a close-up of her face, leaned forward over the tufted balustrade and exclaimed excitedly, "Philippe…I know that girl!"

With his own opera glasses trained on a particular box seat, Philippe absently commented, "What girl?"

"On the stage!" Raoul replied, his heart pounding. "The

brunette chorus girl…there in the lavender gown."

Tearing his gaze away from the young mademoiselle in box sixteen, Philippe turned his glasses toward the stage and asked his brother, "Where is she, Raoul? Point her out to me."

"There," Raoul repeated, "just there…the one in lavender with that group of girls between the trees."

"Ah…yes, the brunette. She is pretty enough I suppose, if you like your women flat-chested and skinny," Philippe replied dryly.

"It's Christine Daaé," Raoul affirmed. "I knew I'd seen her before!"

"And how on earth did you come to know such a creature?" Philippe inquired.

Raoul continued to view the young woman through his opera glasses, as he spoke with a hint of wistfulness in his voice, "Do you recall five years ago, when father took us to the Villa Perros for the summer?"

"Yes, yes," Philippe answered impatiently, "but what has that got to do with the girl?"

For the past five years, Raoul had thought fondly on those enchanted summer days when, for once in his life, he had been permitted to behave as a normal boy. Count Philibert had kept to his rooms during that holiday, and Raoul's elder sisters, Ceceil and Margurite, had spent most of their holiday visiting a favorite aunt. With Philippe engaged in the family's business affairs at the time, Raoul had been free to wander the beaches and villages on his own.

The young Vicomte had grown up without the company of other children his own age. A succession of nannies, his mother, elder sisters and aunts had coddled and spoiled him, while his father had generally ignored him. The Countess de Chagny had died when he was nine, and Raoul had endured a lonely childhood. He had been given every material possession imaginable, but had never been permitted to enjoy the carefree activities of a normal boyhood.

One early summer day when the tide was out, as he was exploring the half-buried carcass of a beached boat, he had happened upon a gentleman and his young daughter flying a kite. The pretty young girl had run after her father, who had sprinted down the water's edge to increase the kite's lagging altitude.

Raoul had kept his distance, watching the charming pair from a pile of driftwood. Suddenly, the wind shifted, and the kite had come spiraling down out of the air, landing practically at his feet. The young girl and her father had then approached him and introduced themselves.

"Good morning, young man," Gustave smiled broadly. "I am Gustave Daaé and this is my daughter, Christine."

Behaving like the perfect gentleman he had been raised to be, Raoul stood to his feet, bowing gallantly with a sweep of his arm as he greeted the strangers, "Good morning, Monsieur, Mademoiselle. I am le Vicomte Raoul de Chagny."

Christine had hovered close to her father, peering at the boy from behind him with a shy and inquisitive smile.

"Well, young Vicomte...perhaps you would like to give it a try!" Gustave laughed, pointing at the crumpled kite that lay face down in the sand.

"I'm afraid I haven't much experience with these," Raoul answered, a trifle embarrassed.

"What?" Gustave questioned the strange boy. "Never flown a kite? Well, now is the perfect time to do so!"

Before Raoul had been able to answer, Gustave had retrieved the kite from the sand and the three of them had taken off running down the beach. Laughing and out of breath, the boy had removed his shoes and stockings, rolled up his trousers, and let the cool ocean spray splash in his face. By the end of the day he had been shirtless and sunburned...and had never been happier!

Following that extraordinary introduction, Raoul had found himself frequently in the company of Daaé and his daughter. On warm evenings, he had been invited to join them for supper in Madame Valleria's beachfront mansion. On such evenings, following a hearty meal, Daaé would regale the children with Nordic stories, accompanied by his violin and the instruments of other local musicians. Raoul had never seen such an odd assortment of students, intellectuals, and professional musicians; but the days had passed pleasantly as he was introduced to a very different world from the privileged environment in which he had been raised.

Whenever Raoul had been able to escape from his sisters and aunts, he and Christine had read books together, taken walks along the shore, and talked of their deceased mothers. Raoul had enjoyed Christine's feminine company, and soon he began to fancy the girl his sweetheart. When he wanted to tease her, he had called her "Little Lotte"; the name of a character in one of their favorite stories about the Angel of Music. Christine had loved the sad story of the little girl who had captured a songbird in a cage. There had been a favorite song that Christine used to sing in those days, but Raoul couldn't quite recall the verse. She had sung it often in the most angelic voice he'd ever heard, and throughout those summer days, Raoul had found himself increasingly drawn to her.

As nineteen year old Vicomte Raoul de Chagny watched Christine from his brother's box in the opera house, he recalled the windy afternoon when a stiff breeze had blown a red scarf loose from her hair, and out into the incoming turquoise waves. Without even thinking, he jumped fully clothed into the foamy surf and retrieved her scarf, then ran back to shore wet and shivering. He recalled that she had blushed prettily, and had even thanked him with a kiss on his cheek. That summer had flown by too quickly, leaving a fourteen year old boy smarting from his first crush. On their last day together, Raoul had kissed her hand and had confessed breathlessly, "I shall never forget you, Mademoiselle!" Christine and her father had packed up and left Perros in late August, shortly before the de Chagny's had returned to their chateau in the countryside. Raoul had often thought of the girl in the five years that had passed, but had sadly come to the conclusion that a poor musician's daughter could never be the sweetheart of a de Chagny.

Staring through the lens, he was once again enchanted by the musician's daughter. She had matured into a true beauty since that summer in Perros, but even from up in the balconies, he could see that she was still the same sweet girl who had been his first love.

In that moment, with his eyes lingering on her lithe form and feminine features, he was inclined to believe that fate had brought her there, and that he must not squander a chance at renewing their acquaintance. Perhaps her father had won a seat with the orchestra, Raoul mused…and if so, he would have an opportunity to see her as often as he wished. It mattered little to him now that she was not from a wealthy family, and he intended not to let her slip through his fingers again.

Smiling to himself, with his thoughts on the chorus girl, Raoul hardly noticed when Philippe's grating voice interrupted his reverie, "Little Brother, you haven't heard a word I've said, have you?"

"Hummmmm?" Raoul mumbled.

With the opera glasses held firmly to his eyes, he gazed down on Christine in unabashed admiration.

Determined to speak with her, he boldly asked, "Philippe, do you suppose we might congratulate the cast afterward? I would like to invite Miss Daaé to supper with us."

Taken aback by the boy's request, Phillipe replied, "Tonight? I'm sorry, dear Brother…but perhaps another time. La Club Diamonte does not serve minors."

Philippe had hoped a suitable young woman would win his brother's attention this evening, but a teenage chorus girl was certainly not what he had in mind. When his father had been alive, no de Chagny male would have been seen in public fraternizing with chorus girls…but how could Philippe refuse his brother on his birthday? Raoul did seem quite taken with the girl, and it was probably nothing more than infatuation, so what would be the harm of at least making introductions? After a moment or two of conversation with the girl, Raoul would realize that she was unsuitable, then the two brothers and their guests would go along to the cabaret as planned.

"I think an introduction might be arranged…but as for supper with the girl…perhaps next weekend would be better," he suggested, patting his brother on the back.

Like a proud father, Erik had watched Christine's debut performance six nights ago, confident that he was responsible for her blossoming talent. He had leaned over the balustrade from box five, watching as she had tentatively stepped out onto the stage and taken her place beside the older and more experienced singers. Surrounded by the lavishly costumed cast, she had seemed like a gosling among swans, dressed in a drab, ungainly gown. Her hair had been pulled back severely in an unattractive coiffure, and the make-up they had applied made her look washed out under the lamps.

Immediately after that first performance, he had sent word to Louise that no expense was to be spared, and that the girl must be more properly costumed for the remainder of the run. Moreover, he had requested that a single pink rose, tied with a white ribbon, was to be left on her nightstand. The rose was a means of communicating his approval, and from that night on, after each performance a single pink rose had appeared.

On this particular night, Erik lounged lazily in box five, his head pressed against the back cushion and his legs stretched out akimbo, as he fully expected to nap through the opera for the sixth time in one week. His sole purpose for being in the house that night was for the sake of Christine, who seemed to thrive on her Angel's attention and praise.

Yanking the flask from his pocket, he unscrewed the lid in anticipation of yet another uninspired performance of *Favola d'Orfeo*. He sipped from the flask as the orchestra butchered the overture, then pulled a notebook from his waistcoat, planning to amuse himself with a ribald libretto for *Don Juan*. Nonchalantly slitting open the curtain to watch Christine's entrance, he nearly choked on his brandy, and was completely unprepared for the vision that now greeted his eyes. Biting down on his lower lip, he drew in his breath sharply and swore aloud as she came into clear view, "Bloody hell, is that…Christine?"

She stepped out onto the stage dressed in an entirely different costume from the rags they had assigned her on previous nights. No longer dressed in a drab and ill-fitting gown, she now seemed to float across the stage, attired in a lovely violet gown, and for the first time ever, she had worn a corset, giving her the hourglass shape and cleavage of an alluring young woman. Sheer chiffon draped in soft folds across her ivory bosom, and her waist-length hair fell in ringlets around her exposed neck and shoulders.

Golden cuffs jeweled her bare arms, with bobbles dangling from her earlobes and tinkling bells chained about her ankles. The subtle colors of peach and rose enhanced her mouth, cheeks, and dark brown eyes, and she was quite easily the most beautiful girl in the cast.

Erik slowly rose from his seat and stared, open mouthed, at her innocent, yet sensual beauty. He steadied himself against a pillar, his lower stomach churning fiercely as he sighed, "My God…she looks so damn womanly. She has breasts!"

Over the years, he had seen Christine's face smudged with tears, her knees scraped and bandaged, and she frequently wore her hair in two long braids tied with ribbons. He had never thought of her as beautiful, only sweet and pretty in a childish fashion, but there on the stage stood a beautiful young girl with small breasts and soft curves. The child he had known had vanished, and in her place was this alluring young woman.

Over the past five years, with more patience and tenderness than he had thought himself capable of, Erik had been developing Christine's voice; elevating her from a child with a naturally pretty voice to a young girl whose voice had become a thing of stunning power, control, and beauty. Under his instruction she had mastered demanding arias, her range and tonality surpassing that of many adult sopranos.

His personal funds had provided her clothing, books, costumes, and occasional gifts. Moreover, he had paid her tuition for the conservatory, and with the assistance of Madame Giry, he had overseen every aspect of her education. Christine had become almost like a daughter to him, and their strange companionship had become the delight of his life. The perpetual gloom of the underground had lifted like a fog, and he now awoke each day in anticipation of hearing again the sound of her voice. There was always something to look forward to, and he felt that he had finally found something of more value than his music. He had been less angry in recent months, less prone to dark spells and outbursts; and he had even become more productive, as he now slept better and had been eating regular meals.

For the past five years, night after night, Erik had been tutoring Christine through the mirror. After her lesson, the two of them would frequently talk as she expressed her thoughts and shared her secrets. Whenever she was confused or sad, she had always confided in her Angel, trusting him with her innermost concerns...but the changes from child to young woman had been slow and subtle, with Erik barely noticing as Christine had transformed into a glowing adolescent. To him, she had remained an innocent, pure, and vulnerable child...a child who needed him. He had effused himself into her through his music, and she now possessed pieces of his soul.

In his eyes, Christine would always be a child, for he had never contemplated her growing up and leaving the opera house. She had matured before his eyes, but he had refused to recognize the inevitable metamorphosis. As long as she remained a child in his eyes, they would be together and he could influence her...he could love her.

"Damn," he swore under his breath. "She's not a little girl anymore."

In that moment, as he watched Christine on the stage, seen through his inexperienced and naive' perspective, she had seemed to grow up overnight, and he was struggling to grasp the significance of this transformation. Confused by a whirlwind of conflicting emotions, he sank down into his seat behind the curtain, aware that something had shifted.

Suddenly, he felt compelled to leave the theater and retire to his room where he could think without all the distractions. *Don Juan* would allow his mind to sink into the warm oblivion of music and brandy...but he had promised Christine that he would be waiting for her after the performance.

"What now?" he muttered into his hands.

He was ghastly tired and curiously agitated, but she would be waiting and it would be wrong to disappoint her.

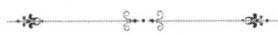

Before the curtain call had ended, while the audience was still applauding, Erik rose up from his chair, flung his cloak over his shoulders and pulled the hood up over his head. With his face completely concealed in the dark hood, he cautiously slipped out of box five, wound his way down the deserted staircase, and dashed toward the corridor behind the stage.

Repeating what had become a ritual, he opened the chamber to the backside of Christine's mirror…only to discover that her room was empty!

A pink rose lay on the nightstand, as it had following the past six performances, but Christine was not there. Supposing she had been delayed and would arrive at any moment, Erik sat down on his stool and reached in his pocket for the flask. He took a few sips and found himself wondering exactly how many times over the last five years he had ventured up to the mirror chamber.

"Perhaps I should have counted," he remarked dryly, taking another sip of brandy.

He tapped his foot while flipping open his pocket watch, growing impatient with Christine's tardiness. It was unlike the girl to keep him waiting, and he could not imagine how she could be so inconsiderate. He stood up and ground his teeth, then stepped out into the corridor and took a few more swigs from the flask. He waited, pacing back and forth for a quarter of an hour, but the girl did not show.

The backstage was swarming with noise and activity as I squeezed through the crowds and into the dressing room quadrant. La Carlotta and the other principals were being showered with flowers and praise, but I was simply fleeing from their admirers to change out of my costume! It had been my first performance wearing a corset and I couldn't wait to get the thing off of me!

Throughout the three-act opera, I had barely been able to breathe! I knew that my Angel would be cross with me, because I simply had not been able to catch my breath. The miserable garment had made it impossible to produce any sort of decent sound, and my range had been cut by a whole octave. Somehow I had managed to stand behind the other girls, and had prayed that no one in the audience would hear me squawking out the notes.

It was an odd sensation wearing the corset for the first time; with the awareness that I had crossed over the threshold of childhood into womanhood. In a matter of months I had gone from a child in braids to a young lady in fancy underclothes and lip rouge! Madame Giry had warned that the corset would take some getting used to, but she had insisted my figure would be greatly enhanced by the whale bone stays. She had not, however, warned me that it would hamper my ability to sing!

It had also been my first performance wearing noticeable make-up, and my reflection in the mirror had pleased me. I fancied the way it had lit up my face and accentuated my dark features, which I thought so plain when compared to the beautiful Meg. But half way through the second act, when drawing out the final Fortissimo, I had nearly fainted...and by the second curtain call, the corset had become sheer torture!

Tugging at my costume, I raced for the dressing room, through the throngs of admirers and well-wishers, but stopped when I heard someone shouting my name, "Mademoiselle Daaé, ah...pardon me, Miss Daaé!"

I looked around, but there were so many people that at first I did not see who was addressing me.

"Miss Daaé!" another shout pierced the commotion. "Mademoiselle Christine!"

I turned to see a handsome gentleman in his late thirties, attired in expensive looking formalwear; with a pearl-gray top hat, a black opera cloak, and white gloves. He had a broad toothy smile, a thin blond mustache, and his gray eyes flashed coldly in the dimly lit hall.

"Miss Daaé, a pleasure to make your acquaintance!" the gentleman spoke with a bow. "We simply had to come backstage and congratulate the cast on this evening's splendid performance!"

I was not unaccustomed to patrons visiting the backstage after a performance, but this gentleman had been quite forward, and I found myself uneasy in his company. However, as a handsome young man stepped out from the crowd, I forgot all about the older fellow. I could not believe my eyes! It was Raoul de Chagny, from the summer of five years ago at Perros! Though he was much taller and had lost all of his boyish awkwardness, I would have known him anywhere! He was not quite as tall as his brother, but ever so much more handsome. His crystal blue eyes were set evenly in a strong forehead, his features fine and symmetrical. He wore no hat over his chin-length brown hair, which fell in soft waves over his right brow and around his shirt collar. His smile was warm, his lips perfectly formed, and his chiseled chin and jaw were clean-shaven. He smiled down at me with a gracious bow and I nearly lost my breath as he addressed me.

"Mademoiselle Daaé," he spoke shyly, "What a happy coincidence, finding you here after all these years!"

He was astonishingly sophisticated; dressed in his evening tailcoat, ivory brocade vest and white ascot. Although five years had passed since that summer by the sea, I could still picture him as a boy, with his trousers rolled up to his knees, wading through the waves and chasing after my scarf. What a dear boy he had been, and now he stood before me; a handsome young man in every way. I could tell that I was blushing furiously, my cheeks felt like flames and I couldn't think of a thing to say! Surprised and happy to see him, I found myself at a loss for words, and simply flung myself into his arms as if we were both still childhood friends.

"Oh, Raoul! I cried, "My dear...dear Raoul!"

He returned my embrace warmly, and from his expression I could see that he was very happy to see me as well.

"Christine, this is my brother, le Comte Philippe," he said jovially. "Philippe, this is Mademoiselle Christine Daaé, daughter of the Swedish violinist, Gustave Daaé.''

"Oh? I'm afraid I've never heard of him," answered the Comte.

I curtsied and smiled, but knew instantly that I did not like Raoul's older brother, who then reached out and drew my hand to his lips with a kiss. There was something unnerving about him, yet I was so entranced by Raoul that I managed a polite reply despite my reticence.

"Pleased to make your acquaintance, Comte," I demurred.

"Ah...Miss Daaé, my brother has told me all about you," Philippe began. "We are celebrating his nineteenth birthday with a night at the opera, and how fortunate that he recognized you in the company! How is it, may I ask, Miss Daaé, that you came to be a chorus girl?"

"Yes, Christine," Raoul continued the inquiry, "is your father with the orchestra this season?"

At the mention of my father, I averted his eyes and realized that Raoul knew nothing of Father's death. I did not wish to discuss my personal affairs in front of his older brother, so I answered quietly, "My father died five years ago, Raoul. I've been living and studying in the opera's dormitory ever since."

A look of compassion came over Raoul's face, and frown lines creased his aristocratic forehead as he gazed sincerely into my eyes.

"Christine, I...I am so sorry for your loss...your father was a great man," he spoke genuinely.

At that moment, a young gentleman accompanied by two fashionably dressed women diverted Philippe's attention, leaving Raoul and me to gawk at each other. I still had no idea what to say to him and began to feel foolish as I stood there wringing my hands. Finally, after several moments, he reached out and took my hand, and his touch sent a tingle up my arm. I found myself giddy and breathless in his company, suddenly incapable of thinking clearly or forming a complete sentence!

The expression in his eyes was intense as his hand gently enveloped my own, and although I had seen many attractive young men, I could not take my eyes off of Raoul's handsome features. His looks were unusual, in some ways even beautiful; with a nose that was neither too large nor too small, and startling blue eyes. There was a soft romantic glow all about him as I opened my mouth to speak, "Raoul, I want..."

I was just about to wish him a happy birthday, but Philippe returned with his elegant companions and cut me off.

"Miss Daaé, I'm afraid we have supper reservations elsewhere. Pleasure meeting you though," he added with a stiff bow.

A noisy group of people emerged with much hollering and laughter, and I saw Raoul's mouth moving in some kind of reply, but I couldn't hear him. Knowing that my Angel would be cross with me for abusing my voice, I shouted over the commotion, "Raoul, it was lovely seeing you again!"

But it was no use. Philippe placed his hand on Raoul's arm and urged him down the hall as the dressing rooms spilled over with guests and revelers. Devastated, I stood watching him being pulled away from me; however, to my joy, just before he was swallowed up in the throng of partygoers, Raoul stopped and called back to me, "Christine! I'm sorry! I'll call for you soon!"

Nodding my head with a smile, I wondered when or if I would ever see him again, and for some moments I stood there, foolishly wishing he would come back. The evening's earlier elation slowly turned to disappointment as I navigated through the crowd and retreated to my dressing room.

"I have better things to do than wait for an ungrateful child!" Erik spat, deciding to leave the mirror chamber, and on his way to being drunk.

After all he had done for her; all the times he had trudged up there in the darkness for her lessons…and this was how she repaid him? Did she have no regard for him? Did she not value the time set aside for her each day without fail? Had he not made sacrifices on her behalf? But perhaps now that she was a young lady, and no longer a child, she had become typically selfish, as most women were!

"Damnation!" he swore.

Grinding his teeth, Erik jabbed a hand through his wig and turned back to snarl at the mirror. However, just as he was about to slam the chamber door closed, Christine finally arrived, walked into her room and sat down on the bed. She had changed out of her costume and into her dressing gown, and had braided her hair for bed. Skulking back to the mirror, Erik was relieved to see her, but he was also angry at her thoughtlessness.

Except for the mysterious expression on her freshly scrubbed face, she looked again like the sweet little girl he had known for the past five years. His initial thought was to scold her soundly, but instead he observed her, fascinated as she sat there, quietly staring down at her hands. Had she not realized the time? She didn't seem anxious or aware of his presence, nor did she move or speak. Surely she had expected him to be there, as he had promised he would...but she seemed oddly distracted.

Suddenly, she raised her eyes and flicked her gaze all around the room until they widened on the clock. Drawing her hands to her face with a gasp, she jumped up from the bed and hurried to the bureau to light her white prayer candle. Moving quickly back to the bed, she lifted the pink rose from the nightstand, held the bud briefly to her nose, then began to twirl the stem nervously between her fingers.

"Angel?" she whispered timidly, tiptoeing toward the mirror, her brows drawn together.

Erik waited, puzzled over what it was that struck him as different about her. Even without the corset, make-up and gown, the girl seemed changed. He decided not to answer her right away, curious to see what she might do next. After a few torturous minutes of his own silence, her lips quivered faintly and she cried out, "Angel, are you here?"

Christine stepped closer and again looked over her shoulder at the clock.

"Angel, please forgive me. I am so sorry that I am..."

"Late!" he completed her sentence, his voice gruff with alcohol.

At the sound of his gravelly voice, Christine looked startled...even a little afraid. He had not intended to speak so harshly, but he was still angry that she had apparently forgotten him. Backing away from the mirror, she lowered her head and stared at her feet, clasping the rose in her hands.

"I apologize for being late, Angel...but please do not be cross with me. I shan't be tardy again, I promise."

He watched as her lower lip trembled faintly, finding it odd that he had even thought to take notice of her lips. Well, of course, the girl had lips...but up until that moment, he had never taken note of their exquisite shape. Her eyes, too, seemed to draw his attention as never before, and he was beginning to regret the harsh tone he had used to greet her...for she was clearly repentant.

Calming his tempers, Erik tried to smile and softened his voice as he spoke up, "Yes, you are late, child. Perhaps you would like to tell your Angel what delayed you?"

Christine nervously raked her bare toes over the carpet, chewing absently on her bottom lip.

"Well, I, ah…I ran into an old childhood friend, and we started talking," she stammered, "and the dressing room was so crowded with guests…and, well, I'm afraid I completely lost track of the time."

"A childhood friend?" Erik replied with interest, relaxing a little. "That's nice, Christine. Tell me about her."

"My friend is a boy, Angel. The boy I told you about who fished my scarf out of the ocean."

Erik vaguely remembered the story, and sat down on the stool as his mood began to improve.

"A boy, is it?" he asked, stroking his chin. "Then, my dear, tell me all about the boy."

Christine smiled in a dramatic fashion that Erik had never seen before. Her eyes were alight and her cheeks flushed, and as if standing in a spotlight, she was suddenly glowing.

"Oh, Angel, his name is Raoul, and he's the most handsome boy I have ever seen!" she enthused, sweeping her arms out to the side. "And he's so kind, and well-mannered and sweet!"

"Handsome? Hmmm…how old is he, my dear?" Erik asked, leaning forward on the stool, slightly agitated.

"Raoul is nineteen, Angel. He is celebrating his birthday tonight."

"Nineteen?" Erik repeated after her, thinking to himself that nineteen was hardly a boy.

"What did the two of you talk about? Old times, I suppose?" Erik tried to make small talk.

"Yes, a little, but we didn't have much time. Raoul was with his older brother, le Comte Philippe, who was anxious to dine with their guests," Christine answered.

"Then, do you fancy him, Christine?" Erik asked, not at all certain he wanted to know the answer.

Christine fiddled with her rose, staring down at the floor with an enigmatic smile. Her long lashes and eyelids concealed her thoughts as she tilted her head to the side and answered shyly, "Yes, Angel...I suppose I do fancy him. I mean, I always have but...well...it's different now. What I mean is, I fancy him in a different way than I did when we were children...if that makes sense," she added with a giggle.

All at once, Erik found himself inexplicably angry, both with Christine and with the boy.

Lashing out at her, he spoke with a harshness he had not intended, "Well, I am not at all pleased by your lack discipline, Christine...therefore, from now on you will refrain from loitering backstage after performances. The drafty hallways endanger your voice, and you must not abuse your vocal chords by chatting incessantly after a night on the stage! I shall now require you to immediately change out of your costume and return directly to your room...is that understood?"

Christine looked confused and hurt; her eyes beginning to water as Erik deliberately increased the volume and sharpness of his voice.

"You will learn, my dear, that you must make sacrifices for your art. Music must always come first! Your voice must be the priority and not your social life! Now, have I made myself clear?" he barked.

In all their time together over the years, he had never spoken in such a harsh manner, and Christine began to cry, her eyes darkening with hurt as her shoulders sagged. He watched as great tears trailed down her cheeks, imprinting shiny streaks on her ivory skin. Her nose reddened and her lips quivered as she raised her head and looked straight into the mirror.

"Angel," she whimpered, "I am sorry I've made you angry; please forgive me!"

Erik had never felt so miserable as he did at that moment, seeing her in tears because of his boorish outburst. He could not comprehend his dark mood, or why he had verbally battered the girl for such a small offense. His need to protect her had obviously gotten the better of him, and he regretted his shrill tone.

Drawing in a deep breath, he smoothed back his hair and placed one hand on the mirror, leaning forward against the glass. She seemed so close to him on the other side, and he found himself gazing into her large brown eyes; now as sad as they had been when he had first seen her through the mirror all those years ago.

"My dear girl," he soothed in his gentle, hypnotic voice, "'Tis I who must apologize to you. Forgive me for raising my voice...but I must be obeyed. Your father entrusted you to my care and appointed me guardian over your gift. I am wise and I know what is best...so do you promise to trust me, my dear, and to do as I ask?"

Christine averted her eyes from the mirror and gazed down at the rose in her hand. With her brown eyes downcast, she spoke so softly that Erik had to press his ear against the glass to hear.

"Yes, Angel," she sighed, "I know that you are very wise and kind, and I will do as you say. I promise, I shall not disappoint you again," she said, crossing her heart.

In that moment, he yearned to reach through the mirror and wipe away her tears, to hold her in his arms as he had done when she was fevered with influenza. She was a strange and delicate creature, whose sensibilities were easily wounded. He had seen this girl cry on many occasions, but for the first time it was he who had been the cause of those tears...and he felt like a beast.

Wishing only to protect her, Erik had convinced himself that, as her Angel, he must watch over and guide her. However, tonight he was a little drunk, and he realized now that he should have left his flask at home! Taking a step back from the mirror, Erik squared his shoulders and raised his chin, confident in her promise.

Chapter 14
Falling Angel

My Angel had forbidden me to linger backstage after performances, but I sometimes caught a glimpse of Raoul and his brother Philippe watching the opera from box twenty-one. On occasion, I thought I saw Raoul looking down at me through his opera glasses, but resigned myself that it had only been my imagination. He was in my thoughts nearly every day, and I could not forget the exquisite feeling of his hand touching mine, or the intense look in his eyes that night in the hallway. My thoughts were in a jumble as I fantasized about Raoul, imagining us together as sweethearts. It was difficult to focus on my dance classes and vocal training, and despite my Angel's orders, I secretly prayed that somehow fate would bring Raoul and me together.

I was tempted to disobey my Angel and wait backstage should Raoul come looking for me again, but after the disappointment I had caused my Angel months ago, I could not bring myself to break my promise. Even when impatient with my clumsy vocal exercises, he never berated me. He had inspired my voice, showing me nothing but kindness. The beautiful pink rose of his approval had never failed to appear magically on my nightstand, and each time I saw the rose following a performance, I envisioned him in his true form; with resplendent white wings and golden hair.

I would picture him setting the rose on my nightstand, and then suddenly disappearing in a flash of glory! How dear those roses had become to me; the petals of each one having been pressed between the pages of my bible, then collected in a crystal bowl beside my bed. The faintest scent of dried roses was a constant reminder of his devotion, and I could not bear the thought of angering him as I had done on the night of Raoul's birthday. My Angel's voice was a remarkable instrument, capable of great beauty and tenderness; but when it was raw with anger, it had the power to inflict me with shame.

Weeks following my wretched tardiness, I began to feel a change in my Angel's affection toward me. I had adhered to his strict guidelines and had worked hard to please him, but his voice and manner had taken on a chilly aloofness. He always arrived for my lessons as scheduled, but we rarely chatted afterward, and I sensed that he no longer wished to spend time with me...that he was only continuing my lessons out of obligation, and not because he enjoyed them. He was very quiet, and even when singing me to sleep each night, his voice was somehow distant. I cannot express the despair I felt at his withdrawal. A light had blazed into my life with my Angel's appearance, but that light was beginning to fade as we drifted further apart. Whenever I questioned him about his coolness toward me, he responded with a sigh, continuing the lesson half-heartedly. If I tried to speak of my affection for Raoul, or tried in any way to share my secret longings, he seemed indifferent, perhaps even annoyed; therefore I no longer confided in him.

With October's arrival, the falling leaves measured a succession of increasingly gloomy days, and dreariness seeped into my soul as I found myself again grieving for my father. Madame and Meg had recognized my malaise, and went about plotting to take my mind off my troubles; whisking me away for walks in my favorite park, or for shopping trips and luncheons.

In an effort to cheer me up, one Sunday afternoon we journeyed in the carriage for a picnic in the park. It had been chilly that morning, but the afternoon air was still pleasant enough for an outing. The opera house had become strangely claustrophobic, and I was grateful for a respite from its dusty oppression.

I had chosen to wear my dark blue woolen dress with matching jacket, my burgundy hooded cloak, a pair of kid gloves, and my button up boots. My hair was pulled back loosely in a ribbon, but stubborn curls had already sprung free and were fluttering about my face in the breeze from the window. Madame had prepared a basket of sandwiches, fruit, and a round loaf of fresh cheese, and as the three of us arrived at the park, I puzzled over my Angel's remoteness, keeping my thoughts to myself.

Flaming autumn trees reflected red and gold on the leaf-strewn pond, and only a few swans and ducks now skimmed through the drifting debris. The blue of the sky had taken on a metallic hue as clouds of lavender and pewter loomed overhead. We spread a blanket across the cool grass and opened our bottle of wine, hoping it wouldn't rain. Meg sat across from me as Madame divided the meal between us, and as always, Meg was cheerful as she chattered between bites.

Sitting beneath the canopy of brilliant fall colors, I wondered what it was about me that I could never seem to grasp happiness for more than a few isolated moments. With each wafting of circumstance, I often felt bent and twisted by forces outside myself; fearing what the future might bring. Would I never learn to be content with life as it was, I asked myself...and why couldn't I be more like Meg, who had a natural aptitude for joy? As long as she was loved by her mother and was surrounded by the opera's eccentric world of ballet and theater, nothing seemed to bother her.

I envied Meg's closeness to her mother. The two were always together, Madame a faithful support and a steady shoulder for Meg's troubles. I wondered how different my life would have been had my mother survived. Would she have been to me what Madame was to Meg? Would she have patiently answered my questions and helped me sort out the mysteries of growing up?

"Christine, really, you must try one of these sandwiches...they are delicious!" Meg spoke between enthusiastic bites, munching her sandwich as if it were the most delicious meal in the world.

"No, thank you, I'm not very hungry," I answered.

Madame cocked an eyebrow as she sipped her wine, shifting her attention back to me.

"I've noticed, my dear, that you haven't been eating much at all. If something is troubling you, Christine, it might help to talk about it," she advised, dabbing the corner of her mouth with a napkin.

I desperately longed to talk about my affection for Raoul and about my Angel's strange behavior, and I feared that if I did not confide in someone soon, I might die from loneliness.

"It is difficult to explain, Madame," I began haltingly, "but I'll try."

Above us, a few autumn leaves released from tree branches, fluttering down onto our blanket, and I was amazed by how easily the words came, once I let myself express what had been bottled up inside.

"Madame, I am ashamed to say that I have angered my…that is to say, my teacher, and he has not yet forgiven my thoughtlessness. He treats me so coldly, and I shall simply die if he will not forgive me. In many ways he has been fatherly towards me, but now he pushes me away and I miss how it used to be between us. I care for him so…and I just don't know how to make things right."

Looking directly into my eyes, Madame silently regarded me, sipped her wine and said, "Perhaps your teacher is unaware of how much you are hurting, my dear. Have you told him so?"

"Each time I try, he changes the subject," I answered.

I selected a few colorful leaves which had fallen on the blanket. Thinking that they would be beautiful dried and pressed on a card for Monsieur E, I placed them gently in the pocket of my cloak as Madame went on.

"I suspect it is merely a misunderstanding. You must be patient with him, Christine. I doubt very much that your teacher would deliberately hurt you. Try to make him understand…make him listen."

"I will try, Madame," I answered, but wondered to myself how a girl like me could make an angel listen to anything.

As our afternoon drew on, the sun emerged from behind the clouds and the threat of rain gave way to warm golden rays. I felt more at ease as we talked; with Madame and Meg attentive as I told them about Raoul, and about how he had held my hand, and how handsome he was.

Madame smiled as I described Raoul's beautiful face, and when I blushed, she teased, "Christine, my dear, I do believe you fancy him."

We lunched and chatted for what seemed like hours, with me feeling much relieved as my soul unbound itself in the crisp autumn air. Meg gossiped and giggled about boys she had found attractive, and Madame described how handsome and charming Meg's father had been when she had first met him. We laughed and talked well into the afternoon, watching as the sun pooled golden between the trees.

When the temperature chilled and shadows lengthened, we packed up our picnic basket and folded the blanket, deciding to walk once more around the park before taking the carriage back to the opera house. With the setting of the sun, I donned my cloak and pulled the hood loosely up over my hair. On our way around the path, I talked about that spring day when we had come to feed the squirrels, and of how I had mistaken the little swan hatchling for a baby duck. We had a laugh, as our cheeks turned rosy in the crisp autumn air.

Rounding the final curve of our walk to the carriage, I noticed two couples strolling through the trees in our direction and nearly fainted when I recognized Raoul and his brother, accompanied by two exquisitely dressed young women. Mortified, I tried to think of an escape, but there was no avoiding an awkward encounter. Without thinking, I pushed back my hood, hoping he would recognize me, and yet terrified that he might not want to see me. My practical clothes and unkempt hair could not possibly compare with Raoul's strikingly beautiful companion; so consequently, with a thousand butterflies wreaking havoc in my stomach, I sucked in my breath and prepared for humiliation. When they were only yards away from us, I could see from Raoul's expression that he had indeed recognized me, and he let go of his companion's arm the moment our eyes met.

"Miss Daaé, how lovely to see you again," said Philippe with a bow. "Out enjoying the afternoon sun, are we?"

"Mademoiselle Christine," Raoul stammered, his blue eyes brilliant against the burnished hues of autumn. "Wonderful to see you again!"

"Raoul," I replied nervously, "I had hoped to see you again, too!"

Raoul's manner toward me was reserved, but warm, and his apparent shyness only endeared him to me all the more. I introduced him to Meg and Madame Giry, then Philippe

209

introduced their companions, Adele and Camile Rousselot.

Meeting these two young women, I wanted to run and hide behind the nearest tree! Compared to Raoul's companion, who was elegantly attired in a claret ankle length long-coat trimmed with luxurious fur, I looked like a church mouse!

The hat she wore was adorned with stylish brown netting, yards of claret colored ribbon, and perky pheasant feathers. Amber jewels glistened from her neck and earlobes, and she had the most beautiful violet eyes and shimmering flaxen hair, piled and twisted in the latest fashion.

Though her clothing and mannerisms were far more sophisticated than mine, I guessed her to be just two or three years older than I, and obviously from an aristocratic family. She and Philippe's companion were sisters, and to my observant eyes, I saw no indication that Raoul cared much for the pretty girl. He barely looked at her as we all made polite conversation, with his eyes trained only on me. I was aware that the longer he stared at me, the more I could feel the heat radiate on my face and neck.

Our little group conversed casually about the opera, the weather, and the latest gossip, with the two young women adding a comment here and there. Throughout the entire conversation, Raoul seemed disinterested, and as I caught his gaze flicking back and forth in my direction, my knees went weak. When at last we had exhausted every suitable topic, my heart sank as Philippe announced, "It is rather good fortune running into you like this, Miss Daaé. Raoul mentioned yesterday that he hoped to have the opportunity to say goodbye before we left."

"Goodbye?" I questioned, raising my eyes to Raoul's.

"Yes," Philippe continued, "I am taking him with me to America for an extended holiday. We sail in three days."

Well, I just stood there like a fool, unable to say a word, dumbfounded by Philippe's miserable news.

"America?" Madame Giry said with interest. "If I may ask, where in America are you staying?"

"A fascinating city called New Orleans, Madame...ever heard of it?" Philippe answered, taking a step forward and thrusting out his chin.

"Yes, as a matter of fact my former-husband, Anton, has

lived there on and off for years…although I believe he currently resides in London."

An unreadable expression passed over Philippe's features as his eyes swept up from Madame's bosom to her face, where upon he smiled in a way that made me uneasy. Taking no notice, Madame engaged with Philippe and the two young women in a discussion about New Orleans, and other travels and destinations; while Meg tugged on the back of my cloak and whispered, "Say something, Christine!"

I finally regained my senses, opened my mouth, and asked Raoul directly, "How long will you and your brother be abroad?"

"For eight months or so," he spoke in his shy manner. "We shall return sometime in June."

Wicked tears burnt behind my eyes, but I was not about to let them betray me. Steeling my nerves, I lifted my chin and smiled my prettiest smile as I bravely told him, "I hope you have a lovely time then!" I spoke evenly, trying to disguise my disappointment.

Suddenly, breaking away from his brother and their companions, Raoul stepped very near to me, bending down until we were so close that I could see the gray flecks in his irises.

His nearness sent my heart racing, and I wanted more than anything for him to kiss me. His blue eyes were almost silver in the cool shade of the copper trees, and I found myself lost in his intense gaze. Copper strands glistened in his dark hair, and his complexion bore a healthy golden cast in the sun's setting rays. Perfect white teeth flashed in his beautiful smile, and he reached out and took my gloved hand, squeezing it gently.

"Mademoiselle Christine, with Madame Giry's permission, I should like to call on you when I return," he said quietly.

I wanted to dance…to cry, to sing and to laugh all at once! He *did* care for me! He wanted to see me again…and I felt as if I were floating two feet above the ground as his eyes narrowed on my face. I longed to throw my arms about him as I had done when we were children…but thought better of it, considering the circumstances.

But eight whole months, I thought to myself…*that is an eternity!*

Looking up through my lashes, I allowed my gaze to linger

on his mouth, smiled demurely, and then quickly averted my eyes.

"I would like that very much, Raoul," I answered.

I could barely breathe as he bowed, lifted my gloved hand to his lips and grazed my fingertips with a soft kiss.

"Till then, Little Lotte," he whispered, so that only I heard what he said.

I did not want him to let go of my hand, but the others had ended their conversation, and Philippe indicated that it was time for their supper engagement. Raoul bowed, I curtsied…we all said our goodbyes, and I watched his shadow trail after him as he disappeared down the walk, thinking to myself that it had been a perfectly lovely day!

Years of living in the opera's underground had afforded Erik the opportunity to create clandestine entrances into nearly every hall and room of the great structure. The building had already been riddled with hidden passages and chambers even before his arrival, so he simply took advantage of what had been devised by others, adding more of his own as the need arose. This allowed him to come and go as he pleased with relative freedom of movement; and as he began exercising more control over the opera's affairs, these passages suited his purpose quite well.

Erik waited until Madame Marie had left for the evening, and then crept out of the closet at the very back of the cluttered workshop, where there was an entire wall of cabinetry. Unfolding his long legs, he stretched to his feet and breathed in the aromas of dusty costumes, new fabric, and starch. The goods he'd requested from Madame Giry had been neatly stacked with her usual note of greeting attached, all waiting on a bench for his approval.

With the temperature dropping, he had sent Madame to a few establishments for items he'd ordered, among them a custom winter cloak to replace last season's worn garment. It had been constructed of the finest wool, and he stroked its voluminous length, admiring the meticulous stitching. The lining was an exclusive imported silk, the color of whipped butter and embellished by a damask pattern. Also included in his parcel were three pair of fine wool trousers...all black, and two white dress shirts. There were five architectural volumes wrapped in brown paper, and a bottle of Raynal Armagnac, his favorite brandy.

Erik was a man of exquisite taste who took pleasure in fine clothing and gentlemanly accoutrements. He loved the fragrance of leather-bound books, and the feeling of a fresh linen shirt against his bare skin. He accentuated his uncommon height and lanky physique with dark woolens, cashmere, silks, and brocades; and would sport only items purchased from the most renown Parisian clothiers. Even though he was generally confined to his rooms in the fifth cellar, Erik always took care with his appearance and toilet, often clean-shaven and smelling of hand milled French honey soap.

Collecting his parcels, he set them neatly on a table, sat himself down in a chair near the gas lamp, and opened Madame Giry's letter. His eyes slowly grazed Louise's missive, reading the letter's content with his expressions ranging from amusement, to surprise, to anger, and then finally a look of utter dejection.

After a few minutes in thought, he dropped the letter on the table with a heavy sigh and hung his head down, raking his hand through his dark hair. Standing up and pacing across the floor, he kicked a few stray items out of his path as he swore aloud, "I had no idea! Damn! I've certainly made a mess of things, haven't I!"

He unfolded the letter and re-read Louise's script, immediately deciding what he must do. Scooping up his parcels, he stomped across the floor and placed his new acquisitions in the closet, then slid the back panel closed. He flipped open his pocket watch and checked the time. He realized that Christine would already be asleep, but this could not wait until morning. He must see her tonight and repair the damage he had unknowingly done to the child.

Winding through the dark passages to the corridor behind the dormitory, Erik thought again on Madame Giry's letter:

My Dear Erik,

These are the items you requested, and I trust they meet with your approval. Monsieur Jordon was not pleased by my late arrival, as he had just closed up shop

213

for the evening; but my classes had gone later than expected, so my tardiness could not be avoided

(However, using my charm and feminine wiles, I convinced him to let me collect your order after hours.)

Now, my friend, there is an urgent matter I must bring to your attention. Are you aware that Christine has been moping about for the last several months? The girl has simply not been herself. She hasn't been eating, and until yesterday had talked to no one about what was troubling her. Finally, with a little coaxing from me, she confided that she fears she has somehow hurt her "Angel", and that you are apparently angry with her. I must say that she is simply devastated, believing that her Angel no longer cares for her. Erik, you must not allow her to languish this way.

If you have done anything to deliberately hurt that child, I shall hold you personally responsible. She is at a delicate age and must be treated with special care. I expect you to do whatever is necessary to convince her of your forgiveness and devotion.

Some advice, my friend...angels do not have tempers!

Yours,
Mme Giry

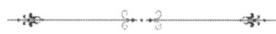

Moments later Erik stood behind the mirror, gazing at Christine's sleeping form in the soft light of the lamp. She lay on her side facing the mirror, her face framed by loose brunette tendrils, and her lashes closed against her ivory cheeks. He had never seen a sight more stirring than this sleeping girl with her soft even breaths, and her hands curled up under her chin.

What had he done to her? In a moment of clarity, he now realized that without intending to, he had indeed pushed Christine away, and he didn't know why he had done it. Her willingness to open her heart to him and to share her private thoughts had once been a joy, but lately he didn't want to know what was on her mind or in her heart. It was all he could do to drag himself up the endless flights of stairs and crawl through the dark passages to her mirror. The effort to see her had become such an irritation that he had even considered breaking off her lessons. Her voice had soared to new heights, its maturing soprano ever more beautiful with each passing month, but as she sounded less like a child and more like a young woman, even her voice had begun to grate against his nerves. Once the girl had spoken of her father, her childhood, and the antics of the opera house; but recently she had turned to topics of romance and of Raoul de Chagny. Erik had grown weary of her romantic musings, and was annoyed...no, sick to death of her girlish prattling about that damn boy. Their conversations now frequently left him surly, and lately after her lessons he had been returning to his lair in a foul temper to begin pounding mercilessly on *Don Juan,* then drinking far too much brandy.

Her company had been making him edgy, resulting in his coolness toward her, and perhaps even unintentional cruelty. To his shame, he saw that now. The more she had reached out for her Angel's affection, the more he had resisted her need for attention and had allowed her to suffer his indifference. He had heard the sadness in her voice but had been oblivious to the fact that *he* had been the cause of it.

Erik was sophisticated in his style and personal taste. He had enriched his years of solitude with detailed study of all the sciences, history, arts, and human behavior. His ability to absorb knowledge in a variety of subjects and interests far exceeded that of the average man, and he was capable of achieving anything his superior mind could conceive. Erik was an accomplished man in his mid-thirties, but experientially, he was as much of an adolescent as Christine; barely out of his boyhood knickers when it came to dealing with a woman's delicate nature. He had only been able to observe females from afar, like creatures under magnifying glass, to be studied and admired, but never understood. He had no experience with these new conflicting emotions, and he was unsure of what it all meant; nor could he understand his body's disturbing physical responses, recently elicited by dreams and thoughts of Christine. He had been struggling to make sense out of a situation that was fast spinning out of control. He did not know his own mind, and was unable to comprehend the changes which had imperceptibly developed within himself as well as Christine.

Why should her school-girl infatuation for a harmless boy bother him? Surely he had considered that at some point the girl would grow up, fall in love with a young man and begin her adult life. *But she is still just a child, and those events are far into the future…or are they?*

"My God," Erik whispered, "she's not a child anymore!"

She was only a year or two away from the age when young women began to marry, have children and make a home for themselves and their family.

"And what then?" Erik sighed, pressing his forehead against the mirror. "If she falls in love and marries, what happens to me?"

What would become of their plans…that is, his plans? What would become of his music, if he did not have her to introduce his work to the world? Backing away from the mirror, Erik stuffed his hands in his pockets and drew a breath through his teeth. He had never thought of Christine as a married woman. His ambition for her was as an artist; a brilliant star with The Paris Opera, who would one day outshine all who had gone before. The dream was within her grasp, her voice and musical artistry developing at a stunning pace. He would compose for her and she would sing his music. She would continue training and living in the opera house, where he could watch over and protect her, and love her for the rest of his life. But what if she chose to marry that boy, or some other young man? What if she abandoned her music and then abandoned him, and what if she chose to leave the opera altogether, or even Paris? How would he live without her?

Christine stirred in the bed and repositioned an arm, her eyelids fluttering in sleep. Raising his head, Erik watched as she appeared to be dreaming, her face as delicate and pretty as a china doll. A wonderful life awaited this girl; a future that Erik was beginning to fear might not include him.

Slowly removing his mask, a startling revelation took shape

in his mind as he mulled over his thoughts.

"And love her for the rest of my life..." he repeated out loud, clutching the mask in his hands.

"Damnation...I do love her!" he muttered.

He could deny it no longer. He loved Christine Daaé, and he could not bear the thought of losing her to Raoul de Chagny, or anyone else, for that matter. She must remain at the opera house! There was no other way. She was happy here. It was her home and his. The Angel of Music must make her understand that the world outside the opera house held nothing for her. Surely she would not leave him for a mere human husband and a life of mediocrity. Surely she would not sacrifice her Angel to become the wife of a sniveling nobleman!

Dropping the mask onto his stool, Erik pressed the palms of his hands on the glass and leaned into the mirror, fogging the smooth surface with his breath. He closed his eyes and began to hum *The Bleeding Rose*, altering his voice until the dark melody seeped through the mirror and into Christine's dreams.

Chapter 15
Passages—August, 1879

On the morning of my seventeenth birthday, I awoke feeling apprehensive and strangely out of synch with the world around me. Madame and Meg had planned a lovely party, complete with entertainment, refreshments, and wine. However, I had no heart for parties and dreaded the dishonesty of acting happy when I felt utterly miserable.

With my darkest childhood nightmares returning, I had not been sleeping well for weeks. These dark dreams had been increasing in frequency, and I found myself fearful of falling asleep, often lying awake for hours as I fought the lull of exhaustion.

My one joy was the time spent with my Angel. After a brief and painful season of distance, we were now closer than ever. Once again he had been permitting me to pour out my heart to him, with all its dramatic shifts and twists. The crystal bowl beside my bed was brimming with rose petals, a fragrant symbol of his pride in my achievements. However, I knew that he alone was responsible for my improvement.

No longer content to hear me perform solo arias, he had chosen beautiful duets for the two of us. We sang together in harmony, and as my voice had matured I was startled by how artfully it blended with my Angel's silvery offering. I could almost feel his joy through the mirror as we sang, but there were still times when a whisper of sadness tainted our sessions, and I could not imagine what could make an angel sad.

He had been teaching me not only the mechanics of using my voice to its full potential; but more importantly, he was teaching me how to find the heart of the song; to convey its passion and sentiment with a dramatic flair. I learned how to become the character I was portraying, reaching beyond myself into the soul of the opera's heroine...and I discovered that I could even make my Angel cry. On at least two occasions, I was certain that I had heard him weeping at the conclusion of our session. I didn't know that angels were capable of tears, but my dear Angel was, which made me revere him even more.

Recently, our heavenly contact had moved beyond the walls of my bedroom, and I often felt his presence throughout the halls and various rooms of the opera. Even when alone in the rehearsal studio, I would sometimes hear the faintest whispering of my name, and oh, how his divine voice speaking my name could drive me to the edge of complete happiness! As I wandered through the dark hallways at night, I would strain to hear him speak my name again and again. I loved knowing that my Angel was not bound by walls or physical restraints; he was omniscient, and could find me anywhere or anytime...and in truth, I needed him more than ever now.

Raoul de Chagny had promised to return in June of my sixteenth year, but eight months had stretched beyond a year, and he and his brother had not returned from America. I had counted the days at first, recording each waking thought of him in my journal; but when the weeks had blurred into months, and then a year had passed without a word, I resigned myself that he might not be coming back at all.

I tortured myself with the thought of Raoul falling in love with someone else, and that perhaps he had even married. I had been trying to forget him, but his dear face would appear in my mind's eye as I secretly fantasized about sharing a life with him.

On the morning of my birthday, I had gone through the motions of getting out of bed and changing into my clothes, but throughout the day I had moped about, doing my chores, catching up on my lessons, and taking lunch with Madame and Meg. By late afternoon, I had retreated to my room to be left alone. As I sat on my bed sulking like a spoiled child, a glance at the clock reminded me that my party was only hours away, and I tried to adjust my attitude by thinking pleasant thoughts. It would be unfair to Madame and Meg if I did not at least try to present a happy face, and after all, according to my Angel I was an actress…but I doubted my ability to fool anyone.

Thankfully, Meg burst through the door with her pretty smile and cheerful voice, immediately putting an end to my tiresome self-pity.

"Christine, aren't you excited?" she beamed. "It's your seventeenth birthday, and my goodness, whatever are you going to wear?"

Meg was two years older than I, but she was also a whole inch shorter and ever so much prettier, in my estimation. While I was all gawky arms and legs, Meg's graceful figure had been sculpted and perfected by the dance. No one could make me forget my troubles like Meg. Her warm smile and pleasant giggle always had the ability to chase away my demons.

"I haven't decided yet, Meg," I replied, dropping my hands into my lap. "I don't feel very festive today, so perhaps I won't dress up at all."

With a pretty little huff, Meg rolled her eyes and chided me playfully, "But, Christine, it's your birthday, silly! Of course you must wear your most beautiful dress!" Leaping across the floor to my wardrobe, she proceeded to empty the hangers of my fanciest gowns, and before we knew it the bed was heaped with petticoats, corsets, and satin skirts. Giggling at her antics, I sat on the edge of the bed and flung a limp wrist to my forehead, a gesture I had seen from Carlotta many times.

"I haven't a thing to wear!" I sighed, feigning the diva.

"Christine Daaé," Meg said in imitation of her mother. "You get up off that bed and put a smile on your face this minute! We have a party to attend!"

To dramatize her command, Meg bent down, took my hands in hers and pulled me to my feet, wrapping me in her arms in the posture of a waltz. As we had done when I first came to live at the opera, we danced across the floor, singing and laughing. She spun me wildly around the room until, at last, we both collapsed on my bed in the mounds of fabric and petticoats. Meg laughed so hard that she slipped off the mattress and landed on the floor with a loud thump, promptly throwing her head back and guffawing in a very unladylike manner!

I clutched my sides, rolled over on my back, then kicked my

legs with fits of giggles until tears ran down my cheeks. Full of mirth, I leapt to my feet, stood up on the bed and tossed garments at Meg until they were strewn across the floor. Our faces were red and our voices raised in merriment, as Meg jumped up on the bed to join me...but we suddenly froze, clamping our mouths shut as Madame Giry burst through the doorway and stared in disbelief at the complete disaster we had made of my room!

"What in heaven's name...? You ladies had better get to the washroom immediately!" Madame scolded, "and when you're finished washing up, you will tidy up this mess!"

"Yes, Madame," we both giggled in concert, as Meg jabbed me in the side with her elbow.

Madame's stern expression softened, and she grinned, surprising us both as she wagged her finger at us playfully and said, "I'm pleased to see that the birthday girl is in fine spirits. Now don't dawdle, you two!"

The minute she closed the door, we burst into hysterics, hugging and laughing until our sides hurt. Finally we lay exhausted on the bed with our thoughts turning again to the party...and dresses, and champagne, and our hair! Gathering up my toiletries and underthings, we toddled out the door, giggling all the way down the hall to the washroom. Half an hour later, we calmly walked back to my room wearing our dressing gowns; with our faces scrubbed and our hair ready to dress for the party. Upon opening the door, I squealed...for there, sitting on my bed, was a large pink and white striped garment box tied in pink satin ribbon! With Meg following, I rushed to the bed, knowing who it was from before I even opened the package. My hands flew up to my face as I grinned at Meg and announced excitedly, "It must be from Monsieur E!"

"Well open it, Christine!" Meg coaxed, pushing me closer to the bed.

Picking up the attached card, I read aloud: "To Christine on her seventeenth birthday. Congratulations, Mademoiselle. May you have a delightful day. Your friend and benefactor, Monsieur E."

"Open the box, Christine!" Meg pestered as I smiled down at the card in my hand.

"All right!" I replied with a wicked grin.

I deliberately took my time lifting the box-top and folding back the many layers of pink tissue. Meg was beside herself with excitement, peeking over my shoulder and urging me to hurry! Slowly, I lifted away the final thin layers of tissue, and what greeted my eyes was a dainty bottle of mimosa cologne, nestled on top of a beautiful pale green dress. The silk dress was embroidered with delicate pink roses all along the pointed edge of the stylish cuirasse bodice, and roses also bordered the hem of the luxurious bustled skirt. The sweetheart neckline was trimmed in ivory lace and cut tastefully to reveal just a little cleavage. Delicate ribbon roses trimmed the ivory sheer puffed sleeves, and tiny ivory rosebud buttons trailed down the pleated bodice front.

"Oh, Christine," Meg sighed, petting the dress with her hand, "it is simply exquisite! Feel how soft it is."

"Yes," I smiled, stroking the green silk with my fingertips, "it is perfect."

"You *are* going to wear it...for the party, I mean!" Meg remarked, with her hands planted on her hips.

"It's perfect, Meg, but how does he always seem to know what pleases me?" I questioned under my breath.

Carefully, I lifted the dress from the box and held it against my body, sashaying across the rug to the mirror and admiring my reflection as Meg stood beside me. The powdery green was lovely with my pale complexion and dark hair, and perfect for the occasion.

"It's simply delicious!" Meg sighed. "You will look like a countess."

Nodding my head, I carefully draped the dress across my arms and laid it on the bed, my thoughts turning introspective as Meg began to scoop the rest of the garments up from the floor, hanging them neatly in the wardrobe.

"You get ready, Christine, and I'll start cleaning up...but then I must be off to make myself presentable," said Meg.

I smiled and replied, "You're such a dear friend, Meg. Whatever would I do without you?"

Grinning wickedly, Meg quipped, "Get into much less trouble, I expect."

I chuckled as I sat down at the cluttered vanity and began to apply my make-up with the various brushes and pots of color displayed across the mirrored tray. Meg and I continued our chatting until the door opened again, and Madame Giry entered the room with her typical half-smile. Taking notice of the dress displayed on my bed, she glided across the floor, and as her tapered fingers trailed across the stitchery, blossoms and leaves, she said, "It would seem, my dear, that Monsieur E. knows your preferences very well."

"Yes, Madame," I agreed. "Monsieur is very generous."

"That he is...that he is, indeed," Madame muttered wistfully, then flicked her eyes up to the clock and reminded us of the time.

"Young ladies, you have precisely one hour and a half to finish getting ready!" Turning to Meg, she added on her way out the door, "Come with me, Meg, and I'll see to your hair."

Following her mother, Meg grinned at me and giggled, "Don't dawdle, Christine!"

With my room back in order and everything quiet again, I pulled the length of my hair loosely to one side, leaving soft ringlets to graze my forehead and ears. Securing a jeweled comb into the side swoop, I hummed to myself and scrutinized my reflection. I pinned a milliner's rose just behind my ear, hopped up from the stool, moved to the full-length mirror, and adjusted the hair pins until I had achieved the desired effect.

I knew that my one remarkable feature was my hair, and it must be perfect. As I combed, prodded and twisted the coiffure into place, gooseflesh rose up on my arms when I heard my name whispered, "Christine..."

As always, the sound of his voice speaking my name left me breathless, and I paused with a smile, pleased by his appearance at my mirror.

"Angel," I whispered back, "today is my birthday!"

"Yes, I know, my dear, happy birthday," he said.

His voice was very soft, and I went back to working on my hair, hoping our conversation would continue.

"Angel," I asked, "will you be at the party...will you see me there?"

He answered sweetly, "I see you everywhere, Christine.

Wherever you go, I am there watching over you."

Standing before the mirror, I tilted my head to the side, eyeing my hair from different angles, then smoothed my hand down the skirt of my dressing gown.

Never satisfied with my appearance, I remarked critically, "I suppose that will have to do."

"You are very beautiful, Christine," he said, his voice barely audible.

Beautiful? I thought to myself. Had I heard him correctly? His words shocked me. Our affection had grown over the years in such a way that we could speak comfortably with each other about nearly everything, yet he had never before said those words to me. The only compliments I had ever received from him were in regards to my voice, and I was stunned that an angel thought me beautiful.

I stared at my reflection, trying to see beauty, but saw, instead, a skinny girl whose breasts were too small and whose eyes were too large. I had only ever thought of myself as 'almost' pretty, and it pleased me to know that he liked the way I looked.

"Do you truly think I'm beautiful?" I asked, needing assurance.

"Yes…very," he replied.

It then occurred to me, for about the hundredth time, that I was speaking to a creature whose face and form I was forbidden to see; for no matter how many times I had asked him…even begged him, my Angel would not permit me to see him. Only an invisible voice was granted to me, and I was suddenly melancholic that he was able to see me, but I would never be given the privilege of seeing him.

"Angel," I pouted, "it is simply not fair!"

"What isn't fair, Christine?" he asked.

"It's not fair that you can see me, but I cannot see you."

He didn't speak, and so I stepped closer to the mirror, staring into the reflection of my own eyes as if they were his.

"Ever since the first year I arrived at the opera house, you have been able to see me whenever you wish…and, well, now I want to see you!" I announced boldly, jutting out my lower lip.

He was silent. I waited, and then…"You may never see me,

Christine, never," he spoke firmly.

Dropping my arms to my sides, and already knowing what his answer would be, I asked stubbornly, "But why not?"

He often fell silent in those awkward moments, and again there was no immediate answer.

Disappointed, I reached over to the vanity for my pink ribbon, and tying it in a soft bow around my neck, I pressed him further, "Will you at least tell me what you look like?"

"What do you imagine I look like?" his reply came without hesitation, the sound of his voice filling the mirror that stood between us.

Ever since that first night when he had introduced himself to me through the mirror, I had visualized the stained glass and statues of angels I had seen in church. Angels were always depicted with luminous white wings, wearing flowing white robes trimmed in royal colors. A halo of light emanated from their holy faces, and golden hair framed their perfect features. I was convinced that my Angel must be far more beautiful than any image painted or sculpted by a man.

"I think you must be the most beautiful angel ever created," I spoke reverently, searching the glass for some evidence of his face.

He did not reply, and as frequently happened between us, a strange intensity permeated the room. Busying myself, I fussed with my hair until he spoke again, "Yes, Christine, it is as you say. I am beautiful and I want you always to think of me that way. You shall never see me, but I have given you my voice…a voice which no other human has heard. My voice is only for you, Christine, and your voice must be only for me."

Twisting a ringlet absently around my finger, I sighed and lowered my head, wishing that I could change his mind.

"Is it enough, Christine?" he asked.

"Is what enough, Angel?" I replied.

"Is it enough that you may hear my voice but never see my face?"

I wondered…what if, despite my begging, he never permitted me to see him? Could I continue, for the rest of my life, speaking to an unseen presence; and yet if he were to show himself one day, would that really change anything between us? We had gone on like this for years, with his voice my only contact. Yes, it was true that I longed to see his face, but if his voice was all I would ever have of him, then it would have to be enough.

"Yes, Angel…I suppose it will be enough…as long as you never leave me," I spoke solemnly. "For I would surely die without the sound of your voice!"

"I shall never leave you, Christine!" he whispered, then added with just a breath, "My dear…I love you."

I stood motionless before the mirror, my mouth gaping open and my cheeks flaming red. He had never spoken such words, and I cannot describe how it felt to hear him say that he loved me. Tears crested in my eyes, and from somewhere inside my belly, I felt a warming sensation.

Blotting my eyes with my handkerchief, I answered, "I love you too, Angel! We shall always be together like this, shan't we?"

"Yes, my dear, as long as you wish it," he assured me.

He sounded different in some way. His phrases were clipped with a certain unevenness of his breath. I could not account for the change in his tone of voice, which became even more mysterious as he resumed our conversation.

"Christine, would you say that our affection for each other has grown from what it once was in the beginning?" he asked.

Bending over the vanity, I selected my pot of lip-rouge, walked over to the mirror and carefully painted a pale rose color on my lips with a fine brush, pursing them together.

"Yes, Angel," I answered, "you are my dearest companion and truest friend."

"And do I make you happy, Christine?" he continued in that unusual voice. "Do you enjoy your lessons and our time together?"

"Oh, Angel, I live for these moments! To talk with you, and to laugh with you! I live for the sound of your voice… and when you sing to me, I want nothing more!"

His voice became more buoyant, with the pitch rising as he spoke again, "I hope I shall always make you happy, Christine, because you have brought more than happiness to…"

Suddenly, the door flew open and I nearly jumped out of my

skin when Meg waltzed into my room, abruptly interrupting my Angel as she swanned through the door, blushing and beautiful in her buttercup yellow party dress.

"Christine," she whispered, wide-eyed, "I thought I heard a man's voice in here!"

Although Meg and I were more like sisters than friends, in all the years of our friendship I had never told her about my Angel. As far as she was concerned, he was just my tutor, the kindly old gentleman I had been taking vocal instruction from for years. I had often considered telling her my secret, but the timing had never seemed quite right.

"Of course you didn't hear a man's voice, silly! It must have been from somewhere down the hall. You know how these old corridors project voices," I said sweetly, hoping to divert her attention. "Meg…you are so beautiful in yellow! Would you please be a dear and help me into my dress?"

"Of course I'm beautiful!" she teased, spreading out her arms with a twirl, "I am a prima ballerina!"

We gathered up my new dress, petticoat, and stockings, and placed them behind the dressing screen where I began to change. Meg helped me into my clothes, fastening the back panels and smoothing out the layers of the dress over my crinoline. I spritzed the mimosa cologne behind my ears and on my wrists, loving the delicate floral fragrance. With everything in place, I rushed out from behind the screen with a swish of silk and a wafting of mimosa, and then tiptoed to the mirror, watching as approval shone in Meg's eyes. Wishing to show off for my Angel, I rose up onto my toes and spun around several times to Meg's applause. Conscious for the first time that I cared about what my Angel thought of my appearance, I was hoping that he was still there and that he would approve of the dress.

Meg stepped up beside me and placed her arm around my waist as we smiled at ourselves in the mirror; she in her vibrant yellow and I in my soft green.

Erik hid in the upper mezzanine, and sat where he could watch the party from behind heavy blue velvet drapery. He had instructed Madame Giry to spare no expense for Christine's birthday gathering and the dining hall had been decorated with bouquets of roses, purchased from the opera's own floral shop. The hall was illuminated by candles, with a spectacular late summer sunset framed by the west wall of windows. Golden light poured in through the paned glass; and Erik relished a rare sight of the gardens outside. The trees and shrubbery were crowned in green, and the sky was ablaze with sunset colors.

Only a few members of the opera company were in attendance so far, but Erik was pleased by the well-wishers who had come to mark the occasion. Mademoiselle Suzanne and Marie were there, along with Jammes, Ginesse, and a few members of the chorus. Joseph Buquet and his wife had come, and two or three stagehands had also arrived with their ladies.

Having brought his own supper along, Erik dined on a pear, a crust of bread, a few slices of cheese, and a rather greasy roasted chicken leg; all of which he had lifted from the kitchen. Licking the grease from his fingers, his mind wandered to an hour ago when he had watched Christine readying herself for the party. He had been pleased by her show of pleasure for his gifts, and had watched as she had adjusted her hair and applied her make-up. It seemed to Erik that each time he saw her she had grown even more beautiful and, anxious to see her in her new dress, he wondered what was keeping them.

Finishing his meal, he wiped his mouth and hands with a napkin and finally, to his relief, Christine, Meg, and Madame Giry all entered the hall to polite applause. With his eyes widening, Erik sat forward in his chair and drug his hand hard across his mouth.

"Damn, look at her!" he whispered, stunned, as always, by her beauty.

The dress was a simple, but elegant, compliment to her willowy figure, with the pale green silk accentuating her dark hair and fine features. Erik was mesmerized by her grace as she seemed to float across the room to greet her guests. The fluid movement of her arms and delicate hands entranced him, and everything about her was soft and alluring. He watched her rose-tinted lips in motion as she spoke to her guests, and her feminine gestures drew his undivided attention.

But as his eyes continued to follow her around the room, Erik was troubled. He had never reacted this way to Christine, not even on that monumental night at the opera when he had first seen her in her grown-up gown and stage make-up. Something dark was stirring within him as his body began to respond with heated discomfort. He allowed his eyes to linger on her soft curves and the creamy white skin of her neck and bosom. His hands were sweating, his pulse raced, and there was a spreading ache in his groin as he moaned her name.

"God help me, I love her," he muttered quietly into the thick drapes. "I know it is morally reprehensible...but I can't help myself!"

In his mind, he had already crossed the bridge between right and wrong, and there was no turning back now. There could be no recapturing the innocent love he had once felt for the child, Christine Daaé, who was now a woman; a desirable, sensual female. Erik had never felt this kind of romantic love before. He had lusted after young women from afar, and had craved sexual pleasure like any man; but what he felt for Christine was more powerful than any infatuation he'd had with a chorus girl or a pretty maid. Erik wanted to touch her skin, to cup her breasts in his hands, and to feel the warmth of her kiss. He had never kissed a woman, and wondered, what would it be like to kiss Christine? How would her lips feel against his? Drawing his fingertip to his mouth, he ran his index finger along the contour of his lower and upper lips and closed his eyes.

He knew from his manuals that lovers used their tongues in deep kissing, and for other sensual pleasures he could only imagine. He had seen drawings and paintings of coital coupling, but what did it actually feel like? Tracing every inch of her with his eyes, he devoured her beauty and engorged his fertile imagination. In his mind's eye, he stripped her of her dress and her corset, picturing her lying naked in his bed, waiting for him. Subconsciously his hand moved to his legs, and pressing the flesh of his inner thighs, his fingers inched closer to his groin.

"This is madness!" he growled. "What in hell am I doing? I'm thirty-eight years old and I have no business thinking about her like this!" he said, yanking his hands away and pounding his fist against a wall. Battling back and forth in his mind, the voice of reason was pitted against his raw sexuality.

"This is a ridiculous game…but I want her! God help me…oh hell, I've got to stop this!" he spat under his breath.

Pulling the flask from his pocket, Erik unscrewed the cap and took a few sips, wiping his mouth with the side of his hand. He stood to his feet and stomped away from the drapes, backing up against the wall with his eyes squeezed shut. For a few seconds he hovered in the darkness of the unlit mezzanine, fighting for control of his body…but Christine's soft laughter echoed up into his ears, and again he found himself drawn hopelessly back to the balustrade. Clinching his fists, he let out a long sigh, crept back to the curtain and parted the drapes.

Christine was arranging morsels of food on a small plate with a serving utensil, and he watched as she placed tiny bites in her mouth with her fingers. Erik smiled as she sat down at the table and was surrounded by a circle of chatting ballet girls and boys. Everything she did excited him, and even watching her in the simple act of eating was a sensual revelation. He observed her interaction with others, studying the play of light and shadow on her delicate bone structure. For over an hour, he spied on Christine and her guests, unable to tear his eyes away as she chatted and dined with her friends and associates.

The double doors to the kitchen swung wide open, and Meg and Madame Giry stepped through the entrance, carrying a large candlelit cake on a silver platter. The pink and white confection was placed on the table in front of Christine, and Erik was captivated by her ethereal beauty in the rosy glow of seventeen candles. Surrounded by the cheers and applause of her guests, Christine blew them out, plucked them from the cake, then licked the residue of icing from her fingers. Erik found himself absently licking his own lips as his mouth began to water.

He watched as Christine began to cut slices of cake, then looked on as Madame Giry stepped behind her, leaned down and whispered something in her ear. Suddenly, a brilliant smile spread across Christine's face, and turning his head, Erik followed her gaze to the dining hall's main entrance, where a handsome, impeccably dressed young man holding a bouquet of extravagant flowers stood in the doorway.

"I apologize for my late arrival!" the young man declared with a bow.

Dropping the knife, Christine jumped up from her chair and swept away from the table with her skirts billowing behind her as she raced toward the door. She flung her arms around the handsome fellow's neck, while Erik watched in confusion and disbelief.

"Oh, Raoul!" she exclaimed, "Where have you been all this time...and however did you find out about the party?"

"So, that's Raoul de Chagny," Erik seethed between clenched teeth, a muscle twitching in his jaw.

"Quite simple, my dear," Madame Giry announced with a conspiratorial grin, "I invited him!"

"But, Raoul," Christine said, "you have been gone for so long. I feared that you might never return!"

Smiling broadly, Raoul made his explanation, "My brother was detained on business in New Orleans. Our ship docked three weeks ago, and I had been recovering from a fever when I received Madame Giry's post."

Shooting up out of his seat from behind the drapes, Erik hardly knew how to respond to the shocking sight of *his* Christine in Raoul de Chagny's embrace. The boy pulled away slightly, only to place his bouquet in her arms, and Erik had never seen her eyes shine as they did when she looked up at the young man's extraordinarily handsome face. *So this is the boy who fished her scarf out of the sea?* At twenty-one years of age and just under six feet tall, the Vicomte possessed an aristocratic bearing, but with none of the usual arrogance that went with the title. He seemed completely taken with Christine, and Erik immediately despised him.

The two were whispering closely while guests mingled in the background, and Erik repositioned himself in an effort to overhear the conversation.

"Damn!" he swore. "What in hell are they prattling on about?"

As Madame Giry and Meg began clearing the table, Christine glided across the floor and whispered something in her guardian's ear. Madame nodded, gave Christine a quick kiss on the cheek, then watched with a smile as the girl grabbed her wrap and rejoined Raoul.

Unseen, Erik slipped out of the dining hall and followed, his heart racing as he pursued the young couple down the long corridor to the theater's backstage.

Christine opened a door, gathered up her skirts, and began climbing the iron staircase that seemed to go on forever. She led Raoul upward, ascending to the highest levels of the opera house. Raoul followed, crouching under the ceiling support timbers, bemused by her ease as she led him through the buttresses, rafters, and joists and into a narrow doorway. He had never seen such a place, nor had he ever been in the company of a young lady who was not afraid to soil her hem or dirty her hands. Watching her negotiate the awkward footing, his eyes lingered on the train of her dress as it flared out behind her. In many ways she was much changed from the little girl he had known seven years ago, and yet she still possessed the otherworldly quality which had drawn him to her that summer in Perros.

They soon arrived at a door which Christine unlatched, and with a push, she opened the door against a blast of incoming fresh air from the opera's expansive rooftop. The evening was pleasantly warm, with just a hint of autumn in the breeze as the horizon was bathed in the receding rays of the sun. A few stars had already appeared in the sky, and a rising moon backlit Apollo's Lyre; the graceful god who offered his golden harp in salute to the makers of music. A vast, rolling carpet of street lights and glowing windows stretched out nineteen stories below, as Christine took Raoul's hand and led him across the roof, where they came to stand beneath the statue.

Having followed Christine up there many times over the years, Erik was already crouched in his hiding place, observing as

Raoul de Chagny brazenly held her hand and gazed into her eyes.

"Christine, the view of Paris from up here is spectacular," Raoul sighed.

"This is where I come when I need to be alone, Raoul," she replied. "I love the lights of the city...and the stars. It's so magical, like being in heaven."

Hardly believing that he was standing with Christine on the rooftop of the opera house, Raoul warned himself that he must be careful with her. Christine was not like other girls, and even though he desired her beyond reason, she must not be overwhelmed by his true intentions.

Mindful of the many times she had retreated to the starry sanctuary of the rooftop, Christine peered through her lashes at Raoul, wondering if she could trust him with her private thoughts. No one but Meg had been privy to her favorite hiding place beneath Apollo's Lyre, but Christine felt calmed by Raoul's serene and reserved manner.

Raoul draped his arm around her and drew her close, his voice soft and steady in her ear. "At last we are alone, Christine. I've wanted to be alone with you from the first night I saw you, on the occasion of my nineteenth birthday," he explained, his fingers clasped around her arm. "Our reunion was much too brief. I scarcely had a moment to speak to you that night...and then in the park last year, well, it was simply impossible. My brother has good intentions, but at times he is misguided."

Christine listened, merely nodding her head as Raoul spoke sincerely, "You see, the young lady was more interested in him than she was in me. I was afraid, Christine, that you might have gotten the wrong impression about myself and Mademoiselle Adele. I assure you, she is just an acquaintance, and I have not seen her since, nor do I intend to." Taking both her hands, Raoul looked directly into Christine's eyes and added, "Christine, you are the only girl who commands the whole of my heart."

Hidden behind the gigantic winged Pegasus, Erik clenched his fists and sucked in his breath, listening in on the hushed conversation.

Raoul furrowed his brow with concern and inquired, "Now, tell me about your father, Christine. I was so sorry to hear of his passing."

She hesitated, looking up briefly at the sky before she answered, "Father died seven years ago in December, Raoul," she whispered. "He had been ill for weeks, and the physicians tried everything to save him. I was at his bedside when he passed, Raoul, and the horror of his death still haunts me to this day."

Closing her eyes, Christine fought back the tears, cleared her throat and resumed, "You can't imagine how difficult it has been to go on without him. At times I still feel that my soul was split in two when he died." Lowering her head, Christine remarked sadly, "Had it not been for Madame Giry, Meg...and my teacher, I would never have recovered."

Raoul pulled her closer, attempting to comfort her, and said, "Christine, I am so sorry. I know how close you and your father were. He was an honorable man who showed me much kindness. You know, I was never happier than when in the company of Maestro Daaé and his daughter...but may I ask, why are you now living here at the opera house?"

As Erik listened, Christine inclined her face toward Raoul and spoke to the Vicomte as if he was her dearest friend. Wedged between the Pegasus and Aphrodite statues, Erik ground his teeth and muttered curses under his breath.

"It was Father's wish that I live in the dormitory and study the arts with Madame Giry," Christine replied. "I have been happy here, but I still miss him, Raoul...and I sometimes wonder if there isn't something wrong with me. There are times when I don't know myself...when I feel as if true happiness always waits beyond my reach."

Christine leaned her forehead into Raoul's shoulder, while he gently stroked the back of her hair. The patterned stars overhead glittered as soft music wafted up to the rooftop from somewhere in the streets below. Imagining that it was he who was holding her, Erik bristled at their physical closeness and the intimate nature of their conversation.

"Christine, my mother died when I was nine," Raoul offered, "and there is still not a day when I don't think of her, so I do understand how you feel. My father?" he huffed coldly, stiffening his spine, "well, the truth is, the man barely acknowledged my existence!"

Raising her head, Christine interjected, "Isn't it strange, Raoul, that both of our parents are gone? I never knew my mother, and you never really knew your father. It's almost as though we were meant to meet that summer day on the beach in Perros."

He gazed down at her with a weak smile, and brushed a curl from her forehead as she went on, "I thought you a strange and sad boy...a boy who had never flown a kite. Was your childhood so unhappy, Raoul? Did your father never show you kindness?"

As Erik thought back on his own miserable childhood, he wanted to slap the Vicomte for his self-indulgent sniveling. The young man hailed from one of the wealthiest families in France. De Chagny had everything; looks, money, prestige...and now it seemed that he would also have Christine...so what the hell was he whining about? The fool had no idea what it meant to suffer! With each passing moment, Erik despised him more, and he was equally angry at Christine for being so easily taken in by the boy's pathetic tale of woe!

"My father was a cold man, Christine, but Mother was the kindest and most gentle woman to all who knew her. Had she not been so generous with her affection for me, I should have died of loneliness."

Lifting her eyes, Christine offered, "I'm sorry, Raoul. But at least you still have your brother and sisters...and I have Madame and Meg who are like family to me now...so neither of us is truly alone, are we?"

Raoul reached out to take hold of Christine's hand, and she accepted, lacing her fingers through his as their conversation was carried away on the evening breeze.

He bent down to sniff her hair and resumed his thoughts, "Yes, we have our own lives now, Christine...and one thing I know for sure is that I want you by my side. I have always known it, Christine, even from that first morning on the beach."

Erik gulped as his eyes started to burn, telling himself that he should have been the one holding her hand, and he wanted to hurt de Chagny for daring to touch her that way.

"I was such an awkward and skinny thing back then, I am surprised you even took a second look at me," Christine laughed.

How easy and comfortable they are with each other, thought Erik. *As if they belonged together.*

Looking out over the city, Raoul confessed, "You were always pretty to me, Christine, even when you made me fetch your scarf from the surf."

Hand in hand, the two peered down over the rooftops as their shared memories resonated between the statues.

"I made you fetch my scarf?" Christine teased. "That isn't how I remember it at all! As I recall, you jumped in after it without a word from me. Father said you were just showing off!"

"Your father was very wise," he chuckled, tugging lightly on her hand. "I had to do something grand to get your attention!"

"Well, you succeeded, Raoul. I couldn't help but laugh when you walked out of the surf dripping wet! Really…it was just a silly scarf," she said, tilting her head sideways with a smile.

"Yes, and I recall, Little Lotte, that you kissed me on the cheek as my reward."

"I was quite brazen for a nine year old, wasn't I?" Christine said with a giggle.

Their voices fell into soft laughter as Erik steeled himself against the knifing pain of their levity. It was clear that Christine's feelings for the boy went beyond infatuation. She cared for him…and the boy obviously thought the world of her.

Who wouldn't? Who wouldn't love her?

Raoul pulled Christine gently around until they stood face to face, and with his heart thumping, he worked up the courage to demonstrate his true affection.

"Perhaps it is time I returned that kiss, Little Lotte," he whispered.

Cradling her head with his hands, Raoul lifted Christine's face to his. Every inch the gentleman, he leaned down, careful not to press his body into hers, then kissed her lightly on the mouth, with their lips touching for only a moment. There was no passion in the kiss, just a chaste and delicate brush of his mouth meeting hers. Christine's eyelids fluttered, and a soft blush bloomed up into her cheeks as her hands lingered on his suit lapels.

Without his awareness, the name "Christine..." had escaped Erik's lips. Crouched behind Pegasus, as he spied on Christine's first kiss, he doubted that, if faced with such an opportunity, he would have been able to resist pressing his body against hers; but the de Chagny boy was just standing there, gazing down at her like a love-sick whelp. Erik would have preferred to see him paw at her, but as it was, the boy's decency made the situation even more intolerable. If de Chagny had been a cad or a clumsy youth, unable to reign in his passions, it would have been easier to hate him...but it appeared that he was, indeed, a handsome and principled young gentleman.

As they broke away from the kiss, Christine took a step backward.

"Raoul, when will I see you again?" she asked, her fingertips barely grazing his chest.

Folding his hands over the top of hers, Raoul replied, "I shall be attending the performance this Saturday. May I take you to supper afterward?"

Christine withdrew her hands and averted his eyes as she said softly, "I'm afraid I can't, Raoul; my teacher won't permit me to socialize after performances. He insists it will tire my voice."

Raoul looked down at her with a puzzled expression and insisted, "I shan't keep you out late, I promise. Now tell me you'll come to supper...I must see you again," he said, capturing her hands and drawing them up to his lips.

"No, Raoul, I can't disappoint him. He is so good to me, and has only my best interests at heart," Christine rebuffed gravely, staring off into the distance as she withdrew her hands once again.

Curious about her comment, Raoul inquired, "Who is this teacher, Christine, and when will I have the pleasure of hearing you sing?"

Separating herself momentarily, Christine walked away from him and stepped closer to the edge of the roof. She pulled the silk wrap more tightly around her shoulders and tilted her head, as if listening to something.

"He is a very great teacher, Raoul, who has a singular knowledge of music. He has been my instructor for seven years now, and he has performed enchantments with my voice. I dare say, I no longer recognize myself when I sing…but he will not permit me to perform in public yet. He tells me that the Paris Opera is unworthy of my voice, and that, until he is ready to reveal my voice to the world, I must commit myself fully to his guidance."

Furrowing his brow, Raoul drew closer and tried to re-establish eye contact.

"What is his name, Christine? Is he connected in some way with the opera?" he questioned.

Christine contemplated revealing her teacher's true identity to Raoul, but if she told him, would he think her mad, she wondered? In Christine's eyes, her Angel was the most natural being; a companion she had grown to love in the void left by her father's death, and with the exception of Madame, she had never told another soul of his existence. Christine feared that to tell Raoul the truth would mean a betrayal of her Angel's most sacred trust, and there were other things about herself…her fears and her dreams, that she had shared with no one but her Angel. Should she now reveal those mysteries to Raoul? Could she trust him to understand her, and to see into her soul as her Angel had done? After a moment of inner deliberation, Christine concluded that the Angel of Music must remain her secret for a while longer.

Observing from the shadows, Erik waited for Christine's answer, ready to destroy any fool who dared to drive a wedge between him and the girl he loved.

Christine removed the wrap from her shoulders and took hold of the fringe. Flipping it loosely before her, she watched as it was caught up in the breeze. A strange expression ignited in her eyes as she spoke wistfully, "When I am in his presence, Raoul, it is like a divine visitation, and in those sublime moments there is no place I would rather be."

Raoul shoved his hands deep inside his pockets and listened, concerned by the intensity of her description of a teacher whose identity she had not disclosed. What could she possibly mean by a divine visitation? Wasn't her teacher just an ordinary voice instructor in spectacles? The sort you might see in any university or concert hall? Even the tone of her voice altered when she spoke of him, and the look in her eyes was disconcerting.

Suddenly replacing the shawl across her shoulders, Christine spun around to face him directly. "I cannot meet with you after the performance, Raoul" she affirmed. "I won't disobey the Maestro!"

Creases reappeared in the Vicomte's forehead as he withdrew a hand from his pocket, raking his fingers through his hair. Before he had a moment to formulate his response, her mood shifted again and she tiptoed closer, saying with a smile and a lilt in her voice, "But there is no performance on Sunday, Raoul. Might we walk in the park after church? I could prepare a picnic for the two of us; that is…if Madame gives her permission."

Shaking off his concerns and encouraged by her invitation, Raoul rejoined Christine and bent down to kiss her forehead, their eyes meeting as she rose up on her toes and kissed his cheek.

Erik exhaled slowly, devastated that she had agreed to see the Vicomte outside her Angel's sphere of influence. His anger simmered as he continued to observe their restrained affections.

"Darling, that would be delightful," Raoul replied. "With Madame's permission, I shall bring the carriage around for you at one o'clock sharp. And don't forget, I will be admiring you from box twenty-one on Saturday night. Will you watch for me, Christine?"

Happily nodding her consent, Christine lifted her eyes to his and smiled. This was more than she had ever hoped for or expected; that Raoul de Chagny would be courting her. Not only was he the most handsome young man she had ever seen, but he was still the same sweet boy she had met by the sea years before; considerate, kind, and ever so well mannered. He made her feel safe, unhurried, and happy, and the wait for Sunday would be unbearable! She would look for him in box twenty-one, all the while wishing to join him for supper afterward, as he had requested; but never again would she disobey her Angel. In any case, she was certain that he would give her permission to meet Raoul on a Sunday afternoon. How could he object to an outing in the park on a day when the opera would be closed?

Nodding her head, Christine answered, "Yes, Raoul. I'll watch for you!"

With a relaxed smile, Raoul took her by the hand and said, "Until Sunday, then, Little Lotte."

Minutes after Christine and Raoul had left the rooftop, Erik crouched down at the statue's base and looking up into the sky, he wished to hell he had never followed them. Each touch and every word spoken between them had inflicted unimaginable pain. For the first time in his life, he was in love, but Christine had inexplicably now fallen in love with someone else. She had poured her heart out to the young man as he, in turn, had poured his heart out to her. Their discovery of each other beneath the stars was more than Erik could bear.

Had Christine been his own daughter, he might have been proud that a young man of de Chagny's status was courting her; but though Erik had at one time felt fatherly affection toward the girl, his intentions for her now were anything but fatherly. Pink infatuation had turned a dark shade of red, and she was all he thought about day and night; all he dreamed of and everything he wanted. He had been painting portraits of her; images of her face and figure to worship and to decorate his home. He had painted her happy, sad, and pensive, with every expression and pose. There were portraits of Christine dressed in satin gowns, with her hair falling around her shoulders, elegant and refined, and he had also sketched her naked, reclining and sensual.

"Christine..." he spoke her name aloud, then chuckled darkly. "She thinks I'm a bloody angel! I'm sick of being her damned angel. I want to be flesh and blood to her! I want to be her lover!"

Recalling their past few years together, he threw his head back and laughed aloud at the absurdity of it all. Had he really entertained the insane notion that there might be something more than affection between himself and Christine? Had he been foolish enough to believe that he could somehow woo her from behind the mirror? Even if she were not in love with the Vicomte, how did he expect to romance her when, in Christine's eyes, the angel was an answer to her prayers; a celestial being who watched over her and who had been training her voice? The irony was not at all lost on him as he contemplated their ridiculous relationship. He had been her Angel of Music for seven years and had deliberately conditioned her into believing his masquerade. It was his own fault that she now saw him as an 'angel' and not as a man with male desires. How had he expected to transition the girl from worshiping the Angel of Music, into loving Erik the man...the man who lived beneath the opera house in a tomb...the man who hid his disfigured face behind a mask...the man who would never be able to offer her a normal life?

Closing his eyes, Erik slowly rose up from his crouched position, trying to convince himself that he did have something of value to offer her. He could give her something of far more value than all of de Chagny's charm and wealth; something the Raoul de Chagnys of the world would never comprehend. He could give her his music!

Music was the great passion he shared with Christine Daaé, the unbreakable chain which had been born of something far deeper than infatuation. Theirs was a music not manufactured by written notes, manmade instruments or a voice; but a music which transcended all human effort. Erik's music now lived and breathed inside Christine. No man would ever know the secrets he had accessed through that music, and it was only a matter of time before the music of her body would be his as well. She was his and his alone, and he was prepared to go to any lengths to possess her!

Leaning against the Apollo's Lyre, he pressed the unmasked side of his face against its cold bronze as he groaned darkly, "Poor Christine, if she only knew that Erik is no goddamned angel!"

Suddenly he cackled out loud, conscious that he had never felt less divine than at that moment. As potent images of Christine's face and form shot fire through his loins, he found himself more closely in tune with the wailing of demons than with the music of angels. Graphic images of violence directed themselves at Raoul de Chagny, and Erik felt constricted and trapped...bound by his passions. He couldn't stomach the thought of descending into his subterranean prison, with its stone walls and suffocating darkness. He needed air and open sky above him… yet even on that rooftop he could feel invisible bars closing around him. He couldn't breathe! He craved a freedom he would never know, and his agitated state of mind recalled his confinement in the gypsy camps.

As he paced across the roof's expanse, Erik muttered under his breath and repeatedly raked his hand through his hair. He threw off his cloak like the unfurling of wings, then pulled off his evening coat and vest, he unbuttoned his dress shirt and watched as it fluttered on the wind, then stopped down to remove his shoes and stockings. Finally, he stood up straight, unfastened his trousers and shorts, pulling them down over his hips, buttocks, and legs. Silhouetted by the ocher moon, Erik's lanky physique was overshadowed by the gigantic statue of Apollo's Lyre, whose perfectly sculpted figure was a mockery of Erik's own distorted features. He reached up to his face and tore off the mask and threw it down spitefully at the statue's feet. Flipping open the opera cloak, he spread it over the roof's surface, and as he laid down on the heavy wool, he felt out of place and time, like a foreigner in his own skin. The summer breeze lightly brushed across his naked body, but he couldn't relax, his arms and legs twitching as he tried to get comfortable.

There were no clothes constricting him now, no dark chambers encompassing him, and no stone vaults pressing down on top of him…but the weight of his sexual desire crushed him as he whispered her name…"Christine."

He moaned in the back of his throat and pressed his hand between his legs, but there would be no release for him tonight. He could not escape the pain of wanting her, nor could he get the image of her, wrapped in de Chagny's arms, out of his mind. Covering the deformed side of his face with his right hand, Erik turned over onto his side, but found no rest beneath Apollo's Lyre.

Chapter 16
Entrances and Exits

Philippe de Chagny stared blankly out the French doors of his executive suite, chewing his cigar and blowing blue columns of smoke up to the ceiling. His apartment in the Hotel de L'Monte showcased a pleasant view of the city, but the view had been immaterial in choosing that particular location. More importantly, this apartment afforded privacy and much needed refuge from his monotonous and demanding duties as the Comte de Chagny.

Following his father's death, Philippe had soon found his obligations to the de Chagny estate a tiresome affair, interfering greatly with his personal interests and the life of leisure he had cultivated after completing his service in the Royal Navy. Out of family duty, he made all the required public appearances, and hired accountants and assistants to manage the estate's finances; maintaining his public image while quietly pursuing his private recreation. With a bit of creative accounting, he had secured a rather large sum for his own private use; however, the guardianship of his younger brother was a role he took quite seriously, and he would make no compromises where Raoul's future was concerned.

The twenty year age difference between Philippe and his brother had established him as a father figure, and from the beginning Philippe had assumed the responsibility of looking out for his much younger sibling. Raoul was a gentle person, who some might have even thought of as weak, and whose transition into manhood had been arrested by the death of his mother and a rather poor attempt at fathering by the elderly Comte. The old man had had no use for a boy whom he believed was tied to his mother's apron strings, and although Philippe was in agreement that perhaps the woman had coddled Raoul, she had merely overcompensated for her son's absentee father. The old Comte had merely tolerated the boy, if he had paid any attention to him at all. Philippe had frequently spoken to the old man on his brother's behalf, only to be told that his little brother would amount to nothing and wasn't worth the effort. Raoul had starved for his father's approval but he had never won it. The old man had died without having said a word of reconciliation, and thus Raoul drew closer to Philippe after their father's death.

As he sucked on his cigar, Philippe considered Raoul's new crush on the Daaé girl. From their first meeting, he had not bought into the girl's innocent act, and was convinced that she had designs on becoming the Vicomte's wife for his money and position. Philippe was aware that his brother's good looks and status attracted many eligible females, and he had seen with his own eyes how Raoul affected nearly every girl he came in contact with. Why, they gazed at him moon-eyed and love-struck; and add to this his wealth and family crest, and there was not a more desirable young bachelor in all of Paris!

Philippe was concerned about the events which had transpired over the past weeks, and had been weighing his options, trying to decided what action, if any, might be taken in order to put an end to Raoul's infatuation with the chorus girl. Thanks to the meddling of Madame Giry, the two had been nearly inseparable since Raoul's return from America. Philippe had hoped that the trip to America might have taken Raoul's attentions away from the girl; but throughout their stay in New Orleans, Raoul had spoken incessantly of her. The attractive young ladies Philippe had introduced him to had made no impact on the boy's obsession with Miss Daaé.

Since their return to Paris, Raoul had attended every performance at the opera house, meeting with Mademoiselle Daaé on numerous occasions, which had led Philippe to suspect that his feelings for the girl were genuine. Well, Philippe simply could not allow this to continue. He had discussed the matter with Raoul, hoping to convince him of his folly; but the discussion had unfortunately turned into a row, with both brothers raising their voices at each other. Raoul had stomped angrily out of Philippe's office, threatening to surrender his share of the de Chagny fortune for the sake of Miss Daaé's hand in marriage.

"Not if I have anything to say about it!" Philippe purred through a puff of cigar smoke.

Philippe knew enough about the girl's unorthodox upbringing to suspect that there might be information that could help his cause; information that could possibly bring about his brother's change of heart...information easily obtained for the right price. The deed would require someone on the inside with access to the opera house, and specifically to Madame Giry's apartments.

Suspecting that there were skeletons moldering in the Daaé family closet, Philippe was convinced that the woman had some sort of history with the girl, and more importantly, with her father who, by all accounts was no more than an itinerate fiddler. As a man of the world acquainted with the wiles of women, Philippe had sensed that Madame Louise Giry was hiding nasty skeletons in her own closet...and he intended to unearth them.

Clenching his teeth around his cigar, Philippe took a long drag before grinding the glowing ash into dust. Strutting across the plush carpet to the divan, he sank down into the cushions, pleased that he now had a plan of action where his brother was concerned. He did not intend to see the young man disgraced and penniless with a houseful of screaming brats and a peculiar chorus girl for a wife!

There was one gentleman Philippe thought might be just the man for the job. He had been with the opera for years and was well respected by the company; but Joseph Buquet had a darker side, as most men did in Philippe's estimation. Now it was simply a matter of sending a post to arrange a meeting.

By early September, the opera had begun preparations for the winter production of *Faust* by Charles-François Gounod. Based on the morality tale penned by Johann Wolfgang von Goethe, *Faust* was a highly demanding opera with a classic story-line about an old philosopher who sells his soul to the devil in exchange for his youth and the beautiful maiden, Marguerite.

The set design was a progressive concept using abstract form, misshapen buildings, primitive scaffolding and a drab, monochromatic color scheme. Some thought it was sheer genius, while others argued that the design was a monstrosity, bobbing their heads and commenting snidely behind the scenes. Despite typical backstage gossip and fears of box office failure, sales for *Faust* were coming along briskly, and many attributed the healthy revenue to Philippe de Chagny, whose patronage was clearly paying off.

Amid the chaos of mounting a new production, to the shock of some cast members and the relief of others, Monsieur Debienne had announced his imminent retirement. The new owners, Armand Moncharmin and Firmin Richard, were set to take the reins officially a few days prior to the grand gala opening. This news had thrown the entire opera house into even more gossip and speculation, as it was rumored that Debienne's wife had discovered another of his liaisons, thus his hasty departure abroad.

Had Debienne's sudden retirement and indiscretions not been enough to keep tongues wagging, after the cast list had been posted in late September, a number of strange incidents had occurred in rapid succession, starting fresh tales about the notorious Opera Ghost. A day never went by when he was not discussed, with some tearful chorus girl insisting that she had heard his maniacal laughter from the opera's lower cellar.

During rehearsal one morning, a canvas fly had mysteriously detached from its pipe and cables, plunging to the stage and narrowly missing Carlotta, who had been warming up for Marguerite's aria in act three. From up in the catwalks, Joseph Buquet had insisted that he had nothing to do with the near tragedy, and in her typical flurry of lace and feathers, Carlotta had stormed out of the theater, demanding that Debienne relieve Buquet of his post.

For his part, Joseph had seen dark shadows frequently lurking about in the catwalks; a flash of black and white leaping from the flies and then disappearing behind the backdrops. On several occasions Buquet had attempted to follow the shadow, but to no avail. The shadow was obscenely nimble and had ably pulled itself up the cables, climbing to stunning heights at an astonishing pace. Buquet had always prided himself on his own physical prowess, but a stout man in his late forties was no match for the shadow, who seemed to have sprouted wings!

The ballet girls had continued to whisper of ghostly shapes in the basement, strange bursts of cold air, doors and cupboards closing of their own accord, and of disembodied voices in the corridors. The apparition had now begun to show himself almost daily, and as his legend grew he was given the name the Phantom of the Opera. Madame Marie, the costume mistress, had been reporting mischief concerning Carlotta's costumes, and Carlotta had received several letters…each one increasingly threatening in tone, all written by the Phantom.

The letters warned of certain disaster if the woman insisted on playing the role of Marguerite, and she was also apprised that the Phantom had chosen a replacement! In her pride, Carlotta thought little of the threats, knowing full well that there was no one else in the company who could take her place, and the diva had said so openly and loudly to anyone who would listen!

One particularly gloomy evening, halfway through his session with La Carlotta, Maestro Reyer had excused himself and rushed off to his offices in search of his score, which had suddenly come up missing. Carlotta had remained behind to work on her aria, "Ah, je ris de me voir", *The Jewel Song*. Alone in the deserted theater with her eyes closed and her arm waving out before her, she sang a capella:

> *Ah, I laugh at my reflection,*
> *So beautiful in this mirror!*
> *Is it you, Marguerite, is it you…?*

Convinced that she was, indeed, the embodiment of the beautiful Marguerite, a role that would win her glowing notices, Carlotta rhapsodized in the sound of her own voice:

> *Answer me, answer me,*
> *Is it you, Marguerite, is it your beautiful face?*

Imagining a mirror in her hand, Carlotta gestured and preened, smiling at her make-believe reflection like Narcissus;

envisioning herself onstage, glittering with jewels as all the audience admired and cheered her. She imagined Marguerite's diamonds dangling from her earlobes and throat, sparkling against her perfect peach flesh and the green velvet of her gown. She pictured herself dipping her hands in the dainty treasure chest, pulling out strands of pearls and chains of emeralds. What a lovely scene it would be, with the spotlight shining down on her red hair and the diamond tiara. Brava…brrrrava! she chanted in her thoughts, caught up in her reverie. When a breath of air brushed the back of her neck, presuming it to be Reyer, Carlotta turned to look at the seat behind, but there was no one there! Muttering to herself in Italian, she supposed that it had merely been a draft in the miserable old building, and continuing to sing, she ignored her misgivings, simply in love with her perfect pitch and heavenly tone. However, after thirty minutes or so, when Reyer had failed to return, the woman began to wonder what was keeping him. She had already sung the piece through several times, and was impatient to hear herself accompanied by the piano. The Maestro could be rather annoying at times, she thought, huffing to herself as she squirmed in the chair out of irritation, but the orchestra would provide a splendid backdrop for her vocal expertise.

As she drummed her nails on the seat armrest, Carlotta huffed again, rose up from the chair and noisily made her way up onto the apron. Her heels clicked loudly as she waddled to center stage, her bustle fanning out like tail-feathers from her backside. Thrusting out her chin and bosom while striking a pose with the imagined mirror, Carlotta launched again into *The Jewel Song*, forcing her voice up into the rafters until the notes vibrated in her eardrums and forehead. With her mouth wide open, vocally reaching for the top of her Bell Canto range, she tossed her head back and raised her arms out before her. An unearthly warble then emitted from her throat, which in Carlotta's own estimation was the most beautiful sound she had ever heard!

Brrrrrava! she trilled in her mind, closing her eyes as her own magnificent voice reverberated all around her…but suddenly, her eyes snapped open and the hair on the back of her neck bristled as from somewhere overhead, strange laughter peeled down into the theater!

"A-ha-haaaaa-ha-ha-ha!!" it echoed coldly.

"Who is there?" she whispered in her thick Italian accent.

Craning her neck, she narrowed her eyes and searched the darkened catwalks, shrugging her fur wrap more tightly around her shoulders.

"Is someone there?" she repeated. Crossing the stage, the heels of her shoes clacked loudly on the hardwoods as she called out, "If that is you, Monsieur Reyer, this is not amusing!"

The silence that followed her outburst tweaked her nerves, and she began to see things in the dark that weren't really there…and other things that were. For many years, the theater had been her preferred domain, but it had suddenly taken on a grim and murky mise-en-scène. Rows of theater seats and the grand tier began to close in around her and statues appeared sinister in the shadows; as if reaching out to ensnare her. Carlotta began to fear a maleficent presence in the hall, as gilt faces seemed to mock her from the theater's Proscenium Arch. Scolding herself for her foolishness, she chuckled nervously and grimaced, clenching her fingers around the mink wrap. She told herself that there was nothing amiss in the theater, that the noise had been an old pipe settling, and began to vocalize again, but suddenly, the gas lamps flickered on and off!

Letting out a shriek, she froze in place on the stage, furious that someone would dare to toy with her. For a moment, she wondered if it was perhaps the old maestro, but she doubted that he would stoop to such juvenile behavior. In Carlotta's eyes, Monsieur Reyer was a foolish old man, to be sure, but not one to play tricks on others. Growing angrier by the moment, Carlotta decided that there was only one man who would taunt her for sport: The Opera Ghost. Long suspecting that Debienne himself had been masquerading as O.G, she was determined that this time she would confront him and thereby uncover his true identity. Who else would be capable of appearing in any room, in any corridor, at any time of day or night? Who else had access to the entire opera complex, and who of the management did she distrust more than him? The two had been at odds frequently over the years, and Carlotta was not stupid. She had known from her very first day with the opera that Debienne despised her; and although to her face he was reasonably polite, he spoke rudely behind her back and had his eye on the Daaé girl as her replacement.

"Ha! Over my dead body!" the woman fumed, "That little toad shall never replace La Carlotta!"

Convinced that Debienne was the ghost, Carlotta slammed her heel down on the stage. He was clearly expecting her to run from the theater, perhaps never to return…but the woman decided to accept his challenge and draw him out!

She straightened her shoulders, and bobbing her head, she shouted, "I dare you to show yourself, Monsieur!"

"Ha-ha-haaaaaaaa!" another ghastly cackle echoed down from the ceiling.

Despite herself, Carlotta felt a cold chill slither down her spine. Thrusting out her chin, she tripped over her halting dialect as she shrieked back at the voice, "You are no ghost, Monsieur Debienne! You are nothing but a coward who enjoys frightening women and children…but you do not frighten me!"

When there was no response, Carlotta raised her voice furiously, "You will never get away with this, Debienne! I shall never leave this opera house, and I shall report your crimes to the inspector!"

"Over my dead body," answered a sardonic, buttery male voice.

Staggering backward, Carlotta drew her hand to her throat and gulped, caught off guard by a voice that sounded nothing like Debienne. This voice was colder than ice and as smooth as silk, and now she was truly frightened. What if her suspicions were mistaken? What if the person masquerading as O.G. was actually someone dangerous; someone who might wish her bodily harm? Up until that moment, she had never heard him speak. His threats and pranks had been delivered in the form of letters, and he had always struck when there were others in the vicinity…but this time she was alone.

As Carlotta considered the distinct possibility that she may have underestimated the Opera Ghost, she heard a great flapping from the copper and blue domed ceiling. Squinting up into the darkness, she gasped aloud as the unlit chandelier began to sway of its own accord, its chains and crystals clinking eerily above her head. Forgetting her brash pronouncement, in a panic the woman gathered up the hem of her skirts and began clacking her heels noisily across the stage to the nearest exit. However, at the precise moment when she reached for the doorknob, Reyer opened the door from the other side, wearing a startled expression as he nearly collided with her! While Reyer scrambled to keep his coffee from spilling, almost fainting at the sight of him Carlotta lashed out in her fiery Italian tongue, "Where have you been, Monsieur? How dare you keep me waiting!"

"My apologies, Signora," Reyer flustered. "I simply cannot locate my score, I…that is, well, I could have sworn…"

"My time is precious, Maestro!" the diva interrupted. "You insult me with your excuses. We are fee-neesh for tonight! You will order my carriage now! I go home!"

Coffee in hand, Reyer gawked in bewilderment as La Carlotta sashayed out the door.

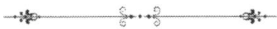

The next afternoon in the perfumed privacy of her dressing room, Carlotta gazed into the mirror as her maids and assistants styled an auburn hairpiece into elaborate twists and braids. She was dressed in a plum colored dressing gown trimmed with pink lace and feathers, her ample cleavage dusted with rice powder, and a heart-shaped beauty mark painted on the swell of her left bosom. Her black eyebrows arched over heavily lined eyelids, and her lips were stained crimson. She was not an overly attractive woman, and the liberal application of make-up did not flatter her large nose or plank-shaped cheeks. She stood admiring her reflection, with her assistants attending to her every whim as she snapped orders.

The diva had been spooked by the events of the previous evening, and pampering from her entourage soothed her frazzled nerves. No longer certain who was responsible for all those ghastly pranks, her intention was to remain locked in her dressing room where she could have an hour to herself before rehearsal.

Carlotta had grown more uneasy throughout the day, jumping at every sound and unexpected movement. Fearful of hearing that voice again, she had refused to be alone in the theater and had insisted that her maid accompany her wherever she went throughout the complex.

As she applied another dusting of powder to her forehead, someone knocked on the door, and Carlotta barked rudely at her maid, "Send them away! I will see no one until rehearsal!"

Tucking a strand of hair behind her ear, Carlotta listened to muffled voices in the hall, presuming a delivery boy had come with flowers, or perhaps a box of chocolates from Piangi, who was wont to spoil her. After no more than a minute, the door closed and with a faint hint of amusement in her eyes, the maid curtsied, then proffered her mistress a sealed envelope. Staring aghast at the all too familiar red seal, Carlotta shrieked and jerked her hand away from the note as if bitten by a serpent, commanding her maid to read the message aloud. Breaking the seal, the young maid folded back the parchment and read the contents:

> *My dear Signora La Carlotta,*
>
> *Your continued disregard for my person may prove hazardous to your health. Be forewarned, my dear; you shall not sing Marguerite. Someone more worthy awaits in the wings. I advise you not to stay late at the theater tonight.*
>
> *Your obedient servant,*
> *O.G.*

As if her powdered face were not already white enough, Carlotta blanched and snatched the letter from her maid's fingers, her mouth twisting in anger. "Who delivered this?" she demanded, her nostrils flaring and her painted eyebrows knit so closely together that they formed one continuous dark slash across her forehead.

"The page," her maid answered, averting her mistress's flashing eyes.

"And did he not say who sent him?" Carlotta fumed, drawing her lips back in a sneer.

"No, Signora, he said only, 'for Signora,'" the maid replied calmly.

Carlotta crumbled the letter in her hand, then spun around and addressed her attendants one by one, "Ha! I am surrounded by imbeciles! No one sees nothing! No one hears nothing! Are you all blind and deaf? Someone must know something!"

Flashing her angry eyes from face to face, Carlotta bore down on her attendants, who merely shook their heads and denied knowledge of their mistress' tormentor.

"I see!" she seethed. "Well, it ends now...and if I discover that any of you hide information about this O.G, you shall find yourselves on the street!"

Clustered together in their group, all the attendants nodded and bobbed their heads mutely as Carlotta gathered up her skirts, whirled around, and stormed from her dressing room, muttering in Italian all the way down the hall.

Carlotta barged into Monsieur Debienne's office unannounced to find him engaged in a meeting. He leaned across his desk, examining what looked like ledgers and legal documents, while two flamboyant men occupied the luxurious leather divan. One was a stout man in his forties with a broad face, multiple chins, and an obviously dyed mustache that completely hid his mouth. His beady eyes were set in a sloping forehead, and dyed black hair fell about his shoulders in waves. He wore a brown tailcoat with burgundy satin lapels, burgundy trousers, and a black satin cravat tied in a large bow. His partner was a tall, slender man in his fifties who sported a shock of curly red hair on his head and a pointed red beard on his rat-like face. Wide lamb chop sideburns dominated his angular cheeks, making his narrow nose look even longer.

On any other occasion, Carlotta might have been intrigued by the presence of such gentlemen, but that afternoon she had little interest in Debienne's business affairs and was determined to have his undivided attention. If he was not the notorious O.G, then it was about time he found out O.G.'s true identity! With no regard for the strangers, she tore across the carpet toward Debienne.

Tossing back her head and thrusting out her chest, her arms flailed wildly as she waved the crinkled missive in Debienne's face and shrieked, "I demand to know who is responsible for this!"

Debienne ignored the woman's tempers with a dismissive wave toward his guests.

"Ah, Signora, you are just in time to interrupt my meeting with the opera's new managers. Allow me to introduce Monsieur Armand Moncharmin and Monsieur Firmin Richard." Speaking jovially, he then turned with a bow and addressed his guests, "Gentlemen, I present to you the opera's star soprano, Signora La Carlotta Giunicelli."

Vaguely amused by Debienne's awkward announcement, Carlotta quickly recovered and fluttered her eyelashes at the strangers.

"Ah-ha!" she said as she waved the note, "Then perhaps you two will put a stop to this conniving ghost...or Phantom...or whoever the hell he is, before I walk out for good!"

The two gentlemen rose to greet the opera's diva, bowing and gesturing lavishly as they gushed, "Ah, Signora Carlotta! At last we meet the grand diva who fills the theater with her admirers!"

Never one to deny a gentleman's compliment, Carlotta curtsied and preened like some ghastly bird, while the new owners continued to pet and grovel. Then suddenly, remembering her original purpose for bursting into the office, she threw the crumbled letter down onto Debienne's desk and stomped her foot on the hardwoods.

"Another threat like this from your friend, the Phantom, Monsieur, and I walk out that door for good!"

Turning on her heel, Carlotta left the two new owners staring, with their mouths hanging open as she stormed out the door.

"What is that woman going on about, Debienne?" asked Firmin, pulling furiously at the point of his beard.

"Yes, what's all this about a ghost or a Phantom?" Armand questioned. "Is the woman having, er...vapors?"

Wishing to avoid the question all together, Debbienne handed Armand a leather ledger and a box of letters tied together with string. The man received the items, looked down at the labels and dates and remarked, "But about this ghost, Debienne...is this a joke?"

Lifting his chin, Debienne glanced nervously at the door and laughed, "Yes it is precisely that, gentlemen! A little opera house humor, if you will."

"Ah, yes...very well then, we don't mind a good joke now and then, do we, Armand?" agreed Firmin, slapping Debienne on the back with a chuckle. "For a minute there, I thought she was serious!" he laughed.

Joining in the laughter, Debienne guided his guests back toward the desk, resumed his business manner, then reached into his vest pocket and retrieved a key. He unlocked a drawer, pulled out a stack of books and placed them on the cluttered desk.

"Look over this memorandum, gentlemen," he entreated. "These are the financial records and my daily log from the past eight years of my tenure as manager. Everything you need to know about The Paris Opera House and its history is within these pages."

Clearing his throat, Debienne glanced again at the doorway, and added, "As for the letters, they are quite self-explanatory. I'm sure you'll manage. Now if you gentlemen will excuse me, certain matters require my immediate attention. Please feel free to use my office for as long as you wish."

With that, Debienne hoped that he had bought himself more time!

Chapter 17
Immortal Lover

Once Erik had confessed his love for Christine, she had begun to utterly consume him. His sexual desire for her had driven him back to the *Don Juan* opera, and when he wasn't instructing her or watching her from somewhere in the opera house, he had surrendered again to his true master; giving *Don Juan* full possession of his body and mind. During these sessions, he would play the seduction scene over and over; imagining Christine in the role of Anelinda and himself as *Don Juan*. The organ would blare as he visualized tearing the bodice from her shoulders, then smearing her neck and breasts with kisses.

Those sessions had tortured him, the music exacting a greater price each time he had played through the score, and as his jealousy of Raoul de Chagny had escalated to dangerous levels, he dominated the instrument…violently forcing it to respond to his skillful hands.

The angel opera Christine had once inspired him to compose had been set aside like a spurned lover; its tender and higher passions rejected by the composer who, upon closer examination, had judged the piece insipid and distastefully sentimental. The untitled manuscript had been placed on a pile of similar works deemed unworthy of his attentions, while he had gone back to serving the bestial soul of *Don Juan*.

Christine had been at the lesson for hours, growing tired and cranky as Erik's patience was beginning to wear thin from the backside of the mirror. She had been singing lifelessly, with her voice sounding limp and her pitch erratic. The *Faust* dress rehearsal was less than one month away, and for days she had been distracted and inattentive at her lessons. Erik had not yet informed her that he was grooming her to perform the role of Marguerite, but was waiting for the right moment when he was certain of her undivided attention. Lately, he had sensed that she was keeping secrets from him, but there were no secrets in his opera house, and her meetings with de Chagny had not gone unnoticed. He had followed her over the weeks to each trysting place, where she and the Vicomte had lunched in the park, and although they looked innocent enough, with de Chagny always behaving like a gentleman, Erik could not tolerate the slightest touch or glance between them.

She had been lying to her Angel on account of Raoul de Chagny, and Erik's jealousy had intensified with each imagined transgression. As Christine and Raoul had become closer, Erik had become more desperate to remove her from the boy's reach. On this night, as he stood behind the mirror with the violin in position, his cloak thrown across the stool and his tailcoat unbuttoned, he was at last preparing to seduce her away from de Chagny and into the arms of the angel.

"Sing it once more, my dear," he spoke calmly, glancing the bow off the strings. "You are not concentrating, Christine, and you are consistently sharp on that A. Let your voice rise on the arioso delicately...do not pounce on it!"

Erik moved in closer to the mirror and projected his voice through the gaps around the frame.

"Your pianissimo is positively puny and your fortissimo on the second stanza is too harsh. Loudly does not mean shrilly. Increase the power on the cadenza, but do not force the voice. Support the breath as I taught you," he instructed.

Gazing at her eyes, Erik could see that she was trying to do as he said, but there was something distant in her expression that angered him. Her body was physically present on the other side of the glass and she could certainly hear him, but he knew that her heart was far from him.

"Again!" he ordered, repeating his introductions over the grinding strings of the violin.

Christine nodded, with her brows knit together in concentration as she acknowledged his commands. Opening her mouth, she straightened her spine and resumed the aria to the violin's sonorous accompaniment.

"No, Mademoiselle Daaé!" he barked, his patience wearing thin. "You are rushing where you should sing andante. Relax your jaw and flatten your tongue on the words, "He loves me"…and your tone is too nasal. Let the pitch move up into the roof of your mouth and resonate there…do not swallow it. Stretch out your vocal chords, Christine, and seize control of your larynx. Concentrate!" he snapped at her,

"I am trying, Angel, but I just can't seem to get it right," she replied, frustrated and tired.

"You know precisely what to do, Christine! Stop making excuses and sing the bloody aria as it was meant to be sung!" he ordered, playing his violin roughly through the verse.

Christine cringed at the harshness of his voice, berating herself for her lack of concentration, but tonight all she could think of was Raoul! At one time she had loved her lessons, wanting nothing more than to hear her Angel's voice and the violin; but now it was Raoul she longed to see…and it was Raoul who occupied her dreams. Each time she looked into his eyes, she became dizzy, often forgetting what she was about to say! He was so very handsome and gentle…and all the things her father had been. Now, whenever they were together, she felt that the world was a friendlier place. Like her father had done, Raoul made her feel safe and loved, and each moment away from him was sheer torture. Had it been in her power to do so, she would have fled from her lesson in search of him; for indeed, he and his brother were known to be somewhere in the opera house at that very moment, meeting the new managers for a late supper! Unable to keep her mind on her music, Christine felt guilty, but what could she do? She was in love! Suddenly, the sound of her Angel's voice broke through her daydreams.

"Once again!" he commanded, and again, she sang the phrase disastrously:

> *He loves me! He adores me!*
> *What tumult in my heart!*
> *The birds sing, the wind shivers.*
> *All the music of nature confirms his approach,*

Sing to me again in rapture . . .

"No, Christine!" Erik interrupted, striking the violin strings with the bow. "Have mercy on my ears!"

Christine hung her head, and with her shoulders drooping, she whispered, "I'm sorry, Angel. I do not mean to disappoint you."

Breathing deeply, Erik set the violin down carefully in the corner and reminded himself that she was more easily persuaded by his soft and hypnotic voice. He must now begin her transition in earnest.

"Sit down on the bed, my dear," he said softly, "I wish to speak with you before we continue."

Christine backed away from the mirror, walked to the edge of the bed and sat down on the rose embroidered comforter, then folded her hands in her lap and looked down at her feet. Erik watched her, noticing that her long hair was pinned up this evening, with ringlets hanging about her shoulders. The lamp light accentuated the contours of her face, and her translucent skin appeared to glow from within. Dark eyes glinted from beneath her delicate eyelids...eyes that were windows to an unfolding and tumultuous soul, which Erik craved to own.

To him, she had never been more beautiful or desirable, with her dressing gown spilling layers of cotton lace across her lap; her nightshift peeking through its opening to reveal a glimpse of tantalizing skin beneath the cotton's fine weave.

He sat down on his stool behind the mirror and removed his mask, stroking his knees rhythmically. Gazing at his beloved, he ached to breach the glass and take her into his arms. He imagined her body naked beneath his, her hair fanned across the bed as their arms and legs entwined. What he wouldn't give for just one night beside her, and one morning to wake up and look into her eyes.

Suppressing his fleshly imaginations, he cleared his throat and inquired, "My dear, may I ask you a question?"

Tilting her head to the side, Christine wrapped a curl around her finger and said, "Yes, of course! You may ask me anything, Angel."

"Christine, who do you sing for?" said Erik, keeping his voice soft and even.

"I sing for the character…just as you taught me, Angel," she replied, twisting the ribbons of her gown nervously. "I sing as Marguerite."

"No, my dear, not in the opera…I mean in your soul. Who do you sing for? Who occupies your thoughts and your dreams?"

Christine hesitated, but he had asked her a direct question, so how could she lie to her Angel?

"I sing for my father."

"No, Christine!" he rebuffed firmly. "You do not sing for your father! I shall ask you once more, and this time I want the truth! For whom do you sing? Who is in your heart and in your thoughts when you sing? Whose face do you see and whose voice do you hear at night when you dream…is it mine?" he pressed.

Confused, Christine was unsure how to answer him. She had never seen his face and wondered why he would ask such a question.

"Angel," Christine stammered, choosing her words without revealing too much, "I do dream of your voice, of course. But how can I dream of a face I have never seen?"

She is clever, Erik thought to himself, his thumb drawing circles on his kneecap. Gentling his voice again, he spoke soothingly, "I have watched you in your sleep, my dear. You dream of someone, and when you sing…you sing for someone. I must know the truth…who is it?"

She had not spoken to him of Raoul for weeks, having promised that she would not see the young man…and technically, she had not disobeyed him. She had made certain that Raoul never called on her during performance days, and their only time together had been spent away from the opera house…yet somehow Christine knew that her Angel would not be pleased. She cared too much for him to lie, but feared his anger.

"I swear to you, my Angel, I have not…" she broke off her sentence.

When he failed to respond, his silence emboldened her to blurt out the truth, "It is Raoul I think of, Angel! I cannot help myself! I know that you do not approve, but I swear to you…I never let him interfere with my music."

As his silence thickened around her, she implored, "Please do not be angry, Angel. I did not mean to deceive you."

Like the cracking of a whip, his voice lashed out in accusation, "You are lying, Christine...even now, the young Vicomte interferes with your progress! Your mind is on him, and not *Faust!* How dare you mock me!" he seethed between clenched teeth.

"No, Angel, I would never do that...but I cannot help myself! Please understand!" she pleaded. "Yes, I do think of Raoul, and I do dream of him...even when I am awake. But I have not missed a single lesson or rehearsal," she protested, wringing her hands together.

Erik could not contain his fury at hearing her speak that boy's name. He had known what her answer would be, but it sickened him, just the same, to hear it from her own treacherous lips.

"Again you lie!" he bellowed, watching as her eyes glimmered with tears. "Your body is here, Christine, but your heart is not! You waste my time and spurn the gift I have given you! Perhaps your father was mistaken in sending me here! Perhaps you *are* unworthy!"

"No, Angel!" she cried, the whites of her eyes reddening, "Please forgive me! I shall try harder, I promise! I shall work twice as hard! Please do not be angry with me!"

Curling his fingers into fists, Erik shot up from the stool and shouted, "You deserve my anger, Christine! I ask so little of you...and yet your selfish desires come before your music and come before me! Only the worthy are chosen, Christine. Only those who sacrifice everything!" he gestured, striking his fist hard against his chest. "If you wish to remain under my wings, then you shall not deny your Angel for Raoul de Chagny, or for any other man! Is that understood?" he demanded, watching as her entire form seemed to shrink before his eyes. "You will serve me! You will sing only for me!"

Shaking at the authority of his voice, Christine deeply regretted her confession. "Please, Angel," she pleaded, "do not shout at me...you know that I cannot bear your wrath!"

Erik breathed hard for some moments, then slowly calmed his temper and slinked back down onto the stool with a heavy sigh.

"Forgive me, Christine, my dear, but you must understand

that no man...no mortal being is worthy of you. You yearn for the Vicomte because you think that you are in love with him...but you are young and inexperienced in the ways of men. Men are vain and foolish creatures, Christine, who will only take advantage of your trusting nature. You must never entrust your heart to any man, for mortal men will only crush it ruthlessly!"

His words only served to confuse her further, for he seemed to be demanding that she never love anyone but her Angel...not even dear, sweet Raoul. Surely he could not mean that!

Raising her eyes to the mirror, Christine tried to explain herself, "But Raoul isn't like that, Angel! He is a good man, and he does not..."

"Do you dare to challenge me, Christine? Haven't I always known what is best for you?" he thundered.

"Yes, Angel," she replied timidly.

"Then be silent!" came his cold reply.

Christine sat quietly, waiting, wiping her tears with the sleeve of her dressing gown.

After a few minutes had passed, Erik then altered his baritenor expertly; sweetening and warming it until it seeped through the mirror and into her room, where it seemed to sit beside her on the bed.

"Christine, you must love me," pleaded the impossible voice at her side.

"I do love you, Angel," she wept in confusion, turning to face the invisible presence. "You know I do!"

Erik watched her intently, gathering up the courage to follow through with his plans. Years of loneliness stretched out before him like an open sore, forcing him to act on impulse; forcing him to crawl out of hiding and to hope for something more. Christine was real to him...not a child or an image, or a perfect angel; but a living, breathing, flesh and blood woman...and he had to try for her. He couldn't give up, even if it meant destroying his own soul and hers in the process. Dissenting inner voices argued over his intentions, but Erik only listened to the voice that spoke what he wanted to hear.

You don't deserve her. Stop this now, before it is too late, a voice warned.

No! She is mine and I deserve some happiness...don't I? I won't stop...I won't! Said the other.

Shaking his head, Erik puffed out his chest and strengthened his resolve. "Then I shall now test you, Christine, and you will prove your love for me!" he announced with renewed confidence, his heart turning to stone against her sensibilities.

Picturing himself as an actor delivering a soliloquy, Erik straightened his back, and thrusting out his chin, he spoke majestically, "You must prove that you love me, Christine, by loving and singing only for me. I alone am worthy of you! I alone deserve to be blessed with the greatness of your voice, because I am its creator! When you sing, you must remember the first time you heard the violin. You must call to mind the first time I sang for you; the joy and ecstasy that carried your soul to the farthest reaches of heaven! Only I can bless you with such joy, Christine! The gift of such ecstasies is mine and mine alone to impart! If you love Raoul de Chagny, Christine, then you are not worthy of your Angel...and your angel shall withdraw from you forever!"

Still staring to her left, Christine bore an expression of complete devastation. In all their years together, he had never once threatened to leave her. For seven years she had thrived in his presence, entrusting her voice and her soul to the great unseen Angel who had lavished his music on her. Their hours together had been all she lived for, his voice like nectar to her soul. She cared for Raoul, yes...and perhaps she loved him; but even so, her love for the angel and her need for his music overpowered all logic. The very notion of his leaving had filled her with despair, and she knew only that she would die were he to remove himself from her life.

"No, no, please...no, Angel!" she cried, falling to her knees and staring up at the empty space on her bed where the voice sat. "Do not leave me! I swear to you that I will sing only for you, and I will love only you! I swear it!"

Christine choked back the tears, her lips quivering as she pleaded with him, "Promise you will never leave me, Angel, or I should die of unhappiness! Oh...beautiful Angel of Music, I will die without you!" she sobbed into her hands.

Like an animal sniffing its prey, Erik was intoxicated by his power over her and was preparing himself to push even further. He knew in his rational mind that he was wrong in coercing her promises and oaths…but he no longer cared. His passion had flared up into an inferno, and he burned with its volcanic demands. Shutting out the dissenting 'other voice', he recklessly invaded Christine's confused and fragile mind.

"I must have your promise, Christine!" he insisted, his voice a wall against her tears. "You must swear to me on your father's grave that you will not love another…that you will not allow your body and soul to be corrupted by the touch of a mortal man! I have seen you with him, my dear. He desires you as a man desires a woman. He touches your hand and kisses your lips, but you must now make him understand that you belong to no man and that no man will ever possess your heart or claim you as a lover!"

With every word he had spoken, Christine's body appeared to collapse on itself; as if each syllable and vowel were a physical weight, pressing her down into the floor where she now knelt.

Erik escalated his verbal assault, his words an irresistible pull on her mind as he whispered, "You were created for better things, my dear. Your soul is destined for greatness beyond your imagination. You have always known it…the truth has lain dormant in your subconscious mind until you were ready to hear it!" he declared, the veins in his neck standing out as his voice pressed upon her. "That destiny is now within your grasp, but only I can give it to you!"

Sucking in his breath, he showed no mercy, his voice the instrument of her violation as he sought to break down her resistance. "You are not meant for earthly happiness, my dear. Your fulfillment will only be complete when you abandon the world of men for the embrace of your immortal Angel!

Erik stood to his feet and raised the volume and power of his lirico-spinto, with each word enunciated to pierce her defenses. "Look at yourself in the mirror, Christine!" he commanded, "You are no longer a child! You are a woman, and you must hear the truth! Your Angel has come to save you from the anguish of imperfect and selfish human love…for only the divine love of your Angel can satisfy the secret longings of your soul, Christine! Only I can give you what you desire!"

Nearly out of breath, Erik grasped onto the mirror frame, abandoning all deportment and principal as his voice hardened with determination, "Do you promise, Christine? Will you swear to me on your father's grave that you will love no other but me?! If you cannot, then I must leave you now and find another more worthy...and you shall never again hear my voice!"

Bowing her head, Christine folded her hands in an attitude of prayer. She raised her swollen eyes to the mirror and wept, begging him desperately, "I cannot live without you, Angel! I could never bear to exist in a world where I am denied the gentleness of your voice and your magnificence! I will swear by anything! I swear it on my father's sacred grave! I swear on my own soul that I will do all you say...give up anyone or anything! I will do anything you wish...only promise that you'll never leave me!"

Erik was triumphant; his chin held high and his body alive with power and control. His heart beat madly as the voice of reason was silenced. He had succeeded. She was sitting like a rag doll on the floor, tears streaming down her cheeks in complete submission. Drawing in his breath, he placed both hands on the glass and leaned into the mirror, his eyes boring through the silver and mercury.

"I must have it, Christine!" he growled.

"What?" she asked in exasperation, raising up on her knees with her arms stretched out before her. "What more do you want from me?"

"I must know that you hold nothing back; that you belong only to me!" he rasped.

Pushing her dangerously to the edge, he continued to toy with her sensitivities. Sharply enunciating and thrusting every syllable in undisguised lust, he demanded, "I want your body and soul, Christine!"

His mercurial voice seemed to shake the walls and rattle the mirror, and Christine collapsed face down onto the floor, cupping her hands tightly over her ears. Never had she heard him speak words like this, and never had his voice been so dark and commanding. She was confused and afraid of what he seemed to be asking of her, and yet she could not resist. Minutes passed in silence, the atmosphere of the room rife with tension as she lay there.

Observing her from behind the mirror, Erik's blood pulsed against his eardrums. He panted with an open mouth as he fought for control of his body, gentling his voice with all the discipline he could muster. Softly imploring, silky and erotic, he began to vocalize *The Bleeding Rose*. The low masculine thrumming vibration resonated in Christine's ears, and she turned over onto her back, her eyes desperately searching as she cried out, "Where are you, Angel? Show yourself to me!"

The solid floorboards then seemed to dissolve beneath her body. She felt weightless, devoid of time and place; sensing a voice that brooded about her, regarding her and intimately touching her soul. Strange music caressed and cajoled her, its melody probing; seeking entrance into the core of her being.

No longer willing or able to resist his breathtaking song, an unfamiliar warmth spread from her breasts down to the dormant music of her awakening as she opened herself to the silken voice. Her eyes shone and a smile lit her countenance as she slowly sat up and spoke aloud, "I am here, Angel!"

Erik watched in a victorious frenzy as she lifted her face, her eyes searching the room for his manifest presence.

"Where are you, Angel?" she cried out. "I must see you now! I beg of you…please show yourself at last!"

His hypnotic skills had fully ensnared her, and he had played her mind as deftly and ruthlessly as he had played the dark music of *Don Juan*.

She is mine, a voice whispered triumphantly in his mind. *Christine is mine.*

Christine listened as the magical singing voice floated away from the bed, then seemed to be singing from inside the mirror. Again, she followed it with her eyes, staring at her own dazed reflection.

Fighting the overwhelming desire to smash the glass with his bare fists and take her forcibly, Erik flexed his fingers and drew in a long breath, exhaling slowly as he pleaded, "Do you love me, Christine?"

"Yes, Angel," she wept, her eyes searching the sheen of the

mirror for some evidence of a face.

"Then come to me!" Erik whispered, lowering his voice and barely concealing the hiss behind the tenderness. "Come closer, Christine!" he commanded.

Tears pooled in his eyes as she at last seemed within his grasp, the reality of possessing her almost tangible. She followed his voice, crawling on her hands and knees and kneeling before the mirror like a sinner before a sacred icon.

"Come closer, still," he groaned, "and lay your face on the mirror, Christine."

As he had instructed, she pressed her tear-soaked cheek against the glass, embracing the mirror as she grasped either side of the frame with her white hands. Erik then laid his own face against hers from the backside of the mirror, his tears streaking down its cool surface as he begged, "Do you love me, Christine?"

"Yes, Angel!" she confessed.

"Say it!" he commanded.

"I love you!" she cried, yearning to see his beloved face as all thoughts of Raoul de Chagny fled her mind.

"Say it again!" he growled from the back of his throat.

"I love you, Angel!" she wept passionately.

"Again!" he commanded, all gentleness now gone.

"I love you! I love you! I swear to God I love you!" she cried out through her tears. "Where are you? Hide from me no more...Angel, let me see you now!"

Breathless and panting, Christine's cheek remained pressed against the mirror, and the suspense pulsated between them as he drew the moment out.

When he had convinced himself that she was utterly his, he infused his voice once again with a strange melting together of eroticism and angelic beauty, and spoke very gently, "And I love you, my beautiful Christine...more than anyone, or anything. I shall never leave you, as long as you obey me implicitly. Now you are worthy, my dear! Worthy of the greatest gift an angel can bestow upon a mortal soul...worthy to see my face, my form...worthy to know me as I am!"

As her eyes sought his shape, Christine was beyond speaking and beyond caring whether she lived or died. She knew only that he was the center of everything. The sound of his voice and the words he had spoken had stripped away all her defenses, and she smiled as he coaxed her, "Stand up, Christine."

Obediently, she rose to her feet and as she did so, her dressing gown gaped open to reveal the nightgown's fragile cotton weave. Spying the flesh of her thigh, Erik gasped, and bringing his fist up to his mouth, he bit his hand until his teeth nearly drew blood.

"Take down your hair," he commanded.

Again, Christine obeyed, removing the pins from her hair and letting it fall loosely around her shoulders. Suddenly, Erik knew that he didn't have much time. He knew that if he stayed there any longer, no flimsy pane of glass or strip of clothing would keep him from taking her. In order for his plan to succeed, he must keep his head, and there was still one more test she must pass before their union was assured.

"Tomorrow you will write to the Vicomte de Chagny and explain why he may not call on you again," Erik spoke evenly…softly, his eyes never leaving the sight of her. "You will plead for his forgiveness and inform him that you are promised to another. You will instruct him to pursue your affections no further, and assure him that you are deliriously happy with your intended…your teacher."

Tracing his index finger across the smudged mirror, Erik wrote her name in the condensation. His voice was steady but his hand shook and his eyes began to water as he went on with his demands.

"You will sing the role of Marguerite on opening night of *Faust*. You will be the most stunning soprano the Paris Opera has ever seen, and vast crowds will stand to applaud your greatness. But you will sing only for me!"

Momentarily closing his eyes, Erik envisioned her debut; heard the music in his mind and saw himself seated in the audience, proudly applauding Christine, his creation. His speaking voice began to take on a musical quality, lilting and quivering as he described the scene.

"Applause will mean nothing! Their empty praise and arms full of flowers will not move you…but I shall be watching, and you shall know that I am all around you…and you will sing only for me."

Reaching her hand out toward the mirror, Christine chanted, "Only for you…"

"After the performance, you will go to your dressing room where your admirers will await to worship you…but you will not linger there, and you shall not permit yourself to be tarnished by their flattery. You will change out of your costume as quickly as possible, and then you shall come alone to this room where I will be waiting. When I see the light of your candle, I will know that you are ready…my love, my dear…ready for me to reveal my beauty; ready for me to bring you into my world!"

Satisfied that she was now fully entranced, Erik sang the *Faust* aria, altering the libretto and shaping his vibrato to the rhythm of a heartbeat.

> *Open to me my beloved!*
> *You burn and you hunger*
> *For the glory of my voice,*
> *You who have slept apart*
> *From my embrace!*
>
> *Don't you hear?*
> *Oh, Christine, my angel*
> *Don't you hear my voice?*
> *My steps draw closer!*
> *My form is at the door!*
> *Your lover calls you,*
> *And you must believe in me…*

Upon hearing his voice as *Faust*, Christine stretched out her arms before her, her eyes glazed and her face uplifted in an expression of ecstasy as she listened.

> *Open to your angel!*
> *The secret lover*
> *Who implores you.*
> *Do not refuse his kiss*
> *Do not deny his touch,*
> *Hear your lover pleading,*

Hear your lover calling,
Let your heart believe in me!
Your heart must believe in me, Christine…

She parted her lips as her own voice answered in kind…singing only for him, with all thoughts of Raoul and the world of men behind her. Her voice effortlessly danced to the ceiling, soaring beyond its physical limitations and mirroring the glory of her Angel's own as she sang Marguerite.

Sing to me again!
How lovely is your voice!
A cup of silver tears,
The chalice of my dreams.
Heaven is jealous of me!
The angels weep for me!
Your voice intoxicates me!
Your touch revives me!
From pleasure and love,
My soul trembles
And my heart
Quivers with joy!
Tomorrow, and forever,
I await your visitation!
Immortal lover do not tarry!
Come to me tomorrow…
Come, immortal lover…come!

Chapter 18
December 1, 1879
Five Days Before the Opening of Faust

While Christine attended her morning classes, Erik had been tinkering with her mirror, using a set of tools borrowed from the opera's shop. Replacing the rusted hardware, he filed down the mirror's bottom and top edges, creating a smoother swivel inward. Finally, he had cleaned and oiled the mechanism and then tested it for easy and soundless operation.

His promise to Madame Giry had briefly come to mind as he'd been working, but it was years ago that he had sworn not to use the mirror's secret entrance, and much had changed since then. Christine was no longer a child and had demonstrated by her recent behavior that she was ready to meet him face to face. He had heard it with his own ears…and not only had she begged to see him, but she had also proclaimed her love as a young woman, and not as a little girl who still believed in fairy stories. Their Angel of Music games were drawing to a close, and Erik contemplated the moment when he would at last walk through that mirror and take her away.

Crossing his arms over his chest, he smirked to himself, pleased by the improvements he had made. With a current of excitement buzzing through his body, he then went to work on the mirror's gloomy chamber, preparing to dazzle her. Pulling on a pair of leather gloves, he leaned over and picked up one of the many mirrors he had "borrowed" from the prop storage. The reedy muscles of his arms, back, and chest strained beneath his damp shirt as he placed the heavy mirror on top of a large canvas drop-cloth. Folding the canvas over the glass, he then struck the mirror repeatedly with a wooden mallet until it lay in glimmering shards at his feet. As he stooped down to pull back the canvas and have a look, he frowned at the image of himself reflected in pieces, his features and mask a puzzle of fragmented silver.

For obvious reasons, he generally avoided looking at himself in mirrors, but for some reason he was fascinated by the distorted face and form scattered about on the floor. Squatting down on his haunches, he selected a shard of glass, held it before his face in his gloved hand and observed the dark and light shapes it reflected. In the gypsy camps he had discovered that mirrors were a world of their own, and that their reflective properties were capable of weaving a mystery or a dream, which was precisely what he intended to do to Christine.

He repeated the mallet process with the remainder of mirrors until a pile of gleaming glass glittered on the canvas. He then grabbed a broad trowel from the tool chest and dipped and scraped it in a bucket of thick cement paste, spreading the mixture across a section of the chamber's stone surface. With sweat beading across his forehead, he carefully set the mirror shards into the cement one by one, fashioning a mirrored mosaic throughout the entire chamber while leaving only the floor and ceiling untouched. The cement was quick drying, which enabled him to complete his task with time to spare before Christine's dance session ended. Standing back to admire his work, he grinned as he visualized the illusion those mirrors would create. He removed the work gloves and remarked, "This will do."

He would leave the mess to clean up later and snapped open his pocket watch, stepped out into the long corridor behind the ballet dormitory and decided that it too, needed some tidying up. He would return that evening and have a go at the place by removing the trash and setting a few more rat traps, but for now, he was hungry! Erik slunk down on his stool and wiped the sweat from his neck and brow with a handkerchief. He removed a green pear from his cloak pocket and bit into it ravenously, licking the tart juice from his lips. Consuming all but the core, he tossed the remains into an empty can and looked at his pocket watch again.

"Time to go," he announced aloud.

As he meticulously secured the cravat around his neck, rolled down his sleeves and fastened his shirt cuffs, Erik considered the more difficult task which now lay ahead. He would have preferred to avoid the confrontation altogether, but would never be able to live with himself if he did not make his intentions known to the one person he respected most in the world. Adjusting his mask, he smoothed the wig hair behind his ears and flipped the cloak across his shoulders. He closed off the back entrance to the chamber, approached the mirror, and listened carefully with his ear to the glass. There were no voices outside Christine's bedroom door, so sliding his fingertips along the length of the frame, he tripped the hidden latches, then silently, with the mere touch of one hand, the mirror swung open on its pivots into Christine's room.

"Much better," he whispered as he stepped through the entrance and pushed the mirror closed behind him.

Stepping across Christine's rug, he gingerly opened her door and peeked down the long, dimly lit hallway, expecting it to be deserted; but upon seeing a familiar face, Erik cursed under his breath, "What in blazes is *he* doing in this wing? Jospeh Buquet has no business in the ballet dormitory!"

He stopped short as he spied the scheneshifter sneaking out of Madame Giry's apartment, then quickly dodged behind Christine's door, rubbing his chin quizzically.

"What business has that buffoon with Louise?" he grumbled to himself, raising one eyebrow.

Waiting a few minutes, he checked again, and seeing that the hallway was now empty, he silently made his way to Madame's door across the hall. Of course, Erik had a master key for every room in the opera's maze, but he wondered how Buquet, a boozing sceneshifter, had gotten hold of the key to Madame's apartment; and moreover, what the devil had the man been up to?

"Likely, a robbery," he growled under his breath while looking over his shoulder.

The moment he slipped his key into the lock and entered the apartment, Erik had to fight off a fit of sneezing, and covered his nose with his hand. The violet and mauve room smelled vaguely musty, with a heavy dose of spicy cologne and lavender soap. It was cluttered with antiques, family keepsakes, and opera memorabilia, and the unmade bed was heaped with clothing. Artifacts and collectibles were strewn across the untidy apartment, and Erik looked about the place wondering how Louise kept track of anything in that mess. Dragging his gloved finger through a fine coating of dust on the bureau, he questioned whether or not Louise kept her valuables in a safe. Thievery in the opera house was not uncommon, but primarily occurred only when residents left belongings lying about or neglected to lock their doors. Surely Louise would have kept her jewels locked away, but in any case, he would certainly bring up the Buquet break-in the moment she returned from rehearsal.

Erik's ire was now stirred up, and he ground his teeth as he recalled the horror stories Buquet had spread about his midnight encounter with O.G. years ago in the opera's underground. Even now, Buquet frequently rehashed the lurid tale for anyone who would listen. Erik had not appreciated his graphic description of O. G's unmasked face, although it was accurate enough.

"Perhaps he is nothing more than a pervert," he remarked dryly. "No matter, I'll get to the bottom of it, and Madame must be informed of the intrusion."

Glancing down at his pocket watch again, Erik removed his cloak and gloves, flung them across an armchair and made himself comfortable in the chaise lounge. He stretched out his legs and laid his head back against the soft velvet cushion, then folded his arms across his chest, awaiting Madame's return.

Erik bit down on his lower lip as he waited, considering the oddness of his presence in Louise's rooms. They had known each other for years, and yet in many ways they were strangers. Shaking his right foot nervously, he glanced about the room, intrigued by the feminine decor and charmed by its unabashed romanticism. In her role as ballet mistress, Louise Giry had earned a Spartan reputation for discipline and order, but it was clear that there was another side to her. She clearly loved dance and the theater, and her room was a veritable museum of the opera's past and present.

Closing his eyes, he breathed in the pungent odors of Louise's surroundings, remembering too, the scent of his mother's cologne. He let his arms rest at his sides as his body gave in to exhaustion. Finally dozing off for a few minutes, a dream fluttered on the back of his eyelids, like laundry on a line; but it wasn't just a dream...no! It was a sound and a place; the sound of flapping banners, the smell of rain, and the scent of his mother's lilac perfume.

Jolting upright, the breaths came hard across his tongue as his eyes sprang open to see Louise standing in the doorway. With her cane in one hand and her dance shoes in the other, she looked like she'd seen a ghost! Trying to recover his wits, Erik blinked his eyes as Madame's shrill voice brought him around. "Monsieur Erik, my heavens, you scared me half to death!" she scolded, dropping her dance shoes to the floor. "What are you doing in my room, and however did you get in here?"

Amused by her curt demeanor, Erik's nightmares receded and his breathing returned to normal as he stretched to his feet and greeted her. "Good afternoon, Madame," he said with a forced smile. He stooped down to collect her dance shoes, then stood up straight, swinging the shoes by their frayed ribbons. "How goes the rehearsals? Ballet coming along well, I presume?"

Letting his eyes roam up and down her frame, Erik appraised her appearance as any man would have done with an attractive woman. Her auburn hair was pinned back in a dancer's knot, and there was a slight sheen of sweat on her high forehead. She wore a black silk skirt and a white embroidered bodice, with a fringed shawl tied across her shoulders.

"Erik, for heaven's sake, you have not answered my question!" Madame replied, narrowing her charcoal-lined eyes to cat slits. "How did you get in here...and what do you want? I am not accustomed to finding strange gentlemen asleep in my quarters!"

"Indeed, Madame? I should think a woman like you would have to beat them off with a stick!" he chuckled.

Flashing a rakish smile, he set the shoes down on the chaise and quipped, "Have you a stick, Louise?"

Despite her irritation at finding him in her room, Louise laughed, thrust out her cane and shook it playfully at him. "Yes, Erik, I have a stick, and if you ever do this to me again, you shall feel the sting of it!"

"That will not be necessary, Louise, as I do not intend to make a habit of breaking into your apartment," Erik began in a more serious tone. "However, there is a certain matter I wish to discuss with you. Please sit down, Madame," he said, gesturing toward an empty chair.

"All right," Madame sighed, "I believe I will sit. Rehearsal was exhausting."

Madame Giry seated herself in the armchair opposite the lounge, and pulling a handkerchief from her skirt pocket, she wiped the sweat from her neck. Erik settled himself again on the chaise, lying on his side and propping himself up on his right elbow. Despite the gravity of his errand, he found himself enjoying the company of this fascinating woman.

"What is it now, Erik, another letter to deliver…more tortures for poor Carlotta?" she smiled wryly.

"No, Madame. This time my business is with you," he announced, his facial muscles becoming taut.

Sighing heavily, Louise remarked, "Erik, please do not call me *Madame.* You make me feel positively ancient."

Appraising her again, he offered a slight nod. "My apologies, Louise. You are certainly not, by any stretch of the imagination, ancient," he said with a warm chuckle.

Erik grinned again as he watched Louise's cheeks flush pink, giving her the glow of a young girl…then reminded himself that he must get down to business. Clearing his throat, he began to state his purpose. "Louise, we have known one another for a long time, and I am eternally in your debt for all you have done for me."

Suddenly realizing that he had never thanked her in so many words, he watched as she lifted her head from the cushion and replied in a soft voice, "You are welcome, Erik!" Then, leaning her head back against the chair, she asked, "But what brings you here today?"

He could see by her relaxed demeanor that she was suspicious of nothing, and continuing his preemptory flattery, he said, "My dear, I do not know how I would have survived all these years without your loyalty and assistance. I value our friendship immensely…"

When Louise's expression remained unchanged, he paused and rubbed his chin, drawing in a long breath before making his point, "…which is why it pains me now to inform you that you are interfering in my plans for Christine."

Louise had been sitting with her eyes closed, her head pressed against the chair cushion. Upon hearing his comment, she opened her eyes and glanced at him sideways as she questioned, "What do you mean, Erik? What plans? Are you referring to her career?"

Erik drew in another long breath through his teeth. Having no idea how to broach the subject, he nervously smoothed out the seam of his trousers, then pinched a piece of lint off the black wool, flicking it with the tip of his finger.

"Louise, as you know, over the years I have come to care very much for the girl...perhaps even more than I realized," he said, somewhat hesitantly.

"Yes, I am aware of that, Erik...and I believe that your tutoring of Christine has been beneficial for you both," she replied.

Falling silent again, Erik fondled his pocket watch as he bit down on his lower lip. "But what if I told you, Madame, that my affections for the girl have, ah...changed?" he said unevenly.

With a raised brow, she asked, "Changed in what way, Erik?"

Contemplating an answer, he sat up on the edge of the lounge, swung his feet to the floor and raked his hand through his hair. "I care very much for Christine...that is, what I mean to say, Madame...is that, I love her," he confessed awkwardly, and then added under his breath, "...as a man loves a woman."

Erik searched her features for understanding, and was crushed when he did not immediately find it.

"You what?!" she said, jolting straight up in her chair, her eyes flashing coldly. "Perhaps I have misunderstood...so please do correct me if I am wrong. Are you telling me that you have fallen in love with Christine...romantically?"

Erik exhaled a slow breath, spreading his hands open on his legs and said, "Yes, Louise. God help, me I have!"

With her mouth half-open and her eyebrows arching high up into her forehead, Madame Giry simply stared at him, hardly believing her own ears. "But, Erik, surely you realize how ridiculous that sounds! Christine is still a child...and you are a grown man!" she argued.

Grinding his teeth, he shot to his feet, with his green eyes darkening in anger.

"Ridiculous, Madame?" he stormed, stomping across the floor. "You find it ridiculous that I have fallen in love? Am I not a man like any man? Have I not the same needs and desires as any normal man? I will grant you…my face may be deformed, but the rest of my anatomy is fully functional and intact."

Turning to face her, he glowered at her defensively and demanded, "Am I to be alone for the rest of my life? Don't I deserve some measure of happiness? And if Christine is such a child, Madame, why the devil have you gone out of your way to throw her into the arms of that pretty boy, Raoul de Chagny!"

"Erik, I merely invited the boy to her party, and he is an appropriate age for…"

"Age has nothing to do with it!" he shouted over her, waving his arms as he tread heavy-footed across the floor. "Young women Christine's age are often matched with older men!"

"Erik, lower your voice or someone will hear…and for goodness sake, please do sit down," Madame sighed, pulling the pins from her hair matter-of-factly.

"No, thank you, I prefer to stand!" he hissed. "Speak the truth, Madame; it is this!" he spat, pointing to his mask. "This is why you object to my attraction…my love for Christine! It is not my age, but my face!"

Louise then realized that she had made a mistake. Upon hearing his bizarre confession, she had not taken into account his sensitivity and high strung nature, but in her own defense, she had simply been unprepared for his news. She *had* been noticing a marked change in Christine's behavior, but had attributed that odd behavior to the girl's infatuation with Raoul. Christine had said absolutely nothing about an unlikely romance with her "teacher".

As she gazed up at him, she decided that she must discover the true nature of Christine's affections for her teacher. Was Erik making false assumptions about her regard for him, or had Christine indeed developed an infatuation for her invisible teacher? At the moment it was clear that he was distraught, therefore, she decided it was best to approach the situation calmly. Resuming their conversation, she posed a question, "Erik, when did you first become aware that your affection for Christine had turned to romantic love?"

Sauntering over to the lounge, he sat down and hung his head in his hands. He inhaled a few deep breaths, calmed himself and waited until he could speak more reasonably. "I don't know, Louise. For over a year now, I have seen her in a different light," he sighed into his open palms. With his shoulders slumped and his voice weary, he continued, "One moment she was a child...and the next...she had become a beautiful young woman for whom I felt an affection...a passion I have never known. In the beginning I denied it. Believe me, Louise, I fought against the whole damn notion, but finally, I had to admit that I had fallen in love with her." Raising his head, he looked directly into Louise's eyes and said, "Madame, as much as I am capable of loving anyone...I love Christine."

Stunned by his words, Louise could not doubt his sincerity, but she did question his grasp of reality. Loosening her long braid, she pulled her fingers through her tangled hair, letting it fall about her shoulders, and then responded, "I can see, Erik, that you are very sincere...but have you thought through all the implications? She knows you as her 'Angel' and teacher. How, may I ask, do you intend to...well, introduce yourself as Erik?"

"Leave that to me, Louise," he answered, lifting his head. "I am a resourceful fellow, as you know."

"But, Erik, surely you can see the impossibility of the situation. Christine needs security. She needs a real home, a family, and children. Erik...you live in the cellars deep below the city...and..."

"I know how and where I live, Madame!" he snapped at her. "Do not treat me like a child!" With his face growing red and the veins of his neck standing out, he fumed, "I intend to marry her, and I will go anywhere, or do anything to supply her needs, even if it means leaving the opera, or Paris! I love her, Louise, and I want her to be my wife. I would never condemn her to live in the cellars, for Christ's sake!"

This was something Louise had always wanted for Erik; that he would somehow find the courage to leave the opera house and make a life for himself in the world of men...but never had she envisioned Christine in that equation! Rising to her feet, she opened a drawer in her vanity and dropped the hairpins into a tray while thinking over how best to respond to him. She must behave rationally, and must not match his temper with her own outrage. Louise pressed him gently, "Erik, has Christine ever implied, in any way, that she fancies you romantically?"

His mouth opened and then closed again as he bit down softly on his lower lip. Staring into the fireplace, he avoided her eyes, watching the yellow flame dance and sway. Louise's question was not unreasonable, but he did not know how to answer her. Christine had spoken certain words...words that he had compelled her to say through devious means, but she *had* spoken them, nonetheless. Her voice and her body had responded to his seduction scene behind the mirror, and to see her standing there, begging him to appear, had been a powerful opiate.

Speaking up with his voice tired and devoid of hypnotic resonance, Erik sounded like a little boy when he answered, "Yes, Madame, I believe she has...or she will, when she comes to know me."

Very slowly, Louise walked across the carpet to stand behind him. She could see the tension in his body as he held his arms stiffly at his sides and kept his spine erect. From the back view, he could have been any attractive and successful man; dressed impeccably from head to toe, with a sheen of dark hair just brushing the back of his white shirt collar. He was a very slender, but tall and broad-shouldered man, of an imposing presence, who might have been a politician, a banker or even a member of the Royal family.

Despite the insurmountable odds against him, Erik was a survivor who had managed to create a life for himself on his own terms, and she had little doubt he would continue to do so. Her heart was moved for him, but Christine was her primary concern now. Christine needed her guardian's protection, and it was up to Louise to convince him that the girl was beyond his reach. Their association must remain that of pupil and teacher, and she would insist that Erik end the angel charade immediately. Christine was to be made aware of his true identity, and Louise would then assist in helping the girl to accept the truth. Christine must see him for who he was in the flesh, mask and all. It was the only way...then if she chose, Erik could continue as her teacher. Louise was convinced that the whole affair must be brought out in the open. Christine was now too old to believe in her father's stories, and poor Erik was too confused to understand the damage that he had already unwittingly inflicted. *I've let this go on for too long*, she scolded herself.

Inclining her chin, Louise chose her words carefully and resumed her inquiry. "How can you be certain of her affections, Erik? Christine is unlike other young women her age. She is very fragile, and what if she does not return your affections...what will you do then? Surely you can see that she has grown quite fond of the Vicomte."

Whipping around, Erik stretched to his full height until he towered over her. "You leave that boy to me, Madame!" he barked.

Holding her ground, Louise straightened her shoulders and raised her eyes to his as he exclaimed, "Am I such a monster that you believe a woman incapable of romantic intentions toward me? And do you really think I would take her against her will? I may be ugly as hell and a wreck of a human being, but I am a gentleman!" he shouted, his voice breaking up with shallow breaths. "I have never forced myself on any woman, and I am wounded that you think me capable of such a despicable crime!" he bellowed.

Secure in the belief that he would never harm her or Christine, Louise was not afraid of his temper. If he did truly love the girl as he professed, there might still be hope in convincing him that a romance was out of the question. Unruffled by Erik's fierce posturing, Louise gave him a reassuring look and laid out her objections calmly. "No, Erik, I do not believe you would ever force yourself on any woman...and I don't know where you got the idea that I was implying such a thing. I realize that you are much too decent a man for that, but I do fear that you might have misinterpreted Christine's regard for you. What can she really know of you, in light of your unusual circumstance? Has she ever seen you?"

Raising an eyebrow and self-consciously stroking his mask, Erik avoided her steady gaze, his eyes darting away from hers as he replied, "No, she has not seen me...not yet."

"And when she does, Erik...?"

"And when she does, she will fear and loathe me!" he cut her off bitterly. "That is what you are implying, is it not, Madame?"

"No, Erik, that's not what I meant at all!" she answered in exasperation. "Would you please stop putting words in my mouth?"

Ignoring her, Erik paced across the floor like a caged animal, while she allowed him to vent his raw emotions openly.

"Is my face...my person, so abhorrent that I shall be denied the love of a woman for the rest of my life, Madame? Don't I at least deserve a chance for love?" he pleaded, looking up at her. "I cannot continue like this! I refuse to go on living like a wretched rat in a shit hole. I fear that I will lose what's left of my faculties if I do not have something or someone besides my bloody music...which incidentally, will never be heard!"

Louise nodded her head, folded her hands in front of her body and decided to give him the courtesy of listening to his plight without interruption.

"Do you know how much music I have composed?" he asked her, waving his arms. "There are hundreds of rotting manuscripts, Louise! Pages and pages of my soul's outpouring that even now turn to mildew! Isn't that an absurd irony? God's cruel and perverse joke on the Phantom of the Opera? Why did the Almighty endow me with music that will never be heard? Why? God help me, Louise. I can't stop composing. I can't stop because music is all I have...all I will ever have!"

Sighing heavily, Louise felt her heart twist within her, just as it had done all those years ago when she had first taken him down into the opera's cellars. She could not give him the answers he sought, nor did she understand why he must suffer so. She wished to comfort him, but was resolved to remain strong for Christine.

With short breaths pulsing sharply across his tongue, Erik shuffled over to the vanity and glowered at his reflection in the mirror. Flipping through a stack of yellowed programs, he came across one from the first Paris Opera production he had seen as a boy. Separating it from the others, he saw that its decayed pages were a testament to his life.

Erik stroked the program with his thumb, lowered his voice

and spoke brokenly, "Do you know what it is like, Madame? All these years alone in that stinking fifth basement? I will tell you. It is a living hell!"

Erik closed his hands around the program, and twisted until the fragile document turned to dust and fell to the floor. Whirling around to face her squarely, he angrily blurted out, "Christine believes I am an angel! But I am far from angelic, Madame! I am a man, and I want a woman to share my life and my bed! Does that appall you, Louise?" he challenged, curling his hands into fists. "Yes, I want Christine in my bed! I want to live like other men in the world above! I am sick of the dark. I am sick of being alone! I am sick to death of the Opera Ghost and of this bloody 'Erik'. Erik is not even my real name, for Christ sake!" he hissed bitterly.

"Then why don't you end it, Erik?" she encouraged him, opening out her hands. "Why don't you end the games and make yourself known to Christine and to the world? Why not leave the cellars and take your place among men as the fine gentleman and composer you are? You are no longer a boy, Erik. You are a grown man, so surely the time for hiding has passed? Perhaps the world is not as cruel as you imagine," she added.

Louise flinched as the unmasked side of Erik's face contorted. He drew his lips back and narrowed his eye to a gleaming white slit. With anger flashing across his features like an electric storm, he lashed out at her, "How can you even suggest such a thing, Louise? If I dared to show this face in polite society, they would either kill me or put me away for life! The world is not as cruel as I imagine? You can have no idea of its cruelty, Louise. Good God...no idea at all!"

Louise observed as he turned his back on her, his shoulders sagging and his arms hanging loosely at his sides in an attitude of defeat. The last thing she had wanted was to hurt him, and he was right; she couldn't possibly know what it had been like for him. Had it not been for his disfigurement, the man could have been honored by dignitaries and royalty; with his music performed in opera houses and music halls the world over. Studying his masked face, she could envision him as he might have been, admired and pursued by many lovers. He possessed remarkable genius and a good heart, but life had denied him the one thing he desired most.

Stepping behind him, Louise gently placed her hand on his arm, and as he turned around to face her, she was shocked to see that the poor man had tears in his eyes.

"Your face is not the issue, my friend," she spoke kindly, "for despite its...uniqueness, I believe many women would find you attractive. At one time, Erik, I even wondered if there might be a harmless flirtation between the two of us."

He gawked at her in disbelief, having had no idea that she had ever entertained such notions.

"I see I have shocked you," she said, reaching out her hand boldly to touch his shoulder. "I know the ways of the world, Erik; I am not innocent. I believe a woman could quite easily fall prey to your charms...that is, if you could learn to live without this," she said softly, extending her hand and daring to touch his mask.

Erik bristled at the touch of her fingers, then grabbed her wrist, bearing down on her diminutive frame as he applied slight pressure to her wrist bones.

"Madame," he addressed her with acid in his voice, "were it not for our friendship, I would never have permitted you to do that! No one touches my mask!"

Releasing her with a grunt, he turned his back and folded his arms across his chest as she persisted in her dialogue.

"Erik, don't you understand? Anyone who truly loved you would accept you as you are...with or without the mask," she said calmly. "Remember, my friend, I have seen you without it. I know what you look like underneath the mask...and I am not repulsed by your naked face. It is *you* who cannot bear the sight of it!"

"Oh, Madame, please spare me the amateur psychiatry," he mocked, turning on her icily. "I saw how you looked at me all those years ago! Do you want to know what I saw in your eyes, Louise? Pity...I saw pity and I have no use for pity...from you or anyone else!"

"No, Erik!" she raised her voice in frustration. "You dear, stubborn man...it was not pity you saw in my eyes. Do you not know the difference between compassion and pity?"

"Aside from you, Madame, I have had little experience with either," he sighed, refusing to look at her.

Trying to reason with him, Louise resumed, "Erik, you cannot condemn the entire world for the cruelty of a few!"

"I shall condemn who I like, and this discussion is over!" he bellowed, slicing his hand through the air as he escalated the pitch and tempo of his words. "I do not require your approval or blessing where Christine is concerned, Louise. Nevertheless, I shall ask you this one favor…please stay out of my way! Do not interfere with my plans, and do not encourage that boy to come sniffing around her! And if I can prove to you that Christine cares for me in the same way that I care for her, will you trust me, Madame? Will you remain my advocate and my confidant? Will you trust me to do the honorable thing? For I assure you; I have every intention of making her happy!"

Louise circled around him until they stood face to face. Peering directly into his eyes, she quickly made up her mind how to proceed with him. She had no intention of encouraging this infatuation, but clearly, she must handle him with delicacy. By his own admission, he would never find the courage to make himself known to the girl, consequently, Louise had come to the conclusion that this was a lonely man's fantasy and nothing more. For the time being, she would play along, all the while keeping an eye out for Christine's best interests. Louise assured herself that Erik was no threat to the girl, and she suspected that, in time he would recover his senses.

Offering a stern nod of her head, Louise replied, "If you promise that no harm will come to her, I shall remain your friend…but Erik," she warned him, "you must curb that temper of yours! And if anything happens to Christine, I shall hold you personally responsible!"

For some moments, nothing was said as Erik appeared deep in thought, but finally, lifting his head, he nodded his assent. Louise absently rubbed her sore wrist, and without warning he grasped her hand and drew the underside of her wrist up to his lips, lightly brushing her skin with a kiss. "I apologize, my dear. I had no right to treat you so roughly."

Stunned by the intimate gesture, Louise disengaged and took a step backward, busying herself with a stack of letters on her vanity. She noticed the clock out of the corner of her eye, surprised by the length of their visit. He seemed in no hurry to leave and she thought it unfortunate that, just as they were becoming better acquainted, she must rush him off before the girls returned from their classes. Nervously stacking letters into a pile, Louise turned to Erik and alerted him, "Erik, the girls will be here the moment their class is over!" She spoke hurriedly, "and I must ask you to leave now. We are not finished with this...but before you go, I want your word that no harm will come to Christine!"

Softening his voice, Erik bowed solemnly and said, "I give you my word. I would not hurt her for the world, Louise."

With her mood lightening, Louise flashed a smile and teased, "Then be off with you, and mind that no one catches you leaving my room or my reputation will be in ruins!"

"And mine too!" he shot back with a grin.

She watched him turn to take his leave, then thinking over their curious conversation, Louise inquired, "Erik, before you go, may I ask...what *is* your Christian name?"

Retrieving his cloak and gloves, he bowed once more and replied, "That, Madame, is a secret I shall take to my grave. Good afternoon, my dear."

Closing the door behind him, Erik quickly headed for Christine's room, but suddenly remembering Joseph Buquet's break-in, he stopped midway down the hall.

"Damn!" he swore, "I neglected to tell Madame about that bloody sceneshifter!"

The intense visit with Louise had completely distracted him, and he now would have to go back there immediately and let her know about the burglary! However, he had no choice but to duck out of sight when he heard Meg and Christine bounding down the staircase.

"It will have to wait until I can leave her a message this evening!" he commented under his breath as he ran for Christine's door.

Chapter 19
December 2, 1879
Four Days Before the Opening of Faust

Over the previous weeks, Erik had spent each spare moment preparing his grotto for Christine's arrival. As he stood at the entrance to his bed chamber, he envisioned himself lying on the bed, with Christine lying beside him in the twilight of candles. For Erik, the marriage bed was a mysterious symbol of the union between a man and a woman and until now, sharing his bed with a lover had been an unattainable dream…but with Christine's debut in *Faust* only days away, he had begun to see that dream as a reality. After making up the bed, he set about adding a few romantic touches to the chamber. He arranged his collection of embroidered Indian pillows against the four poster headboard, then placed urns that had been filled with rose petals across the bureau and night stands. Looking about the chamber, he was suddenly struck with the realization that, if he squinted his eyes, all appeared lush and romantic, but with his eyes open he could see mildew here and there on the stone wall, and not even the scent of the roses could disguise the smell of soil and pond slime. This was the best he could do under the circumstances, however, so turning about, he tried to ignore the gnawing pain in his stomach, telling himself that perhaps she wouldn't notice the sour stench of the underground.

Standing before the open wardrobe, he decided it was not too early to select the appropriate clothing for their introduction. He pulled out several pair of trousers and coats, then laid out the garments on the bed, carefully inspecting every button and seam. Earlier that week he had crafted a new mask just for the occasion, and lifting it from a shelf in the wardrobe, Erik held it reverently in his hands. This one was very different from any of his previous attempts. He had given it realistic human characteristics, with a strong brow and a fleshy upper and lower lid. He had also sculpted a handsome bone structure, sloping the angular cheek down to a fine jaw line.

Placing the mask on the bed, Erik chose his ensemble for Christine's debut, took a lint brush to the trousers and then hung them, together with the appropriate tailcoat, in the center of his wardrobe. After he had put away the remainder of his clothing, he closed the cabinet doors and strode down the stone steps to the organ, where he began selecting music for Christine's arrival. For the first time, she would hear him play the organ and together they would sing the duets and arias he loved. He could scarcely believe that in a few days time he would at last hear the sound of her crystalline voice filling his hollow caverns.

In hopes that the instrument would impress her, he had taken hours to chip and scrape stubborn candle wax from the organ console, using his bare hands to massage lemon oil and wax into the worn mahogany, oak, and cherry wood finishes. He had removed the ink stains and grime from the yellowed keyboard, and hummed to himself as he organized the manuscripts, making neat stacks on the music stand. The organ's pipes and fittings had been polished until the old silver spires gleamed. As Erik stood back to appraise the result, again he was struck by the shabbiness of his furnishings.

Earlier that week, he had snuck into the opera's prop closets, borrowing every candelabra he could transport back to the grotto. Standing like golden sentinels, they were now arranged throughout his rooms, their florets waiting to be filled with hundreds of candles.

He had also taken meticulous care with his washroom; setting out fresh towels and trays of fragrant soaps for his lady. The stone floor, wash basin, and tub had been scrubbed…with bath oils, combs, brushes, and mirrors assembled for her use. Her own personal wardrobe now overflowed with the costly gowns and fashionable accessories he had purchased for her, and Erik was anxious to see a real woman filling out the petticoats and bustled skirts…but would any of this be enough to convince her to stay? he questioned himself.

Struggling to control his nerves and looking for a distraction, Erik stepped down to the library, sat down at the desk and took hold of the monkey music box. His thoughts were only of Christine as he turned the windup key, listening to the disquieting music as it resonated throughout his chambers. Absently humming the melody, he stroked the monkey's moth-eaten fur as the cymbals clinked together. With his attention then turning to the base, he opened the hidden chamber, drew out a small black bag and clasped his fingers around it. Still humming to himself, he loosened the strings and turned the bag upside down, shaking its contents gently. A glittering gold wedding band spilled into the palm of his hand, its dainty beauty magnified by the lamplight. As he watched the flame reflect on the gold and jewels, it occurred to him that he had never expected to fall in love, nor had he ever been able to imagine himself proposing marriage to a beautiful young girl...but now here he was, wondering if she would ever accept it.

He rewound the monkey's tune and placed the ring on the tip of his pinky finger, admiring the eight shimmering diamonds set in the solid gold band.

"One day I shall compose an opera based on that melody," he muttered to the monkey, as the strange music hovered above the lake. Suddenly, Erik experienced a swelling sense of expectation he had never known, and he found himself grinning so much that his cheeks ached. Filled with nervous energy and still clasping the ring in his hand, he wandered down to the lake's rock platform and turned to look back over his rooms. His chambers spoke of his music, his art, his love of books, beauty and knowledge...and soon a woman would bring her feminine loveliness to the place that had been his solitary refuge for over twenty years. Though it was only a cave hidden in the darkness of stone and water, in that moment as his eyes wandered back up to the bed chamber, he was satisfied that all was in readiness for Christine. However, his hopeful anticipation immediately turned again to doubt and anxiety. Over the past weeks the tight rehearsal schedule had severely limited his contact with her. He had watched her from box five during rehearsals, following her as always, but had been forced to settle for stolen glances of her lovely face. Shadowing her throughout the opera house was not nearly as rewarding as talking and singing with her, and he missed their daily rendezvous.

Erik passed along the lakeside and reassured himself that Christine was capable of performing the role of Marguerite to perfection. He wished he could be there in person to witness the shock as cast members and crew heard Christine sing Marguerite for the first time, and he anxiously anticipated the critical acclaim that would follow her debut. Articles would be published about how she had risen from the rank of a chorus girl to star as the opera's triumphant diva, and reporters would swarm her dressing-room, vying for discoveries of any scandal that might be attached to her.

Smirking to himself, Erik raked a hand through his hair, visualizing the managers falling all over themselves to win her affections. There would be promises of gifts, social events in her honor, and unimaginable wealth...but he would never allow her to be seduced by the praises and promises of men.

He closed his fist tightly around the ring and became more agitated, making a mental list in his head of all those who had wronged him. He hated the opera's managers for their complete lack of regard for legitimate music. He hated Carlotta for stealing the limelight...and most of all he hated Raoul de Chagny who, it seemed, was not ready to give up his fantasies about wooing Christine.

Digging his boot heel into the mud, Erik snapped his head up and gritted his teeth angrily. He was aware that the de Chagny boy had made several attempts to see her, but to Erik's relief, she had been either occupied with rehearsals, costume fittings, or completing her schoolwork in the dining hall with Meg. Erik had plans for dealing with the Vicomte in his own way and in his own time; but for the moment, he was pleased that Christine had kept her promise to stay away from the boy!

As his temper eased, he raised his eyes to the ceiling and sighed, "At least I know I can trust her."

Fingering the delicate ring, he noticed that the lake was mirror smooth as it cast watery reflections on every stone surface. The ceiling glimmered with ghostly green light, and as Erik circumspectly gazed across the water and into the misty canals, he could hear water bubbling in the distance where the Seine seeped through cracks and crevasses. He closed his eyes and drew in a cool breath, with the ring possessively wedged between his fingers and thumb. Bouncing the ring in his hand and then closing his fingers around it, he turned away from the lake and hurried upstairs to the library. Sitting down at his desk, he dropped the ring into its pouch and returned it to the monkey's hidden compartment. He let his hand linger on the compartment's gold engravings and artificial gems as he slid the drawer closed. With the ring now tucked safely away, his attention then fell to a stack of paper. Ignoring the knot in his stomach, he pulled a slip of paper from the stack, dipped his pen into the ink pot, and began to compose the first of several letters, speaking aloud as he wrote, "Fondest greetings to my new managers, mm Armand Moncharmin and Firmin Richard. On behalf of the opera and its company, I bid you welcome to my opera house."

Pausing, he scratched his chin with a chuckle. "Too much, do you think?" he asked the monkey music box. Erik nodded his head and commented, "No, I don't think it's too much either."

With another dip of his pen in the ink pot, Erik continued his missive.

"I trust Monsieur Debienne has informed you of my monthly stipend and strict requirements regarding box five, which is to be made exclusively available for my use. I anticipate a long and lucrative association with you both, and will be at your service whenever you have need of me."

Pausing again, Erik tapped his fingers on the blotter, then with arched brow, he glanced again at the music box and said, "Let's have some music, shall we? I always think better with music."

He reached out to wind the key and resumed dictating his note, "Now as to the opening of *Faust*; Signora La Carlotta will unfortunately be ill. Therefore, Christine Daaé shall sing the role of Marguerite. I assure you, gentlemen, Miss Daaé will sing the role magnificently! After her triumphant debut, no one shall remember the toad-throated Carlotta! I will inform you, should anything else come to mind. Your obedient friend, O.G."

Satisfied with the letter's content, Erik folded the parchment and tucked it inside an envelope, then melted a puddle of wax onto the flap. Next, he pressed his signature stamp into the warm wax, blowing lightly until it hardened. Chuckling to himself, he set the letter aside and selected a second parchment, and this one he addressed to the diva:

> *My Dear Carlotta,*
>
> *I sincerely regret that you have taken ill, Signora. Pity that the audience must do without the sound of your lovely voice for the opening of Faust. I do hope your condition improves; however, please do not trouble yourself over the opera's success. My protege will perform Marguerite brilliantly, just until you are well enough to return to the stage, of course. Take your rest, my dear, and know of a certainty that I shall be thinking of you fondly on opening night.*
>
> *Your friend and admirer, O.G.*

I had been in rehearsals for most of the afternoon, and returned to my room tired and troubled. *Faust* was opening in only four more days, and I was still recovering from the shock of being told by my Angel that I was to play the role of Marguerite! His instructions had specified that I was to continue the chorus girl charade until such time as he chose to move forward with my debut; meanwhile I was to tell no one…and the whole affair had been playing havoc with my nerves.

I was capable of singing the score without referencing the book, and I knew her blocking by memory, it's true…however, I was not at all convinced that I could live up to my Angel's expectations. What choice did I have, though, when it appeared that everything was under his control, and that he had become a powerful force, with his influence extending far beyond my mirror?

Back in the quiet of my room and glad to be away from all the commotion, I flicked my eyes up to the mirror and marveled at its ordinary appearance. It was just a sheet of glass framed in gold leaf, and yet only I had knowledge of its powerful magic. Ever since our meeting days ago, when my Angel had come to me in a manner different from all previous visits, I had often found myself standing before it, gazing into its reflections and desperately trying to see a pair of white wings or an angelic face.

Recalling his promise to come to me, I smiled to myself, wondering how he would appear and what he would look like. With butterflies in my tummy, I stepped behind the dressing screen, changed into my night-clothes and sat down on my bed. I leaned my back against the wall and dug my toes into the blankets, and drawing my knees up to my chest, I recalled those exquisite moments by the mirror, puzzling over what had happened to me that night. Much of it I could not remember except that, the next morning, I seemed to have awakened from a beautiful dream.

I remembered his voice; a voice demanding and strangely altered from its usual timbre…but a voice I hungered to hear again and again! How had it changed from soft and angelic to a voice of such urgency, I wondered? He had made me feel new sensations that I was desperate to experience again…yet despite my longing for his next appearance, I feared it just the same. I had never truly felt fear in his presence, and I could not comprehend what had changed between us.

As I glanced furtively about my room, I wondered if he was watching me at that precise moment. I could not feel him there, but it seemed that he was never far away. At one time this had been a comforting thought, but I was no longer certain I felt comforted.

I rose up from the bed, lit a candle and turned up the lamp on my writing desk. Opening the top drawer, I then lifted out sheets of writing paper, a pen and a pot of ink. The clock on my bureau ticked away the minutes as the candle's flame bobbed and dipped, and it occurred to me that while the world outside my door was peaceful and ordinary, my mind was a virtual firestorm. Things were happening too quickly, and my life felt on the verge of monumental change as I sat down at the desk. Over the last few days I had been a sleepwalker, moving through my daily routine in a perpetual haze of comings and goings. What had been real and what was merely a dream, I could not tell. No matter where I was or what I was doing, my thoughts and dreams were only of him. When people spoke to me, it was as though I couldn't hear their voices…as if they spoke from a very great distance. His voice alone resonated in my mind, drawing me apart from everything and everyone.

My Angel had promised that I would see his face and his form, and that he would take me into his magical realm. I had no idea what this promise entailed, but I wanted it more than anything in the world. For seven years he had graced my ears and my heart with his glorious voice, and now I was about see for myself from whence that voice came.

In a strange way, his voice had freed me from my father's grave, and I craved his music as a newborn craves its mother's milk. I was certain that a lovely creature must be the source of that magical voice…yet a few nights ago in front of the mirror, I had heard a stark difference in the sound of it. He had come to me as my teacher that night, but somehow before the night was over, his voice had awakened a quiescent yearning inside me…moving me in ways that cannot be expressed with the spoken word. He was still my Angel, but in those extraordinary moments he had become something more.

Tears began to blur my vision as I started to write the letter I had been dreading all day, but knowing that he would leave me forever if I failed to fulfill his wishes, I had no choice but to obey.

I dropped the pen, despising my heart for its betrayal. I hung my head, searching for the right words. I thought about what I must say to Raoul, knowing all the while that he did not deserve the disappointment I was about to inflict. Only weeks ago we had walked together in the park, where in the sheltering trees, we had held hands and kissed like sweethearts. Our shy kisses had been explorative but never demanding, and all of my troubles had seemed to vanish in his protective embrace.

I must admit that I had never seen a more handsome young man, and in a fashion, Raoul resembled my father. A certain set of his jaw and his wavy dark hair, even his height and stature were similar to Papa's. Although my father's eyes had been brown like mine, Raoul's blue eyes were just as kind as Father's, with never a hint of disapproval or anger. He never rushed me or demanded anything from me that I was not prepared to give, and there was no tension between us, only a tenderness that made me feel safe.

Taking up the pen again, I bit down on my lip and squeezed my eyes closed. My Angel had spoken the truth and I must obey, for was he not a creature sent from heaven…a being of wisdom who was privy to my own destiny? Did he not possess the power to see into my future? Surely he must know what God intended for my life.

I cared for Raoul, and the prospect of hurting him distressed me, yet I must be faithful to my Angel. I told myself that, perhaps after I had proven my loyalty and after the opening of *Faust,* my Angel would relax his demands and give his permission for me to renew my relationship with Raoul. I knew that my Angel loved me, for he had told me so…therefore, wouldn't he want me to be happy?

Filled with a sense of regret, I wrote out the first line, praying that Raoul would forgive me for what I was about to do:

My Dearest Raoul,

How lovely our time together has been in these last few weeks! Remembering those summer days in Perros when Father was still alive has refreshed my soul, and I shall cherish these happy memories for as long as I live.

I regret to inform you that my teacher has required me to refrain from all social activities for the next several weeks. I am to devote myself to rehearsal, and to preparing for the role of Marguerite. Moreover, after seven years as my teacher, the maestro has now made his intentions clear. I am promised to him as I can be promised to no other; but have no fear, my dearest Raoul, for he has made me sublimely happy!

I pray that in time you can forgive me. You shall always be my first love and my dearest friend.

Sincerely,
Christine

I read my own handwriting, blinking back tears as I fought the urge to rip the letter to shreds. Regretfully folding the parchment and slipping it inside an envelope, I set it down on the writing desk, rose up from my chair and shuffled across the rug to the mirror, where I stood staring at my own deceitful eyes. In only four days I would stand on the stage as Marguerite. I would see my Angel's beautiful face…and that was all that mattered.

Chapter 20

December 3, 1879
Three Days Before the Opening of Faust

A sumptuous brunch had been given earlier that morning in honor of Monsieur Debienne's retirement. A white-tie banquet was also to be held on that same evening, where the new mangers would be formally introduced. Debienne had made his speeches at the brunch, where he had received numerous gifts and awards. His final task was to attend a meeting with Firmin and Armand to transfer the books and surrender the keys. Turning the key, he opened the door to his darkened office and turned on the gas lamp with a twist of the brass knob, but there was no corresponding hiss and the globes overhead failed to ignite.

"Wonderful!" he remarked sarcastically. "Evidently there is a malfunction!"

The heavy drapery had been pulled completely shut, leaving only a few dying embers in the hearth to expel what little light there was in the room.

"Good riddance to this drafty old place, and why haven't the maids lit my damn fire?" he grumbled irritably, his eyes adjusting to the dark while he rubbed his hands together. "It's cold in here!"

Shoving a hand in his pocket, Debienne fumbled for a tin of matches to light the oil lamp…when out of nowhere a buttery male voice hissed, "Come in, Monsieur…and if you value your life, do not strike that match. I am armed."

With no warning, the door slammed shut behind Debienne, and the sound of footsteps at his back made the hairs on his head bristle. The blood rushed into his face, and he clenched his fists until his nails dug into the palms of his hands. *How the hell did whoever that is get in here?* he questioned himself, assuming that he was about to be the victim of a robbery.

"I assure you, sir, there is nothing...nothing at all in this office worth stealing," Debienne spoke nervously. "But take whatever you wish."

"I am not here to steal your worthless possessions, sir," the voice replied. "No, I have come on personal business...you see, in light of your retirement, Monsieur, I thought it was time to make proper introductions," the voice spoke politely. "Don't you know me, Monsieur? I am your old friend, O.G! However, I much prefer the Phantom of the Opera. It has more of a dramatic ring, wouldn't you agree?"

Debienne's eyes searched the dark, but saw only the undulating orange glow of the anemic fire.

"Do you often introduce yourself with a weapon in hand, Monsieur?" Debienne inquired, forcing his voice to remain steady.

Again he heard the shifting of fabric, and froze in place when hot breath materialized on the back of his neck! Stumbling forward and feeling his way into the center of the dark room, he squinted in the dark as the voice chuckled softly from behind, "I am never without my weapon, Monsieur. Please do sit down."

"I would if I could see my way to the chair, Monsieur," Debienne quipped.

"Forgive me, sir," the voice answered, "I forget that not all men possess my uncanny night vision. But I advise you to keep your eyes straight ahead."

With no assistance, the drapes slowly opened until a thin shaft of pale winter light gave the room a murky gray cast.

"Is that better, Monsieur?" the voice inquired.

"Yes, thank you, sir," Debienne replied, listening for the direction of the voice as he complied with the intruder.

Spying the silhouette of the desk, Debienne sat down in the chair and tried to remain calm, rooting his feet to the floor. Immediately the curtains were drawn closed, and once again the room was plunged into darkness.

"Now what can I do for you, Monsieur?" he asked, his eyes darting about with apprehension.

"Ah yes...Monsieur, let's get down to business, shall we?" the voice chuckled. "You see, Monsieur, with our years of association drawing to a close, I thought it fitting that we meet face to face…well, in a manner of speaking."

Debienne shifted uneasily in his seat and craned his neck, trying to get a look at the source of the voice, and then asked, "So, you are the infamous Opera Ghost, sir?"

"Indeed, I am," the voice replied. "A pleasure to finally make your acquaintance, Monsieur."

The voice sounded almost amiable, which further grated on Debienne's nerves! If this man was indeed the Opera Ghost, what were his intentions, Debbiene wondered…and would there be violence?

"I wish I could say that the pleasure is all mine, sir," began Debienne, "but given that I cannot see who is speaking to me, I do not find this meeting in the least bit pleasurable!"

"I apologize for my invisibility, sir," the voice mocked. "As you might imagine, invisibility somewhat goes along with my reputation as the Opera Ghost…ghosts being invisible and all!"

"Do you have an aversion to light, Monsieur?" Debienne asked, noting now that the voice seemed to be moving about the room.

"Let's just say I prefer to remain unseen," the voice spoke from behind him.

Snapping his head to the left, Debienne tried to gauge the location of his adversary. "I prefer to see who it is that has broken into my office!" he retorted sharply.

"Pity, then…" replied the voice icily, "…for you shall not see me, Monsieur…that is, if you wish to continue living!"

"Really, Monsieur, I do not have all day!" Debienne growled, growing more cross by the minute. "Please state your business or I shall call for the police!"

Debienne listened as the rustling of fabric seemed to encircle him. He strained his eyes, but to no avail. The shuffling sound inched closer until suddenly, Debienne felt a presence at his back, hotly breathing down his neck!

"I wouldn't do that if I were you," the voice warned in an acid tone. "Do not trifle with me, Monsieur! I am armed with a deadly weapon, which I am prepared to use if you so much as move a muscle!"

Throwing Debienne off his game, the voice immediately took on a more amiable disposition as, with a hint of amusement, it questioned, "Is all this violence really necessary, Monsieur? I came here to make friends, and yet you threaten me!"

As the voice paused, Debienne caught his breath and began weighing his limited options. He had already cleared out the contents of his desk, which had included his revolver; and given that the ghost was apparently armed and standing directly behind him, he thought better of trying to overpower him. Therefore, having reached the conclusion that he had best cooperate, Debienne resigned himself to letting the ghost state his business. Sitting forward in his chair, he conceded uneasily, "Very well...I dare say you have the upper hand, Monsieur, so I suppose I have no choice but to play your game. What is it you want from me?"

"Ah...now that's much better," the voice replied, maintaining a threatening stance behind his victim. Taking note of the knot in his stomach, Debienne suddenly felt something poke his rib as the ghost continued, "I really am an easy fellow to get along with, Monsieur...once you get to know me."

There was a short pause as the voice leaned in closer, his mouth only inches away from Debienne's ear. "Now, I want your word as a gentleman that you will inform the new owners, Firmin and Armand, of our tidy business arrangements. It is crucial that my operation not be interrupted by the new management's stupidity and lack of regard for my person," said the voice.

Debienne had felt a hot breath with each perfectly enunciated word, raising gooseflesh up and down his arms. "I have provided Firmin and Armand with the proper documentation, and I assure you that they will be highly cooperative," Debienne replied, resisting the urge to look over his shoulder.

"That may be so, sir, but I would prefer...shall we say...that you put in a personal word for me...just to ensure that there are no misunderstandings," the ghost suggested.

As the pressure against his rib eased up, Debienne exhaled a long breath, then inhaled sharply as the rustling of a cloak swept past him, with the ghost seeming to glide across the darkened room.

"Yes, yes!" Debienne replied, "I shall do just that! I am meeting with them shortly. You have my word as a gentleman, Monsieur, but I'm afraid I do not know your name."

"Ha-ha-ha!" the ghost chuckled darkly. "You may call me

O.G…or the Phantom."

"But I assume you have a real name, Monsieur?" Debienne inquired, hoping the man might stupidly offer more information.

"My name is none of your business!" the ghost rebuffed, with a hint of humor.

At that moment, Debienne could have sworn that the ghost was smiling. There was something obscenely jovial about his tone of voice, and in Debienne's estimation that made him all the more dangerous. Squinting his eyes, he expected to see a flash of white teeth, but again, the ghost was not to be seen. Debienne was convinced that this so-called "ghost" was indeed a clever criminal and not a supernatural being…yet in that dark room, his mind was beginning to play devilish tricks on him! The room wasn't particularly large, so where in blazes was O.G. hiding?

A loud handclap jolted Debienne halfway out of his seat, followed by a booming and theatrical voice that announced, "Splendid, Monsieur! I am pleased that we had this little chat! Now before I bid you adieu, may I leave you with several posts and entrust you to deliver them to the appropriate parties? It has been a pleasure doing business with you, sir!" the voice said cheerfully, then added, "Oh, and please do give my regards to your lovely wife, who I must say made a splendid dance partner! Lisette is it…?"

The words "lovely wife" hung in the chilled atmosphere as Debienne craned his neck and waited nervously for further instructions.

"Monsieur?" he whispered.

No one answered; so again, he whispered, "Monsieur O.G?"…but the ghost had apparently vanished into thin air!

Greatly relieved, Debienne sank back against his chair while rubbing his hand hard across his mouth, then practically jumped out of his skin when the gas suddenly hissed on. Hurriedly, he leapt up from his chair, then striking a match, he lit the nearest lamp. As his eyes adjusted to the light, Debienne took note that several red stamped envelopes had been left on the desk. Expelling a long breath, he raced to the door, pushed it wide open and then rushed to the opposite side of the room where he yanked the drapes open, inviting daylight into the room.

"I need a drink," he grumbled under his breath as he reached into his suit pocket, pulled out a handkerchief and wiped beads of sweat from his brow. Just then, Madame Giry appeared outside the door, accompanied by Firmin and Armand. Taking long strides across the rug, Debienne motioned for them to join him.

"Good morning, Monsieur!" the rat-faced, red-headed Firmin exclaimed, extending his hand.

Visibly shaken by the Phantom's visit, Debienne reached out and grasped the man's hand a little too firmly as he greeted, "Come in, come in gentlemen, and please have a seat."

Debienne sat down in his chair trying to recover his composure, while Firmin and Armand took the two leather armchairs opposite the desk. With a note clasped in one hand, Madame Giry stood back and observed her former and current male employers. Clearing his throat as he stuffed the handkerchief back in his pocket, Debienne turned to address his successors, then noticed the ballet mistress standing in the doorway, and asked, "Before we begin, gentlemen, Madame Giry, what can I do for you?"

Louise answered with a half-smile, "Well, Monsieur, perhaps you should attend to your other business first. I don't mind waiting."

Nodding his head, Debienne replied, "Very well, Madame, but will you please sit down? I am uncomfortable with a woman standing while I sit."

Irritated by the events of that morning and wishing to be free from the opera house for good, Debienne forced a smile as Louise entered the office. He found it impossible to avoid watching the woman as she appeared to float across the floor, her skirts brushing the rug with no sight of shoes or feet. Debienne's eyes followed as Louise curtsied, fluffed out her bustle, then quietly sat down on the burgundy leather divan across from the window, holding her spine perfectly straight and her chin erect.

Acknowledging her with a nod, he stood to his feet and assembled a stack of leather-bound ledgers, then gathered up a box of letters from the book case. "Gentlemen, I presume you have gone over these and have found everything to be in order?" he asked, hoping to avoid further discussion.

Although he appeared to be going about business as usual, the truth was he no longer gave a damn about what became of the Opera Ghost or the Paris Opera House, and he was almost tempted to walk out the door. He had been looking forward to retirement and had been contemplating the places he would travel and the activities he would enjoy. Of course, his wife's wishes must be considered too, but fortunately she was often preoccupied by children and sundry family affairs. He could already taste his freedom from the nagging Carlotta, quarreling directors, and the petty management problems that had continually plagued him as manager; a position he had never wanted, but one which his in-laws had procured.

As Debienne ignored his guests and envisioned himself traveling the world, Armand made a show of clearing his throat until the former manager's attention snapped back to the business at hand.

"Ah, yes, Monsieur Debienne," Armand began, "about that entry in your memorandum…and, er…these odd communications from this O.G. person."

"Yes…the O.G. person," Debienne sighed under his breath.

"Well, yes, perhaps you would care to explain these notations written in red…this one, for example…" said Firmin, standing to his feet. Reaching across the desk, Firmin pulled the black memorandum from the stack of ledgers and opened it to a particular page. Pointing to a hand-scribbled notation, he read aloud, "As payment to Monsieur O.G. for his musical works, twenty thousand francs are to be remitted on the first of each month and hand delivered by a third party. In addition, box five on the grand tier is to be permanently reserved exclusively for Monsieur O.G. and his guests. All box and ticket personnel shall heretofore be notified that box five is never to be sold."

"Yes, Monsieur?" Debienne said, looking blankly across the desk at the new managers.

Fingering his great black mustache, Armand asked nervously, "Would you care to explain exactly what service this man was paid for, and why is there no record of an actual opera composed by someone with the initials of O.G…and what, perchance, does O.G. stand for?"

With a muscle twitching in his jaw, Debienne avoided the question, saying only, "Gentlemen, I would advise you to make the payment without question if you wish your theater to operate without incident."

"Incident, Monsieur?" asked Firmin, his thin mouth gaping

open. "What sort of incident are you referring to? Do you mean to say this man is blackmailing the opera house?"

Losing his patience and wanting desperately to take his leave, Debienne stepped away from the desk and paced across the Persian rug.

"Gentlemen, you have read my notes and I assume that you also read the letters from Monsieur O.G. My advice is that, unless you care to find out what an "incident" is, you immediately comply with his requests. I have nothing more to add to this discussion."

"But surely you cannot expect us to ignore this rubbish, Monsieur!" Armand insisted, pounding his fist on the desk top. "Whoever this is, he is breaking the law and I intend to uncover his identity and have him arrested for harassment and extortion!"

"Yes, Monsieur," said Debienne, "that would seem the logical course of action; however, there is just one problem."

"And what is that?" asked Firmin, his beady eyes trained on Debienne's handsome features.

Debienne's eyes shifted and he moved closer to the door, ready to bolt from the room at a moment's notice. Meanwhile, as Madame Giry watched the confrontation without comment, tracing her fingers across the note in her hands, a hint of amusement lit her smoky eyes.

"Monsieur O.G. is apparently invisible!" Debienne announced, as if it were the most natural statement in the world. "I tell you, gentlemen, the opera house is thought to be haunted and more than half of our performers are convinced that Monsieur O.G. is a ghost; the Opera Ghost…to be precise."

By this point in the proceedings, Debienne could have cared less what these two men thought of him, and therefore he had nothing to lose. Let them sort the whole mess out for themselves! He was washing his hands of O.G, and the whole miserable place.

"Oh come, Monsieur, surely you do not believe that this extortionist is actually the ghost everyone's been going on about!" Firmin replied.

"Of course not!" laughed Debienne. "He is no more a ghost than you or I…but although there is plenty of evidence that he exists, no one can see him. And what is more," he added with a wide grin, "I had a visit from him this very morning in this office! He stood in this room not more than twenty minutes ago! He spoke to me as I am speaking to you now…but I never saw a soul…so whether he is a ghost or a man is not the point. The point is that he will wreak havoc unless you give in to his demands!"

Beginning to think that Debienne had lost his mind, Firmin pulled at his beard and shouted, "Well, if indeed you could not see anyone, where is the proof he was even in here, Monsieur?"

"There is your proof!" Debienne barked, pointing to the letters that were spread across his desk.

"These look like the letters in your box, Monsieur," said Armand.

"Of course they do, Armand!" replied Debienne. "They are from the very same person; Monsieur O.G. himself delivered them into my keeping just this day! He asked that I hand them over to the appropriate party…and so, gentlemen, I am fulfilling his wishes, as I have always done…and as I suggest you do!"

Firmin's eyes nervously darted around the room while Armand stood to his feet and refuted, "Well, why in the hell didn't you detain him just now, Debienne? Or call for the police and have the bastard arrested? I find it preposterous that this has been going on all these years, and yet you people have done nothing to stop it!"

"I assure you, gentlemen, we have tried…however, it is somewhat difficult to arrest a man whose whereabouts are unknown!"

"See here, Debienne, how do we know that you yourself are not responsible for this ruse? Perhaps this scheme has been of your own doing!" Firmin accused, rising up from his chair.

"Yes! Perhaps you invented the Opera Ghost stories and extorted the funds for your own use!" Armand chimed in.

With the three gentlemen glowering at one another, and having been ignored throughout the conversation, Madame Giry drew a hand up to her mouth and coughed as Debienne expelled his breath and rebuffed, "I expect you shall discover the answer to that question after I have left this establishment! In the meantime, I advise you to read these letters!"

Snatching the two letters from his desk, Debienne thrust them out to the new managers, who stood gawking at the envelopes.

"This envelope is addressed to me by name!" spoke a confused Firmin, reluctantly pulling his letter from Debienne's hand.

"Mine as well," replied Armand.

"Gentlemen, I suggest that you stop staring at the damn things and open them!"

As Armand shook his head in bewilderment, Firmin read the letter aloud, "Fondest Greetings, Monsieur Firmin and Monsieur Armand. On behalf of the opera and its company, I bid you welcome. I trust that Monsieur Debienne has informed you of my monthly salary and special arrangement regarding box five. I anticipate a long and lucrative association with you both…"

Here, looking up from the letter, Firmin paused to glare at Debienne, who was tapping his foot on the floorboards and staring out the window.

"A polite sort of fellow, isn't he? The ghost, I mean," Firmin quipped sarcastically.

"Just read the rest of it, Firmin!" Armand snapped.

Nodding irritably at his partner, Firmin resumed, "Now, as to the opening of Faust: in the event of Signora La Carlotta's illness, Christine Daaé will sing the role of Marguerite. I assure you, gentlemen, Miss Daaé will make a splendid understudy. I will inform you should anything else come to mind. A friendly reminder gentleman, if you choose not to comply, a disaster beyond your imagination will occur. I remain your obedient…."

Before Firmin had a chance to read the rest, Armand sprang to his feet, raking a hand through his dyed black locks as his rounded cheeks turned purplish red. "This is outrageous!" he fumed, "I'll not be bullied by this man!"

"You will comply, Monsieur, if you know what's good for you!" replied Debienne, eyeing the coat tree.

"I certainly will not!" argued Armand. "Box five is one of the most costly seats in the house, and each time I have attended the opera, it appears to be empty! Rounding on Debienne, Armand pointed his finger and shouted, "This is a significant loss of revenue, and in my estimation that makes you, sir, a poor businessman!"

Personal insults had been flung at Debienne, which in any other decade of his life would have been equal to throwing down the gauntlet. His spine stiffened almost imperceptibly, but Debienne did not flinch, nor did his facial expressions betray his thoughts. He knew what these men were up against; consequently, their opinion of him was of little consequence. Let them endure a season of the confounded notes, the threats, complaints from Carlotta, and expensive scenery destroyed or stolen! Let them contend with drunken sceneshifters, demanding board members, deadlines, and unreasonable budgets!

We'll just see who the poor businessman is! Debienne vented to himself.

Finally, when there was a break in the heated conversation, Madame Giry stood to her feet, cleared her throat and addressed the managers. "I assure you, Monsieurs, box five is never empty on performance nights," she said firmly. "If you don't believe me, ask the police inspector. He has been called upon many times to investigate disruptions in box five."

"Thank you for the suggestion, Madame," replied Firmin curtly. "We intend to do just that, followed up by a thorough investigation of this matter. Meanwhile, box five will be sold for the grand gala performance, and for each night thereafter!"

"Well, go ahead and try it," laughed Debienne, "and just see what happens!"

Shocked by the former manager's disrespectful tone, Armand bristled, shook the letter in Debienne's face and demanded, "Never mind box five! What is all this about using an unknown for the diva's understudy?"

Pulling his overcoat on, Debienne commented under his breath, "As you will discover, gentlemen, O.G. has no fondness for La Carlotta, and Miss Daaé is a personal favorite of his."

Firmin waved his arm indignantly and asked, "Do you mean to say that in addition to extortion and terrifying people, he has the audacity to meddle with casting decisions?"

"Gentlemen," Madame Giry interrupted, "You will find that Monsieur O.G. is quite gifted, which brings me to my purpose for attending this meeting."

"Yes, what is it now, Madame?" came Debienne's weary reply.

Taking a step toward the desk, Louise held out her envelope and announced, "This note was delivered to the secretary this morning by Signora Carlotta's personal maid."

Rolling his eyes, Firmin seated himself and crossed one leg over the other as he asked, "Dear God, another demand from the diva?

Very well…what does it say, Madame?"

"Yes, please, do read it, Madame," Debienne requested flatly.

Firmin fidgeted with his shirt cuffs and Armand smoothed his mustache with two sausage-shaped fingers as Madame opened the seal and read in her softest alto register, "I regret to inform the management, staff, and entire company of the Paris Opera that Signora La Carlotta has been taken ill with an extreme case of food poisoning. The physician has advised complete rest until further notice. As there is no understudy for Marguerite, Carlotta requests a postponement of two weeks, with the production to reopen when she is well enough to return in the starring role."

Adding no comment of her own, Madame refolded the letter and set it on top of the desk, where Firmin instantly snatched it up. "Oh my God!" he cursed, his face going white. "We cannot open with an unknown! As I see it, we have no choice but to postpone the opening until La Carlotta is well!"

"The house is sold out, for Christ sake!" shouted Armand. "We will have to refund the entire audience!"

Without blinking an eye, Madame offered, "As per O.G.'s messages, gentlemen, I suggest you send for Christine Daaé immediately!"

With panic flashing in his eyes, Firmin asked nervously, "Is she any good, Debienne?"

"I've no idea if she can handle Marguerite! She's never performed a leading role!" Debienne answered, tugging an enormous set of keys noisily from the pocket of his coat. "She's nothing but a young girl who has sung in the chorus for just under two years…an orphan, and Madame Giry's charge."

Rising up from his chair, Firmin flashed cold eyes on Debienne and thrust out his bearded chin, "Are you implying that this chorus girl is to fill the shoes of the popular diva? You've both gone mad!"

"Christine has been privately coached since she came here seven years ago, gentlemen," Madame spoke solemnly. "I promise you…she is a rare talent. Shall I fetch her for you?"

Softening his voice, Armand addressed Louise, "So, are you saying that the young lady is capable, Madame?"

"More than capable, Monsieur," she assured him with a nod. "She is a prodigy."

"Well, I suppose we have no choice but to give her a listen!" Firmin replied, exasperated.

The room was suddenly a place of nervous energy and panic as Firmin and Armand blustered about, exchanging whispered conversation, while grabbing up the ledgers and their own hastily written notes. Desk drawers were opened and slammed shut as files were placed in attache cases...and Debienne stood back to watch the drama unfold with a faint smile playing upon his lips.

"Now see here, Madame," Firmin issued orders, pulling on his gloves, "please arrange for the young lady to meet us on stage in an hour, and have someone locate Maestro Reyer...we'll need his expertise...and if he approves, she will be assigned the role."

With a puff of breath across his thin lips, Firmin caught the eye of Monsieur Armand and said with a sigh, "I need a drink, Armand...care to join me?"

Nodding his head vigorously, Armand quickly gathered his hat and cloak and replied, "Absolutely!"

As the new managers made their way toward the door, Debienne dropped the keys onto the desk with a loud clatter, scooped up his cloak, bowed with his hat in-hand, and made his way to the exit; and without looking back he announced, "Well, gentlemen, it appears that you have matters under control. Farewell, Madame Giry, farewell gentlemen...I must now take my leave!"

And with that, Debienne breathed a sigh of relief as he walked out of his office for the last time!

Chapter 21
December 4, 1879
Two Days Before the Opening of Faust

The first winter snow of the season had blanketed all of Paris that morning, overlaying courtyards and streets with crunchy slush. Buildings and trees glistened as the afternoon sunlight pierced through a shroud of pale gray clouds. Upon the announcement that La Carlotta was too ill to play Marguerite, the opera house had erupted in noisy pandemonium, and when it was also announced that an unknown chorus girl had been chosen as her replacement, there had been a near-mutiny as a few of the more experienced sopranos who had been passed over, began to spread rumors that Christine had only gotten the role because she was known to be sleeping with Raoul de Chagny!

With her mind on the evening's performance, Christine had tried her best to ignore the gossip, mentally mulling over her blocking and the libretto as she waited in the wings. Upon her introduction to the cast, she walked out onto the stage to luke-warm applause, knowing that many in the company were skeptical. Attired in a rather plain frock of an ordinary color, her hair pulled back in a ribbon, there was not a shred of conceit about her as she found her mark. She locked her eyes on the grand tier, displaying remarkable poise for one so young and inexperienced. Christine closed her eyes and recalled her Angel's warning that she must sing only for him…that he was the only one worthy of her voice, and that, the only approval she needed was his. Imagining him out there in the auditorium, she relaxed with a deep breath and calmly gestured her readiness to Maestro Reyer.

The Maestro gave the signal, the piano introduction for *The Jewel Song* began, and with all eyes watching, to the shock of the cast and crew, Christine Yvette Daae sang an exquisite

Marguerite! Her voice was effortless, her intonation sheer perfection, and her lyric soprano scaled the material beautifully. Her portrayal of the character was informed with all the warmth and effervescence that Carlotta's lacked, proving that she was a dramatic actress, as well as an accomplished vocalist.

At the song's conclusion, the entire cast applauded and whistled. Even the most critical of the company, Hugo Robert and Eugene Sargent, were seen smiling broadly, for no one at the opera house had ever heard a voice so singularly pure. As Christine blushed and curtsied demurely, chatter spread throughout the auditorium, with everyone stating their surprise that such a voice had unknowingly been in their midst for seven years!

Following her historic audition, Christine was then whisked away to the costume department and hastily measured for her gowns. As she reviewed the blocking and stage directions with the director and Madame Giry, Madame Marie ripped out seams, preparing to alter Carlotta's gowns to fit the younger girl's slender frame. Christine was fitted with wigs, make-up artists matched her foundation and powders, while Monsieur Reyer, who was stunned at her preparedness and vocal expertise, led her through the entire score.

The old Maestro couldn't imagine who in Paris had coached this young voice to its crystalline beauty, and without success, questioned her about the man's identity.

Meanwhile, with their sweat stained sleeves rolled up, stagehands feverishly cranked the huge "Mouth of Hell" into place, as Buquet and his sceneshifters double-checked the rigging and cables, supervising the lowering of enormous backdrops. The piano pinged over the sound of hammers and shouting, as the ballet girls stretched at the barre, with Madame Giry leading them through their routines.

The aromas of baking bread and fresh coffee made their way up to the backstage as cooks prepared supper in the kitchens, and the opera's new managers nervously paced in their office, terrified that the show would be a resounding flop! As they discussed Debienne's bizarre revelation about the Opera Ghost and his blackmailing schemes, Armand found himself glancing over his shoulder from time to time…but to his relief, thus far, there had been no unusual incidents. By all appearances, if the Opera Ghost was anywhere in the vicinity he was thankfully keeping to himself!

Across town in his brother's penthouse at the swanky hotel De L' Monte, Raoul de Chagny's downcast expression stood out sharply against a room flooded with winter sunlight. The morning had begun with scattered snow showers, but by afternoon the sun had broken through with a vengeance, thawing icicles and turning the snow into dirty slush.

The Vicomte sat in an occasional chair, staring down at a letter he had read at least twenty times. He kept hoping that he had misunderstood her message, or that somehow the words would change with another reading; but no matter how many times his eyes grazed her graceful handwriting, Christine's message made him colder than the slushy cityscape outside the window.

Up until now, he had not thought Christine capable of cruelty…but her message could not have been clearer; she was in love with someone else. Raoul was angry and hurt as he thought back over the last few weeks, and could not imagine what he had done wrong. He had made every effort to to please her, and had been under the impression that, she too, felt something for him…something more than the playful affection they once shared as children. But with this shocking development, he couldn't help but question her motives. Had he been just a play-thing for her? Had their kisses been meaningless to her, and had she only pretended to care for him?

Raising a hand to his mouth, Raoul rubbed a knuckle across his lips and anxiously glanced up at Philippe, who lounged on the sofa, eyes closed, smoking a cigar. Having heard Christine's rejection letter for himself, Philippe was secretly pleased. This damaging letter might make things go much easier on his end. Perhaps now it would be unnecessary to use the information he had been acquiring from Joseph Buquet; for although Philippe was a ruthless man when he needed to be, he had no desire to cause his little brother further distress. Consequently, he had already made up his mind that this information would only be revealed if Raoul's romance with the Daaé girl progressed to a proposal of marriage.

Cracking his eyes open, Philippe glanced sideways at his brother's slumped form in the chair, and he felt genuinely sorry for the boy. Raoul was a decent young man, given to high moral standards and lofty romantic notions, but Christine Daaé was the kind of girl one used as a diversion and nothing more. She had no family, no money, no social standing, and absolutely nothing to recommend her. Like most chorus girls, she would likely sell her affections for favors; and when she had grown too old and unattractive to perform with the opera, she would land in a third rate cabaret or dance hall.

"I simply do not understand," Raoul muttered under his breath, his face buried in his hands. "She never once hinted that there was someone else!"

"Perhaps you misunderstood her standing with this teacher, Raoul," said Philippe. "Or perhaps she deliberately deceived you."

Shifting in his seat, Raoul looked out the window and watched the sun disappear behind a cloud, saying nothing in response to the cynical remark. In a matter of minutes, the weather had suddenly changed again, with a bank of heavy clouds now looming on the horizon. Light snow mixed with rain began to pelt the windows, and as the sky darkened, the elegant hotel room fell into shadows.

"Christine isn't like that," he whispered. "She is not that kind of girl."

Philippe flicked his cigar in the ash tray, grabbed a book and began absently thumbing through its pages. "Trust me, Raoul, given time and the right circumstances, they're all like that!" he commented darkly, picking a piece of cigar paper from his teeth.

"You don't know her as I do, Philippe," Raoul rejoined, turning to face his brother defensively. "Christine is the sweetest girl in the world…and I'm convinced that there must be more to this."

"She threw you over for another man, what more do you need

to know?" Philippe said without looking away from his book.

"But something doesn't quite add up," Raoul remarked, leaning forward in the chair. "We were getting along beautifully, and I believe that she was falling in love with me. I know you don't approve, Philippe, but I love Christine and refuse to let her go without a fight."

Unmoved by his brother's sentiment, Philippe stared down at the open book without reading. Raoul's response to the note was not unexpected. He could see that his brother had fallen hard for the Daaé girl, but at present, given that events seemed to be taking their natural course, he would bide his time. It would do no good to argue with Raoul over Christine's unsuitability. The boy was simply too infatuated to be reasonable.

"Well, what do you intend to do then, Raoul?" Philippe asked dryly. "What do you know about Miss Daaé's teacher?"

Raoul set the letter down on a marble-topped table, stroking his chin as he explained, "Christine has told me very little about him. All I know is that they have been acquainted for a number of years, but I had no idea there was more to it than that."

Raising his eyes again to the dreary scene outside the window, Raoul continued speaking, more to himself than to his brother, "Now that I think about it, she does speak affectionately about him...however, I pictured a hoary-haired professor of music, and certainly not my romantic rival!"

Philippe stood to his feet, strode to the bar and poured himself a cognac. "Would you care for a drink?" he asked.

Raoul sighed deeply as he rose up from the chair and picked up Christine's letter from the table. With his shoulders slouching and his footsteps slow and heavy, he joined his brother at the bar. "Ordinarily, Philippe, I would say no. I have no desire to repeat Father's mistakes, and the smell of alcohol has always been repugnant to me..." he confessed.

Speaking quietly as he looked down at the letter clutched in his hand, Raoul added, "...but tonight, yes, I will have a drink."

Philippe poured another glass, handed it to Raoul, and the two clinked their glasses together with Philippe offering a toast. "To Father...wherever he is! May he receive his just reward," he mocked bitterly, then drained his glass and poured himself another.

"Philippe, I know that you despised Father but I wish you wouldn't speak of him with such open contempt!" said Raoul, peering down into his glass.

"Even now you refuse to speak against him, Raoul," Philippe remarked, setting his drink down on the bar, and dragging his index finger around the rim of the glass. "You are a better man than I, Raoul...a better man than I."

Raoul patted his brother lightly on the back, and advised, "He's gone, Philippe. Let him rest in peace."

Philippe shrugged and walked across the plush rug, plopping down on the sofa with a grunt. He stretched his legs out to the cocktail table and crossed his arms behind his head as he questioned his brother, "How do you do it, Raoul?"

"How do I do what?"

"How do you persist in that damn good nature of yours?" Philippe chuckled.

Strolling back to the window, Raoul pulled back the drapes and watched as snow began to fall, with the sloppy flakes quickly accumulating on rooftops and tree branches.

"I simply believe the past is behind us...that's all," he replied, slipping Christine's letter into his coat pocket.

"Well, it is not that simple," Philippe said flatly.

"It is as simple as you choose to make it, Brother," Raoul set forth thoughtfully. "Mother taught us that forgiveness purges the soul, while bitterness corrupts it."

Philippe propped himself up and turned his body to recline on the sofa, then questioned his brother, "Then you intend to forgive Miss Daaé, just like that...no questions asked?"

"Yes, and if she wishes it, I will remain her friend," Raoul asserted, squaring his shoulders with a proud lift of his chin.

Making a grinding sound in the back of his throat, Philippe turned his head toward the window and grumbled, "If it were me, I would not give her the time of day! You deserve better!"

"Philippe," Raoul quipped, trying to be cheerful, "what you need is a wife and children...someone to bring out your softer side."

Philippe sat up and gawked at his brother, cynical laughter rolling off his tongue as he retorted, "Ha! When hell freezes over!

My unmarried status suits me just fine, my dear boy. As long as I can have any woman I desire between the sheets I've no need for a wife!"

"Is that all you care about, Philippe...sex I mean?" asked Raoul, frown lines wrinkling his brow.

"What else are women good for but companionship and sex?" Philippe asked, amused. "I have no interest in children and I don't need a woman to mother me, nor do I fancy the complexities of marriage."

Raoul crossed his arms in front of his chest, and leaned against the window frame. "How about love, Philippe, doesn't everyone need to be loved?" he asked.

Philippe sat up and swung his legs down from the sofa, lit another cigar, taking several puffs. The bluish smoke snaked up to the paneled ceiling as he carried on the conversation, "You pine for true love if that is what you want, Raoul; as for me, I'll just take the sex...and speaking of sex, Raoul, do you actually intend to remain a virgin until your wedding night?"

Raoul de Chagny did not immediately answer, and instead, stared out the window, his attention given to a passersby walking below in the snowy streets. Drawing a hand up to his forehead, he raked his fingers through his hair and answered with a very soft voice, "I'm afraid it's too late for that."

Shocked by his brother's comment, Philippe sat up straight and snapped his head around, leveling his gaze to his brother's eyes as he inquired, "You mean, you and the chorus girl have...?

"It wasn't her," Raoul interrupted.

Intrigued, Philippe stood to his feet and joined his brother at the window.

"Who then, anyone I know?" he asked, his curiosity piqued.

"No," Raoul said flatly, tracing his finger through condensation on the window.

"You're not going to tell me, are you?" Philippe drawled disappointedly.

Shaking his head, Raoul continued to stare down at the street below. "No I am not. She was a decent girl I suppose, but she's certainly no Christine. I now regret the whole affair."

Clapping a hand on his brother's back, Philippe pushed for

more information, "Will you at least tell me when it happened?"

"No!" Raoul replied, smoothing back a curl from his forehead. "Now can we please change the subject?"

Philippe stared incredulously and wondered how many other secrets his little brother had kept from him.

"Subject dropped," he said, his words slightly slurred. "You are aware, Raoul, that your sweetheart is filling in for the diva Carlotta on opening night of *Faust*."

Inhaling a heavy breath, Raoul clenched his jaw, then pulled Christine's letter out of his pocket and unfolded it. Reading the first line again, he answered solemnly, "Yes, I am aware of that. The moment she leaves the stage I intend to be waiting for her...and this time I will not take 'no' for an answer!"

Chapter 22
December 5, 1870
One Day Before the Opening of Faust

The candles had burned down to a soft glow, and although it was early morning, the underground caverns were as dark as midnight. Faint reflections glimmered across the dark lake as Erik's boat rocked with a rhythmic slosh. The *Don Juan* manuscript was laid out across the music stand, and his mask sat beside a half-empty glass of brandy. Pen and ink drawings were scattered over the desk, depicting Christine in one hundred different poses and expressions. The notes and cards she had made for her anonymous benefactor were stacked nearby, where over the years he had read and cherished each one.

Across from the library in his bed chamber, Erik lay asleep in the old four-poster bed, with blankets and darkness wrapped around his reclining form. The fog of dreaming held him it its thrall, as his legs twitched beneath the bedding, and his eyelids fluttered under the influence of distorted memories.

He was an infant, gazing drowsily into his mother's blue eyes. She held him in her arms and rocked him gently as she sang a lullaby. He suckled at her breast, listening to the peaceful thrumming of her heartbeat as she stroked his cheek, cooing her baby to sleep.

Making soft gurgling sounds in the back of his throat, Erik turned over onto his other side and grasped the pillow to his chest as the dream propelled the infant forward in time. Suddenly he was a child, crawling on his hands and knees alone in a dark corridor. "Mama, Mama!" he cried out…but no one came for him. Unaware that she was gone, the child began to sob, tottering up to his feet as he again, desperately screamed for her, "Mama, Mama!"

Groping through the darkness for a door of escape, he found that the hallway had no openings, no doors or windows. All at once a flash of light temporarily blinded him, forcing the little boy to teeter backwards and to squeeze his eyes shut against the glare.

Erik moaned into his pillow, the sheets twisting around his body as he tossed and turned in his sleep. Down the corridor the little boy ran, crying and screaming hysterically, but when at last he reached the end of the corridor, only a mirror awaited him there. The little boy did not look up, but stared down at his hands to see that they had transformed into the hands of an adult man. The dream had carried him from infancy to childhood, and finally to adulthood, and now he stood gawking at his hands as if they belonged to a stranger.

The muscles in Erik's face twitched, and his arms and legs jerked under the sheets. His eyes fluttered open, then closed again as sleep deepened around him.

In the dream Erik gathered his courage, and slowly lifting his eyes he looked up at the mirror where, on the other side of the glass he beheld a beautiful young woman. She wore a formal gown, and her hair tumbled about her shoulders in chestnut ringlets. The sight of her face made his heart ache, and he instantly knew her name. "Christine," he moaned, as his eyelids quivered in sleep.

Examining the edges of the frame for a passage into the mirror, he found no hidden latches and called out to her again, but she did not respond as his whispered cries were lost in the void between sleep and reality. Sitting on her bed unaware of his presence, Christine looked down at the floor. Desperate to join her on the other side, he pounded on the mirror with the flat of his hands and shouted, "Christine, Christine!"

Upon hearing him at last, she arose from the bed and walked slowly across her room, the hem of her gown trailing on the carpet behind her. She stood so close to the glass that he could see the bluish veins in her neck and the bronze sunbursts of her irises. Pressing her delicate hand onto her side of the mirror, she matched her fingers to his.

As dream Erik tried to find a way to Christine, sleeping Erik tossed and turned in the bed. Gritting his teeth, dream Erik pounded on the mirror until it began to fracture into hairline cracks and wide fissures. He moaned her name repeatedly as he battered the glass with his fists. Finally, he reared back with a primal yell and lunged forward, striking the mirror with full force! In a silent explosion of razor-sharp fragments, the mirror shattered and glass flew at him, tearing his flesh as it lodged into his skin. Ignoring his pain and the blood that dripped down into his eyes, he thrashed his way through the mirror's jagged remains into Christine's room, where he found her lying dead in a pool of blood with a shard of glass piercing her heart.

Erik's eyes snapped open. He bolted upright and gasped for air. "Oh Christ!" he swore.

Wiping his brow and neck with a corner of the sheet, he shot out of bed and paced wildly, grumbling to himself as he tried to shake off the nightmare.

"Damn it to hell!" he swore again, his head throbbing. "Damn it to bloody hell…I will have her and no one will stop me!"

Barefoot and naked, Erik staggered to the outcropping and dove into the lake's icy waters headfirst, disappearing into into murky green darkness. Submerged under water, he held his breath until his ears ached and his lungs began to burn, then resurfaced gasping for air. He glided through the cold water, returned to shore and wearily crawled back up onto the landing.

As he dried his arms and legs with a towel, he wrestled his thoughts back to more pleasant considerations, reminding himself that tomorrow night Christine would be his. Tomorrow night he would take her through the mirror, and nothing would prevent him from having her for his own. It was only fair that she should be his, he told himself…for hadn't he been patient and waited until she was ready to know him face to face? She had begged him to show himself that night, but despite her pleading, and for her own sake, he had exercised restraint. How simple it would have been to have entered her room through the mirror, to have scooped her up into his arms and to have carried her away. But for her sake he had remained solidly inside the chamber, and for her sake he was affording her more time to prepare.

After vigorously rubbing the towel over his head, Erik wrapped it around his waist, and as doubts continued to assault his mind, he pushed them aside, thinking only of what tomorrow night would bring: a woman in his arms, a lover in his bed.

Shivering with the cold, he made his way to the organ platform, picked up the glass of leftover brandy, and sipped it slowly. With the glass still in hand, he walked up the stone staircase to his bed chamber, pulled on his robe and knotted the sash around his waist.

As the brandy warmed him, he drained his glass, set it down and lit a candle. He needed his music now. He needed to distract himself from his doubts, and music was the only way. Carrying the candle down the steps to his organ, he flung the back of his robe out behind him and sat down on the bench, bowing his head in thought.

What if upon discovering that he was not an angel from heaven, but a reclusive man with half a soul and a hideously deformed face, she should reject him? He couldn't keep her entranced forever...so what if upon waking from his carefully constructed dream, she turned away in hatred? How would he survive if she refused to him love her?

"She must love me," he moaned. "If she won't have me...then it is over! I cannot and will not spend the rest of my days alone!"

Erik lifted the heavy *Don Juan* manuscript from the music stand, closed the dusty pages with a soft thud, then deposited the great tome on the organ console. He then drew in his breath, flexed his fingers and again bowed his head, this time summoning the new opera. This would be the first time he had attempted to play the angel composition in months, but he needed no written score to recall its melody. With eyes closed, he struck a majestic, splintering chord that shook the pipes with full-throated ferocity. Almost immediately, the music began to purge his torments, and within a matter of minutes he had vanquished the nightmares. Arching his back, his head wove from side to side as his feet danced across the pedals. With his fingers deftly flying across the keys, he swayed and dipped over the instrument until his chambers thundered with a joyful, soaring music!

He murmured her name like the words of a magic spell, as the celestial angel composition reverberated from stone to water, charging the chamber with the opera that she had inspired!

Chapter 23
December 6, 1879
Morning of the Opening of Faust

Slowly opening my eyes, I became aware of a knot in the pit of my stomach. Fighting to keep my nerves under control, I lay there thinking that I had never been more terrified! The week of rehearsals had gone smoothly, and I was gratified by the reception the cast had given my interpretation of Marguerite, nevertheless, those had only been rehearsals and tonight for the first time I would perform for a live audience of hundreds. Father and I had performed throughout Europe, but never for an audience the size of the Paris Opera. Those who had come to hear us were common folk, peasants, workers, and merchants; not to be compared with the elite of Parisian society.

La Carlotta's illness had been broadcast in all the papers, and the audience would be expecting her understudy to sing with a voice similar in tone and style to hers. However, the Angel of Music disliked the woman's bombastic voice, and had therefore, shaped mine into a distinctly different voice; free of overly dramatic portamento and wide fluctuating vibrato. He had honed my soprano until from lowest to highest pitch, I had learned to flex my voice, shortening or lengthening the vocal chords for nearly flawless control.

Under my Angel's guidance, my voice now flowed from octave to octave, with no noticeable shifts in my passagio. He had trained my chest, middle, and head voice to blend imperceptibly, and had instructed that I never force the highest notes across my tongue, or swallow them in the back of my throat, as some did. Moreover, he had taught me to raise my soft palate, which prevented my soubrette from sounding harsh or shrill to the ear. In the beginning of the training process, it had all been very technical and tedious, but over the years I had begun to recognize the difference between my voice and the notable sopranos of that day. Of course, my voice was the result of my Angel's work and dedication, therefore, I now saw it as a miracle and nothing of my own merit.

Lying with my knees drawn up to my chest and the side of my face pressed into the pillow, I closed my eyes, silently praying for his guidance, and wishing that he would visit me once more before the curtain. I knew that, if he could just once more tell me that he was pleased, the inner voices of doubt and fear would be silenced. It did not matter in the least to me how the audience received my performance, for I had no desire or need to win them over; caring only that he would approve. I cared only that I would give him joy, and that he would be proud of me. My voice was his creation and those who heard me tonight would be hearing an angel's voice. He had transformed my childish soprano into an instrument that was no longer mine. Later that night I would stand before the footlights, and my Angel would be singing through me, for I was merely the chosen vessel of his glory!

Opening my eyes I looked up at the mirror, stretched out my arms and legs, still feeling a trifle sore from the overlong rehearsals. I stood up and stepped into my slippers, then lifted my dressing gown from the bedstead, surprised to see a single rose tucked into the pocket. My eyes darted all around the room and then back to the mirror, as I questioned why had he left a red rose, when before he had always given me pink roses? And why was it tied with a black ribbon, when the ribbon had always been white? Pulling the rose from my pocket, I flinched as a thorn hooked the delicate skin of my thumb, and drawing my thumb to my lips, I sucked the trickle of blood until the bleeding subsided.

Unlike the fruity scent of pink roses, the red rose exuded a rich, heady fragrance, far more exotic than the pink variety. As I stroked the velvety petals and pressed the rose to my cheek, I noted that it appeared nearly black at its thickly petaled cortex. Delighting in its fragrant silkiness against my cheek, I walked across the room to the bureau, set my rose in a glass of water, and admired the perfect symmetry of enfolding layers. The deep red color dominated the soft pinks and ivory of my room, and everything else paled in comparison to the striking red rose, which I would soon display in my hair that evening as Marguerite.

Chapter 24
Evening of December 6, 1879
The Opening of Faust

Patrons and first-time attendees swelled into the opera's grand entrance, despite the heavy snow and a sudden announcement that La Carlotta Giunicelli had been replaced by an understudy. The grand foyer glittered with the gowns and jeweled tiaras worn by Paris' most fashionably dressed women, and arm in arm, couples were escorted to their seats as the grand tier filled with international dignitaries and the opera's elite.

Seated in box twenty-one, Raoul and Philippe de Chagny cut debonaire figures in their white ties and tails. Phlilippe sported a gleaming chapeau supérieur, while Raoul's head was bare, with his dark hair handsomely styled. Unaware that many young ladies had taken note of his arrival, the Vicomte wore a pinched expression; his brows knit together and his lips tightly pursed. The seat beside him was spilling over with a bouquet of exquisite flowers, wrapped together with a wide pink satin ribbon. Throughout the day he had been rehearsing what he would say to Christine, and regardless of his promise to behave as a gentleman, he was determined to get some answers. He needed to know the true cause of her rejection, and he felt himself deserving of more than a written note. He wanted to see her eyes, and he needed to know more about the man to whom she had promised herself. It had taken him many years to find her again, and he was not about to let her slip away so easily.

Philippe leaned back in his seat, disinterestedly flipping through the program and thinking over the day's events. Adjusting the vision field of his opera glasses, he scanned the crowd for a certain young lady with whom he had arranged a dalliance following the performance. She was late to arrive, however, so Philippe entertained himself by staring down the lens at other young women who caught his eye. When that sport had become tedious, he then set the opera glasses down and glanced at his pocket watch, pleased that a full ten minutes remained before curtain. Reaching for his coat and rising up from his chair, Philippe prepared to step out to the men's lounge for a smoke.

"Join me for a cigar, Little Brother?" he drawled.

Repositioning Christine's bouquet, Raoul protected the white lilies from being crushed as Philippe walked by, then answered glumly, "No Philippe...I prefer to stay here, but you go ahead."

As Philippe strode out the back door, Raoul gazed down at the bouquet, anxious for the evening's performance to begin. Turning his attention across the auditorium, he glanced at box five with a puzzled expression. Given that the box was rumored to be owned by a reclusive old gentleman, he was surprised to see that it was now occupied by a charming young couple. The curtains had been pulled wide open, and Raoul watched as two more couples joined the party and took their seats. Raoul speculated that the old fellow who owned the box had apparently neglected to show, and it must have then been sold to the young couple and their guests. Catching the young man's eye, Raoul nodded and smiled, supposing that they were about the same age. A tinge of envy tightened his throat as he observed the couple who were seated closely together, obviously in love and quite possibly married. He was thankful when his envious musing was cut short as a bell sounded, alerting the audience that the curtain would rise in five minutes.

The orchestra then made their way down into the pit, with musicians opening cases and collecting their instruments. Excitement rippled through the theater as strings, flutes, and blaring horns began their tuning regime. Minutes later, as the last of the audience filed in, the lamps were extinguished and the chatter died down to whispers.

All heads turned as Maestro Reyer strode regally down the center aisle, dressed in white tie and tails, with a baton clutched in his white gloved hand. A spotlight followed him as he took his place at the podium, then finally, as the audience drew in a collective breath, the Maestro tapped his baton and the orchestra began a prelude to the overture.

The young newlywed couple and their companions were about to settle into box five for an evening of music and theater. Their private box was one of the most elegant in the galleries, appointed in lush red velvet, with the walls covered in quilted brocade. Carved armchairs were upholstered in maroon damask, and a six-foot tall golden angel stood regally at the back of the small room. Golden wall sconces gave the luxurious nook a warm and cozy glow, providing the perfect view overlooking the stage. Monsieur Andre helped his young bride remove her fur wrap and placed his arm around her shoulder, kissing her discretely on the cheek.

"How were you able to acquire these lovely seats on short notice, Andre?" the young bride asked her husband.

"Ahhhh, it was by good fortune!" he answered proudly. "You see, due to the owner's illness, the box was available for sale, I was at the head of a waiting list in the event of cancelations…and so here we are!"

"Well, this is certainly lovely way to end to our honeymoon," the young bride sighed, nestling her head on her husband's shoulder. Andre leaned in and kissed her on the lips, and for an unguarded moment, the newlyweds forgot everything else around them. Suddenly, however, a peal of cold laughter disrupted the romantic coziness of box five.

"A-ha-haaa! He-he-heeeee!" the voice cackled.

"What was that!" the young woman exclaimed, pulling away from the kiss and jolting upright in her chair.

"I've no idea," her husband replied calmly. "Perhaps a draft?"

After a few seconds of quiet, the young couple relaxed again, supposing the sound had been from a down-draft or the settling of old pipes. They looked over the opera's synopsis and cuddled as the orchestra played below. Seated behind them, the rest of their party engaged in light conversation, with the women pulling fans from their handbags and flicking them open with theatrical flourish.

"A-haaa-ha-ha-ha," came the laughter again, sounding closer this time. The young newlyweds looked nervously about, obviously disturbed by the unearthly noise.

"That is no draft, my friend, it sounds like someone laughing!" one of the male guests remarked. 'Perhaps one of our neighbors?"

"But who would do something so childish?" the young bride asked her husband, wide-eyed and wringing her dainty hands.

"I don't know, dear..." he replied reassuringly, patting her knee. "...but if it continues, I shall have a word with the management!"

Standing to his feet, Andre leaned across the rail and looked to his left and right at the parties in boxes four and five. Seeing nothing that would suggest one of these people had been responsible for the noise, he moved his chair closer to his bride's and took her hands in his, trying to reassure her that everything would be all right. Meanwhile, the patrons in the adjoining boxes had taken notice of the conversation, and were now leaning over their own balustrades in curiosity.

"Don't worry, darling," Andre whispered, gently squeezing her gloved fingers. "I'm sure it was nothing. These old buildings are known for drafts and...."

Andre, however, was unable to complete his thought as every person in box five then heard a distinctive a male voice, which seemed to speak from an empty chair near the exit!

"I am not a nothing, Monsieur!" said the voice in elegant French. "Have you never heard of me, Monsieur? I am the Phantom of the Opera!"

"What the hell?" Monsieur Andre swore, standing quickly to his feet. "Did you hear that, Georges?" the young man asked his friend.

"Yes, I did!" Georges answered, jumping up from his seat. "What is this, a joke? Did you set this up for our amusement, Andre?"

Before Andre had a chance to defend himself against the accusation, the voice answered with a hiss, "I assure you, Monsieur, this is no laughing matter! You will kindly vacate my box immediately, or I shall have to throw you out! The opera is about to begin!"

Having heard enough of the threatening voice, Andre gruffly searched for its source throughout the box. He checked behind drapes, underneath chairs, peering through the back door into the darkened hallway, then turned around to the others in exasperation.

"I swear to God, there is no one here!" he replied, shrugging his shoulders.

"But of course there is, Monsieur!" the voice mocked, now speaking from Andre's empty chair. "I am seated beside your lovely wife…and I must say…her perfume is as lovely as she is!"

Staring aghast at the empty chair, the young bride jumped to her feet and joined her husband at the back of the room. "Oh my heavens, Andre…please take me home now!"

"Yes…let's get out of here!" said Andre, assisting his terrified bride out the door.

The other two women scrambled from their seats in a panic, as the men rushed about collecting their gloves, wraps, handbags and opera cloaks.

By then the occupants of the surrounding tiers had heard the commotion, and were leaning over their balconies for a better view.

Just as the young couple and their guests fled from box five, the voice spoke most amiably from directly behind them, "Have a lovely evening, ladies and gents…and by all means, do pass on my compliments to the management!"

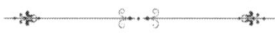

The audience applauded as the prelude concluded and the orchestra began the invigorating overture for *Faust*. Box five's curtains were slowly drawn closed, and the little room fell silent. Erik locked the back door from the inside, pulled his chair up closer to the balustrade and removed his opera cloak and gloves, tossing them across a chair. Sitting down, he slit open the drapes, took up his opera glasses and watched anxiously as the curtain opened onto a darkened stage.

There was immediate applause when the footlights flared up brightly as the audience took in its first glimpse of the stunning set. Oversized books stacked twelve feet high, formed crooked towers; their spines labeled with the works of Dante, William Shakespeare, Homer, and Plato. Perched on the pinnacle at stage right and left, were demonic and angelic figures who would serve as witnesses to the unfolding drama. At center stage the opera's protagonist *Faust*, a balding old man in philosopher's robes, sat atop a pile of decaying books. Behind him, painted in drab hues of gray and brown, a gigantic gothic building loomed high up into the catwalks.

Its windows, doors, and architectural flourishes had been constructed at odd angles, informing the set with a surreal and melted appearance. The painted backdrop depicted a dismal gray sky with splashes of abstract color, and an ochre colored sun that gave no warmth to the proceedings. An open gargoyle's mouth the size of a small house, was the set's most startling feature. With jagged teeth jutting from its upper and lower jaws, "The Mouth of Hell" glowed red from the inside, while rolling fog seeped from its throat, poured across the stage, and crept over the apron in fine wisps.

Costumed as the old philosopher *Faust*, Piangi struggled to his feet and crawled down the book tower by way of a ladder invisible to the audience. Leaning on a walking stick, he hobbled downstage as his powerful tenor voice rang out across the theater.

There is nothing to live for…all is vanity!
I search for wisdom in vain!
I have searched the world's books for truth
But find only passions and appetites
I seek wisdom from the creator…but he is silent
He speaks not in my ear
Where are you, Almighty God, do you not hear?
Can you not see?

I see nothing! I know nothing!
If am blind then, You...Almighty God, are deaf!

As *Faust* poured out his bitter complaint on the stage, Erik waited for Christine's appearance, impatiently thrumming his fingers on his knees. Having spied on the set and backdrop construction, he agreed that they *were* impressive, but in his opinion Piangi had been miscast. His vocals were strong, but he was too bulky to play a frail old man convincingly. With a bored sigh, Erik leaned back in his chair while keeping one eye on the activity below, absently watching as *Faust* pleaded his case, shaking his fists at the heavens with his accusation:

God Almighty, what can you do for me?
Will you restore love, youth and faith to this old man?
Be dammed, oh human pleasures!
Damned be the chains of youth and longing!
Chains that make me grovel and beg!
Grovel and beg!
With every hour my hope passes in vain,
I no longer dream of love or of battles;
I am old, and no more a dreamer
All is lost! I am a fool! I am damned!
Damned, be these books, damned be wisdom and faith!
If the Almighty will not hear me...then come to me, Satan!
Come to me!

Old man *Faust* hobbled and cursed, angry with God and his frail body. Costumed in shades of gray and black, the demon chorus and wraith dancers then slithered onto the stage, flanking the old man on either side. They thrashed and swirled about him until, surrounded by their swelling and chanting ranks, he was barely visible.

Erik closed his eyes and showed little interest, stretching out his legs in boredom. The music faded in his ears as the opera dulled into a backdrop for the mad swirl of his own conflicting thoughts. In less than two hours he would take Christine Daaé through the mirror, and although he had dreamt of this moment for months, now that it was upon him, he couldn't stop shaking. He took the flask from his pocket and sipped his brandy, with no intention of drinking to excess, only enough to quell his nerves. Throughout the day he had paced like a nervous groom, making repeated visits up to the mirror chamber, calculating the length of the journey from the mirror down to his rooms. He had gone over his plans and fussed over the condition of his grotto, and had then spent the afternoon punishing the organ with *Don Juan* to the point of complete exhaustion. Feeling sleepiness take hold as the action continued onstage, Erik leaned his head against the back of the chair, closed his eyes and dozed off.

Accompanied by the ominous rumble of bassoons, french horns, and kettle drums, Hugo Robert made his entrance as Mephistopheles through the glowing gargoyle's mouth. The tall handsome baritone was arrayed in regal red velvet robes trimmed with jewels and fringe. Upon his head he wore a wide brimmed red velvet hat, made to look even more impressive by the huge feather plumbs attached to the crown. The audience seemed amused as he strutted forth from the glowing Hell's Mouth; singing gaily, holding a gold goblet in his right hand, and brandishing a great silver sword at his hip.

> *I am here, my brother! Why should you be surprised?*
> *You called for me, and I have come to serve you!*
> *Sword at my side, feather in my hat*
> *My cup is full of treasures for your pleasure*
> *I wear rich garments...for in truth, I am a gentleman, and no devil!*
> *Therefor, doctor, what do you ask of me?*
> *Shall I give you wealth...power, or is it love you seek?*
> *Speak your desire, man, and I shall grant it!*

The dark plot played out on the stage, as *Faust* bargained for youth, power and maidens. Mephistopheles seduced him into selling his soul by showing him a vision of the beautiful and young Marguerite. *Faust* cut his thumb with a knife, signed the document in blood and drank enchanted wine from the devil's goblet. *Faust* was then changed from a frail old man into the handsome and virile man of his youth, and despite his stoutness, Piangi cut a fine figure with his trim beard and flowing dark hair. No longer bent over and halting, when he emerged from the gargoyle's mouth, he struck an elegant pose in his black velvet breeches and grand coat of blue silk.

Stirred awake by the change of scene, Erik opened his eyes just in time to see the latticed window light up to reveal the silhouette of a young maiden spinning at a wheel. Marguerite was only in shadow, but Erik clutched his chest at the mere sight of her, and from that moment on, he knew of nothing else that transpired on the stage, save Christine.

As Act Two unfolded, he inhaled a deep breath when Marguerite was finally introduced in her garden. Rose colored lighting haloed her features and she wore a maiden's gown in shades of green, with the velvet basque bodice accentuating her tiny waist and delicately boned figure. Her eyes were painted and lined, but even false eyelashes and heavy stage make-up could not detract from her ethereal beauty. Wearing a jeweled crown on her head, the many glittering necklaces, bracelets and rings flashed in the lights as she danced and twirled about the stage, modeling the jewelry that *Faust* had given her.

From Erik's vantage point in box five, he observed that all eyes in the audience were riveted upon her as she began to sing *The Jewel Song*:

Is that me in the looking glass?
Ah...I cannot recognize myself!
So beautiful am I,
Is this mirror enchanted?
Is it you, Marguerite, it is you?

Effortlessly, her voice enraptured the hall, her flawless soprano bringing smiles of surprise and enjoyment to the audience. Erik had heard her sing countless times over the years, but never like this. Never with such rapturous abandon, and never in a venue where her voice was allowed to reach its full potential.

Will he find me beautiful?
With these jewels in my ears and around my neck?
I look like a princess and not a maiden.
What is the cause of this metamorphosis?
No...no, tis no longer my face;
Ah...I can't recognize myself!
So beautiful in this mirror!

The second act flew by, with Erik hanging on every note Christine sang. He removed his mask and a crooked smile lit up his deformed features as her voice called to him like a siren song. Throughout the performance he alternately laughed and wept, every emotion making him feel vitally alive. Never had he felt so completely human or more perfectly divine.

During the final scenes of Act Two, Erik watched transfixed as Marguerite was callously seduced by the bewitched *Faust*, who had drunk dark magic from the golden cup of Mephistopheles, and had then impregnated the maiden with his demon child. In the climactic moments of scene three, Christine as Marguerite, stood center stage in a tattered gray gown awaiting her judgment. Marguerite's beautiful curls had been shorn, with her bare scalp visible through uneven clumps of hair. Iron prison bars were then lowered down from the flies onto the stage, surrounding her on all four sides.

The judge pronounced her guilty for the murder of her infant child, and the court then condemned her to execution by hanging. Falling on her knees to plead for forgiveness, Christine's entire body shuddered, and her face appeared etched with torment in the harsh lighting. Her soprano voice began to break with sobs, yet it managed to soar as she pleaded for mercy, with genuine tears glistening down her cheeks:

My God, save me!
My God, I implore you!
Holy angels, radiant angels,
Carry my soul to my Savior!

Holy God forgive me!
Holy God, to you I abandon myself!
Holy angels, radiant angels,
Carry my soul to the bosom of Heaven!

Christine lifted her face into the lights, and Erik fought back his own tears, hiding behind the red curtains in box five. His lifelong dream had been embodied by that historical performance, and at last he had made himself known to the world through her. As she sang for the audience, it was he who was singing through her…and as the applause continued long after her aria's conclusion, he received the applause for himself, knowing that while he must remain hidden in the shadows, she would now stand center stage; a dazzling new star in the footlights of Paris. He had put her there and he would keep her there.

"Brava!" he whispered hoarsely, his voice breaking in gulps of air, "Brava, Christine

Marguerite was then surrounded by the entire chorus of angels, her soul redeemed and delivered to heaven. The angel chorus sang joyfully as white wings enfolded the maiden.

She is saved! Christ is brought to life!
Christ is reborn!
Peace and joy to disciples of the King!
Christ has been resurrected!
Christ is resurrected!
Christ is brought to life!

Maestro Reyer bowed in tribute to the young singer, blinking back tears as the audience rose to its feet. In the privacy of their box, the new managers, Firmin and Armand, popped open a bottle of champagne and congratulated themselves on the great success of the opera and their discovery of the pretty ingenue, Christine Daaé. Raoul de Chagny stood up from his seat, applauding and shouting vigorously while Philippe begrudgingly nodded and clapped. Leaving box five, Erik swept his cloak off the chair and swung it across his shoulders. He then slipped out the back exit with haste, and descended into darkness before the crowds began to disperse.

Deafening applause and shouts of "Brava!" brought the house down as flowers were laid at Christine's feet and bouquets heaped into her arms.

Piangi and Hugo Robert stood on either side of her, supporting her fainting weight when she grew lightheaded; and assisting her as she curtsied in the spotlight. Bearing a distant gaze, she looked out across the audience and hardly heard the applause as she whispered breathlessly...

"Angel...where are you?"

La Fin~Book One

Chanson de l'Ange continues:

Book Two: The Bleeding Rose
Book Three: Angel's Song

www.chansondelange.com

Enjoy an excerpt from:

An Epic Retelling of The Phantom of The Opera

Chanson de l'Ange

Book Two:
The Bleeding Rose

Prologue

From the moment I had come to live at the opera house, I had been surrounded by mirrors. They were everywhere! The rehearsal studio had boasted an entire wall of mirrors, and each day as Madame Giry had taken us through our routines and exercises, those mirrors reflected our progress, but they had also reminded us of how much more we had to learn.

There were mirrors in Madame's apartment, in her parlor, and in the bedrooms. Over the years I had enjoyed watching as she would sit at her vanity, applying her make-up and styling her hair; magically transforming herself from a plain, middle-aged woman into the mysterious lady with cats-eyes and auburn hair.

Even the dining hall had been outfitted with mirrors and for Meg and me, the reflections of animated diners had been amusing as we had watched them converse and horse around! Then there were the gaudy mirrors in the Grand Foyer, the backstage mirrors, the dressing room and wardrobe mirrors...all having their own unique appearance and function...but naturally, the mirror I loved best was the one that hung in my own room.

It was a full eight feet tall and was decorated with an exquisitely carved gold-leafed frame. The carving was a design of leaves and vines, with clusters of grapes and lavish, swirling patterns...and ever since my first night at the opera house, it had watched over my growing up years; my heartaches and my joys. That mirror had played a significant role in my little rose-colored world, and even before my introduction to the Angel of Music, I had been captivated by the strange notion that, if I were to place my hand on the glass in just the right way, the mirror might transport me into some magical realm.

My bedroom mirror had also shown me the various sides of myself as, from day to day, my reflection would change with my moods and the advancing years. Through the mirror's silver stare, I had witnessed my transition from girlhood into womanhood, with both my past and future projected in my ever-changing face. Gazing into the mirror, I could see both the little girl I once was and the woman I was becoming, and it occurs to me now as I reflect upon what was to come and what had already been…that our memories are mirrors.

Like our memories, mirrors do not always reflect our true selves; for how can they when it is through our eyes alone that we may observe? Likewise, the memories we reflect upon as we grow older can be distorted by our myopic vision of the world and the events that have shaped us. I often wonder what it would be like to step outside myself just once; to see the real me as others do. Would I be pleased, or would I be ashamed? I do fancy how the mirror makes my skin appear to glow, and the softness it lends to my weary features…so perhaps it's best I never know how others perceive me, and perhaps memories are meant to be softened in the telling…

Chapter 1
December 6, 1879
Through The Mirror

After the third curtain call, my legs began to wobble and Piangi caught me just as I started to lose my balance. People shouted and cheered, crowding in all around me, but I couldn't discern their voices as the backstage became a jumble of noise.

When I couldn't walk on my own, dear Piangi picked me up in his arms and carried me out into the corridor toward the dressing rooms, pressing his way through the patrons. Smiles blurred past me and I buried my face in his neck to shut out the cheers as more and more well-wishers flooded the hallways. Desperate for quiet, I cupped my hands over my ears, but the laughter and shouting roared in my head as Piangi fought his way to my door.

Throughout the evening I had performed as though in a dream…as if I had left my body and had observed the entire opera from a great distance. With only one thought persisting throughout the course of my performance: *I am singing for you.* I had spoken these words over and over in my mind, knowing that because of him, my performance as Marguerite had been truly magnificent!

While singing the score and interacting with the other actors, I had sensed that he was there in the theater, and I had told myself that my performance must be perfect…though not for the audience, but only for him. It was because of him that I could feel Marguerite's pain, and it was the result of his coaching that I had been able to communicate her remorse and suffering at her lover's betrayal. For among other valuable lessons, my Angel had taught me that music was the innermost language of the soul.

Piangi then forced his way through the burgeoning crowds, ordering them to clear a path. "Miss Daaé needs air!" I heard him shout in his broken English. "Please make way for the child!"

Finally, we arrived at the dressing room door, only to find it completely blocked by audience and cast members who had come to congratulate me.

Raising my head, I opened my eyes as Raoul de Chagny shouted over the uproar, "Christine! Please, I must speak with you!"

Suddenly, Madame Giry was beside us, pushing people out of the way. "Miss Daaé can see no one!" she hollered over the din. "Please, back away from the door!"

"Madame Giry!" Raoul persisted, his head bobbing above the crowd, "If I could just have a word!"

"Not now, Vicomte!" she scolded. "Come back in twenty minutes. Christine will see you then."

A rushing of air brushed past me as the dressing room door was flung open and Piangi sat me down on the chaise, while Madame Giry pulled off my shoes and began untying the ribbons of my bodice. Tugging the dress sleeves down from my shoulders, she unhooked the top fasteners of my corset and then loosened the back laces, helping me to breathe more freely.

Carlotta's dressing room had been temporarily reserved for my use and the entire space had been decorated with bouquets and vases of flowers. Many candles burned from atop the vanity and tables, and the fragrance of roses, violets and freesia tickled my nose. The pale blue wallpaper was almost entirely plastered with the diva's theater banners, cards, and mementos; with one huge portrait of the diva herself dominating the wall opposite the mirror. Thickly piled rugs covered the floor, and a three-paneled dressing screen stood in the corner beside a large wardrobe.

The room was too lavish for my preference, but it served as a refuge from the commotion in the hall, and I was grateful that the furnishings and rugs muted the antics of a rowdy cast and crew, bent on getting drunk and celebrating till dawn!

"Thank you, Signor," Madame spoke to Piangi. "I'll see to the girl…you may go now."

"Yes, Madame," Piangi said with a bow.

The broad-faced tenor then stooped down and gently kissed my forehead. "You were magnificent, Mademoiselle…" he spoke in clumsy French, "…simply magnificent!"

I nodded my thanks and smiled weakly as Madame tried to untangle my lacings. Piangi shut the door behind him as he joined the commotion in the hallway, while Madame continued to assist me, gently inquiring, "Christine, can you sit up, my dear? We must get you out of your costume."

I sat up on the chaise, and having no strength to remove my own clothing, I permitted her to tend to me. An unusual fatigue had come over me and as I tried to recover my strength, my thoughts turned to what the coming hours might bring. Glancing up at Carlotta's Italian clock, I took note of the time, thankful that I still had half-an-hour before I must return to my room.

There was a light tap on the door, and from out in the corridor, Meg shouted, "Please, Mama, may I come in?"

Madame unhooked the last fastener, and I exhaled in relief as the corset fell away, allowing my lungs to fully expand.

"Yes, dear, come in!" Madame answered.

Meg breezed into the room, tiptoed across the floor to the chaise and planted a kiss on my cheek. "Oh Christine!" she exclaimed, "You were stunning! I'm so proud of you!"

Still wearing the white under-gown of her angel costume, her cheeks were flushed, her makeup was smeared from sweating, and she had wrapped a heavy woolen shawl around her shoulders for extra warmth as her body cooled down.

"Meg, be a dear and fetch Christine a glass of water," Louise coaxed her daughter.

"Yes, Mama," Meg replied, prancing over to the vanity.

Returning with a full glass, she sat beside me and proffered the water, which I then drank down in a few unladylike gulps, begging for more.

After I had emptied nearly half the pitcher, my head began to clear and I was feeling much improved. The dizziness gradually subsided, and after a few moments I sat up, squaring my shoulders and taking deep breaths as Meg refilled the pitcher from Carlotta's water closet.

"You were terribly dehydrated, dear! Dehydration and the excitement are what made you faint," Madame informed me, lightly stroking my cheek.

"I am much better now, Madame," I assured her, having finally found my voice again.

Listening to the chiming clock, I checked the time again and my stomach began to flutter wildly as the hour of my Angel's visitation approached.

"Why don't you lie back for a while, Christine," she suggested. "A little rest before the gala would do you some good."

"Oh, no, Madame! I can't rest, and I'm not going to the gala tonight!" I blurted out, jumping to my feet...still a trifle unsteady, but regaining my senses. "I have to change! He'll be expecting me soon and I must not be late!"

Regarding me with a wary look in her eyes, Madame rose to her feet and began clearing my garments away

Scooping my corset and shift up from the floor, Madame commented, "I'm sure the Vicomte won't mind if you take a few more minutes to recover."

"No, Madame...I was not talking about Raoul...I am meeting my teacher!" I answered wistfully.

For a moment Madame said nothing, then raised one eyebrow and touched my chin with the tip of her finger. A shadow passed over her eyes as she pressed her lips together tightly and addressed Meg, "Meg, my dear, will you leave us for a moment?...and please inform the Vicomte that Christine is too exhausted for visitors tonight."

"Yes, Mama," Meg curtsied and said with a pretty smile. "Christine, you will tell me everything tomorrow...won't you?"

"Yes, of course I will...silly! Haven't I always?" I lied, forcing a grin.

As Meg closed the door behind her, Madame came to stand directly in front of me, and placing her hands on my shoulders, she leveled her gaze to mine, speaking with concern, "Christine, are you truly meeting your teacher alone tonight?"

"Yes, Madame! He is waiting for me now!" I answered breathlessly, hardly able to contain my mounting excitement. Madame was correct. I had been dehydrated. The performance had simply been draining, but the water had revived me, and now I was desperate to get out of my costume and into something more suitable for meeting my Angel.

"And you will meet him of your own accord?" Madame asked with a dour expression.

"Of course, Madame...but I am already terribly late and I shan't disappoint him," I answered, seating myself at the vanity.

She stood behind me and pulled out the pins that had secured my curls to the wig's fine webbing. Carefully, I then removed the skull cap, breathing a sigh of relief as the wig peeled away.

Rubbing her hands through my scalp, she loosened the curls, coaxing a wide-toothed comb gingerly through my hair. Madame's attentions had always been a comfort to me, and although professional hairdressers ordinarily assisted principal players, it was pleasant chatting together as she pulled her fingers through the length of my curls. Leaning back, I was filled by a sense of peace, imagining that this is what my mother would have done had she lived.

"Christine, are you certain that it is wise to meet your teacher without a chaperone? Madame said, a frown etching her features. "After all, what do you know of him?"

"I know that he is wise and kind, Madame, and that he would never harm me," I replied, gazing at the mirror.

Saying nothing more and patting my back gently, Madame set the comb and brush on the vanity, left the room briefly, and then returned with a steaming tea kettle. Filling the washbasin with freshly heated water, she helped me peel off the false eyelashes and then I leaned over the basin, scrubbing my face with a wash cloth until an oily residue of greasepaint congealed on top of the water. The steamy water on my skin felt delightful, and I scrubbed until the last remnants of pancake makeup and heavy eyeliner had been removed. Madame then handed me a towel and I dried my face, frowning in the mirror at my naked complexion. Using cheek and lip-rouge almost daily had left me feeling myself plain and unattractive without it, and I wondered what my Angel would prefer. Would he fancy me with just a touch of color, or might he prefer my face natural?

Deciding to wear just a touch of rouge and light lipstick, I quickly applied the color while Madame coiffed my hair, pulling back and securing the sides with two combs.

As I continued my beauty regime, I was suddenly struck that the girl looking back at me was very different from the girl I had been only two days ago. My face was flushed and my eyes were full of secrets, and just like Marguerite in her jewels, I scarcely recognized my own reflection!

As Madame put the finishing touches on my hair, unsmiling, she nodded her head and said quietly, "Let's get you into your dress."

We stood up together and I stepped behind the dressing screen to change. I had brought my pale-green birthday dress to wear for the evening, and Madame helped me out of my chemise and drawers.

Changing into fresh under things, I slipped on a clean corset, holding my breath as Madame pulled the laces taut until my hips and waist were properly cinched. To the corset I added my petticoats and the dress, which Madame then buttoned up the back. Standing before Carlotta's full-length mirror, I turned sideways with a sigh and fluffed the bustled three-tiered skirt. It seemed to me that I had transformed overnight from a girl into a young woman, and I smiled hesitantly at the image, not quite comfortable with the dramatic changes taking place in my life.

"Lovely, my dear," Madame said reservedly, reaching out to stroke the fine silk.

I loved the dress because the color suited me and because it had been Monsieur E.'s birthday gift, and I hoped it would win my Angel's approval, but I couldn't help thinking how odd it was that I was no longer choosing my fashions to please myself or anyone else in the world of mortals. I was attempting to look beautiful for someone I had never met face to face, and I could not imagine how a mere mortal girl in a pretty dress could impress an angel!

"Everything is about to change," I muttered under my breath.

"Pardon?" Madame asked.

Giggling nervously, I shook my head and smiled, "Oh nothing, Madame. I was just thinking out loud."

Suddenly my throat became as dry as cotton, but my water glass was empty. "Madame, I need another drink of water!" I blurted awkwardly, stepping from behind the screen and dashing back to the vanity. Pouring another glass, I sipped slowly, being careful not to smear my freshly painted lips. Just then, there was a light tap on the door and Madame left off her straightening up of the dressing room to see who it was. Unlocking the door, she made certain that no one else entered with Meg, who was carrying a lovely bouquet of flowers that were bundled together by a pink satin ribbon.

"The Vicomte asked me to give you these, Christine," she grinned, placing the large bouquet in my arms. "He asked me to give you this, as well."

She handed me a gift card, which I promptly tucked into the flowers without even glancing at it.

"I'll read it later," I spoke impatiently.

With her smile fading, Meg insisted, "But they are from Raoul! He's waiting just outside the door, so shouldn't you at least read the note? I think he's expecting you to join him at the gala," she added.

Before I could answer, Madame made my excuses, "Meg darling, do go out there and tell the Vicomte that Christine will see him first thing in the morning…but for now, she is not feeling well and must be off to bed."

Assuming that Raoul and I were still sweethearts, Meg's expression was one of confusion. I had made up my mind to tell her the truth as soon as possible, but at that precise momentI was anxious to fly out the door and I had no patience to deal with Meg, or Raoul…or anyone!

"Meg, what is it like out there?" I asked, my palms sweating and the pulse pounding in my ears, "Have the crowds thinned out?"

With her typically upbeat outlook on the rebound, leaning closer, Meg gleefully confided, "Besides the Vicomte, there are still a few stragglers in the corridor…namely, Nanette and one of her beaus! They are…well, you know…kissing," she giggled. "You should see it, Christine! She is acting disgracefully, but he's so handsome…so who can blame her? And Marie says that he's at least four years older than Nanette," she gushed, as Madame Giry rolled her eyes with a good-natured chuckle.

Ignoring Meg's gossip, I extracted myself gracefully from the conversation and tiptoed across the room toward the back exit.

"We'll talk later, Meg…but I have to be going now!" I exclaimed.

"Christine, don't forget your cloak!" Madame reminded me, lifting my burgundy cloak from the coat tree. She placed it across my shoulders and fastened the neck, then pulled the wide hood up over my hair and kissed my cheek. Taking both of my hands in hers, she stared directly into my eyes and advised, "If you need me, Christine, you know where to find me."

Smiling weakly, I collected a lamp and stepped out into the back corridor with my heart hammering hard in my chest, as chills pinged up and down my arms.

Avoiding the noisy gala on the mezzanine, I wound my way through the opera's maze of corridors, breathing a sigh of relief when I finally reached the deserted dormitory wing. Confident that everyone else was still upstairs, I tiptoed to the end of the darkened hall, inhaled sharply, then unlocked and slowly creaked my door open. Not knowing what to expect as I stepped into my rosy room, I held my breath as I shut and bolted the door behind me. I saw nothing out of the ordinary…but the strange stillness gave me a sense that something was about to happen.

There was no light save the lamp in my hand, and as I walked toward my bed, the pink glow of my walls was a welcome relief from Carlotta's lush quarters.

Scrutinizing the room which had been mine for seven years, I took note of the rose-patterned rug, the embroidered comforter, my wardrobe, the screen, and the damask chair. Wondering if I would ever again return to the opera house, I felt unwanted tears dampening my lashes as I thought back on the love I had known in that old building. Madame and Meg had been like family to me, and I wasn't certain I was ready to leave them behind. Considering the prospect that I might never see them again, I began to question where my Angel would be taking me.

I glanced at the clock on my bureau and knew that I was mere moments away from his arrival. The breath quickened in my throat as I thought about running back to Madame Giry and Meg before it was too late. I was beginning to feel uneasy, and as I stood in the center of the room, my eyes darted toward the door, and then back to the mirror. I could hear snow pelting the window and the faint howl of wind up in the eves, as all around me, sights and sounds attested to a routine life, but this was no ordinary winter evening. Anticipation had somehow changed into fear…and suddenly, just as I was about to make my escape, I heard his voice calling my name and my fear vanished.

Setting the lamp on my nightstand, I removed the glass chimney and lit my prayer candle. As the wavering flame cast long shadows across the walls, I seated myself on the bed and whispered, "I'm here, Angel!"

Boring my eyes into the mirror, I held my breath as gently, sweetly, he began to sing our aria from *Faust*:

> *Open to me my beloved,*
> *You burn and you hunger…*

Rising up slowly from the bed, I gazed all around the room as his voice seemed to pass through the walls, and with my heart about to burst, I clutched my cloak to my breast until my knuckles whitened. The candle guttered, my pulse raced and tears pooled in my eyes at the sound of his voice!

> *For the glory of my voice*
> *You who have slept apart*
> *From my embrace…*

"Oh, dear God," I cried out, suddenly afraid again. Ready to flee from the room, I tried to turn away from the mirror, but his voice held me there and I did not move a single muscle.

> *Do you not hear?*
> *Oh, Christine, my angel…*
> *Do you not hear my voice?*

My feet felt heavy, as though encased in concrete, and I stood there like a statue as his voice spun its web around me.

> *My steps draw closer,*
> *My form is at the door,*
> *Thus your lover calls you...*
> *And your heart must believe in me!*

Lifting my chin and closing my eyes, I took one sluggish step toward the mirror, and with my arms outstretched, I called to him, "I hear you! I believe in you!"

> *Open to your angel,*
> *The secret lover,*
> *Who implores you,*
> *Do not refuse his kiss...*
> *Do not deny his touch!*

Taking two more steps forward, I walked toward the mirror like a slave, my hands and fingers extended straight out before me as I cried out, "No, dear Angel! I will not deny you!"

> *Your lover pleads,*
> *Your lover calls,*
> *Let your heart believe in me...*
> *Your heart must believe in me, Christine!*

With tears trailing down my cheeks, I pleaded, "I believe in you! Come to me, Angel!"

"Sing to me!" he commanded...but for some reason, I hesitated. My voice was tired from the performance, my throat was dry, and I was afraid that if I sang for him, he would be cross with me. Staring ahead at the mirror with my lips pressed together, I nearly jumped out of my skin when his voice became an instant pressure against my will.

"Sing to me, Christine!" he commanded.

Unable to resist again, I sucked in my breath, and praying that he would be pleased, I sang Marguerite's recitative:

Sing to me again,
How lovely is your voice!
A silver cup of tears...
The chalice of my dreams!

From behind the mirror, his voice joined mine and a sonorous melody pulsed between us, with he, the cello and I, the violin.

Heaven is jealous of me!
The angels weep for me!
Your voice intoxicates me;
Your touch revives me!

His voice grew louder, charging the room with glory as the walls, the ceiling, and the air vibrated with the power of his coming. I sang Marguerite's libretto and meant every word:

Is it for love
That my soul trembles,
And my heart...
Quivers with joy?

All at once the weariness left my body, and I felt energized...as light as a feather...and as if I could fly! With the music dancing between us, I peered into the mirror to see that my eyes were lit from within, and every inch of my body tingled as my entire being responded to his nearness. My lips were moist, my cheeks flushed, and scarcely able to stand...I was ready to collapse at his feet as I sang out the final verse:

Today, and forever,
I await your visitation,
Immortal lover, do not tarry,
Come to me now...
Ah, come immortal lover...come!

I worshiped at the mirror, now prepared to turn my back on everyone and everything that had gone before. All thought of an ordinary life vanished as I wept in absolute submission to his voice. My part in the song ended, but his voice continued to whirr and buzz in my ears like a swarm of bees. I grew dizzy and attempted to cry out in answer to him, but I was beyond singing or speaking as thick sobs caught like cotton in my throat.

With my eyes riveted on the mirror, I gasped audibly as the glass appeared to melt like wax, then a blast of cold wind rushed into my room, blowing through my cloak, extinguishing the candle and plunging the room into darkness!

For a few moments I remained breathless and immobilized, until a faint glow began to light up the mirror! I watched in disbelief as it flared up into a huge flame…a dancing, golden flame that seemed to set the mirror afire! I stared in awe as fragments of silver materialized and began to swirl around the flame like fireflies.

The silver fragments cast rainbow prisms that bobbed and dipped across the walls, the floor and ceiling of my room. They splintered across my body and clothing, and extending my hands out before me, I grinned like a little girl as the fairy lights touched on my fingers in turquoise, magenta, and yellow!

As I beheld the miraculous lights perform their enchanting dance, my Angel's voice grew clearer and stronger, pulling me ever closer to the mirror as he sang, "Come to me!"

Like a spirit, I obeyed as my body seemed to float across the floor. I squinted my eyes and stared dumbfounded, as a tall, dark form materialized from out of the dancing lights!! He wore a dark cloak that flapped about his body like black wings, and with the exception of his pearly white face, he was dressed entirely in black. I staggered on my feet as his pale hand reached out to beckon me, and the breath left my body, with my legs giving way as I tried to grasp it. Falling backward against something solid, I was then lifted up and enfolded in warmth, as all around me the world went soft and dreamy. Laying my head against his shoulder, I closed my eyes as he drew his wings around me and carried me into the heart of dancing lights.

Gently, he pulled the hood of my cloak up over my head, and as I felt his hand barely grazed my cheek, I closed my eyes and knew no more.

When I opened my eyes again, I awoke to a gentle rocking motion and heard the sounds of dripping water all around me. I opened my eyes to see that I was in some sort of boat, lying on a bed of pillows and covered with fur blankets. The air on my face was so cold that I could see my breath in puffs of vapor, and it took several blinks before I could focus on our location. Grateful for the warmth, I clutched the furs tightly to my body and yawned.

The figure who had come through my mirror now stood with his back to me, and seemed tall and imposing against the eerie greenness of our surroundings. Sitting up just enough to peer over the edge of the boat, I saw that we were gliding through an ancient canal whose ceiling was made of jagged limestone rock formations. Cool mist rolled across the water's surface as a lantern swayed from the prow, casting yellow reflections onto the green waters and creating strange shadows throughout the ancient vaults.

As the tall figure turned to look over his shoulder at me for the first time, I sucked in my breath, startled by his austere bearing. His eyes flashed sternly against the dark cloak and white face, but as I scrutinized his appearance more carefully, I realized that half of his face was covered by some sort of mask. The other side was a pale face with a strong jaw, long straight nose, noble forehead and black arched brow, and although he had not threatened me in any way, I was beginning to feel uneasy in the presence of a creature who certainly looked nothing like the angel I had imagined.

When he saw that I was awake and looking up at him, he tilted his head slightly, drew the side of his finger to his lips and commanded, "Sleep."

Ever so softly dulling my mind, that strange vibration again pulsed in my ears; and as I struggled to stay awake, an irresistible drowsiness overtook me. Surrendering to his voice, I felt myself sinking down into a deep sleep.

Find *The Bleeding Rose* on Amazon
and at www.chansondelange.com

About the Author

Paisley Swan Stewart

Inspired by her favorite author CS Lewis, Paisley Swan Stewart describes herself as a person of magical thinking. She spent her youth performing in musical theater and studying classical voice. She began writing songs and poetry in her early teens, and is an accomplished colored pencil artist who once sold her artwork through her family owned and operated gift shop-gallery. Paisley notes that her writing is often influenced by her personal faith in Jesus Christ, and her diverse artistic interests.

Paisley and her husband of 35 years reside in a modest home in the beautiful Pacific NW. When not busy with home improvements, the couple enjoy spending time with their closest friends, and taking walks in their favorite local park. Between them, they have 3 grown sons and 2 grandchildren. Paisley and her husband are currently making the most of his retirement by landscaping their property, and by enjoying the many doves, hummingbirds, wild birds and squirrels that visit their yard.

An avid fan of social networking, in the winter of 2005, Paisley began regularly communicating with her readers when she first submitted *Chanson de l'Ange* in a chapter by chapter format on a Phantom of the Opera fiction website. Nestled with a laptop in her comfortable chair, on any given day Paisley continues her outreach to fans and friends as she plots the intricacies of her next novel.

Made in the USA
Lexington, KY
05 June 2014